Praise for Relentless A

"Relentless is VERY REAL."

"A pure winner from cover to cover."
—Courtney Carreras, *YRB* magazine on *The Last Kingpin*

"Gripping." —*The New York Times* on *Push*

"Fascinating. Relentless has made the best out of a stretch of unpleasant time and adversity…a commendable effort."
—Wayne Gilman, WBLS News Director on *Push*

"Relentless redefines the art of storytelling…while seamlessly capturing the truth and hard-core reality of Harlem's desperation and struggle."
[illegible] Johnson, Founder of
the [illegible] Literature Book Club

"Relentless is seriously getting [illegible]." [illegible]

"Relentless writes provocative stories that raise many questions but presents stories that everyone can relate to."
—*Da Breakfuss Club*

"Relentless is on the forefront of a movement called street-lit."
—*Hollywood Reporter*

"One of the leaders of a 'hip hop literature' revolution."
—*Daily News*

"Self-publishing street-lit phenomenon Aaron serves up a smoldering batch of raw erotica and criminality."
—*Publishers Weekly*

ST. MARTIN'S PAPERBACKS TITLES
By Relentless Aaron

Rappers 'R In Danger

Platinum Dolls

Seems Like You're Ready

Sugar Daddy

Triple Threat

To Live and Die in Harlem

The Last Kingpin

Push

RAPPERS 'R IN DANGER

AN URBAN DRAMA

Relentless Aaron

St. Martin's Paperbacks

This is a work of fiction. All of the characters, organizations, and events portrayed in this novel are either products of the author's imagination or are used fictitiously.

RAPPERS 'R IN DANGER

For information address St. Martin's Press, 175 Fifth Avenue, New York, NY 10010.

ISBN: 0-312-94970-7
EAN: 978-0-312-94970-9

Printed in the United States of America

Relentless Content, Inc. trade paperback edition / June 2004
St. Martin's Paperbacks edition / June 2009

St. Martin's Paperbacks are published by St. Martin's Press, 175 Fifth Avenue, New York, NY 10010.

10 9 8 7 6 5 4 3 2 1

Special Dedications

To my friends and mentors: By now you're all tired of seeing your names in print, so I'll just say, *you know who you are*. To Tiny Wood (my close friend & confidant): Thank you for your support and focus.

To Julie and family, and to Emory and Tekia Jones: Thank you all for your faith in me. Thank you to Michael Shapiro, Larry, Kevon and Gail at Culture Plus, Karen and Eric at A&B Books, Nati at African World Books, Carol and Brenda of C&B Books, Curt Southerland, Darryl Stith, Adianna, DTG, Joanie, Kevin, Lance, Lou, Mechel . . . and especially you, Renee McRea. Thank you for adopting me! To Makeda at Jazzmyne Public Relations: I picture you on a hammock, about to blast off (again) as you read this! Be clear . . . I'm a fan of yours too! Thank you so much.

To Lorna at ARC bookclub, Naiim, Mr. Perkins, Mr. Reeves, Rick, Ruth, Tiffany, Courtney Carreras at YRB Mag (you rock!). Thank you all.

To the many bookstores around the world who carry Relentless content: Thank you for affording me space on your shelves. I intend to cause a major increase to your bottom line.

And last, but certainly not least:
Thank you to my family, friends, and fans. It is you all who keep me driven.

Foreword

by Tiny Wood, legendary concert promoter

The witty lyrics that we hear today are full of power. No matter who the rapper is, their words have all come as a result of *someone's* experience, whether it's from a rapper's imagination, or incidents of the past, the rhymes still have their own legs as they walk into the consciences of our youth. This particular story takes this scenario from A to Z, in the most profound "what if" tale that I've ever read. Relentless works these characters and the twists in the ongoing plot as if he were weaving down the basketball court and winding up for a slam dunk. You will thoroughly enjoy this captivating drama, regardless of your like or dislike for rap music, since *Rappers 'R in Danger* is really a metaphor for life and its everyday coincidences. As a longtime fan of the hip-hop world, and as a participant in its early growth, I wanted to acknowledge Relentless for bringing the world such an important story. However, I also wanted to join him in acknowledging some of the forefathers, specifically the club and concert promoters who have helped to propel hip-hop into the universe it is today, the entrepreneurs who rarely (if ever) receive the "props" they've deserved from the beginning. To the many promoters representing the tri-state area, who so determinedly dedicated themselves to successfully and professionally presenting the art of hip-hop—from the clubs to concert halls, old school to the new.

Yes, the skeptics were wrong, because rap lives on!!!

The Promoters:

To name just a few: Sal Abbatiello "The Fever," Antoinette Productions, Black Door, Vito Bruno and Roman Ricardo/D.R.B. Productions, Disco Masters Productions/w "the Electrifying Jimmy D.," the Dow Twins, Elmo, Scotty Flash, Gilmore Productions, God Father Productions, M. Morton Hall, Al Haymon Presents, Pete D. J. Jones, John and Steve Juliano, Tony Cooper, Stagger Lee Productions, Daved Levy, Man Dip/Lite Productions, Herman M. and Friends, Sparky Martin, Gene Pendergrass, Charles Potts, Don Powell Productions, Sylvia & Joey Robinson, Jerry Roebuck, Rush Productions, Charles Statler, Sun Song Productions, Richard T/The T Connection, T.P. and B. Productions, Reggie Wells, Winston Collection, and those who have contributed to Tiny Wood Productions.

Special Acknowledgments:

Bachelors in Blue, Faces, Jeff Lavino, David Maldondo, Ralph Mercado Production, Phil Peters Presents, Joe Taino/Taino Entertainment Corp., George Woods Presents and the one & only Maria Davis. Sound System technicians included The Disco Twins, Infinity Sound Machine, D.J. Marino (R.I.P.), Eddie Rivera/I.D.R.C. (R.I.P.) Finally, I want to acknowledge and "shout out" Cara Lewis formerly of Norby Walters & Associates, and Paulette Cunningham/"The Fever."

You all have contributed heavily to the world of hip-hop, and you are not to be forgotten.

Tiny Wood

Chapter One

All of the drama started right here, on Queens Boulevard, in broad daylight. The three hoods—Brice, Cooksie, and Ringo—were about to "bust a move," as they called it. However, to the rest of the world, this was but a "robbery in progress." All last week Brice was saying, "We gonna bust this move! We gonna bust this move!" And he had been promoting the escapade almost every hour since then, repeating himself like a scratched CD. So now here they were, the three of them, about to play God with the lives of others—and with their *own* lives.

When Brice spoke on this five days earlier, he was charged like a hot wire, doing his damnedest to stop Ringo from the low-budget rap demo he had scheduled for the same day. Not that he was hating on Ringo's aspirations, but Brice needed another body to execute this event that he had planned so many times in his dreams.

"Yo—fuck that rap shit, dawg. We gonna bust this move over on the boulevard. I'm tellin' you . . . one score like this, and you'll have *way* more money in one day than some record deal can get you. Word."

"Not if I go platinum."

Brice laughed at the idea.

"Nigga, you must be smokin' crack if you think you can all of a sudden do a demo, get a record deal, and sell a million records. Don't you know the odds? Huh? A nigga wanna be a basketball player or a rap star, but the real deal is that there's a billion otha muh fuckas who want the same thing. It's a fuckin' pot luck game, dawg."

"What if I'm one in a billion?"

"Well, if you are, then let's do this shit, so I can get some money and invest in you. 'Cause without the dough, your ass ain't even goin' ghetto gold!"

Brice was cracking up. Cooksie (and eventually Ringo) couldn't help but join in until they all created a chorus of laughter. When Ringo calmed down some, he said, "I ain't never shot nobody before, Brice. That's not even in my flow."

Cooksie added, "We ain't gonna *shoot* nobody, right Brice? I mean, you telling us this check cashing joint is sweet, and the guns are just for show . . . *right*?" Even Cooksie needed some assurance, evidenced by his uncertain tone of voice.

"No doubt," Brice told both friends as he passed around a forty-ounce beer. Ringo sat adjacent to Brice and Cooksie as the three checked out a cheesy drawing—the layout of the Just Right Check Exchange—on a sheet of paper between them.

"And besides, the guns won't even be loaded," he went on to say.

"No?"

"Why should they be? Them people will be so scared shitless they'll hand the money over just like we say." All three homeboys, none of them older than eighteen, agreed to execute the plan on the following Thursday.

"Okay, check it," warned Brice. "The armored car should be there by twelve thirty. My girl says that it gets real slow by one o'clock, when the lunch crowd goes back to work. So, that's when we move."

"When the lunch crowd gets back?" asked Cooksie.

"No, *stupid*. At one o'clock, when it gets slow." Brice slapped Cooksie upside the back of his head.

ONE WEEK EARLIER AT SUMIIA'S
GRANDMA'S HOUSE

Sumiia Johnson was a nineteen-year-old that Brice claimed possession of. She started out as an acquaintance—a friend of a friend, really. But as of a month earlier, Brice began to pour on the charm, at precisely the time he found out that she worked as a cashier at the Just Right Check Exchange.

"You gotta watch this guy called Simmons," Sumiia told Brice, the morning after their marathon of uninhibited sex. "That guy swears he's John Wayne or somebody. He even spins his gun around on his finger like that horse on the Cartoon Network."

"You mean Quickdraw McGraw?"

"Yup."

"Don't worry, I gotcha. The dark-skinneded one with the eyes like they about to shoot out of his face." Brice had spent a few days checking things already and pretty much knew the who's and what's relating to the check cashing franchise.

"Yup."

"And he probably works out two times a day, huh?" Brice guessed.

"Maybe three," said Sumiia in a tone of warning. "Or so he says."

"Yeah, yeah. But all that muscle ain't gonna stop this here." Brice reached down by the side of the sofa. He showed her a machine pistol—or the "baby whop," as Brice called it.

"If he gets anywhere within two hundred yards o' this . . ." Brice made a *whoo-ee* expression.

"Brice—"

Brice covered Sumiia's mouth with his hand.

"Shhh, before you wake your grandma."

She still managed to pry Brice's hand away. "I thought you said you'd keep that in the car?"

"Right. I know what I said, boo. But your grandma don't live in no goddamned gated community. A nigga gotta protect what's his."

"Oh? And what do you consider yours?" asked Sumiia.

"You ain't gonna start that black feminist mess again, are you?"

"What's that? A feminist?"

"Just something my brother tells me about in his prison letters. He says y'all mess things up real bad."

Sumiia sucked her teeth.

"Whatever, nigger. I don't see no ring on my—"

"Whatchu call me?"

"Nigger?" she repeated while crossing her arms over her bare breasts. Sumiia barely finished her sentence before Brice slapped her face. Emotions welled up in her eyes and throat while the tears flowed spontaneously. Eventually, Brice felt it was safe to remove his hand. The last thing he needed was her grandma all up in his business.

"But last night you told me to call you—"

"That was my dick talking, stupid. And I didn't say nig*ger*, I said nig*ga*. There's a difference, dummy."

Sumiia held her cheek and began to sob, however softly, however hopelessly. This wasn't the worst she'd been through, messin' with one hood or another from around the way. And regardless of all the craziness here, the two were still intimately positioned, with Brice hovering over her, with both their naked bodies still mashing against one another there on her grandma's couch.

"Now, to answer your question," Brice went on to say, "ever since I've been sticking this power drill up in your ice cream, I considered you mine." Only now did Brice realize that he had the baby whop in his hand and that Sumiia was cutting her eyes at the threat of it. Afraid, but steaming.

"Now." Brice slid the nose of the weapon along her tear-stained cheeks, along the slopes of her breasts, and down between her legs. "Now. Whose pussy is this?" He asked the question while underneath the sheets his "power tool" muscled its way back into . . . her . . . ice . . . cream. *Umphhh.* Brice grunted his relief amid her sighs and sobs. And Sumiia more or less agreed with this ruffian's activities (or she was merely overcome by his imposing will), even grabbing ahold of him while he fucked her mind and body. When the sex was over Brice wondered if Sumiia would change her mind and maybe blow the whole plan. After all, he needed her. Had he finally gone overboard?

"Listen, baby, all I'm doin' is lookin' out. You never know, feel me? And as far as you 'n' me go, baby, I've made my decision. As soon as this score's over I'mma lace you with a fat diamond ring." Sumiia looked at Brice with some doubt—one of those expressions that spoke a thousand words.

"Okay, let's do it like this. Remember I told you the day before last, how I ain't going down on no girl unless she was sho' nuff gonna be mine?"

"Yeah. And it's been a one-way deal ever since."

"So would you . . . would you believe me if . . ."

Brice kissed his way down Sumiia's neck, her collarbone, and around her nipples, working his way down below the navel.

". . . I *showed* you . . . instead of just . . . words?" Sumiia giggled as Brice disappeared under the sheet.

"Stop . . . you know I'm—unhh—messy, *oooh* . . . you're not—oh God," she squealed. "You're—not—*serious*." She could no longer speak, too caught up in the rapture. Her eyes eventually squeezed shut, feeling that this was so right, that this was heaven.

Brice merely wanted Sumiia to keep her mouth shut and to go with the flow. So if eating her pussy real good was all he had to do, then so be it. As long as she followed instructions so he and his boys could get paid.

Sumiia shuddered something like six times before Brice was done. He went to wipe the nasty musk from his mouth and returned to see her gleaming at him with those sultry eyes. She reached out for him and fondled his limp penis.

"Come on, girl. We had *enough*."

"But don't you want me to—"

"No, no baby," said Bryce, easing her face away from his shriveled up dick. "I just wanna hold you," he lied. "Don't worry, you ain't neva gotta lift anotha finger while I'm around. I'm 'bout to move you and your grandma up out the hood."

From then on, the two snuggled on the couch,

"Now, who's your man?" he asked, no weapon this time.

"You are, boo."

"I won't get any more of that feminist shit?"

"Are you kiddin'? The way you did the damn thing down there?" Sumiia was half kidding. She sighed and continued to say, "Shit, boo. I'd be a fool to let *you* go. I belong to you, from my toenails to my nose hairs."

"Good. Now tell me more about how they move that dough at your job. . . ."

MIDDAY, THURSDAY

The sky brokered in a pleasant, sunny day—the kind of day that made life seem perfect, as if nothing could go wrong.

"Why we gotta do this in broad daylight, Brice? There's more exposure out here than a two-page spread in *The Source*."

"It's like I say, Ringo. Nobody would expect anything like this in the daytime. Remember the element of surprise they talked about in that book *To Live and Die in Harlem*—"

Cooksie jumped in and said, "That nigga Push was a bad mothafucka."

Ringo looked back over the car seat at Cooksie, scowling at him.

"Man, you know you didn't read that shit."

"That nigga high-speed reads," said Brice.

Ringo cackled out loud, more to relieve the anxiety than anything else.

Cooksie retorted, twisting his lips.

"I'm just sayin' that Push a bad boy."

"Are we all done with the Queens Boulevard book review? We got a fuckin' move to make here. *Anyway*, my whole point is, it's so busy out here, everybody doin' their own thing . . . it's perfect. We'll get lost in all this mess once the shit hits the fan." Brice turned a more concentrated look toward Ringo.

"Don't tell me you're gettin' cold feet at the last minute."

"Please, dawg. I'm just coverin' my ass. If I don't, nobody will."

"True that," answered Brice with a poker face.

"Look. It's the truck," said Cooksie. "Right on time, just like your girl said."

"That's my girl," Brice growled to himself. Then to the others he said, "now, as soon as they leave, as soon as big eyes comes back from droppin' the checks off at the bank, we make our move. Pull around the corner, Cooksie." Brice was unable to take his eyes off of the armored truck that was now double-parked in front of the various storefronts.

MEANWHILE: FARTHER DOWN QUEENS BOULEVARD

It seemed like forever that Jesse Champagne had been working to get to this point. Finally she was about to have her record deal: a sizable budget, a sizable advance, the guarantee of at least two music videos, and a nationwide promotional tour. It was all so right. And all she had to do was sign on the dotted line. Done deal.

"You okay, Jesse?" Kianna put her hand to her best friend's shoulder.

"I'm good. I just . . . do you all mind if I take a break? Just five minutes is all I need."

The emotions were too much for her to bear. The lawyers, her agent, the various executives from the record company—all of them were present. But more important, Aunt Sara's sage advice meant more than all of this . . .

Always take a time-out before you make a serious decision, her aunt had told her since she was a child. *Follow your heart and your instincts but never feel rushed or pressured into anything.*

And so Jesse, now a nineteen-year-old woman with plenty of good fortune to go with her looks and talent, left the record company's conference room, headed for the elevators. Kianna was on her tail.

"What's the matter, Jesse? I'm right here."

"Kianna, I can't explain. It's not something I can't discuss with you. You know you're my girl 'n' all. But this is just . . . it's something personal; a private thing. Like . . . I gotta do this alone. Some quiet time for myself, that's all."

"Well okay. I . . . you sure you're okay? You don't need me?"

"I'll be fine," said Jesse, already in the elevator car. "Trust me. Just a little fresh air is all I need. It's so stuffy in there. So many eyes on me, ya know?" The elevator doors closed as Jesse promised to return shortly.

* * *

Today was Jesse's day. She was ripe and radiant with her flawless bronze complexion and long tresses of golden brown hair spiraling wildly and voluminously, as if all that hair had sprouted from her head into a sculpted bush. Her eyes were wide and alluring. Her nose had a glistening diamond stud on the right side, and her lips were juicy looking, like she had some delicious fruit in front of those kiss-me cheeks and that contoured jawline. And even though Jesse was in deep thought—even with that slinky, shapely bod clothed in a tailored, career-woman's jacket and matching white skirt, she had a certain youthful pizzazz.

Jesse was a walking, talking billboard; it was all in her attitude and her presence. And even out here on busy, sunny Queens Boulevard, it all added up to the obvious: She was a superstar.

But little did Jesse know that her little time-out from that stuffy conference room would not only disrupt her opportunity for fame and fortune, but would also change her life.

For a stickup that was supposed to be so "sweet," Brice and his tagalongs were certainly armed to the hilt. Ringo was carrying what Brice called the Enforcer. It was actually a .45-caliber automatic pistol, similar to what a police officer might keep as a sidearm, except that it had grooves in the grip that molded to Ringo's hand and fingers real nicely. Cooksie, on the other hand, was dressed like a cowboy. He had two pistols, both of which were easily purchased at a Nashville, Tennessee, gun show. At the time he was shopping at the show, Cooksie didn't have enough for two pieces of major hardware, so he purchased one—the Desert Eagle—and the less expensive .45, which the vendor said was a favorite of the GIs from WWII to Vietnam.

Naturally, Brice had the baby wop for point-blank shooting and "wettin' shit up." All of the weapons were a welcome element of security for the time being, whether wedged in a holster under Cooksie's arms, or stuck in the waist of Ringo's jeans, or on a leather strap, like the Uzi hanging down at Brice's side. Not to mention that these three jobless, hopeless fucks also had the nerve to have on Windbreakers that were blinding and bright so that (Brice said) they'd blend in with the colors and reflections of this brilliant summer's day. And for disguises, if things weren't already stupid and strange, Brice passed out masquerade masks—something that the rich folks wore at costume balls, with feathers and all.

"Here, Ringo." Brice passed his partner a full magazine of ammunition. "Just slap that in the handle there."

"Man—you betta stop. I thought we said—"

"Fuck what we said. The plans changed. Didn't you tell 'em, Cooksie?"

"Tell me *what*?" asked Ringo, swinging his head to and fro.

Cooksie avoided eye contact.

"There he is," said Brice, ignoring Ringo as if he were some shopper who'd been turned down for a refund. There was no time to think . . . only time to move. Simmons, the carrier/security guard they referred to as "Big Eyes" was returning from a check-drop at the bank down the block. At the same time, Brice, Ringo, and Cooksie went to take their positions at varying intervals—ten or so feet apart—along the sidewalk that led to the entrance of the Just Right Check Exchange. Brice was closest to the storefront, then Cooksie and Ringo. Ringo was supposed to feed a quarter into a meter for a car that wasn't his. But now that he thought about it, he couldn't even find that quarter.

"Yo, chief, you happen to have change for a dollar?" Ringo didn't have to work hard at pretending, since Big Eyes didn't answer; he just wagged his head and kept it moving. Once he passed, Ringo called out, "Big Eyes!"

"What the fuck you say?" He finally turned his attention to Ringo.

"You heard me," said Ringo. "All I did was ask you for a quarter."

"Forget your own godamned quarter. And if I was you, I'd watch my mouth."

Ringo was concerned that the man was so close, using his pointer finger to get his message across. But he also remembered what Brice said: "He's on the job, so don't worry. He can't touch you unless you threaten him—he'll lose his gun permit . . . and his job."

"Whateva," said Ringo, still bracing himself before the larger man. Big Eyes simply looked Ringo up and down, laughed, and spun away.

Brice was ten or so feet closer to the exchange, digging into a trash can for empty cans and bottles. Already, he had grabbed six or seven of them, containers that would supposedly earn him some tax-free money, a far cry from the hundred grand waiting a few storefronts away. Just as Big Eyes was passing Brice-the-pauper, a short Asian woman pushed her way through the Tin-Pan Chinese restaurant's front door, broom in hand.

"You go from hay-a," she demanded, raising the broom, ready to swat Brice like a fly. "You no make a mess!"

Brice wanted to backslap this woman with her bad timing; she was interfering with his hundred-grand stickup. But he maintained his demeanor, knowing how close he was from pay-dirt. In the long run, he'd laugh about this woman while counting his money.

Half ignoring the woman, Brice gave her a full view of the back of his bright yellow Windbreaker while he continued to peek through the garbage. At the same time he mumbled under his breath, something about his right to hunt for bottles. Big Eyes was approaching Cooksie's area now, while Cooksie leafed through a number of dollar bills, still picking others up from the ground where he coincidentally dropped them at the entrance to Just Right. From his kneeling position he could see big-eyed Simmons coming, still with a little disgust across his face. Meanwhile, none of the three armed robbers were sure whether Simmons would bend down to assist Cooksie, or if he'd step over and around him. It was a coin-toss conclusion that they'd have to be prepared for.

"Dag, you just gonna step by me like I don't exist?"

In his cold tone, Simmons said, "Hurry and pick that up, man. I need this doorway clear."

"I'mma make sure I report y'all to the Better Business Institute," said Cooksie, knowing he had fucked up the name.

Simmons rolled his big eyes to the sky and proceeded to unhook the keys from a belt loop of his trousers. Eventually he used the keys to unlock the front door instead of waiting to be buzzed in.

"'Scuse me, y'all got change up in there?" It was Ringo now who had hurried behind Simmons.

"See the lady at the—" Simmons' reply was interrupted by the hard object poking his side. He had made the mistake of taking his eyes off of Cooksie, and now there were three guns pointing at him, and all of the weapons were hidden from the busy street.

The masquerade masks were being worn by now, and it made things obvious enough for Simmons to curse, finally drawing his own conclusions about the oddities—the three strangers: at the meter, the garbage can, and on bended knee at the front entrance. But of course, all of those thoughts were things to figure out *before—before* it was too late, *before* the guns, and *before* Simmons could kick himself in the ass for the stupid spell. Yes, that was all *before*. But this was *now*.

"Move inside, chief. And don't think about playin' hero either, 'cause it's *your* blood that'll be on the sidewalk. You can bet on that shit." Once inside the establishment, the three recognized their first small problem. There was a woman in the corner of the lobby, and she was holding an infant as she negotiated her cable bill on the pay phone. Brice didn't have to think twice. Casually, he stepped over by the woman.

"Sorry, lady. Time's up."

And he pressed the pay phone's weathered tongue, terminating the call.

"Now go have a seat and keep quiet. Ain't nobody gonna hurt you." Brice was sure the woman noticed the gun since she pulled her baby closer and obeyed without so much as a whimper. All the while, Brice wondered if the proprietor or the cashiers had figured this out yet. He also wondered how much time they had as he sort of assisted the trembling woman over to a metal trash can, on top of which she sat her wide ass. She nervously stroked and rocked her infant, less like a child and more like a good luck charm.

Across the lobby, Cooksie had one of his pistols tight against the big-eyed courier's spine, forcing him to open a second door to the far end of the three cashiers' windows. Ringo saw to the other two customers in the lobby—bodies that blocked most of the activity from the cashier's view. There was an elderly woman who was busy entering a code into an electronic keypad, and a man in a blazer and tie, apparently cashing a check. None of the customers was aware of the robbery in progress, and that was just fine. Brice went to join Cooksie now, and he thought of pistol-whipping Big Eyes upside the head to prevent any heroism. But instead, he figured he'd save the employee until he needed to threaten violence—in case the others didn't do as they were told. By any means necessary, they were gonna leave this place with more money than they'd ever seen in their lives. But so far so good. For now, everything was working marvelously. The Just Right Check Exchange was under siege.

"Ladies, as soon as possible, I need you to back away from them windows and put your hands where I can see them," said Brice. "Where's the boss? Where's Lydia?" While Brice was working off of his inside information, Cooksie was also following the plan in step-by-step detail, and at the same time pat-searching Simmons for weapons. He found two of them: a 357 Magnum in a holster under his left arm, and a palm-sized 9 mm strapped to his ankle. Cooksie wouldn't dare bend down for the second gun, making himself vulnerable. Somebody already made that mistake once today.

"Take that off," Cooksie ordered, prodding Big Eyes with some war veteran's .45 caliber. "Ah-ah-ahh, just drop the gun on the floor . . . good. Now call Lydia in here. Call her now!" he growled.

All of a sudden—with a gun in his hand—Cooksie was a beast.

"Miss Lydia! Miss Lydia!" There was no answer. And everyone in the room seemed confused for a moment.

"Yo, B!" Cooksie shouted, keeping with the pact they made earlier—*no names during the holdup. First initials only.*

Ringo had things under control out in the front lobby while Brice and Cooksie tried to make sense of the missing proprietress.

"Wassup?" asked Brice.

"Ain't no Lydia comin' out. She might not be here."

Brice did some quick thinking before finally looking toward Sumiia.

"You. Go open the office door. Move it." And to the other cashier he said, "*You* . . . lay down on the floor." The blonde seemed to have a problem with that—maybe the floor was too dirty.

"*Now!*" Brice insisted.

As she was told, Sumiia went to the office door and tried the handle.

"It's locked," she announced, but she said it with an underlying warning that only Brice could sense.

"Shit." Brice grunted.

And out of nowhere, the shit he talked about avoiding began to hit the fan. The office door swung open and an extremely thin white woman marched into view with a gun in hand. Her presence was shocking, like she'd just come from a Lucky Charms convention. Her black hair was greased back and she was dressed like a one-woman circus or freak show. If not the convention, then perhaps she just enjoyed dressing like a leprechaun in her full-length, lime-green neon jacket (a cape, really) that she wore with the flaps open, exposing her rail-thin frame in neon-pink slacks and some paisley printed blouse. Completing the woman's loud presence were pumps that matched her cape, pink nail polish to match her pants, and lipstick, too. And—*Jesus*—the lipstick not only dressed her lips, but the outer edges of her ears as well.

Before Brice could make sense of this, before he could apply too much thought to what low-budget porno flick she must've popped out of, there was his salvation to consider. He dived to the floor, knocking over a table with cash and various mechanical devices, in hopes of dodging this woman's counterattack. Bullets riddled the table, and there were screams from the cashiers, as well as from the woman out in the lobby.

"You got the right one, fucker!" Lydia yelled. By now, Brice figured Lydia to be his worst enemy. And when there was breathing room between her flying bullets, he returned fire. From where he was lying on the floor, he could see the neon-green shoes. He aligned the Uzi and let it rip with a rapid-fire blast that sounded something like amplified popping corn.

The woman's squeal filled the room as she collapsed. Gun smoke also stained the air while the blast already had a number of ears ringing. When Brice got up to inspect, he not only found the leprechaun bludgeoned on the floor yet still moving, but he also found Sumiia on the floor. Her eyes were already spilling tears, begging for help as her hands grabbed her belly.

Cooksie had backed against the wall, papered with bounced checks and money order blacklists, pointing both guns at Simmons.

Finally, Ringo appeared through the doorway.

"Brice! *Look out!*" he shouted.

Brice had no time to curse Ringo for using his real name, nor did he have time to respond. The woman had her gun in hand, already pointed, discharging two rounds.

Brice went spinning backward, hit by at least one of the bullets. Ringo's reflex was instant. He stepped up to Lydia the freak and fired all ten rounds, plus the one in the chamber. He was still pulling the trigger, no ammunition left, long after the woman was finished.

Cooksie uttered a mad holler when he saw that Brice had been hit and that Ringo was frozen with fear. His response to the mishap was to cut down Simmons. He turned into a madman, and for no reason but rage, he pumped two slugs into the large man's back. Another into his skull. Cooksie then hopped over the fallen body to help Brice.

"The freak bitch shot me, Cooks."

Cooksie made a brief examination and saw that Brice was merely grazed about the chest. He checked for other wounds and found none.

"Yo, man. You gonna be all right—word." He helped Brice to his feet. "We gotta get outta here, yo. Ringo, shake it off." Again, Cooksie with the disregard for name calling.

"Shit," Brice muttered when he saw through one of the cashier's windows. The customers had made a mad rush out of the front entrance.

"Brice . . . help me . . ."

Sumiia.

"Yo, we gotta jet. Fuck that money," said Ringo, his eyes searching back and forth, and his body rattling like a tall glass of ice.

"Grab the mothafuckin money!" protested Brice with his weapon nearly pointed at Ringo. He then crouched down to Sumiia, who was crying.

"Damn, baby," was all Brice could come up with as he calculated things.

"My stomach, Brice. It hurts."

Her hands were messy with blood. There were two others dead. She had been shot. And no doubt, the customers were outside on the sidewalk now, tellin' the whole world about the robbery. This wasn't exactly the walk in the park he had anticipated.

Shit . . .

"It's gonna be all right, baby. Close your eyes and squeeze real tight."

"O-kay . . . ," she choked.

Brice looked back over his shoulder. His boys were handling business. The second cashier was nearby; surely she'd seen and heard everything from her fetal position on the floor.

The leprechaun's 9 mm was close by and Brice crawled some to pick it up. He came back to Sumiia, bent down to kiss her forehead and tear-stained cheeks.

"You're gonna live forever, baby. Just a little longer—help will be here." Brice had one more look around before he brought the palm-sized gun to Sumiia's temple at close range. He then pulled the trigger, and blood spit out through the opposite side of her head.

As if Sumiia could still hear him, Brice said, "It's the best thing, baby. Trust me." Cooksie and Ringo jumped at the sound of the gunshot.

"Aw shit, Brice! God*damn*!"

"Whatchu expect me to do? She was in pain, dude! Let me handle the heavy shit. Y'all just scoop that dough up and check the front. See if it's clear to jet." Then Brice said to himself, "*Aw shit*? Aw shit is *right*. Can't tell *me* how to do this shit." Ringo and Cooksie looked at each other, unsure of how they even found themselves in this trap with this psycho.

Still on the floor, the blonde's eyes were wide with terror. She began screaming continuously now that Brice was approaching. Quick to shoot her, Brice put a stop to her noise. He then shook his head, somehow disbelieving his own actions.

"Let's be out," demanded Cooksie, hastily stuffing the last handful of cash into the second knapsack.

Jesse Champagne's desire to clear her mind for some decision-making somehow spiraled out of control—no less than a silver dollar dropping into a well, smacking against its walls toward certain loss. A certain end.

There was a small crowd that gathered on the sidewalk, by the parking meters at the curb. Jesse couldn't tell if they were pointing at a bunch of TVs there in the window of Everyday Electronixx, or if perhaps there was an in-store celebrity appearance.

But who would be appearing here inside of the check cashing outlet?

No matter, the idea of an in-store appearance made her bubbly inside. So she stopped to get a peek. It wouldn't be long before that was her, with appearances in every major city. Of course, there were other things to complete first: the contract . . . meetings with producers in Pleasantville, Brooklyn, Mt. Vernon, Atlanta, and L.A. But she couldn't wait till the hard work paid off.

Wow. L.A. I'm really going to L.A. Soul Train, B.E.T.!

Traffic was at a standstill on Queens Boulevard, and it seemed to be heaviest where Jesse was walking. Meanwhile, she was having an important conversation with her conscience.

Don't be hasty, Jesse. L.A. will come soon enough . . . Right now you've got to clear your mind . . . decisions . . .

And just to think, all of these people on the sidewalk—the drivers gazing from their cars, and the proprietors in their store windows—they had no idea who was strolling past them.

In a few months they'll know . . . and they'll be climbing over one another to get my autograph.

Jesse digressed from her "clear thinking" once again. However, in the great kaleidoscope of life, she wasn't too far from the mark. The talent this woman had could rival most others the world over. The singing and dancing made her a songbird that could flutter in the wind. Her ability to play sixteen instruments—not counting her beautiful voice or the way she handled a harmonica—meant she had more talent and potential in the tip of her finger than most others could claim in their entire body.

But it was during this daze—this state of wonder that she was caught up in, the fascination for the day itself—that Jesse was thrown for a spin and hurled into the center of the sudden events before her. A blue and white police vehicle came to a screeching halt there in the street. Another whipped around into reverse, its wheels also burning rubber against the boulevard's asphalt until he came to an awkward halt. A third vehicle skidded and barely missed a head-on collision with the first vehicle. Two more vehicles—both of them unmarked, egg-shaped sedans—were positioned in a jagged arrow that was directed toward the crowded sidewalk.

Jesse froze, as though this were her first time on stage. She was that pie-eyed deer, spellbound by bright headlights. Only this was daylight, and she was no animal. This was Jesse, the aspiring entertainer . . . the butterfly whose performance level was magic. Most anyone would call this unbelievable, how so much chaotic activity could come stomping down so far and so fast, sucking this harmless woman into its violent path.

BACK INSIDE

"Fuck that! We go for ours," barked Brice. "I ain't gettin' stuck in here—we good as dead. They only five cars out there. So I say we go out blastin' at *whateva*. Ain't no way they'll be expectin' that. *Here*." He passed Ringo the 9 mm—the one belonging to the dead proprietor—and without hesitation, Brice turned around and began blasting through the windows of Just Right with the Uzi.

Ringo experienced an instant of indecision, but he ultimately went along with Cooksie and Brice, bolting through the door with that fuck-it mentality and a new title: murderer.

"CLEAR THE SIDEWALK—NOW!" an officer's voice squawked over the squad cars loudspeaker. The sound of the announcement bounced and echoed off of the various surrounding buildings, creating the illusion that this wide artery of daily commerce was but a canyon where the mayhem escalated with each passing second. Pedestrians scattered, fell over one another, and ducked as best they could out of harm's way. The gunmen—whether they knew it or not—had a field of protection in these frightened bystanders; obstructions which made it impossible for police officers to fire at will. Two of the gunmen grabbed innocent women as their living shields while they continued pelting police vehicles and other cars with their wild gunplay. Officers crouched behind their wide-open car doors as bullets pinged and panged along the metal, fiberglass, and chrome surfaces.

"Back the fuck up! *Back up!* I swear to God, I'll shoot this bitch. I *will*!" threatened one gunman. In the meantime, officers duckwalked around various vehicles, trying to get a better shot at the guy as he moved in front of the Tin-Pan restaurant. Pulling the woman close to him so that they were body to body, the gunman seemed to have an easy time of it, snatching her up as if she were light as a feather, or else weak and out of shape. He had his arm around her neck now, sure to keep her wedged between himself and certain fate.

"P-please," the hostage struggled to say. "Don't doth-this to me."

"Shut up. Shut the *fuck* up!" As the gunman grunted in the woman's ear, his teeth clenched and his eyes darted every which way. He did his best to eye everything all at once. And the woman was more obedient now, moving in step with her captor toward the end of the block. At the same time he was saying things in her ear, outside of any officer's ability to hear.

Ringo was breathing so heavily that he could barely get a word out.

"Do what I tell you and—"

They must've thought he was blind, and that he couldn't see the cop circling around the opposite way. He pulled the woman closer, inhaling the perfume from her neck as he gave instructions.

"—you won't get hurt." Ringo couldn't even convince *himself* of that, with his senses spinning so turbulently, to the point that he was in a vacuum, playing every second of this by ear.

In haste, he fired wild shots at the crawlspace under the van until there was a pain-filled wail. He fired another in the direction of the car, guessing that he could ward off the cop in hiding. Sirens continued to approach from a distance, making this more of a hopeless encounter, increasing Ringo's level of desperation.

Gunfire was also constant farther down the block, in the opposite direction from where Ringo was moving. Cooksie and Brice were doing battle with 5-O, shattering the windows of nearby storefronts and surrounding vehicles. A pedestrian was struck down. Another was wounded. In the space of a few seconds, this popular commercial strip went from an orderly economic melting pot to a deadly war zone. It was a scene that astounded gridlocked drivers, shell-shocked shoppers, and business owners, who cleared employees and patrons from the forefront of their stores. It was a nightmarish episode that none of these folks could've imagined, but one over which they'd likely lose sleep for weeks and months and years to come.

There was a surprise shot that came at Ringo, and the woman he held hostage went limp. A blotch of red stained her white business suit somewhere at her waist. That's when he felt himself dragging dead weight and realized: *Oh fuck! They shot her! Mothafuck!* It seemed that po-po was also playing it "by any means necessary."

No other choice left him, Ringo raised both of his weapons, leaving the young woman slumped on the sidewalk, and he blasted at anyone in sight. Things happened fast, and before he knew it he was sprinting around the corner.

This was a breath of fresh air for Ringo, since all of that

mayhem was somewhere behind him. None of the cops (as far as he could tell) were following him yet. But he was sharp enough to know they'd be right behind him, armed to the hilt. *Would they blame me for that woman?* he couldn't help wondering, even as he huffed and swallowed and ran for his life, doing his best to keep the knapsack from falling off his back.

The block down which Ringo sprinted was one of those narrow Queens streets that allowed for just one lane of traffic, and that was perfect for him. Just one or two pedestrians were strolling in the distance—not even in his way.

Constantly checking for 5-O over his shoulder, Ringo continued on like a football team's wide receiver, breaking between parked cars, then across the street toward a schoolyard with its side wall mural of Malcolm X and Dr. King shaking hands. He was confident that nobody could match his speed, and it was impossible for any police vehicles to come after him since there was some traffic crawling slowly toward Queens Boulevard. Not wanting to take his escape for granted, Ringo imagined one cop radioing another, reporting his location, direction, and description. Sure that someone had seen him enter the schoolyard, Ringo ducked into a cove where a water fountain extended from the wall, and where a door—maybe to a storeroom or something—was positioned. Out of breath, with his back against the wall, Ringo felt like a big, bright announcement in his sky blue jacket. He removed the knapsack, then the jacket, and he finally knelt down to repackage his part of the prize money. His attention shifting every which way, Ringo felt 100 pounds lighter, and yet there was still his 160-pound heart banging in his chest. Turning the jacket inside out so that the white lining now showed, Ringo wrapped sacks of cash from the knapsack—a sure "red flag" for authorities—and he filled the jacket. He tied the whole thing into a neat hobo's sack and tossed it over his shoulder with the sleeves as a handle. Only briefly did Ringo look up and see the quote under Malcolm and Martin: *Give Peace a Chance.* But it was a saying that, by this point, came too late. Ringo only had room to be afraid, not inspired.

"*Shit,*" he told himself, only *now* realizing he still had the damned masquerade mask on. He flung it and began his casual walk through the rest of the schoolyard to the next block.

The sirens were more annoying now, to the degree that they seemed to close in from every direction. Up ahead, blue and white squad cars raced along Queens Boulevard, and yet they seemed to overlook Ringo as he finally made it back to the strip—the *last* place he thought they'd be looking.

A moment later, Ringo was inside the Nu Being barbershop, waiting patiently for a haircut, praying that none of the cops were smart enough to check an establishment five or six blocks away from the commotion. He was relieved when one of the barbers gestured that it was his turn, and even more so once the sheet was covering him.

"Take it all off," instructed Ringo, ready to live up to the full meaning of "new being."

While the barber began his scalping, Ringo expressed interest in the makeshift boutique in the rear of the shop.

"By the way, how much for those cargo pants and sports jersey?" As if the cost was an issue. Less than ten minutes later Ringo was wearing new clothes with a shimmering scalp. And an hour later, he was comfortably waiting at the Dunkin Donuts shop on Hillside Avenue, the rendezvous that the three agreed on in the event anything went wrong. And it seemed that everything possible had gone wrong. After a four-hour wait, Brice and Cooksie never showed up at the donut shop.

Chapter Two

The Queens community was outraged about the Just Right robbery. The killings, the hostage crisis, and the shootout were all covered by the media, including the *Post* and *Newsday*, newspapers that had three- and four-page pictorial features and follow-ups on the police investigation in the weeks that followed.

There were six dead as a result of the robbery, including Devon Pitt—aka Cooksie—who tried to use a child for a shield but was shot down from behind. There was one bystander shot down in the blizzard of crossfire, and of course, the two cashiers, big-eyed Simmons, and Lydia, the Just Right proprietor.

All of the funerals except Cooksie's were conducted in one lengthy ceremony that included appearances by the mayor and governor of New York. At the same time, police sketches of the suspects aired on regional shows morning, noon, and night. The drawings weren't exact but accurate enough for close friends and family to speculate.

Ringo and Brice weren't able to establish communication and assumed that they were both fugitives.

It wasn't a remark that was taken seriously at the time, but what Cooksie said before the robbery meant the world right now.

Ringo had asked, "What happens if we don't make it to Dunkin Donuts?"

Then Brice said, "With all that money on you, you'd *better* make it."

"Well, what if ? What's the backup plan?"

"Fuck, Ringo. We can keep making backup plan after backup plan after backup plan. I'm sayin' if you don't make it to the donut shop, then somethin' went *seriously* wrong."

"Yeah," said Cooksie. "And that means we get out of Dodge."

So that was it. They had to go into hiding. Brice had $38,000 in cash; Ringo had $58,000. There was more than enough to survive, to stay out of sight until things cooled down. Whenever that was. Brice had already burned most of his family ties, and since Sumiia was dead, there wasn't even a girlfriend to turn to for that tension relief. And he dared not visit the friends who made the love connection between him and Sumiia; better that they just consider him missing.

With no time to waste, Brice grabbed the few things from the room he rented, and he took a taxi to Newark, New Jersey. There he'd concoct some kind of hustle. After all, anything was possible with so much money in his hands.

Ringo had the very same options as Brice; that is, he had none at all.

His only family was a father who drank and gambled, but who managed to keep his job at a local barbershop. Usually, his take-home pay was enough to carry the rent for the apartment he and Ringo shared, and there was always a little something in the refrigerator, but he'd drink and gamble the rest away.

Ringo saw to it that next time his pop opened the refrigerator there'd be a surprise waiting. He also bade farewell to the two girlfriends he juggled. Donia was the easier of the two.

He told her, "I want to take you to Atlanta with me, D, but it isn't in the budget."

"How long will it take?" she asked him. Ringo struggled. "I can't say. They had me working with a few producers, one after the other. It could take awhile."

"Can . . . can I visit you? I can get the money from my savings account."

The suggestion caught Ringo off guard.

"I suppose so. But let's cross that bridge when we get to it. Right now, I just wanted to call out of respect, know what I mean? I gotta do this, and I gotta do it now."

Donia said she understood.

Jordan wasn't as naive as Donia. She wouldn't go for the cock-and-bull story about the Atlanta recording sessions. With her exotic looks and quick wit all up in Ringo's face, Jordan put up a fight.

"I'm coming too," she said once he had explained about his dying grandmother. "I'll leave this job right now if I have to."

The response was so sincere that he wished he had followed his first instinct, to do this by phone instead of at her job, a diner on Guy R. Brewer Boulevard.

"Can't do it, boo."

"Can't? *Can't?!* How you gonna cut me out of something so important—something so personal as family? I thought you said I was family too? After all I . . . after all we . . ." Jordan couldn't seem to utter the words and just fell apart in front of him.

"Don't do this, Jordan. Maybe we can work something out," Ringo lied.

He didn't want her to quit her job, but he said he'd appreciate her asking for emergency leave. And that evening—eight hours after the robbery—Ringo was in Jordan's studio apartment, twisting her out until the wee hours of the morning.

By sunup, Ringo was on a Metro-North commuter train, headed toward Connecticut. He had no specific reason for choosing Connecticut, except that he was one state away, not too close, and yet not too far. Besides, the trip was a cinch: There were too many people mulling through Grand Central Terminal for him to be noticed, and the train was an express—last stop, Bridgeport, Connecticut. Little did Ringo know that Bridgeport had one of the highest murder rates in the United States.

With a canvas sack of very few belongings, Ringo took a taxi from the Bridgeport station.

"Take me to the nearest motel," he told the driver.

"The nearest? You sure? There's a Quality Inn Hotel a few blocks—"

"Ehhh . . . a hotel is too rich for my taste. Plus they probably want credit cards and all that jazz."

"Oh," said the driver, and he kept his mouth shut for the rest of the ten-minute drive.

The State Street Motor Inn was the closest motel, just west of the train station, and convenient for Ringo since he had no car.

The area was crowded with one- and two-family homes that didn't seem capable of standing up to a strong wind. If a property was fortunate enough to have a front yard, it was small, unmanicured, or downright unfriendly to the eyes.

Even in the ambitious weather, these streets appeared to be abused by time; the sidewalks were soiled by litter, dog shit, or both; and one homeowner's attempt to set an example by cleaning up didn't make a dent as far as improving such a damned atmosphere.

The area's residents, many of them anyway, apparently fit right in with their surroundings. The trend was promiscuous women; unimaginable Bebe's kids; gangs of teenagers who fought (and killed) over turf, girls, or who said what; and endless aspiring mixtape deejays, at home without jobs, with time enough to blast the entire block with an intolerable volume of rap music, or some old school or reggae artist whose hook was repeated over and over and over again.

Ringo quickly realized what the sour taste was in the cab driver's mouth, and yet he didn't mind his new home—noise pollution and other such annoyances included. As far as he was concerned, this was a hood just like his hood back home. There were patterns of ignorance, pain, and misery, as well as moments of joy and laughter here, just as there were in Queens or Brooklyn.

What mattered most was that this was his second chance at life. He kept thinking back to how crazy he was to grab that pretty girl, and how it was even crazier for that cop to shoot her.

He wondered if she was alive and if she was one of those who contributed to the police sketch. He wouldn't blame her if she did.

Shit. That bullet had my name on it.

Or maybe it didn't. But if all of those recurring images of Queens Boulevard weren't enough to haunt him, then there was always the Just Right proprietor and how he had shot her repeatedly.

In his mind, no matter what readjustments he was experiencing as he settled in Bridgeport, he kept rationalizing how he'd saved Brice's life and that his shooting the woman was a matter of self-defense. But in his heart there was no lying; he knew that what he'd done was wrong, wrong, wrong. And there was no way to fix any of it. No way to turn back time and bow out before the day began.

He'd have been working on his craft in the studio. However, the cards didn't play out that way. Instead of building on his rap career, he succeeded at killing someone. And now he was Ringo, the murderer.

The Motor Inn was a one-level collection of one-and-a-half-room studio residences that at one time must have been delivered on flatbed trucks as pre-fab homes before they were somehow attached to create one big gray horseshoe with a parking lot at its center.

Every last one of the living spaces was occupied by a welfare recipient, whether it was an elderly man or woman, or a single mom with four children sired by three different deadbeat dads.

All in all, the combination of various residents made for a soup of joblessness, domestic disputes, and aimless suffering.

At night and especially on weekends, there was the pattern of drinking, drugging, and partying—activities that helped chase the misery away.

Ringo began to think that his being here might've been a bad decision, what with the police visits to the inn at least two or three times a week. But on second thought, he realized that the troubles here served as the perfect diversion—a consistent one—that mostly steered clear of 41E, his home in this gray puzzle of shamelessness.

Irony and luck were the ingredients that allowed him to claim 41E in the first place, since it just so happened that a resident had been arrested days earlier for distribution of narcotics, leaving the inn's only vacancy—a convenience in Ringo's desperate situation. All he wanted was a roof over his head and a mattress to lay on. Somewhere to hibernate. Ringo knew that sooner or later he'd have to step away from the inn for one reason or another and that in doing so, he'd likely be leaving his belongings (especially his cash) unattended. So one or two solutions came to mind.

He'd either get himself a man-eating dog—a less-desirable option, since it would probably have the inn's manager knocking at his door—or else he'd have to befriend a trustworthy woman who could be convenient for both sex and to keep his temporary residence safe.

Until then, he remained a homebody, only strolling across the street to the very mini-mall where there was a laundromat, a fast-food chicken joint called Nelly's Wings, and a post office that also served as a two-table pool hall as well as a high-priced convenience store.

Ringo took that first stroll on the day of his arrival, buying an order of wings from Nelly's and a quart of Coke from the all-purpose post office. Owned and operated by a woman everyone called Momma Jo, the establishment seemed very homely, where a person could hang their coat and stay awhile. A television was set to BET while a compact stereo was set to Hot 97, which was still within range, since New York City was only forty-five minutes away.

Ringo caught an eyeful of an attractive girl who helped at the cash register, and made a point not to express any obvious interest in her that first day. It felt like too typical a gesture to address her with any more than a customer's interest, something she might expect from any young man from around the way.

In a business-as-usual manner, Ringo made brief eye contact with her, he thanked her for his change, and pivoted off purposefully.

Still, Ringo couldn't help how his senses were sucked in by the redbone beauty's allure.

Two days later, Ringo stopped into Momma Jo's for a gang of cleaning supplies since the inn manager did a horrible job, if he did any job at all in getting 41E into shape.

"A little cleaning today?" the redbone cutie asked as she totaled his items. With an exhausted sigh, Ringo answered, "Yeah, somebody's gotta do it."

"You're over at the Motor Inn, aren't you?"

Ringo saved the embarrassed expression he had ready and simply answered, "Yup."

"You seem down. Everything all right?"

"Oh, I'm good. Just at the starting gate to a helluva job—I'll take that *Essence* magazine, too, thanks."

"For the lady in your life?"

"No. More for the lady in me."

"Huh?" she snapped, flashing her peculiar eyes.

"A little science my uncle taught me—how we're all made up of the x and y chromosomes . . . that little something from our mothers and fathers."

"I—see," she said, still unconvinced.

"It's just that I've spent most of my life around Pop, and not enough time around women. That's why, I guess, there's no lady in my life."

"Okay, I get it. So you're trying to learn about women, I guess by reading *Essence*."

"It's a start, I figure. At least when the time comes, I'll know what's important to you guys . . . the things you like . . . what makes you feel fulfilled?" The cashier was attempting to fit the *Essence* magazine into the bag of cleaning supplies and it fell to the counter.

"Fulfilled," she said, somewhat unaware of her actions. She was staring now. Ringo retrieved the magazine and slipped it into the bag between the two rolls of paper towels. In the meantime, he nodded and took out his wallet, wondering if he'd said too much.

Ringo's wallet was thick with at least a thousand dollars in small and large bills wedged in its folds.

"This should cover it," said Ringo, passing her a twenty-dollar bill and wishing she'd stop staring.

"Oh—I . . . you wouldn't happen to have anything smaller, would you? Kinda slow around here."

Ringo was too busy trying to impress her to be disturbed by inconveniences.

"I don't think so," he replied, almost absentmindedly.

"But tell you what, I can come back later for the change. Besides, I might even need a few more things, Miss . . . ?"

"Oh. Sorry. What was it you said?"

Ringo snickered under his breath, sure not to belittle her, and he repeated himself.

"Sure. I—yeah that'll be fine. You are right across the street."

"Forty-one-E," Ringo added. And glided out of Momma Jo's, betting his every last cent that she was watching.

Ringo smiled as he crossed State Street. His game was working. It was only a matter of time before his long, hard New York influence was received by her soft, warm, and impressionable Connecticut-bred welcome wagon.

While considering his next play—and not yet aware of the young lady's name—Ringo kept himself busy with his own massive cleanup.

The paneled walls were tarnished with nicotine, as were the lighting fixtures and ceilings. So Ringo mixed hot water and Pine-Sol in a bucket, and with a scrub brush he attacked everything in sight.

As the layers of grime were scrubbed away, Ringo couldn't help but be amazed at how anyone could sleep in this place, inhaling the foul odors and fumes day and night.

It didn't take long for him to realize that the cleaning was also aggravating things, the fumes being reborn. So he opened the front door and a window to air the room out.

This would make it four times that he peeked across the street hoping that he'd get a glimpse of her, Momma Jo's helper. But if he couldn't see her, at least he could recall her in his imagination as he cleaned.

"I wish to God I had a steam-clean machine
I'd wax this job like a one-man football team
with all this muck on the walls, this damn nicotine
I can't see this place fit for no human bein' . . .

So for now I'll be the inn keeper's housemaid
I'll buy the Spic and Span, the Lysol, the bleach, and
Raid I'll be Cindafella and clean this place all day,
but I'll do it while I dream about the cutie 'cross the way."

"Can a girl rent your services?" said a voice from behind Ringo. And he would've jumped, shaken by the surprise. But this was such a pleasant surprise, one that triggered a smile.

"*Whoa* . . . scared me," Ringo lied.

"Sorry. I just came over to bring your change and the door was open."

"Of course," said Ringo, trying to hide any trace of street slang and ready to go to most any extreme to win her over. "I forgot all about it. I kinda got lost in my work."

"Gee, come to think of it, I've never seen the inside of one of these rooms. I thought it was much smaller."

Ringo looked it over as if for the first time.

"Almost like a mini apartment, isn't it? Oh—watch your step. The bucket," Ringo warned. *No, you did not just come inside.*

"Sorry, I can't offer you a seat. I can hardly lay or sit on the mattress, as soft as it is . . . I'm afraid I might sink."

She put her hand over her mouth.

"I'm—I'm sorry. I didn't mean to laugh."

"Oh, it's okay. This is all a joke . . . for now, anyway. Did you say you had—?"

"Sorry again. Here ya go. Eleven dollars and—"

"Eleven dollars? I gave you a twenty."

She offered a guilty smile. "I have—a receipt for you with all—"

"No, no. I'm not doubting you. I was just surprised, that's all. You go ahead and keep that."

"Oh no. I couldn't—"

"Ringo."

"Excuse me?"

"I'm Ringo," he said, extending his hand. "I just figured we haven't been properly introduced."

"Yes. Well, Ringo, this is too much to be a tip."

And too little to be anything more, he thought.

"Depends on who's doing the tipping, doesn't it? And I'm sorry. I didn't get your name," Ringo tossed in the casual request.

"And I didn't give you my name," she replied, and put the money on the bed. "Mister, I don't know who you are, or what drugs you sell, but you can't buy me. And I don't know what made you think I was for sale."

Without another word she left, pulling the door shut behind her.

I'll be DAMNED if she didn't just diss me.

Ringo copped an attitude for an instant, then he smiled and went back to cleaning and rapping.

"I like you, girl, but you won't get away so easy,
I didn't come to Bridgeport for you to treat me greasy,
I'll take my time, no matter how much you tease me,
but when I smash that ass, shit's gonna be off the heezy!"

Ringo laughed deliriously and wondered if that little interaction was the boy-meets-girl portion of their forthcoming relationship.

Chapter Three

Tom Kellogg, the manager and inn keeper, had his office at the front of the horseshoe. He also lived there as far as Ringo could tell, since there was a counter in the office, a simple couch in the lobby, and then a door that obviously separated his work from his domestic life.

Ringo went to see Kellogg to ask if he could toss out the bed that came with the room.

When he rang the bell at the counter it took all of five minutes for the hillbilly type to show his face. And if not for the announcement from behind that dividing door—"I'll be right out!"—Ringo would have come back another time. When Kellogg emerged from back there he was in shorts and a T-shirt, revealing more flab than Ringo cared to see around his legs, arms, and what bounced about his chest. One of his legs had the tattoo of a young girl—maybe his daughter—with her long hair and pretty eyes, nowhere near resembling Kellogg.

"Sorry to disturb you," mentioned Ringo, and he suddenly forgot why he'd even come to the office. It was the sight of the black girl, back there in Kellogg's crib. The man hadn't closed the door, and Ringo could see her buttoning her blouse—pink, silky, and form-fitting.

"No problem a'tall," said Kellogg, realizing where Ringo's attention had turned.

"What can"—he shut the door—"I do for you?" And there was the quaint smile.

His eyes shifting back to what he quickly assessed as a dirty old man, Ringo went on with his request.

"Uh, yeah. I was just wondering, if you didn't mind, I wanted to get rid of that bed in my room."

With certain denial already in his eyes, Kellogg began to answer.

"Well, Mr. Jenkins—"

The discussion was interrupted when the door swung open.

"See ya next week, Kellogg."

"Yeah, next week, Tangi. And don't be late."

Kellogg had some of the devilish pride seeping from his grin. And Tangi rolled her eyes in response as she strutted by barefoot, with her strap-up sandals in hand.

When she passed Ringo there was a certain guilt about her, in the way she avoided eye contact and reached up with her free hand to smooth her hastily-tied-back hair.

"So, Mr. Jenkins . . ." There was contempt in his tone. "You say you wanna get rid of my bed? That bed cost me money, sir."

"I'm sure," said Ringo, his eyes pulling away from Tangi's backyard in motion. "But I wouldn't mind replacing it myself." Ringo had to get used to being called Greg Jenkins. He felt Kellogg's vibe, and that he was aware that the name was phony. But he also got the idea that such fabrication was okay with the man; that he'd accept whatever pretenses as long as the rent was paid on time.

"Whoa. With your own money?"

"Yes, sir."

"Shit, son. We oughta go into business together. Hell no, I don't mind if you buy a bed. It's gonna be a good one, I'm sure." Kellogg was questioning as well as presuming, but he was gradually politicking as well.

"I mean, you wouldn't get somethin' cheap that would break down after a couple of weeks."

Ringo kept the comment he had to himself.

"No. Of course not, Mr. Kellogg. I'll spend some good money. I'll even make sure to come back to you with the receipt."

"Hmmm." Kellogg stroked his shaved chin. "And you'll leave the bed here if you should have to up 'n' leave?"

"Absolutely."

"Well then, I'll tell you what. You give me the receipt, and I'll even go half with you on the cost." Not expecting any such generous assistance, Ringo wondered what Kellogg had to gain by having the receipt. Maybe something regarding taxes, Ringo guessed. But then he shrugged that off, unfamiliar himself with paying taxes.

"You're a good businessman, Kellogg. I don't care what they say about you." And Ringo got out of there, leaving Kellogg with that strange expression, maybe unable to decipher the full meaning behind the comment.

Butter and Sweets were Kellogg's hired help who shared in the grounds keeping, tending to the trash, sweeping the large parking lot, and doing maintenance—fixing sinks, unclogging toilets, and changing locks whenever residents moved out. Ringo hadn't lived at the inn for long enough to see it himself, but he could imagine these two bulky men executing some no-more-excuses evictions on behalf of a sometimes ruthless innkeeper. Just as soon as Butter and Sweets completed their day's work, they came to remove the crusty, sagging bed from Ringo's room. And while they were at it, Ringo had them take out the seedy easy chair as well.

"Here, guys," Ringo said, handing the two men a few bills.

"What's that for?" asked Butter. "Kellogg pays us for this."

Ringo appreciated the man's honesty and said, "That's fine. This is just something extra for the two of you. Here, take it. Please."

"Man. This is a whole week's pay, mister.

What're you, rich or somethin'?"

"I wish."

By 6 p.m., a truck had rolled up into the Motor Inn's parking lot—which was almost empty since most residents were without automobiles—frightening the children, who generally knew this as their safe playground. The arrival of the truck was another relief for Ringo, since he had such a time of persuading the furniture store.

Earlier in the day he flipped through the local newspaper and spotted a pullout from the Furniture Outlet that bragged:

DELIVERY TO YOUR DOORSTEP. However, the salesperson on the phone made up some poor excuse.

"Sorry. The inn is out of range for deliveries." And Ringo thought back to the cab driver when he'd asked to be taken to the nearest motel: *Are you sure?*

"I'm paying cash," Ringo told the salesman.

"Honestly, sir, you sound quite sincere, but you should know that we've been burned once or twice before when callers ordered by phone. And . . . well, not for nothin', but you're asking us to deliver to the State Street Motor Inn? I mean, wouldn't *you* think that was fishy? And you're on a pay phone to boot? I wasn't born yesterday."

The line went dead.

"Motha—" Ringo slammed down the phone and put more money in the slot.

"Listen. Don't piss me off. Your ad says you sell furniture. Your ad says *delivery to your doorstep*. Now, why the f—Why would I waste money in a pay phone if this was a prank call? I need some damned furniture!"

"Easy, mister. I'll tell you what. How about coming down to the store to leave a deposit. Surely, a man who can order a thousand dollars worth of furniture, sight unseen, can drive down—" Ringo mashed his hand over his face, thinking about sleeping on the floor, all because of the rude salesman.

"No, mister. I don't have a phone. I don't have a car, and I can't order the stuff over the Internet, but I have enough cash in my hands to pay your salary for a year. . . ."

There was a silence on the line as Ringo figured out another way to do this without having to leave State Street.

"Tell *you* what . . . I'll send someone down in a taxi with the money. Would that be good enough?"

"Well then, now you're talking."

"All right then. Have my order ready by five o'clock." Ringo hung up the phone and then, finally, he understood the reputation that the inn and its neighborhood had earned.

Now that the truck was here, with Butter and Sweets on hand for the job, a small audience gathered.

The children all stood by in awe, as if this was Christmas.

Meanwhile, other residents peeked out of their windows or otherwise boldly stood outside of their doorways with their bodies almost folded, or else chatting with neighbors and pointing.

Suddenly Ringo had become a stageshow—it was attention that he never anticipated or wanted. *Damn. It's just a few pieces of furniture—not like I'm building another Disney World.*

"Okay, kids, go and play. Let the men do their work," he said, making his way through the crowd, interested in getting a look at the furniture he'd be paying half for.

"You like it?"

"Yeah—yeah, I guess I do. But we never talked about an easy chair and table," said Kellogg.

"I know, Mr. Kellogg. I haven't changed the deal—just give me half on the bed and the rest is on me."

"Well shit, young man. Ain't gotta tell me twice." And he pulled out some money to tip the driver. The way he peeled off the bills was so obviously done, to show all of the spectators that he was the one paying for these things.

Ringo snickered and told himself, *Whatever makes you happy, Kellogg.*

By Ringo's third day at the inn, the novelty of Nelly's Wings had worn off. Ringo began to diversify his meals, choosing alternatives from a series of other fast food restaurants, including Chinese, Japanese, Caribbean, and Italian. And naturally there were pizzas and hoagie sandwiches from Subway.

The meals didn't hurt his pockets any, just a mere fifty dollars a day for the convenience.

There was also the payphone use that was becoming a nuisance—the change, waiting for another user to complete his or her call, and most important, there was no call-back number listed on the device. Besides that, the phone was out in the open, where he swore that the many residents of the inn were spying on him, and maybe even clocking his every activity.

In the game of secrecy, of going underground and hibernating, Ringo was sure doing a poor job of things.

He eventually found a cell phone company, also in the local paper, that claimed to make "house calls."

Soon, he had a cell phone with his own phone number in the name of Greg Jenkins, and plenty of privacy to go with it.

More comfortable now in his clean living quarters, Ringo spent hours focusing on some goals. Sure, he was a prisoner of sorts, but it was according to his leisure, with all of the conveniences of a long-term vacation. He read books like *Holler If You Hear Me,* by Michael Eric Dyson; *When Chickenheads Come Home to Roost*, by Joan Morgan; and just about the whole Donald Goines catalog. He read about civil rights struggles, racial conflict, and every Nelson George book, whether it was about the music industry or not.

To break up the monotony, Ringo watched his new nineteen-inch television cable service—compliments of Kellogg—and he'd keep his stereo (also new) tuned to New York's hip-hop radio personalities and the latest music in current rotation.

Most important, Ringo spent hour upon uninterrupted hour writing new rhymes and reciting them with a stopwatch in hand, since a song only lasts so long before losing a listener's attention.

After two weeks of being Ringo, the homebody, it was a thrill to hear a knock at his door. He was sure that he was out of danger, and that the Just Right tragedy was behind him. So he hoped it was the pretty girl from Momma Jo's, coming back to apologize. Ringo didn't even take the time to ask who it was—he just pulled open the door.

"Hi. I . . . uh . . . well, this is for you. A little welcome bag I put together." It was the girl he'd seen in Kellogg's home office the other day. Ringo would've checked his watch if he had had one on. *A welcome bag?*

"I guess it's better late than never," he said, trying to keep from being sarcastic. "You wanna come in? I would appreciate some friendly company about now."

She gave a nervous nod and Ringo took the so-called welcome bag—nothing more than a brown shopping bag—and he set it down, not wanting to open it in front of his guest.

"You're *working* for Tom Kellogg, aren't you? I remember you from his office. What's your name?"

"Tangi Stokes," she answered, and thanked Ringo for inviting her inside, but not before checking over her shoulder to see who might be watching.

"Wow, you really hooked your place up."

"No big deal," Ringo said, thinking again about the finances he'd calculated earlier—in two weeks he'd spent just over $3,000 of his $58,000, not including the two thousand dollars he'd left for his pop. And before the money disappeared, before it got as low as $50,000, Ringo made a commitment to himself: he'd have to start making money instead of just spending it. He had to consider long-term survival, not just short-term living.

"I been meaning to stop by earlier, but you seemed busy. Don't you go out?"

"Yeah, now and then. But I *was* busy—you're right. Whoever stayed in this place last left it a mess, like a pig pen."

"I can't tell," Tangi said, still impressed, her eyes dancing through the room.

"You live here at the inn too, don't you?"

"Yup," she said, with her hand caressing her neck and collarbone. "Down in twenty-two-A." Ringo thought of how the complex was sectioned in six parts—A through F.

"Oh, 'kay. That's near the back. You're there with family?"

"Mmm hmm. My momma and two brothas. They both knuckleheads—younger than me."

"How old are you, Tangi?" Ringo was looking closer now—her God-given assets outlined by the black halter top and denim shorts. The Nike sneakers she wore were new—enough to still live on the store shelf.

If she is a whore, at least she keeps herself together.

"Eighteen," she replied in shy fashion.

"And cute, too." Ringo threw in the compliment as he reached into his miniature icebox. "Coke?"

"Thank you," she said as she took the soda. "I mean, for the props. I try to keep it tight, ya know? Momma says a girl's always gotta be on top of her glam game, whether poor, rich, or in between." Tangi snickered. "Ma is crazy."

"Even so, she must know what she's talkin' about. Bet she looks as good as you."

"Ma holds it down. But when we go to the club it's me that

gets most of the numbers. She might beat me out once in a while, but all the niggas say I'm hot like fire."

Ringo was thinking how Tangi opened her mouth to speak, with practically her whole life story spilling out. She was becoming more transparent. In the mood to listen and learn, Ringo asked, "Just how often do you go around with welcome bags?" He wondered if he had misjudged the girl, and he took up her brown bag. It was all fresh fruit, something anybody could be thankful for. Apples, oranges, pears, and bananas.

"Or—am I the first one to get a bag of fruit?" Before Tangi could answer, an idea tapped on Ringo's shoulder. Something told him that Tangi's mom put her up to this, that she helped her daughter put the bag together, that she gave her a few pointers, swatted her on the ass, and said: *Go get 'em, girl!*

The thought amused Ringo, aware that he might appear to be a good catch to the nosy residents (the spies) at the inn.

But then, Tangi didn't seem like a con artist to him. And even if she was, her eyes reflected the truth . . . she wasn't addressing him as just any stranger, and she probably figured him to be a city nigga (another way of saying city slicker)—likely some of the talk that went on behind his back. She probably saw him as someone who knew the talk and the walk, someone who could see through most characters.

The revelation pushed Ringo to answer his own question. He said, "Not that I'd be mad at you for just wantin' to kick it with me. I needed some company anyway, for real."

Tangi seemed impressed and said nothing. Her eyes wandered again.

Meanwhile, Ringo studied her. He inspected every contour and curve, and he wasn't ashamed in doing so. To say the least, he was thrilled at how she was presenting herself for his approval. And he didn't have to be city slick to know she was also making herself available to him.

She was checking out the stereo system and rack of CDs now. And her back was to him, with that same tight ass that was shouting as it passed by him in Kellogg's office.

Kellogg . . . she was buttoning her shirt . . . she was barefoot.

But she was in Ringo's company now, looking refreshed and open-minded. And besides, Ringo hadn't been with a woman in two weeks—enough reason for him to ignore the thought of her and the inn keeper.

For now, he had to think things over and consider how he'd play his cards. It was a battle between his loneliness and his objectives.

Yes, he needed someone around to keep an eye on things.

There'd be that convenience he needed, of sex with no strings attached. But at what cost? Who was this girl really? What kind of drama did she have hidden, tucked away between her folds?

Ringo was hit with that image again—Tangi in the shorts and T-shirt, the sandals in one hand, the other hand smoothing back her rushed hairdo, that guilt on her face . . . *See you next week, Tangi . . . and don't be late*, Kellogg had said.

Oh brother.

Forgetting that scene wasn't as easy as he'd thought.

"How come you ain't got no girlfriend?" she asked.

Thinking quickly, Ringo said, "I ain't really been checkin' for no girls. I'm on a mission."

"It's like that?" Tangi turned her eyes from the CDs she held, the expression implying something might be peculiar about him.

Ringo chuckled. "No—I'm not gay, so get that out of your head. When I say I'm not checkin' for girls, it's because, one, I'm not into girls, I'm into women. And two, I'm too busy, period."

"What you busy doin'?" Tangi asked, as if she had been keeping a record of his comings and goings.

"I rap."

"What, like, gangsta rap? Or that pop shit?"

Ringo chuckled again.

"Since you put it that way, it's something like hard-core sex and violence."

Ringo swore he was seeing things, how her nipples made further impressions under the black halter top.

Tangi's face lit up.

"Can you do a rhyme for me?"

Ringo laughed loud enough for folks to hear him out in the parking lot."

"Ha ha ha ha. You are fu—nny! Do a rhyme?"

Tangi frowned. "I'm *serious.* I love rap. Old school, new school—everything. *Please?*"

"*Well, I would bust a rhyme but it's not the time/*
I'm not in the mood . . . to be spittin' hard lines."

Tangi smiled so much it must've hurt.

Once she realized Ringo was rhyming, she turned vibrant, so excited she didn't know what to do with herself.

Ringo went on:

"*What I'd rather do*
And I don't mean to be crass
I'd like to kiss you up and down
Get my hands on your ass.

You pretty like a flower,
where'd you come from
And are you sellin' any cookies?
'Cause I'm hungry for some."

Tangi was shivering something awful. Not only were her nipples hard, but she was moist enough to form a big ole wet spot in her shorts. Her mouth opened slightly and her eyes bugged out some.

Finally, she had to swallow.

No, he didn't just say.

Tangi's heart fluttered and she lost focus. She found it hard to speak.

"So? Did you like it?"

"You . . . just made that up? Right here and now? I mean, were you serious?" Tangi's voice trembled.

Ringo shrugged. An awkward moment followed, during which the two made their own internal decisions. Ringo spoke first.

"Well?"

"Um . . . yeah. I . . . I liked it. I *loved* it."

"What part"—Ringo approached Tangi—"did you like best? About me kissin' you up and down? Or . . . my hands on your ass?"

Tangi blushed and she became uncomfortable standing still, as if she'd fall apart if not for her clothing.

"Or . . . maybe you liked how I called you pretty like a flower."

Tangi's eyes twinkled like sparkling diamonds in Ringo's tight grip. She was feeling soft and gushy now, wanting to be touched and controlled by him. Close enough to warm her with his breathing and his body heat, Ringo leaned in to her with his hands clasped behind his back.

The very edges of his lips grazed Tangi's cheek as he went to whisper in her ear, tickling her with his words.

"Where you want it? The bed? The floor? Or up against the wall?"

"I . . . I . . ." Tangi swallowed her words instead of them leaving her mouth. "I don't know." At the same time her breathing was heavy and uncontrolled against Ringo's neck.

"You feel like makin' some music together?"

"I—I guess . . . Yeah," she sighed. Ringo nibbled on Tangi's earlobe and she stood there, with her hands at her sides and her loins quivering. Excited himself, Ringo choreographed his moves, blowing on Tangi's neck, working his way around her and then wrapping his arms around her waist. He pulled her gently against the rock in his pants and slid his hands up over her breast. So far, in the battle between loneliness and objectives, loneliness was whippin' ass in a big way.

"You sure your momma wouldn't mind?"

Tangi smiled, then told him the truth.

"She's the one who sent me," she admitted. She turned around so that they were face-to-face, and clasped her hands behind his neck.

Ringo stood a foot taller than Tangi, and she was five and a half feet. A long kiss connected the two, their tongues busy in every corner of their mouths until they were familiar with each other's taste.

Ringo led most of the activity, his hands exploring her body until her halter top was untied and shed to the floor. He got a hungry man's look at Tangi's perky breasts, not sagging the least bit, and unique with large nipples—wide as half dollars and swollen like dark ant hills atop her mahogany brown skin.

Tangi was jittery with Ringo examining her like this, and she crossed her arms. Ringo gently swept her arms back to her sides, exercising his willpower.

"Come-eer," he murmured, leering at Tangi through lizard-like slits, one brow notoriously arched. She obeyed, slithering up to him and closing the distance.

There was a brief, not affectionate kiss this time. Ringo followed it by scooping her off her feet and laying her on his brand-new bed.

"Take this off, girl," said Ringo as he stripped out of his own clothes. And he stood there in his fitted briefs telling himself that this was too easy. But at the same time he needed companionship, someone to keep his affection muscles strong and his well of passion from going dry.

He crawled down on top of her, drawn in by the surrender in her eyes—so deep with desire, and yet betraying traces of innocence.

He kissed and licked along the nape of her neck and under her chin. She smelled good enough to eat, even perspiring like she was.

"What do you—do with—that man?" Ringo asked between the grunting, their bodies twisting about for position, and their mouths eating at this and that pleasure point.

"Uhmph . . . ohh . . . oooh . . . what—man?"

Ringo ate his way between her breasts, moving southbound toward her center.

"Kellogg."

"Once in a while—I, unhhh . . . help out with the rent, ooh, baby that's sooo good."

Ringo stopped to look her in the eye.

Tangi said, "It ain't nothin', really. I don't even feel nothin' when I'm with him."

"Once in a while? What's that supposed to mean?"

"Once, sometimes twice a month. Why you trippin'?" Tangi asked, as if fucking the landlord to pay the rent was the most normal occurrence in the world.

"And your mother knows about this?"

"Please. He used to do it with Momma, but he said he got tired of the same old pussy. Then Momma talked to me."

"Damn, girl. Your mother gives you away like that? How long this been goin' on?"

"About two years, since my pop was killed around the corner. But I only did it with him since two months ago."

"That shit is triflin', Tangi." And Ringo slumped over onto his back, yet to enter her.

Both of them laid there and stared up at the ceiling. A moment later Tangi sniffled. Ringo wondered if that, too, was practiced—part of a performance she knew well.

Eventually it got to him and he turned toward her.

"Hard knock life, huh?"

"But I'm strong. I'm a woman."

"Then why do I get the feeling you don't believe in yourself? You don't sound real with it, like you been sayin' those words for a long time."

"I *do* believe it."

"No, you don't."

"How could you say that? You hardly know me."

And that was a hell of a thing to say at a time like this. In one sense, she was right. And it was much too mature a point for her to make. Too conscious. However, on the other side of the coin, she was right on target, since that was exactly what Ringo wanted: No strings attached.

He didn't care to know about this girl's past escapades (with or without her mother, the pimp), or about her rent romps with Tom Kellogg, or her lack of self-esteem that got her into these situations from jumpstreet.

All of these things were none of Ringo's business, and too

much information for a man who just wanted to splash around in a woman's bowl of cream, a man who was supposed to be invisible and unattached to anything.

And now that he had a chance to think twice about it, the idea turned sour—too insensitive a state of mind, especially after reading the *Chickenheads* book.

As if reading his mind, Tangi asked, "You want me to go?"

"Yeah, you better."

And as soon as Tangi left, Ringo found the copy of *Essence* he'd bought from across the street, and he finished relieving himself with long, imaginative strokes. With as much skin as the magazine featured, it felt like the right thing to do, like this was the perfect alternative.

Chapter Four

THE MONEY MELTED down to $51,000. and that's just how Ringo saw it—a block of ice sitting out in the hot sun, dripping slowly to nothing. Meanwhile, Ringo buried himself in reading, therefore channeling his sexual frustrations, and mostly forgetting about his attempts with the two local girls.

He seldom went to Momma Jo's these days since Butter didn't mind running errands, however indebted he felt to Ringo for the money received after moving those few pieces of furniture. And it was for the best that Tangi was avoiding 41E, because this was becoming an acceptable introverted lifestyle. A safe one that beat out a jail cell by a long shot.

It was three months into Ringo's residency at the inn that he lost his cable signal. The weather was pleasant and there was no reason, as far as Ringo could tell, why the cable should be off. This was also not the first time it happened, however it was easily connected once Ringo contacted Kellogg.

Ringo had the funny feeling that Kellogg cut the cable in a way to have residents call or come to see him in person. Either this was a devil's tactic for getting some quick response for whatever reason, or Kellogg was lonely and wanted attention. But, of course, that was only a guess.

"Shit." Ringo realized that one of his favorite shows, *Behind the Music*, was about to rebroadcast the feature they produced on Tupac. He phoned Kellogg, however the answering machine was taking all calls.

So, in order for him not to miss his show, Ringo made a short trek across the lot headed for the management office.

The sky was gray, not quite pitch-black, and the moon was such a perfect circle, so radiant and glowing, that Ringo thought the universe had to be in good working order.

The moon also helped to illuminate the grounds about the inn, since Kellogg didn't go out of his way by any means to provide lighting.

At least the front office had its neon sign flashing: NO VACANCY. And there was a lamp on over the door, just as it was with most other residences in the complex. Inside the office was dark since it was obviously closed for the night.

Ringo knew that Kellogg's residence was behind the office, so he shuffled around back and knocked on the door.

His knock fell softly against the door and it gave a few inches. He wondered if it was hastily closed, just another advertisement on behalf of Kellogg, the slob.

There was a whimper, but it was loud enough to be a cry.

Ringo looked back over his shoulder, then this way, then that, to be sure that his creeping was his secret alone.

His conscience was clear regarding what he was—a peeping Tom, a trespasser. But to be considered an intruder was the least of his concerns; after all, hadn't he already broken some of the most critical of the ten commandments?

Now he heard a distressed voice.

"No. Not *there*!" Then a muffled scream.

Tangi.

Ringo shut the door behind him and followed the sounds, the husky breathing and muffled cries. Kellogg's residence was somewhat larger than the other dwellings at the inn, but not so much that Ringo couldn't navigate.

Some light was fanning out from under a bedroom door.

"Take it easy, Kellogg," beckoned a female's voice. And again, Ringo assumed it was Tangi's performance. The mere idea of it both excited and nauseated him.

More muffled cries. Skin being slapped. Again, but louder.

Damn. Ringo couldn't wait to match the imagery with the sounds. When alas he did, he had to rub his eyes.

Tangi was lying on her stomach, on the bed. Kellogg was standing behind her, holding her thighs as he continuously pounded her insides—a finish momentum, with no affection and no compassion. Ringo couldn't be certain, but it looked like he was going in and out of her ass.

But the bigger surprise was that the two were not alone.

There was another woman kneeling on the bed watching while holding Tangi down, restraining her and covering her mouth.

Ringo stood there, his own mouth agape, stuck somewhere between disbelief and fascination.

Her moms?

The older woman was the spitting image of Tangi—an older version. And now Ringo got a better look at Tangi's face: tears and anguish.

Goddamn!

Without a word, Ringo snatched Kellogg by the neck. There was a grunt as Ringo thrust the older man into a wall.

"What the—"

"Get off her!" Ringo ordered.

"Who the fuck is you? Who the fuck is this, Kelly?" Tangi's mother asked.

Ringo assumed "Kelly" was a pet name—a little too personal for his taste.

"Don't worry about who *I* am, just raise up off that girl before I start wuppin' yo' ass!"

"This is my daughter, *asshole*. I'll do what I—"

Ringo had already begun his approach, and now he backslapped Tangi's mother in midsentence. She let out a shriek as she fell back on the bed.

"You okay?" Ringo asked Tangi.

She nodded tearfully and clung to Ringo as he lifted her up from the bed with nothing but a sheet to cover her abused body.

"Look at her. You lay a hand on this girl again and shit's gonna get ugly around here. Your party's over."

"You can't just come in here and—"

"Oh, but yes I can. And go ahead, call five-o if you want.

We'll see how the newspapers like the headlines: The Inn keeper and the young girl on their front page."

Then, to Tangi's mom, Ringo said, "Not to mention you, endangering the welfare of a minor."

Tangi cried like a baby as Ringo carried her back to his place. Her sobs were muffled with her face turned into his chest. He looked around, wondering how many were spying now, wondering if this type of abuse was going on all along, for the sake of paying the rent.

Inside of 41E, Ringo set Tangi down on his bed, keeping her covered, and he went to draw a warm bath for her.

No words were exchanged, just the duties of nursing Tangi. He didn't have anything in the way of first aid, but he was gentle and kind to her, something she desperately needed.

"I read somewhere that water heals everything," said Ringo, doing his best to assure his friend. And he gave her hot tea to help soothe her nerves.

Tangi, Tangi, Tangi.

"Can you get out of the tub on your own?"

Ringo asked after handing her the cup.

"Mmmhmm . . ."

"Good. I'll be in the next room if you need me."

He caressed her head and kissed the bridge of her nose, then turned to leave the bathroom.

"Mr. Jenkins?"

Ringo turned to answer, suddenly wanting to tell her the truth.

"Ringo. Call me Ringo, okay?"

"Well, thank you, Ringo."

"Don't mention it," he said.

In the next room Ringo huffed and squeezed his eyes closed, asking some higher power for the tolerance to put up with this.

And to top it all off, he forgot about the cable problem, so his VH-1 *Behind the Music* Tupac feature was a no-go. Ringo flopped down on his bed and tried to make sense of things.

Later, Tangi sat apart from Ringo, trying to get into the movie he had playing.

"You must think I'm a slut," she said after she told herself, *To hell with the movie.*

The comment hung in the air for some time until Ringo eventually picked up the remote to lower the volume on the TV.

"That depends."

"Depends? On what?"

"It depends. Was that *everybody's* idea? I mean, how'd you end up like that? With your moms?"

"She tricked me."

"Humph—" It was a high-pitched response. "Ain't that a bitch. Tricked you. *How?*"

"She told me to go see Kelly."

Ringo shook his head frantically. "Kelly? You mean *Kellogg*? 'Cause I ain't tryin' to get to know him as *Kelly*. Know what I'm sayin'?" Ringo took a deep breath.

"Okay. Well then, Kellogg. She told me to go and see him. It was just supposed to be me and him, like always."

"Another rent party, huh?"

Tangi didn't appreciate the way he said that. She said, "Well, he hit me. And while I was cryin' he told me to phone Momma. Then Momma came over and got all mad at me, but I could see she was fakin'. Plus she . . ."

Ringo waited as long as he could.

"Plus she *what*?"

"She sick."

"Sick? That triflin' wench is *demented*."

"No, really," Tangi pled her mother's case. "She has this . . . problem."

Ringo came to his own conclusion.

"Drugs," he said.

Tangi was silent and went back to watching the silent Samuel Jackson flick.

"Tangi, even the worst case, even the most drugged-up mother . . . damn, girl." Ringo's thoughts were shifting from one place to the next.

"I ain't never heard of the shit I just seen you mixed up in. She's pimpin' you *and* beatin' your ass. And tell the truth, how old are you *really*?"

Tangi's lids closed in slow motion and her head wagged ever so gradually, like she couldn't believe what she was about to say. Her hand touched her bruised cheek to feel it still throbbing.

"Here, put this on it," Ringo said, handing her an ice pack. "And you still ain't answered me."

Tangi mumbled an intentionally inaudible reply.

"Excuse me? What was that? I ain't wearin' my hearin' aid."

"*Sixteen, okay*? Damn."

Ringo turned to stone as he appraised Tangi with new eyes—a fresh point of view.

Sixteen years old!? Fuck. I could be in jail right now.

Ringo began to experience a whirlwind of thoughts. What was it that saved him? What miracle? Was it that he followed his heart in order to pull away from Tangi when she made herself available to him nearly three months earlier?

What stopped him from thinking with his head—the one *below* his belt? And if that something was discipline, or some sixth sense, then what stopped him from using that when he needed it most, on the fateful day on Queens Boulevard?

His thoughts strayed back to Tangi. Ringo was headstrong and not about to have these two adults abuse this girl.

For the period of time that Tangi had her eyes closed, Ringo found himself staring at her—not questioning her intentions or her strengths and weaknesses. No, Ringo was looking deeper, past the pretty face and physical features . . . past the dead skin, the muscle tissue and blood vessels, right through her skeleton, until he imagined a ticking device where her brain might be. Seeing past all these layers was a frightening experience, even creating the beginnings of a cold sweat.

Jesus. I'm reading too fucking much.

Ringo wasn't even educated enough (not by traditional means, anyhow) to make sense of what he was experiencing, but the seeds of wonder were there. Wasn't Tangi merely a name? A life force that ate, breathed, digested, and evolved? A machine that somehow learned to survive, to maintain itself for the purpose of embodying expressions, thoughts, and conscious energy?

Ringo didn't even know Tangi's entire background, and still he could taste where she'd come from, the road she must've traveled. He didn't need to do any more than recall the frustrations of his own experience. Back in Queens, the apartment building where he grew up was full of issues: the baby-momma drama, the drug use, the drug abuse. Social services and social workers, police, housing police, and the Department of Child Welfare. The juvenile justice system.

The images raced through his consciousness (whether he experienced these things directly or indirectly) like a fast-forward video montage. Just to think he could escape all of that, all that was his past. To think that this was his way out of the ghetto. What a dumb idea *that* was.

But, like all things, Ringo was evolving. The only question was whether it was for better or worse. To dream up his goal was one thing.

SO YOU WANNA BE A RAPPER? an advertisement asked. And there were the three talent shows he won back to back that got his hopes up.

"Get smart, Ringo. The only way you're ever gonna be respected is if you come hard. You gotta go at it from a position of strength. Power. That means money," Brice, the pessimist, said.

"Whatever," Ringo had said to Brice. "I'll get two jobs if I have to. Even three."

"You know what your problem is? It's your heart. You ain't got the heart to take what you want," Brice charged. "Whitey done took what he wanted for years, and he even sugarcoated it all so we young dudes would just swallow it like some sweet-'n'-sour candy. Nah, *fuck* that. You gotta *take* what you want, troop."

That one conversation led to an out-of-state stickup. They robbed a drug dealer's cash—close to $22,000—and split the money into three parts. But $7,000 was chump change in the real world of car notes and mortgages. So they went at it again, this time breaking into a store full of electronics.

What they were able to snatch within the space of fifteen minutes amounted to less than chump change once it was liquidated, so it turned out to be a futile effort—a lesson that made them reconsider risks versus net gain.

Then came the Just Right Check Exchange. Considering how he got away from his past and assumed a new identity for a second chance at life, and considering the way he stumbled upon Tangi's situation, becoming a sort of savior, Ringo could now see the bigger picture. He had come full circle; just like Brice used Ringo, so too was Tangi being used by her moms.

"Tangi, the real deal is I need to be calling the police. Your moms needs to be in jail . . . in therapy—*somethin'*."

Tangi gasped and stood up with fear in her eyes.

"Where you goin'?" asked Ringo.

"I'm outta here. If I knew you was gonna turn me in—"

"Wait a minute. Turn you in? *You* didn't do nothin' wrong."

"Yeah, but if the police find out about Momma, I'm done. I ain't old enough, so they gonna put me in a home. A jail with legal guardians."

Ringo jumped up and gently grabbed her wrist.

"How do you know all this? They took you from your moms before?"

"No. But they did my friend Tashina that way. Her nut-ass pops was puttin' her in the tub with a neighbor's little boy and he took pictures 'n' stuff. The police put her pops in jail and Tashina went to some house on the north side. But I'm not tryin' to go on the north side."

"Tangi,Tangi,Tangi. Relax. You ain't goin' to no north side. I was just speakin' my mind. I didn't say I was *gonna* call five-o."

"Why not?"

Ringo tried to think up a good answer. No dice. "I'm just not."

"And you ain't callin' Social Services?"

"No."

"How come?"

Ringo enjoyed Tangi's curiosity about things, but *damn*, she was getting on his nerves with all the questions.

"Because I don't wanna see nothin' bad happen to you. I . . . I wanna see you do big things with your life, not end up in the street sellin' your body."

Tangi sucked her teeth and had that 'round-the-way-girl attitude goin'. "Never would I do that."

Ringo wanted to tell Tangi what a contradiction she just presented, but instead he closed his eyes. She had a lot to learn.

"Sit down, Tangi. Please make yourself at home." Ringo could see that some of the threat had lifted, replaced by a degree of trust. And now she wouldn't stop looking at him.

"You think you'll be all right if I leave for a half hour? I wanna stop by a drugstore to pick you up some things; somethin' to help you heal up."

"Do you have any other movies? This one's kinda boring."

"Boring? Black fighter pilots are part of our history, girl. You gotta know where you come from to know where you are, and where you're goin'.

"Still . . . ," Tangi pleaded.

"You should watch it from the beginning. You might—"

"Naw, that's aight. How 'bout this one?"

"*Love and Basketball.*" Ringo wagged his head and went on to say, "See that's exactly why I'm gonna be rich one day, 'cause all niggas wanna know about is sex, violence, and sports."

"What about love?"

"Sex, love, same thing. Somebody just changes the word when they need to. The real deal is sex, girl—like they say in this book. Here, you might wanna check this out. There's a lot of readin' there, but the bottom line she gets to talkin' about is sex. There's power in it, girl. Without it, we wouldn't be here. And the day you learn to use the power, you'll be on top."

Ringo knew that he was risking a lot by leaving Tangi alone in his place, but it was a chance he felt he needed to take. He'd either misjudge her now and suffer the loss of some clothes and furnishings—and the bag of money was hidden under his bed—or he'd end up with someone trustworthy and faithful in the long run.

The long run. Ringo wondered how long that would be.

This was a strange feeling, this first outing from the Motor Inn since he'd arrived that first day by taxi. Again he hired a taxi—no sense in flashing his driver's license, or even attempting to drive—to take him downtown.

His first stop was to CVS, where he bought tubes of Preparation H and Neosporin, one ointment for Tangi's sore ass, another for her bruised face. After CVS, he stopped by the supermarket for some much-needed groceries, videos, and CDs. He also picked up a few of the latest crime fiction novels to read when he wasn't rapping, writing, or watching TV.

Finally, he grabbed a few bouquets of flowers from the rear of the supermarket, along with a ceramic vase to sit them in.

I wonder if Tangi has ever received flowers.

At the check-out line, Ringo was shook when he saw the time. Once the cab he called arrived, he hurried to pack the backseat and the trunk with his purchases. There was barely room for him and the driver.

"You're the same driver who picked me up at the train station a few months ago."

"Right, right, okay. I remember. I thought you was familiar when I got you today."

Ringo gave a closer look at the driver's license and attempted to pronounce the driver's name.

"No, that's Rojo—as in row a boat and Joe. Rojo."

"Okay, 'cause I was about to call you Roger."

"Actually, you could call me what you want, as long as it's good news."

Ringo liked this guy. And he figured he might use his services more often—like a private car service.

"Can I call you Kujo?"

"What—like the killer dog? I like that!"

"That's a bet. Kujo it is. Step on it, Kujo."

Sweets was available to lend a hand, and Kujo helped as well, while Ringo managed to unlock the door with one arm hugging a bag of groceries.

"It's me," Ringo announced, hoping to see Tangi as he left her, comfortable watching *Love and Basketball*. But that wasn't the case. There was laughter inside, even before the door swung all the way open. Tangi wasn't alone.

"Well, excuse me. I see we've made a friend," Ringo announced as he set the bag down.

"Porsha says y'all already met, so I didn't think it was—"

"Nah, it's okay, Tangi." *Porsha . . . that's her name.*

"Where you want these, boss?"

"Right there in Tangi's lap, Sweets. Thanks."

"Oh sh—" Tangi's hand covered her mouth, holding in what looked to be a lifetime worth of emotion. Her eyes watered as she cuddled the flowers like an infant child.

"Nobody *ever* . . ." Tangi jumped up and down and Porsha had an open-mouthed smile wide enough to fit an apple in. The two screamed and rejoiced until they tumbled onto the bed. Ringo counted maybe six oh-my-God's during the outburst, before Tangi eventually hopped up from the bed to rush Ringo.

It took just one footfall before Tangi felt pain, and she buckled.

"Tangi!" shouted Porsha, realizing what was happening.

Ringo gasped her name as well when both he and Sweets lunged to catch her fall.

"You have to take it easy," explained Ringo as they all helped Tangi back to the bed.

Tangi clung to Ringo, not wanting to let go. At the same time, Ringo and Porsha locked eyes.

"I guess I had you all wrong, mister."

"You can call me Ringo."

"And you can call *me* stupid for how I acted when I came through before."

"Don't sweat it, Porsha. I *can* call you Porsha, can't I?" Ringo didn't require an answer while Porsha raked both sets of fingers through her hair. He couldn't help but notice how her breast lifted some; how her armpits showed themselves. It was so sensual a motion that it effortlessly turned him on.

Kujo came in with the last of the groceries when Porsha finally spoke. Things were calm now.

"I'm really sorry, Ringo. *Really* sorry. You've been like a prince charming to Tangi. A hero. And I had to be blind to miss that, 'cause there ain't none of them around here."

Ringo thanked Kujo with a nod.

"I can handle things from here, Sweets," said Ringo. And once they left he picked through the bags to find the ceramic vase, he shuffled over to the kitchenette—nothing but a sink, a counter, a hot plate, and a couple of cabinets up on the wall—and he filled the vase with water.

"Where in the world did you come from?" Porsha asked, still with amazement in her eyes as she assisted Ringo.

"Listen, what I did was no big deal. Any real man woulda done what I did."

"Shit, you said *that* right. Any man. Trouble is, *real* men are hard to find," said Porsha, apparently with some pain and suffering behind her testimony. "The jerks around here are just niggas tryin' to get over one way or another. They want shit for free. They want what's in the panties for free."

"Sounds personal," said Ringo.

"Not really. That's just the way it is here. We don't have too much to choose from. And what we do have is, it's *boring*."

"Everything ain't always what it seems," warned Ringo. "And I didn't come here to solve all of your man problems. I'm human, and I got a heart. But trust me, I ain't perfect."

"Well, hell, you make it sound like you're the devil, mista. But if that's the case . . ."

Porsha was near Tangi now, and the two indulged in a high five. "Then send me into the flames." The girls hooted like spectators, with Ringo the male exotic dancer who was about to drop his drawers. And maybe he didn't go that far, but for sure, things had suddenly changed in Bridgeport.

RINGO WAS NO longer a solo act. Sweets and Butter, both of them big-bodied men, became available for most any task. Kujo was on call for errands and quick trips to the supermarket, and he taxied any of Ringo's new friends to wherever they wanted to go.

Porsha dropped by frequently now that Tangi was more or less Ringo's permanent house guest. The only times Tangi was away was to go to work and to make sure her mother hadn't drunk or drugged herself to death. Other than that, she made herself at home, sleeping on Ringo's bed during the day and leaving at night when he slept.

"You got me curious, Tangi. Three weeks I've gotten to know you and I still don't know where you disappear to at night. To tell you the truth—"

"Helloo," chirped Porsha, floating through the front door like some carefree, weightless butterfly. Ringo had that question mark expression going until he remembered he had made a spare key for his new friends to use. More than just that, Porsha had that glow about her; something special was happening to her, and it was obvious in her every gesture.

"I didn't break up anything important, did I?" Porsha asked, planting a kiss on Tangi's forehead and then gravitating toward Ringo, who she kissed on the very corner of his mouth with her slightly parted lips.

These kisses had grown from pecks to promises over the past weeks, waiting only for the right time, that next level. The ball was in Ringo's court.

"Oh no," said Tangi.

"Bzzzt. Wrong answer," said Ringo. "I was just asking Tangi where she goes three or four nights a week. Don't get me wrong, I'm not her pops or anything, and I know she's a young *woman* and all, but I can't help but worry."

"Tangi, you said you'd tell him." Porsha had her hands on her hips.

"Tell me? Tell me what?"

Tangi sucked her teeth and said, "I know, I know. I guess I was just waiting for the right time."

"The right time? The right time for what? Could somebody please stop ignoring me and let me know what the fuck is going on?" Ringo's cursing turned the request into a demand.

"Tangi . . . if you don't, I will," Portia threatened.

Tangi rolled her eyes at Porsha in a way that said, *You make me sick.*

"I didn't know how you'd take it, if you'd look at me like a slut."

"Come on—*me*? If anything, I'd give you advice. I'd give you guidance. Besides, nothing shocks me these days. Nothing."

Ringo braced himself for the worst, wondering if the girl, after all she'd been through, was performing tricks. Or worse.

"I dance topless at a place called The Last Kiss."

"Dance? *Dance?* Is that all? Damn, Tangi, you had me thinkin' you were out there sellin' your body."

"Sometimes it feels that way," she said.

"Every time I get on stage somebody's touchin' me."

"Whaddayou mean, *touchin'* you?"

"Well, they come up to tip me, the money usually folded so that I won't know how much it is—but I already know it's a dollar—and they stick it in my thong with their fingers all near my kitty. Or they smack my ass or whatever."

Ringo and Porsha were still-life subjects, glued to the words before they unfolded from Tangi's lips.

"But I don't sleep with 'em. I mean, I did go home with one dude before—but it's not like I'm hookin'. It's just that sometimes we have to show everything."

"Everything?"

"It's topless six nights a week. But on Saturday nights they have the CDP's."

"CDP's?"

Ringo couldn't make sense of the acronym.

"Closed door parties."

"Oh, and that's where it all comes off, huh?"

Tangi gave a guilty shrug, having shared her best-kept secret.

"At sixteen years old," said Ringo with lifted eyebrows.

"They don't know I'm sixteen."

"Sixteen," he repeated.

"I'll be eighteen in a year and a half," she protested, as if that made a difference.

"Five-o don't care about November. They go by what's on your ID *now*. And that's all they'll see when they bust this Last Kiss place with their CDP's."

Porsha joined in. "I've been sayin' that all along, Ringo. But the girl is hard-headed. I'm just waitin' for the day I get the jailhouse phone call: '*Could you bail me out, Porsha?*' "

"I *told you*, Porsha—"

"Yeah, I know. Heard it all before. Ben pays off the cops,

there's cops that work there, blah, blah, blah. Tell it to the judge."

Ringo asked, "What do you do with the money you make, Tangi?"

"Momma . . . she—"

Ringo put his hand up. "Save it. I'm about tired of my momma this, my momma that. Shit, girl, you ever consider choppin' off one of your arms or legs for that no good b—"

"Ringo," Porsha intervened, "the woman's sick."

"Sick? Yeah, she's sick, all right. Sick in the head. Why ain't she at the hospital if she's so sick? I ain't heard you talk about doctors or medication. Oh, my bad. She's *already* using medication."

"Ringo—," Porsha interrupted, trying to protect Tangi's feelings.

"No. It's okay, Porsha. He's right. I've been kinda feelin' this way the whole time. He's just keepin' it real."

"Listen, you two, I wanna talk to you about somethin'," said Ringo, persuading the girls to close into an intimate huddle. Ringo propped his hand on Porsha's knee.

"Now, you both know I rap and that I'm trying to go somewhere with it." Ringo didn't say this, but it was because of Tangi living with him, and Porsha's frequent visits, that he was afforded the liberty to make some moves. He'd been able to get away and hunt around for the various pieces that would help him with the big picture.

"See, I've been checkin' out certain producers downtown, tryin' to put together my own CD, hopefully within the next few months. Of course, this ain't no overnight process. I gotta review different music tracks, then I need to make a deal with a studio to master the whole thing, then there's the duplication of the CDs. A whole bunch of stuff. The bottom line is, I'm gonna need a few trusty people in my corner—ya know, to help me handle things."

Excitement grew in the eyes of Ringo's new friends. Even *he* wasn't clear as to why he'd need them—he just knew he would when the time came.

"So, why am I telling you this now? Because it's coming real close to blast off. I can already see myself in the studio within the next couple of weeks."

"What do you need us to do, Ringo?"

"Porsha, I need you to do what you've been doing. Giving support. Except now, instead of just stopping over to see Tangi and hang out, you'll have an agenda. And sooner than you think, I'll be payin' you both for your help."

"Aw damn!" said Tangi, ready to riot. "Ringo's gettin' ready to be on *Rap City.*"

"But Ringo, I'll help you for free. This isn't about money for me," Porsha said.

Tangi made a funny face, but didn't waiver from her position. "Whatever. I just know I'm tryin' to be sitting right next to my boy when it comes to the Source Awards and *106 & Park*, too."

"Okay, chill," said Ringo. "Business first."

"What, boo? You don't wanna be on BET? MTV?" asked Tangi.

"Well, yeah, I . . . all that stuff sounds good. But there's too much work to do. Too much to be thinkin' about before the awards 'n' shit."

Porsha said, "Still, I read somewhere that you gotta think big because it takes the same amount of effort to think small."

"Okay—see, that's good. That's the attitude I'm lookin' for. That's why I need you two. Support."

"Ooh, can I be your background singer?" offered Tangi. "Your hype man." After she saw Ringo's face, she changed her mind.

"Okay, then maybe I can get your coffee, or hold your towels?"

"Cut the shit, Tangi. You're all the hype—and headaches—I'll ever need. Just chill. I'll let you know what you can do when the time comes." Then to both he said, "I just wanted you all to have some hope to keep in your back pockets whenever it comes to decisions. I don't want you to do anything hasty because I need you."

"I'm in your corner, Ringo. Whatever you want," Porsha said.

"I've never been needed before," said Tangi.

"Unless you count Ben callin' me up on stage."

Oh brother, thought Ringo.

Chapter Five

MORE OFTEN, and more openly, Ringo was on the grind, meeting young deejays (who were aspiring producers) at the seediest nightspots in Bridgeport. The Cadillac Club. No Man's Land. Catmandoo. Most of these clubs were holes in the wall with an impoverished variety of drinks to choose from, a bass-heavy sound system, and the same ol' fashions.

Ringo noticed both of the two extremes when it came to the women: Some wore tight short-shorts or skirts with a bikini top or blouse that left little to the imagination, while others wore baggy clothing and posted like tomboys, with hats to the back. Brothas had on mostly baggy wear as well, with the whole bling-bling show going on. Fakes, phonies, and frauds in a few cases but toting their unfriendly expressions as a defensive mechanism.

"I'm supposed to meet with DJ Solo," Ringo told a bouncer who stood outside of the front entrance.

Club Domino had a number of dominos that were bigger than life-size on the marquee above the doorway. The dominos were somebody's bright idea: instead of letters to spell the club name, let's use the real thing.

"Sure you are. Same as everybody else in line."

"Can you let him know I'm out here? He'll confirm—"

"Dude. You see all these people out here waitin' to get in? My job is to check IDs, check for weapons, and maintain security. Do I look like an errand boy to you?"

Ringo could hear the message underlying the words: *You're*

a nuisance. Go get in line like everybody else. And he wasn't looking to make a scene, even if his ego was challenged—there was too much on the line, like his liberty and his business objectives. The bouncer's macho shit was also a reminder for Ringo that his talent didn't necessarily make him more important than the next person.

Ringo also realized, as he joined the line of patrons, that he'd be depending on these very club-goers to buy his music when the time came. So, no matter how frustrating, this was one of those early lessons that he'd need to remember, a lesson in humility.

"See?" said the bouncer with a dry smile. "Now, was that so hard?"

Ringo faked a smile and nodded, trying hard not to appear bitter, then he paid the admission and passed through the turnstile.

One day this will change and I'll get the respect I deserve.

An old Wu Tang Clan track got Ringo's head bobbing as he moved farther into the small club. The place felt like the inside of a drum, shaking Ringo, the music pumping vibrations up into his legs.

A waist-high wall partitioned off an area where a crowd of tight-faced men stood around a pool table. On the other side of that wall, behind the men, was a bar and even more bodies, shoulder to shoulder, many of them wanting service from the same charismatic bartender, who had the same effortless smile shining for everyone.

Ringo negotiated his way toward the rear of the club where the deejay was enclosed in a shed built in the corner. Posters and photos dressed the walls behind the stout, goateed twenty-something, who shamelessly announced DJ *Solo!*—echo included—between this record and the next. It was an irritating effect, but Ringo easily looked past that and made his approach.

The jock wasn't alone. He had an Asian girl in there, much younger, who was smoking and dancing and even blowing him nicotine-rich kisses. *Deejay Solo! Solo! Solo!*

Ringo listened for the skills: the taste Solo showed in his music selections and transitions between records. He knew that it took a certain wizardry to choose records from a library of perhaps thousands of artists and even many more titles, just to recall the tempos and melodies, record after record, hour after hour was no walk in the park. And if the deejay didn't have his game down tight, the dance floor, or even the entire club, could become empty rather quickly.

When he was satisfied that Solo wasn't just another egomaniac who knew how to blend records, Ringo entered the deejay's workspace.

"Yo, wassup? I'm Ringo."

Solo was already bobbing his head with the music, so Ringo wasn't sure if he was acknowledging him or not.

Ringo went on to say, "I two-wayed you earlier in the week, about my projects."

"Yeah—okay. I remember. Sorry, I get a lotta cats who say this 'n' that. It gets to the point where it all sounds the same after a while. Hold on, Sunlight, give us some space back here. I'll catch you later."

"Okay, Solo. Want a drink?" she asked.

"Nah," he told her. Then to Ringo, "You?"

"Nah, I'm good."

Solo made a face and Sunlight quickly left the two alone.

"Her name is *Sunlight*?

"That's the name I gave her, 'cause I already mess with two different chicks named Lisa."

"Oh." Ringo chuckled. "I get it. So her real name is Lisa."

"To her moms and pops. But to me she's Sunlight. Then I got Midnight and Greenlight."

Ringo crowed. "Greenlight?"

"Yup. Ever see a Japanese girl with green eyes?"

Ringo wagged his head no.

"Well, when you run into as many girls as I do, you see it all. So, you spit?"

"Yeah," Ringo replied, happy they could finally get to the point. In the meantime, he was checking out the photos on Solo's walls.

"You nice?"

"The nicest," Ringo said. "Everybody *says* they the nicest.

But I'm the only one who needs to have a picture in the dictionary, the definition of the nicest."

"*Awww* shit," cried Solo, with the *oh yeah* smile. And without thinking, he turned his attention back to the turntables. He fooled with a second record, scratching it some before letting it go, until it played on its own.

"You got a demo?"

"I been there already, dawg. I done all the talent shows, did all the demo shopping with mad A 'n' R jokers. All the major labels, nah mean? They all bit at me, but they be lookin' for certain stuff. Only, I ain't no average cat."

"I hear you," said Solo, obviously measuring Ringo.

"See, I'm ready to do my thing independent."

"Okay. You wanna go to an independent label?"

"Nah. I'm talkin' my own independent release. I'm checkin' for strong tracks. I'mma spit my joints. I'mma master, duplicate, package, and sell 'em myself. Even if I gotta sell 'em outta my pocket."

"Damn. You sure know the routine—like you know what you talkin' about, dawg."

"No doubt. And I'm not just talkin'. I'm ready to buy the hot tracks today," Ringo confirmed.

"Today?"

"*Right* now—especially if it's hittin'. I want it. I want the whole joint. One price, no points."

"How many tracks you lookin' for?"

Ringo shrugged. "For real, I'm ready to do an EP first—like three songs on the first CD. I'mma press, like, a thousand of 'em, and sell the disc for, like, four bucks."

"You got your duplication house lined up yet?"

"Not yet. I have some phone numbers and an idea of their prices."

"I might be able to help you with that. I know a company that does the whole package, from the duplicating, to the jewel boxes—"

"I want cardboard. Plastic cost too much."

"Whatever; then they got these slick cardboard sleeves."

"Exactly."

"You sound sure of yourself."

"Sure enough to put my money where my mouth is."

Solo had an idea behind his eyes.

"You freestyle?" Solo asked, more or less challenging Ringo.

"You ain't said nothin' but a word," said Ringo.

"You sure you don't want that drink first?"

"No coke, no crack, no drinks required.
I still spit rhymes until I'm tired—
No braggin, no slackin' and jackin for me,
just bust that instrumental, drop the beat, G . . ."

Ringo stopped to make a face. *Let's go.*

"Awwwe shit!"

After two more records, Solo played a classic Dr. Dre instrumental and handed Ringo a live microphone. Ringo worked up a bounce to the music and the attitude of an angry dog.

"In the Domino . . . Club Domino . . . what what, off the top of the dome Ringo-Solo collabo. Here we go . . .

"It's like midnight, club tight
chicks bootylicious
I got a just-right spit fight
Ringo's straight vicious
you ain't never heard word games
like this here
'Cause you never heard Ringo
And it's time to be clear

You never hear these lines
from no one else
'Cause they been upstairs sittin'
on my mental shelf.

My man Solo said freestyle
and here I am
No need for gun bustin'
'Less you make me mad,

Then I have to Glock it
With the nine in my pocket,
The Magnum, I have to rock it
The twelve-gage, I cock it.

Yo' best bet is stay in line
Don't ever violate, Jake,
If you come, don't come wrong
My wrath is worse than fate

I don't spit just to rhyme
I live life just to spit
I'm just really lettin' stress off
insteada straight killin' shit

Respect the skills, son, step aside,
Betta let a nigga eat
My head is hot, the tongues on fire
Whack emcees, retreat."

Solo mixed in the next record, then turned to give Ringo the thumbs-up handshake along with the shoulder-to-shoulder hug.

"Respect, respect. You *definitely* got the skills, dawg."

"Thanks, man. All I need is some serious tracks and it's on."

"I'm feelin' you. Yo, can't front; I got like four tracks that I can say fit your style. But like two of 'em are all the way complete. One of those you're gonna need clearance on."

"So, basically, you got one track."

"Yeah. But don't sleep on the second one. It's a guaranteed hit. I used a hook from an old Spinners joint."

"Spinners?"

"I'm tellin' you, you gotta hear it. You'll see what I mean."

The two talked for a few minutes more before Solo called Sunlight to the deejay booth. Sunlight showed up slightly winded.

"Ringo, right?"

Ringo nodded.

"You're fantastic. Hot. Like, *blazing*! Can I get your autograph?"

Ringo shared a look with Solo. Solo urged Ringo to satisfy the request.

"You better get used to it. Before you know it they'll be comin' at you by the carloads," said Solo.

Ringo softened from his stone-faced expression and took a black magic marker from Solo.

"You got somethin' you want me to sign?"

"Yeah. *Here*." And Sunlight pulled down her blouse so that most of her breast was showing. Again, Ringo looked to Solo, this time with wide-eyed disbelief.

Solo shrugged, no skin off of his back. So Ringo proceeded with the autograph.

"You know this is a permanent marker," warned Ringo. Meanwhile, more fans gathered nearby.

"Good," said Sunlight. "Then I *can* wash it."

Ringo gave a strange smile. *Whatever you say, girl.*

Solo put an MP3 player on and pulled down the wooden window—it closed like a garage door would—so that the club full of people wouldn't know one way or the other that he had taken a break.

"Boom. Watch the booth for me, Sunlight." Then, to the would-be fans soliciting for Ringo's John Hancock, "Ladies, you're gonna have to catch him later. We got business to take care of. Come on, let us by." Back to Sunlight, Solo said, "Any problems, I'll be in the Jeep." He kissed her head and led Ringo away, through the back door of the club.

Minutes later, the two were in Solo's Land Rover Jeep, heads bopping back and forth to the music. Ringo spoke loud enough to be heard over the music.

"This is the one that don't need clearance?"

"Yeah! I mean, I could do some other things with it if you want. But—"

"Hell no! You can't change this. This here is ten thousand volts to the brain! How much you want?"

"Shit, I ain't trying—" Solo reached to lower the volume. Now his voice was lowered. "I ain't tryin' to be no millionaire offa you, yo. I got plenty more beats like this. It flows like water whenever I'm in the studio—except Bridgeport been dry like the Sahara."

Ringo couldn't tell him that Bridgeport was dry, not with a local deejay holdin' a luxury Jeep such as the one he was sitting in. But then, he had to remind himself that, as it was in his own situation, money didn't always come from the most legitimate avenues. And that was the first red flag—a warning sign.

"I can let it go for, like, six hundred. I'll get credited on the track, right?"

Ringo wasn't sharp enough to see through Solo's closing question: the question that virtually assumes a done deal by involving the buyer *before* money changes hands. Instead, he fed into Solo's inquiry.

"No question. Whatever I print on—the CD, the sleeve, whatever you want. Just no points, 'cause I don't want no strings attached to nobody, especially since *I'm* the one who's gonna be out there pushin' the work. I'm the reason it's gonna sell or not. Feel me? And what I sell, I keep."

"Yeah, yeah. I'm cool with it. I understand."

"Is the other track hard like this?"

"Harder," Solo said, and he switched CDs. Ringo's mind raced in the dead silence. Then the drums beating like a tribal war song kicked in. Ringo nodded. And when the music was over, he offered Solo a total of one thousand dollars for his tracks. Cash and a handshake was how the deal was done. No paperwork, no muss, no fuss.

The next day, Ringo went to one of Bridgeport's only recording studios and met with a producer named Bongo. He explained that he wanted to rent studio time and that he needed a hot engineer to help him. Ringo listened to the music Bongo had and offered to engineer *and* produce the work.

"You gotta do a radio-friendly cut too," suggested Bongo.

"I'm not really checkin' for radio, Bongo. I'm sellin' my stuff to the streets, in the gutters, if I have to."

"What about the mix shows and college radio? How are cats gonna hear your work if you don't get exposure?"

Ringo didn't consider that.

"Tell you what. We can do the street mixes, radio-ready cuts, *and* the instrumentals on the same CD. That way, you'll have six cuts on the same disc. And I won't charge you for the extra studio time."

"What's the catch?"

"Ain't no catch, man. I just wanna see you happy with your CD."

Decisions.

"I'll do the whole deal for two grand," said Bongo. "We can knock out the project within a few days, and before you know it you'll have your masters in hand."

"Two grand. No additional charges?"

"I've done this a bunch o' times, Ringo. Maybe two or three within the last month alone—I can't even count how many it's been in the past year. It's a cinch. All you gotta do is say the word and I'm in your corner."

Ringo could've asked to review more samples of Bongo's work, but he decided to go with his gut feeling. Bongo was his man.

It was time for Ringo to go into his "zone," where nothing and nobody mattered except his end goal. His focus was all about his recording session for "Push," a rap he made up after reading the book by the same title. His other rap was called "Just Cause," which was expected to be Ringo's introduction to the world. The music had been produced by Solo and the chorus line was catchy:

Just cause,
It was only a matter of time,
Just cause,
Ringo's in the house, so let me shine,
Just cause,
Don't think that this is just a rhyme,
Just cause,
This is my grind, my life or death climb.

* * *

The studio sessions lasted two weeks, and there were some post-production hours that Bongo threw in at no cost.

If Ringo didn't take the trip back to State Street each day, then he'd sleep on a couch in the studio, determined to work however hard, however long to complete the project without compromising its quality.

When the sessions were done, Ringo shot right over to I-MIX, the duplication house that Solo suggested. The company was all the way up in Hartford, maybe forty minutes north, and the enterprise was set up in the basement of an industrial building—not exactly a Main Street operation—with nuisance vines growing along the outside walls, potholed pavement and walkways, and rust-ridden doors. Ringo had a mind to make a U-turn and high-tail it back to Bridgeport, where he had a list of alternatives on standby. However, Solo assured him that these guys were dependable and speedy. So Ringo stuck with it. He ignored the cheesy surroundings and came to realize that this was definitely a duplication outfit, with boxes of CDs stacked against most every wall, dozens of CD-burning machines, and even some gold plaques posted, all of them commemorating I-Mix's involvement in the sales of underground rock and rap artists.

Ringo didn't recognize the names, but there were familiar faces. Furthermore, he was aware that the music industry was flooded with performers—some who were here one minute and gone the next; others who stuck around for much longer. Still, those staples of achievement, with claims of selling 500,000 units for this or that performer were intoxicating.

That'll be me on those plaques soon. And then the platinum plaques after that.

"We can have two thousand CDs ready for you by Thursday," said the I-Mix representative.

"What about the cardboard sleeves?"

"Everything will be ready by Thursday C.O.D. Did you bring a photo for me like we said on the phone?"

"Right here," said Ringo, handing the man a photo.

"Good deal. See you Thursday?"

"Thursday it is," said Ringo, charged up like a runaway locomotive.

He returned to Bridgeport with a sample of his work in hand. The cardboard sleeve was a prototype that a graphics girl printed prematurely, but it was a decent reproduction of what the presentation would look like come Thursday.

The computer image of Ringo's half-face and the title of his breakout song "Just Cause" were superimposed to complement each other so that it wasn't a sales pitch but a natural fusion.

Sweets was alone when Ringo opened the door of 41E.

"Hey, boss. The girls asked me to stay here 'till you came in. Hey, Kujo."

Kujo waved.

"No problem. Any calls?" asked Ringo.

"Nope," said Sweets with some laughter.

The phone had been installed only the day before, and virtually nobody had the number.

"What's good on cable?"

"Ain't nothin'. A bunch o' wildcats on Animal Planet. I swear, they smart as shit, boss."

"Where's Porsha?"

"Over at Momma Jo's, closin' the store. Tangi went to work early."

Ringo sighed, feeling as if there was nobody to share his success, however small.

"Well, the CD's done," he said.

"Hey! Congratulations. So, no more trips downtown?"

"A few, but we're almost home free." As he said that, the idea of Tangi at work concerned him. He was so close to paydirt and didn't want any harm to come to her in the meantime.

"You ain't gotta leave, Sweets. I'm goin' over to see Porsha. Kujo, hang out for a minute."

Sweets sat back down. "Cool, boss. I was gonna order some Domino's pizza. You want some?"

"Save me a couple slices," said Ringo on his way through the door again.

"Deal," said Sweets, already on the phone with a shameless smile. Kujo rubbed his belly and licked his lips.

Across the street, the lights inside of Momma Jo's were dying one at a time—closing time.

Ringo watched Porsha and Momma Jo as he crossed State Street. He hurried when he saw the two reach for the pull-down gate.

"Hey hey hey! I got it!" Ringo announced, intentionally surprising the women so that they'd stop to turn around.

"Ringo!"

"Hey, Porsha. Hey, Momma Jo."

Momma Jo cast a glance at Porsha, showing how impressed she was by Ringo. Ringo was humbled, pulling down the gate on his own.

"Well, thank you, young man."

"My pleasure, ma'am," replied Ringo, minding his manners.

Porsha was a snake awaiting her attack, and once Ringo turned around she was in his arms with a hungry hug and kiss.

Momma Jo seemed to enjoy the two.

"What's all this for?" Ringo asked.

"For the rap terror, the woman getter, the record setter, the panty wetter . . ."

"Ahhh, that'll be good night from me," said Momma Jo, mumbling "Mmm mmm mmm," as she stepped off.

"Good night," said Ringo. Then to Porsha, "You been in my tapes again?"

"Are you kiddin'?" Porsha was wearing an earthtone tube top, weathered blue jeans, and a pair of Baby Phat boots. She slipped a cassette tape from her waistband; it had been flush against her navel. "Baby, your words are *a part* of me."

Ringo looked past the dramatic pillow-talk drawl that Porsha meant to seduce him with.

He was more concerned with—

"Porsha? You didn't—did you copy this? Does anybody else have my stuff?"

"Of *course* not. I know how important your work is."

Ringo searched Porsha's eyes, wondering if she was being truthful.

"Then you wouldn't have made no copies without sayin' somethin' first." Ringo had the cassette in his hand now and he didn't intend on returning it.

"Boo? I just wanted somethin' to listen to at work. Can you blame me for wantin' your voice with me twenty-four seven?"

"Mmm hmm. You sure know how to sweet-talk somebody."

The fear dissolved from Porsha's eyes. "I can do a lot more than just talk."

Ringo shut his eyes, took a deep breath, and came up a new man. Or at least he tried to.

"Sorry I snapped at you. It's just been some long hours in the studio. We're done. Finally."

Porsha jumped up and down, with her arms still around Ringo. Her breasts brushed against him.

"So," Porsha fingered Ringo's chest and her voice turned smitten and sensual. "What do you say we spend some intimate time together? Tangi's workin'. We can tell Sweets to find somewhere else to watch cable TV."

"Actually, I had something else in mind," said Ringo.

"Oooh, now, *that* sounds like a plan," said Porsha, and she pressed her lips to his.

Ringo pulled away as if something frightened him.

"Porsha, you have to make me a promise."

"So soon? I thought you said no commitments."

"Porsha, I'm serious."

"Okay, what?" She saw the sincerity in his eyes.

"Don't ever make copies of my work again without my approval." As Ringo said this his hands tightly gripped Porsha's arms. He also shook her as he spoke.

"Ringo—you're *hurting* me."

"Promise me!"

"I'm *sorry*. I *promise*."

Ringo let her go, surprised himself at how he'd flipped back and forth, from kind to angry. Now he shook his head to clear his mind.

"Come on," Ringo said, giving Porsha no choice as he towed her along.

Porsha assumed that Ringo was taking her to his room, afraid of what he might do to her.

She'd been involved with at least two boyfriends in the past who were either physically or verbally abusive, and the past few minutes reminded her of those times. How could copying a tape get him so wound up?

No. Not Ringo. Please, not Ringo.

It was her assumption that he might want her for sex, finally. But he was being so abrupt, so rough with her. And this wasn't how she dreamed it, this wasn't how she wanted it.

Not while he's angry at me.

Porsha was overcome with relief when Ringo guided her not to 41E but to Kujo's car.

"Thanks for waiting, Kujo. Let's go."

"You got it, boss."

There in the backseat of the cab, Porsha was pulled to Ringo's side, and he stroked the back of her head, combing his fingertips through her hair. It was a small thing, but it felt good and natural, and it also eased the tension that clouded her thinking. She wondered if this petting and stroking was his way of saying he loved her, or if love was too strong a word, did he at least adore her? Or maybe that, too, was more than his life's luggage would allow. Maybe his hard-knock experiences were blocking such emotions.

"Porsha, you need to trust me."

"I do trust you, Ringo."

"No. Hear me out. I been through some rough times—times where shit got outta hand. But it was always something that I could've prevented or changed. And I'm not perfect, but I know that my decisions are the truth—good or bad. So you need to know that control of my life, my work, and who I choose to associate with are things that are very important to me. For real, they're things that could kill me or they could save my life."

Porsha was looking so hard into Ringo's eyes that she began to lose focus of him—a sort of dizzy state of mind.

"You're looking at me like I'm crazy, and maybe I am. Maybe I'm just buggin', but most times what comes out of my mouth is the truth. Something I don't have no control of."

Porsha snuggled up to Ringo. In a way, it prevented her from having to look him in the eyes, It stopped him from looking right through to her soul. But she was also at home here, so close to his body, inhaling what she could of him. Here, she could breeze past those undesirable thoughts and concerns. Here, there were no worries.

This is a good man. I just know it. . . .

Fifteen minutes passed, and now the cab snaked down a road lined with warehouses, factories, and assorted lots with trucks, building supplies, and piles of gravel or sand. Toward the end of this road was a split-level ranch-style building, sky blue, with a few neon beer signs hung in most of its tiny windows. A sign overhead read THE LAST KISS.

"Ringo," Porsha protested, but it was far from a serious tone. "We can't go in here. This is where Tangi works."

"Exactly," said Ringo as the cab pulled into a parking space.

Porsha pulled at Ringo's sleeve. "Ringo, don't make me do this. I've never been here before."

"First time for everything. You comin', Kujo?"

"Wouldn't miss it for the world, boss."

Chapter Six

"That'll be ten dollars each for the gentlemen. No charge for the young lady," said the doorman.

The expression on Porsha's face said, *Don't do me no favors.* Meanwhile, the energy inside of The Last Kiss was immediately engaging to Ringo's senses. The music had a rampant tempo, there were hoards of men congregated in almost every corner, and on two stages were six dancers, gyrating, slithering, and pretending to masturbate in an all-out effort to be the center of attention. The air was filled with hoots, whistles, and catcalls from what seemed like sex-starved men, most of whom drank, tossed dollar bills, and fantasized about more than their eyes could see. Ringo, Kujo, and Porsha took seats toward the rear of the club, and a waitress wasted no time in approaching them for their drink orders.

"I don't see her," said Ringo.

"Who we lookin' for?" asked Kujo.

"A pretty, brown-skinned girl. Oh, about her height with hair like . . . *There she is.*"

"GENTLEMEN, GIVE A BIG LAST KISS WELCOME TO CHOCOLATE, RETURNING TO THE MAIN STAGE!"

"*Ahhh . . . Cho-co-late!*"

"Easy, mister. That's my friend you're blowin' kisses at," said Porsha with her unthreatening attitude.

"Kujo, you go on and blow kisses all you want. Porsha, you need to chill. What're you gonna do, tell off every dude up in here? 'Cause, if you look around you, they're doin' a whole lot more than blowin' kisses. Look over there."

Ringo indicated an older man whose bone structure around his jawline and cheeks was recognizable. His eyes peered out from deep ditch slits and his hair was matted down, perhaps with oil. He also had one hand between his legs, and his tongue was flipping out of his mouth, compulsively licking the air in front of him. Porsha started to get up and say something, but Ringo reached out and grabbed her arm. In Porsha's ear, he said, "Don't do nothin' stupid."

"We gotta get her out of here, Ringo. Really she don't belong in this place with all these nasty old men."

"But didn't we just have this conversation a few weeks ago? About decisions? Maybe now you'll open your eyes."

Tangi, aka Chocolate, shimmied out onto the stage in a turquoise thong and bikini top. Her hair was twisted into one whip of a braid that hung down to the small of her back.

"Do you believe this girl?" said Porsha. "That ain't her hair. And what's up with the black lipstick and the reading glasses? That girl don't *read*."

"You know that's all costume, Porsha. Plus, I kinda like the hoop earrings myself. They throw you off a little . . . she looks like she's thirty years old up there, except for the hoop earrings and, well, her tits."

"Excuse you, mister rap terror, panty wetter . . . you need to take your eyes off of *those*."

Ringo said, "What do you expect? They're right there in our face."

Meanwhile, Kujo was in his own world.

"Yes! *Cho-co-late!*" Kujo whistled as loud as he could, yet his excitement was no more and no less than the dozens of other men. Tangi teased the audience for a bit before she unveiled her healthy headlights.

"Hot momma!" someone shouted.

"What I would do to get my hands on that pair there!" another patron called out.

"Ay yo! You got you a sista, Chocolate?!"

Porsha had her legs crossed and one hand was spread over her face. It was her way of making herself invisible in this all-new environment. But she couldn't help being embarrassed for

Tangi, and herself as well, since it was no secret that men were checkin' her out too. "Do we have to watch this?"

"Porsha, where has your head been? Buried in the sand? There's stuff like this, and worse, on TV."

"Yeah, but that's different."

"Why? Because this is up close and personal?"

"No. Because Tangi is my friend. *Your* friend, and yes, that's *very* personal."

Tangi bent over now, and an audience member stepped forward to stick a dollar bill under the centerpiece of her thong. Tangi then strutted off with George Washington between her ass cheeks. There were many other tips placed under her thong, with a slap on the ass here, a caress along the thigh there. When a slow song played, Tangi went down on her knees and simulated oral sex with a customer's Heineken bottle. After that, she laid on her back, spreading her legs to every extreme.

"Maybe you're right," said Ringo. "I don't really wanna see this. Come on, Kujo."

"But—"

"Kujo."

Kujo wheeled the taxicab into the State Street Inn parking lot to drop off Porsha and Ringo. Ringo passed him two hundred dollars for three days' pay and instructed him to go pick up Tangi at the end of the night. Kujo brandished a sunlit smile.

"That means bring her back here, Kujo. Nothing but."

Kujo said, "No problem." But he didn't appear to read between the lines.

"Kujo, the girl is only sixteen. So get your mind outta the gutter."

Kujo's smile soon became a frown, and he drove off, leaving the two in the moonlit lot.

"I'm glad you took me there, Ringo. I didn't know *what* she was doing in there—now that I do, and if I have my way, she won't ever be going back."

"And if I have my way, we'll be leaving this place soon," said Ringo.

"Leaving?" asked Porsha.

There was just the two of them outside, with the sounds of passing cars along State Street and some couple arguing down the way. A barking dog joined in and a baby began to wail. Ringo rolled his eyes.

"You mean, on a vacation?" Porsha nudged him.

"No, I mean a life. Some bigger opportunities than Momma Jo or The Last Kiss or room forty-one-E."

"Wooo, you got real deep all of a sudden."

"Wanna see deep?"

Porsha blushed, assuming that Ringo meant sex. But Ringo took out his sample CD and showed her.

"Wow. This looks good. Can we listen to it?

Can we—?" Porsha suddenly had Ringo's two fingers against her lips.

"I was hoping we could do more than just listen to it," Ringo said. "I was hoping we could *celebrate* to it. You . . . and me . . . in 41E."

The rhyme caught Porsha off guard, and her blush turned to a proud, crooked grin.

"Do you ever quit being talented?" asked Porsha, but she didn't require an answer. Her arms reached around Ringo and she kissed him, slipping most of her tongue in his mouth. It was more than a promise. This time, it was a firm go.

When Ringo opened the door there was Sweets with a guilty look on his face—he had eaten most of the Domino's pizza.

"Don't worry, Sweets. We can always order more," said Ringo, hoping to make the man feel better.

"But right now," Ringo picked up the remote control and turned off the television. "We're gonna need to be alone."

Sweets immediately got the message and got up to leave. When the door closed behind him, it was as if someone had pressed the start button. Ringo and Porsha were all over each other. She pulled off his clothes. He pulled off hers. He had the pressure of erasing the past, of trying to make his career work, of worrying about finances, police detectives, and whether or not he was even considered a fugitive. There were all of these concerns to unload.

Porsha, on the other hand, had dreams for a bright future, anything beyond Bridgeport. And it wasn't as if she didn't feel proud about her hometown—that couldn't be helped. What Porsha *did* want was to experience more of the world. And for now, that was what Ringo was to her. He was her Mr. Right and she was that young woman in heat.

Both of them acted like hungry animals, only with sensuality and passion and selfish aggression. Everything felt right about this. Porsha was consuming Ringo's mind as much as he was penetrating her body.

In the end, Ringo and Porsha were complete with so much satisfied flesh and an uninhibited closeness that they had never before experienced.

Chapter Seven

With each passing week there was a new reality to face. First and foremost, Ringo had to do something about transportation. Getting shuttled around in a taxicab was already lame. But with so much new activity, it was becoming increasingly inconvenient to call on Kujo. He'd rather have something stable, something he could even use as a sort of mobile office. From the day he left New York he wanted to buy his own car. But that would require his name, social security number, and other critical data. It would also require a driver's license, something that, once it was computed, would certainly tell the whole world where James "Ringo" Valentine was hiding.

It had been more than six months since the mess at the Just Right Check Exchange. And still, every second of the mayhem was fresh on his mind, like an open wound throbbing with pain.

Ringo had not seen any New York newspapers, nor was there anything on *America's Most Wanted*, a must-see for him. However, his imagination stretched now and again, thinking that there could be an ongoing manhunt. And he'd stop by Momma Jo's every now and again to see if there were any changes with the FBI's most wanted postings. It was the only way he could stay informed.

To further protect his secret, he shaved his head bald, telling the others it was a part of his "new image." A pair of tinted glasses usually completed his daily disguise.

"How about I buy you a truck?" Ringo said to Kujo after some careful planning. "All I need you to do is be my driver, available at all times to take us where we need to go. Long trips, short trips, whatever."

"I still got my bills to pay, boss. My rent and child support. Gotta take care of my kid."

"I'll still pay you, Kujo. Plus you can use the truck yourself, maybe do some stuff on the side for some extra cash."

Kujo thought about that. Then Ringo said, "But I doubt you'll have time for the extra stuff when I blow up."

That flash of hope pushed Kujo to agree.

"Sounds like a deal to me," said Kujo. "Besides, a successful rapper needs a strong driver-slash-bodyguard by his side, don't he?" Kujo saw more than an empty promise in Ringo's offer, especially with all the cash the rapper was dishing out. He even knew of someone around the way who had a like-new, black Chevy Suburban for sale. Plus, the guy only wanted half the price in cash, in monthly payments.

Ringo got a kick out of Kujo's quick fix and went along with the deal.

With the transportation out of the way, it was promotion time. Porsha made phone calls to local clubs, mapping out a string of unpaid performances, while Kujo drove Ringo to various music stores in Bridgeport, Norwalk, Stamford, and Hartford. Between stops, Kujo suggested that Ringo take a stab at some New York outlets. Ringo turned the idea down flatly.

"One state at a time, Kujo."

And that was the end of that idea.

"You got any radio play on this?"

"What label distributes you? Because we already have agreements with most of them."

"How long will this sit on my shelf?"

"What's my cut?"

These were the same questions that Ringo immediately had to address with each store owner. It was a challenge that he never anticipated. As far as Ringo knew, all he'd need to do is produce the work, and stores would be more than happy to stock his product.

Nizz-aw. What Ringo had to do now was to put his passion

behind his product. He had to pour on the charm and sell his product without being too much of a salesman. People hate salesmen because there are so damned many of them, everywhere you turn. So Ringo needed to put a face, a voice, and a personality behind his product. He had to recognize that it was *he* that was for sale and not a CD with beats and rhymes. There were millions of rappers, but there was just one Ringo.

"Well, this is a little different from the average album. See, I've put my life savings into this project, and now I'm *this* close to signing a monster recording contract. I'm talking national syndication, air play on four hundred radio stations and major distribution and marketing. The only thing is, they want me to sign on the dotted line. They want me to commit to a thirty-city concert tour—almost two shows a night." Ringo's energy was sharp and focused. He knew just what to say, what buttons to push.

The typical response was, "That sounds like a good deal. Why don't you go ahead and sign?"

"It's the money. They're only offering me a hundred and seventy-five thousand, and I know damned well my deal is worth a quarter mill up front."

"But if it means getting your music in rotation, don't you think it's worth it?"

"Maybe. Maybe not. But why should I rush into it? I'm already making money hand over fist." Besides, I just got an offer for a bigger tour, a *total* show, with dancers, fireworks, and a live band."

"Mmm hmm. Sounds *big*. How many singles did you say you sold so far?"

"A hundred and forty thousand. But I'm doing my own distribution—me and my small network of family members. I'm just now getting to your area, and I thought it was important to meet the mom and pop owners first. You guys have been my bread and butter."

"I'm glad *somebody* recognizes that. Say, I'll take a couple dozen copies. You think you could arrange an in-store appearance? Maybe when your song goes top ten?"

"You ain't said nothin' but a word. I'll make sure to talk it over with my promotions director, Ms. Porsha Lindsey."

Less than three weeks later, Porsha asked, "Now that the CDs are in fifteen stores, how will people know to buy them without advertising?"

Advertising had become an issue for Ringo. There weren't too many sources that hip-hop heads could turn to for information about local artists, and the national publications such as *The Source, VIBE*, and *XXL* were much too expensive. One full-page advertisement in any of the big magazines would quickly eat up his pile of money—a pile that was already disappearing, slowly but surely.

Porsha went on to say, "I called The Music Hut down in Stamford and spoke with a salesgirl I know personally. She told me that they haven't even gotten a bite. All twelve CDs are still in stock."

"Good. You keep in touch with your friend. We'll see what she says after we go to plan B."

"Plan B? I didn't know we had a plan B," said Porsha.

"Tangi, I need six teenagers who live around here. Tell 'em you got a job for them. They'll make money, plus they'll get a free CD."

"Okay," said Tangi.

"Then what?" asked Porsha.

"Then on Saturday, the day after my showcase at Catmandoo, Kujo is gonna take the group—we'll call 'em our street team—they'll go to each music store and all they're gonna buy is copies of my CD. *Every single one*."

Porsha protested. "But, Ringo that's gonna cost—"

"It doesn't matter what it's gonna cost. Does it look to you like a brotha's got financial problems? Does it?"

Tangi turned her head toward Porsha, her eyes asking if Porsha was sleeping, and why did she have to go and ask a question like that? Porsha could only summon her own blind faith.

"What*ever*," she finally replied.

"Good. Now here's our itinerary for the week. Butter's gonna pick up the fliers tomorrow. We got a few kids to post them on poles, bulletin boards, and car windshields during the next month and a half. We need those press releases, Porsha—"

"Got it."

"And we'll get complimentary CDs to the music critics at the regional newspapers and magazines."

"Are you sure you don't want me to call *VIBE*, *XXL* or *The Source*?" Porsha asked. Ringo merely shot her an aggravated look. She said, "Okay—relax. Just double-checkin'. Did you set up any other performances? "Nobody wants to pay, Ringo. They're still saying the same thing: *We need to hear some radio airplay before we pay anything*." But they will bring you in for a promotional performance.

Ringo turned to Tangi. "How about that contact you said you had? Somebody you say you met at the club."

"I'm workin' on it. I should know somethin' tomorrow."

"Good. We gotta get some airplay. That should give us a nice jump-start."

Ringo wasn't aware of it, but Tangi's mind was somewhere else at the moment, the determination in her eyes somehow guaranteeing airplay.

Chapter Eight

The others vacated 41E, which was now clearly a cluttered business office, to tend to their respective tasks.

Posting fliers, moving the street team from city to city and carefully securing some radio airplay kept the group busy, leaving Ringo and Porsha to focus on executive phone calls, to strategize, and to do whatever it is that they did while they were alone.

It was pretty well understood by now that the two were bedfellows, and that they needed their breathing room, their space, where they could sex it up. After all, a smile on Ringo's face in the midst of so much day-to-day grinding satisfied the whole camp. If the boss was happy, so was everyone else.

But something was on Porsha's mind for all these months. Something more than just sex and Ringo's independent rap career.

"Ringo?"

"Yeah, boo." Ringo didn't look up from the figures he was calculating, tapping keys on the electronic device in a feverish attempt to make ends meet.

Porsha felt herself getting cold feet again, and it caused Ringo to stop what he was doing.

"What is it?" He pressed her to spit it out.

"It's the money."

Ringo was stuck there for a time, but he abruptly shifted gears and returned to the figures.

"What about it?" he said, having some idea of what she meant.

"I just wondered . . . where it was all coming from. I mean . . ." Porsha searched her mind for the right words—maybe something to lighten the tension her inquiry caused. "You're not wild like other rappers—not *all* rappers—and I never dated a rapper before—I mean . . . just, well, I guess—" Porsha's words died with an exhale. "Oh, I don't know *what* I mean."

Ringo still hadn't looked up, however he locked his fingers together and rested his chin on them, contemplating.

Porsha went on. "Tell me you hit the lottery or something. An inheritance. Your father's rich. I mean, Ringo, tell me anything except—"

"Except what, Porsha?"

"Are you doing something illegal?"

"Did it feel illegal when you put on that Gucci leather coat? Or when you pull that handbag on your shoulder? Or how 'bout the necklace I got you? Does that feel illegal?"

"No," Porsha muttered.

"Well, did it taste illegal when I took you out to dinner last night? Huh? Or how 'bout the night before?"

"No, Ringo. I—"

"Then how 'bout those dozen roses you asked me to get for Momma Jo's birthday? They didn't look illegal, did they?"

"Ringo, you don't have to—"

"No. You're right. I don't have to answer questions about my money. And really, when it comes down to it, my money ain't really none of your business. Maybe you just need to shut your mouth and be happy with the way things are." Porsha lifted herself up from the easy chair and marched toward the door. She didn't appreciate the way Ringo spoke to her.

"Come back here," demanded Ringo, against his own wishes. And he caught her in time to grab her arm, spinning her around to face him. "What—is—your—*problem*?"

"YOU! YOU'RE MY PROBLEM! DON'T YOU GET IT? I WON'T BE ANOTHER DRUG DEALER'S GIRLFRIEND! I WILL NOT WATCH YOU GO TO JAIL AND LEAVE ME ALONE! I'M A WOMAN WITH HOPES AND DREAMS, IN CASE YOU HAVEN'T NOTICED, MISTER RINGO-THE-RAPPER, OR GREG JENKINS, OR *WHATEVER* YOUR

NAME IS. I'M NOT A TOY THAT YOU CAN FLIP AROUND ANY WHICH WAY YOU PLEASE, UNTIL YOU DONE WITH ME!"

Porsha had snatched her arm from Ringo's grip, turning to leave the room, but Ringo pulled her back to him. She tried to fight her way out of his embrace, but couldn't break away. He wouldn't let her. Porsha eventually collapsed against Ringo's chest, her pounding fists softening their blows, until she became a trembling, distressed mass of flesh in his arms.

"Easy, baby, easy. Come sit down. Let's talk."

Porsha told Ringo about one of her ex-boyfriends, Russell. He was her only other lover—there was an earlier experience, but that was hardly love—who also had a lot of money. He also dressed her expensively, wined and dined her, and even put a twelve-carat diamond ring on her finger. Porsha was just seventeen years old at the time, and she knew these circumstances to be normal. Guys treated their girls like "tricks," often putting them in fly-girl outfits and dressing their wrist, fingers, or necks with expensive jewels.

After all, this was the hood. And "winning" a local hustler was a sure way for a chickenhead to make her comeup.

"Don't say that," said Ringo. "You ain't no chickenhead."

"Why not? That's what they all say about us, especially when you're young and don't have any direction. When you're dumb and don't know any better you'll drop to your knees to suck any dick with cash and a car."

"Is that what you did?" asked Ringo, too abruptly.

Porsha lowered her head and as she did, tears dropped.

It was a picture that was worth a thousand words; the guilt of an entire generation of lost girls on her shoulders.

Ringo allowed Porsha a chance to air out her feelings, pulling her against his chest and saying nothing for a time.

"Look, Porsha. What is the past is the past. I'm not holding any of that against you. What I do want you to know is this is a new day. You're with me now. So, how could you be a chickenhead?"

Porsha sniffled. "But it's starting to feel like the same thing. I fell for you; you have all this money . . ."

"But, boo, if I remember right, you chewed me out when I first met you. You saw me flash some money—remember I told you to keep the tip?"

Porsha found some humor in the recollection.

"And look how long it took before we went to bed—*months*! You had me waitin' like your stuff was *all that*."

"It *is* all that," Porsha confirmed. Ringo rolled his eyes in a playful way. But Porsha wasn't playful when she punched him in the chest.

"Ouch!"

"You take that back, Ringo."

"Okay, *damn*, you packin' a punch, girl."

"Well, don't be talkin' greasy about my stuff then."

Ringo took Porsha and growled in her ear. "Your stuff is like sweet barbecue, baby. No bullshit."

And just like that, they were at it again, over and under each other like hungry flesh-eating carnivores. They went from the couch to the bed to the floor, never quite removing all of their clothing, and yet they released enough cum to soil both their clothes and the carpet.

"It's a good thing we don't smoke," suggested Porsha once she found the energy to say something.

"Whaddayou mean?"

"Don't lovers do that after sex? Smoke?"

"I don't."

"I know," said Porsha. "You cuddle." She had a two-thousand-watt smile on her face.

Hours went by until Butter and Sweets returned with the results of the day.

"Anybody home?"

"We're in here," Ringo shouted from the bathroom.

"Want us to come back later?"

Butter and Sweets shared an expression, both of them jumping to the obvious conclusion. *In the bathroom*? There was a giggle behind the door, followed by splashing water. *Wow. In the tub!*

"You can open the door and watch for all I care," shouted Ringo.

Porsha's shrieking laugh followed.

"We better come back, Sweets."

"Yeah, 'cause they trippin' up in here."

"You so *crazy*," said Porsha.

"And you love it. Tell the truth."

"I do. Oooh, that feels good," she said, closing her eyes and feeling spoiled with Ringo's hands massaging her back and shoulders.

They were in the bathtub now—a tight squeeze for two, who were ready to share the same toilet, as passionate as they were about each other.

"So tell me more about Russell. You said it was four months."

"But don't concentrate on that, boo. It was more a bad choice than anything else. We had some good times. Sex—not love. And I got pregnant . . ."

She got a chill just saying the words, recalling the encounter.

"When he found out he was gonna be a father he said he would quit the drug game. He promised me the world, including marriage, a home, and a family, but it was a pipe dream. A few days later an army of those federal agents came in. They did somethin' they call a *sweep*, took so many brothas off the streets that Bridgeport was like a ghost town."

"Did this hafta do with the murders?"

"Yup. The little boy was killed because he witnessed another killing. Then the mayor called them feds in and everything was crazy. Everybody they arrested was threatened with life in prison—and a whole bunch of 'em did a lotta tellin'."

"I heard."

"So Russell ended up one of the losers. He got forty years. No chance for parole. And I wasn't even one week pregnant. I . . . I had no choice, Ringo. My father left us when we were little, and I didn't have a chance to have a daddy in my life. I just . . . I didn't want that for my kid."

Porsha told Ringo about her decision to have the pregnancy

terminated, and how there was bad blood between her and her mother over the whole controversy.

Since that time, Porsha steered clear of the social scene. She ignored any passes that young men made at her and buried herself in the day-to-day reality of helping Momma Jo run the post office. Tangi had become a close friend and confidant—there was nothing else Porsha needed.

"And then you came along. Ringo, you knocked me off of my feet," admitted Porsha. "What you did for Tangi . . . you were a *hero.* I told you we don't have men like you around here. I felt like you were a wind and I had to put up my sail, otherwise I could be left behind. Remember that rapper? I forget his name, but he said opportunity only comes once in a lifetime. I never forgot that. And here you are. Opportunity." Porsha did her best to turn herself around. She at least managed to be face-to-face with him, regardless of how uncomfortable.

"But now it's like déjà vu. I see some of Russell in you, Ringo. You might not understand my point, but I'm just letting you know what's in my heart. You always say to be honest with you—so here I am. And I need to know I'm wrong, Ringo. I've shared as much of myself with you as I could. Ringo, we're not even using rubbers—and that's not, like, me bein' ignorant or anything. It's just that I'm real serious about you. About us. Ringo, I need to know that we're not headed for the same dead end."

Ringo felt Porsha's body trembling there in the bathtub. She wasn't a woman who he wanted to feed small talk to—she was nothing like Jordan or Donia, his girlfriends he bullshitted back in Queens.

"I didn't think I'd need to get into this with you, Porsha. I wanted things to go smoothly—no questions asked. But I see that's harder than I thought."

Ringo took a much-needed deep breath.

"No, Porsha. I'm not dealing drugs. I'm not even doing anything illegal. And no, I didn't inherit money from any rich father. I come from a broke-ass family that sometimes shared a can of beans when there was nothin' else to eat. I had one brother, older than me, and all I can remember is wearing his clothes when he outgrew them. Then he and moms died in a car accident, and it was just me and pops."

Porsha put her head against Ringo and let her mind wander, putting images together with the words he spoke—seeing it all there on the mildewed tile.

"I dropped out of school in the tenth grade, started hustling, stealing shit like bikes, mail, and even house pets. When I got older, the stealing got more serious. One of those situations got out of hand. I made some money—and that's really all I can tell you. But the thing is, I made a decision to change my life. No more small scams or petty thefts. No more risking my life. That's why I came here, Porsha. And my name is Ringo. My boys been callin' me that since I was three feet high.

"Porsha, all I care about is rhymin'. All I want is a piece of this hip-hop game. I got skills. Everybody says it. I listen to a lot of these fake-ass boys on the scene, rappin' about their big cars, diamonds, and houses. But how could they have all that, and they ain't sell a hundred thousand units yet? That kills me how niggas be frontin'—even if a record label advanced a hundred grand, even two fifty—*whatever*. It ain't nothin' but a *loan*. If they can't sell enough CDs to pay back that money, then their rap career is over, or they might try to disguise themselves and come out under another name. Or maybe they'll try to sell CDs on their own.

But the whole thing is smoke and mirrors, baby. It's funny to me how the whackest rappers are posin' like they millionaires.

"I'm not sayin' I'm the greatest rapper of all time. I ain't Biggie or Tupac or Jay-Z or L.L., but there's enough cake out there for me to have and share with my team—feel me? I can keep all the profit as an independent artist, and I don't need to answer to *nobody*. I can eat without worrying about repaying some record company's advance. *I am my record company*. And it is just a matter of time before I build my own fan base. Just like you wanna listen to my stuff, others will too. Just support me, baby. Just stand by my side like a soldier and lemme push this product. Watch my smoke, 'cause I can make this happen. *I know I can*."

Ringo hugged Porsha as if it was their last.

"I need you, Porsha. You're a strong black woman—like my moms was. I need you to keep me grounded so I don't fall for the temptations out there. Rappers got baby mommas all over the place. They blow their money and end up workin' at the gas station or the tollbooth. Maybe they get caught up doin' dirt, and they end up in jail."

Porsha listened to Ringo's testimonies and convictions. She stared into his eyes to hopefully see into his trusts.

Certain things saddened her, while other things inspired her.

There was also that dangerous element hiding. An evasive secret that haunted her and kept an air of concern brewing in her conscience. But bigger than that was the passion and determination reaching through the words, through the space between them, and it tugged at Porsha's heart.

His independence captivated her. His determination was perplexing, a force and magnetism that she'd never known.

Here was a man who went through some hard times, like she had. He survived, like she had. And now, he was rebuilding and, as far as she could tell, doing a helluva job at it.

This rap CD could've been a new invention that Ringo developed. It could've been a line of clothing he designed, or even a book he wrote. What it really was, was a vehicle to establish his foundation. His future.

Most other men she knew relied on a paycheck that, regardless of what they thought, wasn't guaranteed. Some other men she knew had easy street jobs that weren't challenging, only requiring their physical presence—city jobs that were smaller elements of a bigger machine.

Compared to Ringo and the work she observed him perform so far, a lot of the men she had been exposed to were living to *get over*. But nobody that she ever met chased his dreams so passionately, like Ringo. With him, it was a life-or-death battle. Success seemed inevitable.

Together with his good looks and tough spirit, it was a combination that left Porsha with one choice. He was the man that she could love. And so she did, fully and completely.

Chapter Nine

CATMANDOO operated in a house that was once occupied by three families until it was converted into a nightclub. Most of the houses in the area, including Catmandoo, were wood-frame dwellings that had aluminum or stucco siding, made unique only by their colors.

On Lyon's Avenue, the block where the club was located, the homes represented many a pastel color. Sky blue. Canary green. Lemon. Bone white. And there were the most outrageous colors—a bubble-gum pink and a reddish purple that a rainstorm turned into a bloody horror.

Catmandoo was battleship gray, with three levels, a walkway that divided the front lawn in half, and a discreet wooden sign that hung off of the mailbox. The property was also fenced off from the homes to its left and right.

Bridgeport's mayor had recently been indicted and arrested for the years of corruption in City Hall, so the fact that Catmandoo was an unauthorized business in a residential zone was the least of anyone's concerns.

Not only that, but neighbors were employed there, the Block Watch program was paid for, and there were free barbecues all summer long—a sort of series of block parties that the area residents anticipated every year.

A home for college parties, high school proms, and monthly talent shows, Catmandoo attracted a crowd of folks who mostly knew one another by name, and who looked forward to congregating, dancing, and lounging in such a stress free environment.

"Yes, I know Ringo doesn't ring a bell right now, but you know how it is in Bridgeport. We're always last when it comes to anything good—especially if there's gonna be a lot of press involved. Yes sir, *of course* there's gonna be press. But more importantly, were expecting a video to play on BET and MTV at the top of the hour for a whole weekend," said Porsha. Ringo was ready to punch the wall until Porsha put her hand over the mouthpiece of the telephone.

"Relax, Ringo." Her voice was hushed. "I didn't say *whose* video." Then she went back to the phone call. "Well, I wouldn't wanna see you getting left out of all the media hype, especially with such a huge act coming to our hometown. Yes, sure, we can guarantee exclusivity. There's no specific contract, but I really want this to work out for everyone. A *binder*?"

Porsha's eyes swept 41E to meet with Ringo's, and she mouthed the word: *Binder?*

When the call ended, Porsha squealed with delight.

"What is it? What binder did he mean?" Ringo asked.

"*His!* He wants to pay us a thousand dollars, Ringo!"

"*Yes!*" Ringo exalted, slamming a fist into his open palm, then lifting Porsha up off of her feet. She was still telling him good news as he let her down and gave her mighty kisses.

"They're getting us a stretch . . . limo, and . . . they're gonna . . . hire . . . a caterer."

Ringo stopped the kissing to say, "You did that, baby. That's *your* work."

Porsha struck a pose, with her hands on her hips, one shoulder raised some, while she turned her chin that way, eyes fluttering.

"Oh what, you Halle Berry now?" asked Ringo, taken aback by Porsha's exaggerated pride.

"No. *Better* than Halle," she replied through squinted eyes.

Ringo couldn't help being overwhelmed. He impulsively tacked Porsha to the bed and wrestled her short skirt off of her hips, and her knees back to her ears. Ringo buried his face in Porsha's vagina until she begged him to enter her. A half hour later he did just that.

* * *

IT WAS SHOWTIME at Catmandoo. Kujo followed the black stretch limo in the Suburban, and Ringo's entire workforce was on hand as his entourage. The line outside of the club easily fell in love with the illusion before them, the obvious fame and importance of this big-time performer who would be putting on a show for them tonight.

"Another hip-hop millionaire. He must be paid!"

"Wow. He actually came here? For us?"

"He got two women on his arms! Daaaamn!"

The smoke and mirrors were working. Catmandoo's staff laid out the proverbial red carpet for Ringo and company, providing them with a private room where two tables of catered food was ready and waiting. Hot and cold platters. Barbecued chicken wings. Cold shrimp and cocktail sauce. Fruits and vegetables. Cakes and cookies. Beverages of every variety, as well as four bottles of champagne—Krug, Dom P., Cristal, and Moët—all in ice buckets.

All through the night, excessive announcements were barked over the sound system: *Only one hour away from Bridgeport's first platinum recording artist!*

Fifteen minutes until showtime! Get ready for Ringo! The next rap superstar!

Come midnight, the music was faded out and the lights dimmed more than they had been. The stage area on the first floor—otherwise known as the living room, dining room, and kitchen combined—was mobbed, with little or no room to move.

Nobody seemed to care that the person next to them was so close, only that Ringo, whose face appeared on posters tacked and taped throughout the club, was about to make his appearance.

"Bridgeport! ARE—YOU—READY!!!"

The energy spread like a virus, as the house full of spectators screamed and hollered and roared in one deafening wave of a response.

"YOU'RE ABOUT TO SEE HIM ON BET . . . ON MTV . . . ON YOUR TV. . . . HIS LYRICAL SKILLS ARE BITING . . . HIS MESSAGES WILL TOUCH YOUR SOUL,

AND HE'S BEEN QUOTED AS SAYING, I'M HERE TO SHUT THE RAP GAME DOWN! LADIES . . . GENTLEMEN . . . BRIDGEPORT . . . GIVE IT UP FOR RINGO!"

"I was born the rap terror
tongue out, nothin' to cry about
before my first breath
they already put the word out.

They told the perpetrators
that the truth had arrived
they warned the phony lyricists
'Y'all ran out of time.'

Well, whoever put the flag up
I'm here to bring it on
I was meant for this challenge
I was built to be strong

No rhyme out of reach
No beat I can't rock to,
Spend your money on whack cats?
No—that, I'll put a stop to.

Follow me, the pied piper
your homegrown earthquake
spittin' rhymes to get your mind right
raps to make your butt shake

Have you changin' your mind
about movies, about DVDs . . .
Why do anything else
when you can watch me make history?

I live on the southside
of this hip-hop city
Ain't no room for flowers
and no place for pity

I got neighbors that pop
they rock, dance, and sing,
But I was born to make noise
'cause rough ridin's my thing."

The music and the beat that accompanied Ringo's rap had faded out so that his last few lines were a cappella, with each word delivered clear and deliberate. It was merely his introduction, and yet the crowd went bonkers, cheering and whistling for more.

"All right, check it . . . check it . . . Is Bridgeport in the house!? I said . . . is Bridgeport in—the—house!!?"

Again the crowd roared, feeling Ringo's energy.

"Well stay right there,
hold your applause.
while I give you a little
taste of . . . JUST CAUSE!"

Ringo's segueway was followed by the beat: His instrumental track was a catchy old-school melody that got everyone's head bopping. He performed for forty minutes, including his hit "Just Cause," then "Push," the second cut on his CD. The crowd went wild. Ringo also freestyled for the audience, asking random audience members to shout out subjects for him to rap about.

"Come on, gimme a subject. Any subject," Ringo announced into the mic as he toweled off the sweat from his face and neck. A few camera flashes captured the moment.

"Bridgeport! Rap about *Bridgeport.*"

"Okay! You got it. Bridgeport. Bust a beat for me, deejay." Ringo took a deep breath, bopped his head, and lifted the mic to his lips.

"Bridgeport is a place
where the beat is the law
The mayor just got knocked
so this gots to be raw

The feds swept the streets
they said dead or alive
some suckas took the fall
but the strong still survive

And who killed that boy
all for money and drugs?
They done lost their minds,
like some coward-ass thugs

Tryin' to clean up their mess
'cause murder was the case
now look at them fools
a prison lost in space

But you called out Bridgeport
so I'll bust the rap
Straight freestyle from Ringo
the whole world on my back

I been to Cadillac, No Man's,
and the Domino, too
But ain't nowhere poppin'
like the Catmandoo

I gotta thank you Bridgeport
for givin' a thug love
you opened up your arms
and I just can't get enough

But I can't floss forever
'Cause there ain't enough time
I gotta get off this stage
and get back on my grind.

"Give it up for Ringo!"

The *ooh*s and *aah*s filled the house, making it hard to hear.

They shouted for more, more, more! But Ringo didn't return. Instead, he stripped down to his shorts in a private room, where Porsha and Tangi were waiting with towels and ice water.

After changing into a fresh jersey and dungarees, he was escorted to a den area in the house that was designated as a VIP area.

A table was set up with CDs and photos where Ringo autographed everything from CD cases to sweaty palms and even other body parts. By one thirty in the morning, ten CDs had been sold.

Ringo and his group left Catmandoo floating on air. Kujo and Porsha were the only two who didn't get pissy drunk back at the State Street Motor Inn. Butter and Sweets pretended to get tipsy, but they were drinking Welch's Grape Juice. Everyone realized they were putting on an act and it only added to the joy and celebration. "For He's a Jolly Good Fellow" was sung at least three times before everyone fell asleep on the floor, couch, bed, or easy chair.

This would be remembered as one of the good ol' days.

When Ringo woke up late the next afternoon, Porsha was already up and busy on the phone. The room was spick-and-span and they were alone.

"Where's Tangi?"

"Who knows?" said Porsha. "She said something about a meeting—supposed to get some confirmation on the radio time. Hey! Guess what?"

"But I thought . . . didn't she have some kind of meeting last week?"

Porsha shrugged. "Beats me, Ringo. Listen! I have good news."

"Okay, what? But please, stop yelling. My head is killin' me."

"The Music Hut called. They ran out of CDs," Porsha said.

"Shit," said Ringo, aggravation showing as he struggled to sit up on the bed.

"But isn't that good news?"

"No. I mean, I'm not cursing the news. It's the ringing in my ears. I feel like I got hit by a train.

"Wait a minute," Ringo said, remembering something. "Of course they sold out, Porsha. Kujo and Butter took the street—"

"Ringo, Kujo and Butter didn't take anybody anywhere. Trust me when I tell you that everybody's asleep."

"Then how did they run out of product?" Ringo rubbed his head, hardly feeling anything.

Porsha said, "Ringo, all I know is that the store manager wants three dozen more CDs."

"Whoa. I *must* be dreamin'."

"It's no dream, baby. You must have pushed Bridgeport's buttons last night. Word of mouth gets around quick here. Three of my friends even came out of the woodwork, askin' if they could meet you. And I ain't spoke to them tramps in years."

Ringo fell back against the pillows, his eyes closing and opening as he tried to make sense of this. Maybe his dream was beginning to come to life.

Chapter Ten

It was fundamental.

All Ringo needed to do was make more live appearances at other Connecticut nightclubs. He could use the Catmandoo success to support him at the next event, like a job reference, until the CDs were sold out. And maybe he'd repeat the performances and produce a new CD to sell as well.

Porsha turned into Ringo's publicist, spreading word through the hood, calling other clubs and record shops, and booking Ringo for both paid and unpaid performances. It became clear that the pay for a performance was not nearly as important as reaching and capturing a potential fan in person. Even more important, Ringo enjoyed performing. It was a nighttime occupation; it kept him busy and kept his bank roll from disappearing altogether. Quiet as it was kept, Ringo would perform for free all the time if it was feasible.

For four months, Ringo performed on Fridays and Saturdays. His CDs sold out and he needed more. On one of those busy Friday mornings Porsha came rushing through the door. It startled Ringo to the point that he nearly lunged for the gun he had hidden between his mattresses.

"Oh my God—ohmygod! Look!"

"Damn, girl! You almost gave me a heart attack!" Porsha was too busy poking her finger at a magazine to notice. Photos of Ringo were printed along with the liner note, ON THE COMEUP: Rapper Ringo wows audience in Bridgeport, Connecticut.

"What magazine is . . ." Ringo turned to the magazine's cover to reveal the popular *Source* brand name.

"There musta been a photographer at one of the shows."

"*One*? There's three different photos here, Porsha. This one I *know* is the Catmandoo show. Remember the white hockey jersey I wore? With the double zeros? And here. This is the black jersey I think I wore at No Man's Land."

Porsha hugged up closer to Ringo for a better look at the pictures.

"This is too good to be true. How? I know they didn't follow us show to show. Plus, I ain't no superstar to get this much of a push so soon. Did you have anything to do with this?"

"Ringo, you're buggin'. It's only the comeup page. Anybody new can be in there, can't they?"

"You didn't answer me, Porsha. Did you—"

"Don't be silly. I'm a beginner here, takin' lessons from you. I don't have no juice with *The Source. Please.* I *wish*."

Ringo studied Porsha and swallowed a laugh. She was right. She was but a local from Bridgeport. Hard enough to find a man, much less arrange free publicity in a national rap magazine.

Ringo's attention shifted back to *The Source*. He thought about Queens and wondered if the photos might bring him bad luck. It had been almost one year since the holdup. *Besides*, Ringo told himself, *this is a hip-hop magazine. Nobody would be looking here for an armed robber*. And then he smiled, remembering that he had a mask on that day. Feeling silly and paranoid, Ringo kissed Porsha's forehead and got back to more immediate concerns.

Performances. The Catmandoo wanted him back. The Music Hut's manager wanted Ringo to come and perform inside of his store—they'd have a stage built and everything. And a dozen other clubs wanted Ringo, having recognized his name from the good press.

Porsha suggested that T-shirts be made to help promote the single; JUST CAUSE would be printed on the front and RINGO on the back. The T-shirts, Porsha said, could be given away at performances, but people would surely wear the shirts to parties, school, and maybe even during sex. Ringo's reply was, "Hmmm. Imagine that."

It was during one of Ringo's daily workouts—push-ups, crunches, and various stretches—that the phone rang. Porsha was over at Momma Jo's picking up a few things and Tangi was fast asleep.

"I need a damn secretary," Ringo told himself as he went for the phone, still breathing heavy from his tenth set of exercises.

"Hello, may I help you?" Ringo's grunting was more of an inquiry.

"Hey. Is Chocolate there?"

"Chocolate? I'm afraid . . ." Ringo's mind eventually clicked and he looked over at Tangi. "You have the wrong number—there's no Chocolate here." Ringo was about to hang up.

"Are you the rapper?" the caller asked.

"Who is this?" asked Ringo, still wanting air in his lungs.

"I—uhh, well, I do the show at Stamford. WFMV? We play your song." Ringo said nothing. His mind wandered, trying to make the associations: Chocolate. Stamford.

The song.

"Oh. Are you the guy she's supposed to be dealing with for airplay?"

"*Supposed* to be dealing with? Listen, I don't mean to squash your ego, playa. But I think I oughta get a little more respect for squeezing your bullshit song on my radio show. Now put the girl on the phone."

"Who the—Yo, dawg. You don't know me from a hole in the wall. Don't get me twisted with any ol' rapper who needs you and your punk-ass airtime. I suggest you change your attitude—" Ringo was cut short.

"Man, I don't need this bullshit. Tell the bitch the pussy wasn't worth shit anyway. *And* you can kiss your airplay goodbye." The line went dead. Ringo stared at the phone, then at Tangi. He wanted to slam the phone but he contained his rage and set the receiver down gently. His heart jumped when it rang again. *Motha fucka*. Ringo snatched up the phone.

"Listen, you son of a bitch! I'm ten seconds from—"

"Hello. I beg your pardon?" It was a different voice, a higher pitch with a nasal tone. Ringo was fried in frustration.

"Excuse me; I thought you were someone else."

"I see. Well, this is Irwin Johnson, staff writer and music critic here at *The Source* magazine."

"You the guy that ran the photos in the last issue?"

"Well, that was a woman who runs our "On the Comeup" features. I just write reviews, myself. She's the one who gave me your number, actually. She also said I should ask for a woman named Porsha. Is she there?"

"Not now," said Ringo, trying to determine the direction of the phone call. "Is there somethin' I can do for you?"

"I was just wondering if you could send me a copy of the single, 'Just Cause.' Or is there somewhere I can find it on the Internet?"

"I guess I could have Porsha send you a copy." Ringo's mind was dragging, still stuck on the idea of his music not being on the Internet. It was an idea that he thought about but never had time to address.

"Ahh, Mr. Johnson, what do you need a copy for? You thinkin' about reviewing my song?"

"*Your* song? Is this Ringo I'm talkin' to?"

Ringo exhaled.

"In the flesh. This is Ringo, the one in the photo. The one who wrote 'Just Cause.' " As Ringo explained this, he flipped through the magazine, looking for Irwin Johnson's name where the staff was listed. There it was: IRWIN JOHNSON—staff writer.

"Do you consider this a local project? Is that how you've been pushing your song?" It was a good guess on Irwin's part.

"Mostly."

"Because from what I've heard about your song, there's a potential to be much bigger than just a local thing. But I wouldn't be able to give you my strongest critique on the work till I've had a chance to review it thoroughly."

Ringo was discouraged about the idea.

"I don't know. I'm kinda happy with the way things are goin' now."

"Listen, Ringo, not to be too bold, but I rarely make calls like this. Rarely. Usually it's people callin' me—tryin' to put bugs in my ear. This magazine is the biggest resource in the hip-hop culture—"

Before Johnson got a chance to ramble on, Ringo cut in.

"I know what *The Source* is," he insisted, as if he'd be a fool otherwise.

"Okay, then please believe me when I tell you that I'm flooded by tapes and CDs ev-er-y day. Every kind of rapper you could imagine, from every corner of the world, wants a review. I'm just calling on the strength of our photographer's word. She says your stuff is the bomb. Fresh, hot. Whatever word you wanna use. I just need a sample, if you don't mind."

Ideas bounced around inside of Ringo's head like rubber balls in search of escape. There had to be a catch. Finally, Ringo said, "Whatever." And he jotted down Irwin Johnson's address and phone number. As Ringo completed the call, Tangi yawned.

"What time is it?" she asked as she stretched like a contortion artist.

"It's too late, that's what time it is."

Tangi was satisfied with the response—and then she wasn't once she was fully conscious. "*What*?"

Ringo went to sit on the bed where Tangi was now seated, her legs pulled to her chest.

"Ya know, I was just thinkin' about somethin' maybe you could help me out with."

"Okay—cool. Wassup?"

Ringo took a deep breath and cupped a hand over his chin. "You think this radio time is helpin' us any? I'm sayin'—how many listeners do you think are really interested in our stuff?"

Tangi squeezed the sleep from her eyes, grinding the ball of her palm in one socket, then the other. "What do you mean, *are they really interested?* I thought we had to get airplay so the clubs and the stores would believe in the song."

"Did I say that?" asked Ringo.

"Yes. You said that."

"Well, I just don't think we need radio. I think the shows I do are enough. Radio has just been a waste of our time when it really comes down to it." *Please fall for the bullshit, Tangi.*

"Wha—? A waste of—Ringo! We're on ten stations now. People call in to request the songs."

"Tangi, *we* call in to request the songs."

"Okay—yeah, but some others do too."

"Well, I don't care. I say drop the radio campaign." Tangi had an awful look on her face and Ringo swore he heard her say something.

"What was that? I didn't hear you."

"I was just sayin', *good . . . less work for us*."

"Exactly," Ringo answered, trying not to condemn her with his eyes. "Get dressed. I'm havin' Kujo take us to your favorite restaurant."

"Ringo, I ain't got no favorite restaurant."

"Well, we'll *find* you one," he said, running his hand over her mismanaged hair, and pulling her head to him, cuddling it on his shoulder. This felt good. Instead of getting all upset at Tangi for doing what she did, he consoled her. Whatever she did with that guy to get the music played on the radio, Ringo was grateful for—and that was even a different way to look at things—but now that he found out, the nonsense had to stop. *No more desperate measures, Tangi. Please don't do anything else that you'll regret in the long run.*

The next day, Kujo drove Ringo out to Hartford to pick up the reorder, and an additional five thousand CDs. It was an investment that whittled his cash on hand to just below $8,000. However, the way things were going, Ringo could foresee selling all five thousand pieces for a profit to exceed $10,000. It was sure money.

"Sounds like you're doin' real good, Ringo. This makes, what? Ten thousand CDs in how many months? Wow. I wish we were partners," said the technician at I-Mix Studios.

"No, that number isn't right. We're only at seven thousand but, no. No partners. I'm gonna keep doin' the independent thing. Thanks anyway for the offer."

The technician shrugged his shoulders. "Okie dokie. But you're the first indie to do over ten in such a short—"

"I told you we're only at seven. You have the numbers wrong."

"Oh. Well. Yeah, maybe I'm mixing you up with somebody else."

"Maybe so," said Ringo. And he left with the cases of CDs loaded in the back of the Suburban. As Kujo directed the truck away from I-Mix, Ringo expressed his pride through a happy grin.

"Everybody wants to be my partner now that things are cookin'. Damn. Why can't dudes just fall back and play their position? It's always, *Lemme get a piece of the action.*"

Kujo said, "They don't see your hard work, boss."

"Where I'm from, we call that *catchin' the vapors.*"

"I always wondered about that, boss."

"What's that?"

"Where you're from. You never told me."

That's because some things are better left unsaid, Ringo thought.

"I'm from the planet Earth, Kujo. Just like you. Everything else is unimportant. Now how about a slice of pizza before you get back on the thruway?"

"Helluv an idea," said Kujo, somewhat oblivious to the change in subject.

The corner where Joe's Pizza was located also had a fried chicken franchise, a tailor, and a barbershop. There was also a street vendor out on the sidewalk, in front of those outer businesses, as if he had carte blanche, or that the other businesses were irrelevant. Ringo left Kujo in the Suburban and went for the pizza.

"Four slices. Two with sausage and extra cheese. The other two with mushrooms, onions, and peppers."

"Would you like extra cheese on the second two as well?" asked the pizza guy.

"Nah. My stomach would kick my ass and I'd end up with a

headache," said Ringo, finding his own humor to be hilarious. Then he laid a ten-dollar bill on the counter. While waiting for the food, Ringo wandered toward the front of the shop, his attention eventually falling on the vendor. From Ringo's perspective there behind the wall of glass, he happened to be right behind the vendor, who was looking at a table full of CDs and tapes.

Oh shit!

Ringo's eyes grew wide with amazement, and it was a matter of seconds before he bolted through the entrance of the pizza shop to confront the vendor. He took up one of the CDs, his eyes locked on the graphic image. It was as though he was looking in a mirror, only it was a fuzzy black-and-white reproduction of himself. *A bootleg!* Ringo heard of bootlegging—how someone got ahold of an artist's product before it hit stores, often selling poor copies of their music for a fraction of the price.

But so soon? How? Everything is controlled by me.

"How you doing, sir? What can I help you with today?" The vendor was polite to Ringo, not even aware of the resemblance between the artist featured on his product and the man standing before him. It was a greeting that quickly disarmed Ringo of his hate and rage.

"These. Where did you get these?" asked Ringo. At first, the vendor didn't understand. But Ringo was quick to hold up the CD. The vendor soon turned nervous and appeared to brace himself for trouble.

"I only sell music, sir. Just make honest living to feed family. Don't want trouble." The vendor's hands were raised, palms upturned and spread apart, pleading. Ringo felt as though he had a weapon on the vendor, but he didn't. The only weapon was in his eyes; the determination and concern he expressed was a fearsome combination.

"Where'd you get these?" Ringo repeated the question, this time with his brows furrowed.

"Solo. He sell me many CD and tape. I pay cash, then I sell on street. Please, I don't want trouble."

Solo. That mothafucka.

"What's up, Boss?" It was Kujo who came up behind Ringo. And now the vendor broke a sweat, looking up and down the street, maybe for help. Ringo was quiet, assessing the vendor and his tabletop operation, wondering if he was lying—ready to smash his whole enterprise with a foot-stomping tantrum if he was.

"You sure you didn't get this stuff from I-Mix?"

"I-Mix? Neva heard of I-Mix. I buy only from Solo, all the time. Me, my brotha, maybe ten more vendors too." Ringo bit his lip, a painful means of holding his steam. Kujo cocked his head, only now realizing what was going on. Ringo's CDs were there on the vendor's table, but they didn't look authentic—not like the ones Kujo was accustomed to seeing. Kujo clasped his fingers and inverted them so that his knuckles cracked. It might be time for him to prove his duty and honor to his boss.

Ringo turned to Kujo with a disappointed expression, except there was a lack of urgency, as if he'd suddenly changed his mind. To the vendor, Ringo said, "You don't mind if I have one of these, do you?"

"Here, sir, you can have all." The man scooped up the dozen or so CDs, just a fraction of his banquet of bootlegs. "I very sorry." The vendor held out the CDs for Ringo to take.

Ringo smirked; he took just one.

"No, no, you go ahead and make your money. Knock yourself out. Just remember me when you get rich." Ringo slapped Kujo on the shoulder and stared at the bootleg copy is his hand, amused by the things he was learning about his new business—the shadiness of it all. The vendor called out to Ringo before he reentered the pizza shop.

"Excuse, Mista Ringo? Please, sir, can you sign for me? To my daughter?" The vendor held out another bootleg copy, hoping for an autograph. "She love Ringo!"

Ringo could've broken out laughing at the vendor, with his uncomfortable smile and balls of steel. Now he wagged his head and smiled.

"What's her name?" Ringo asked, taking a magic marker from his pocket and then the CD from the vendor. The man had to spell out the name for Ringo, but Ringo also scribbled out a personal note: *Support your favorite rapper . . . buy the real thing!* And Ringo scripted his usual—a fancy *R*.

For the rest of the week Ringo was busy dropping off CDs to the various music outlets, all the while fighting an urge to shoot back to State Street, grab his gun, and wage holy hell on DJ Solo, and even the scum up at I-Mix Studios. How else could Solo duplicate the CDs if not for their help? And besides, it was Solo who suggested I-Mix in the first place.

What a fool I was to trust him so easily. I should've known something was fishy when I saw Solo's expensive truck. Above all, Ringo wondered how much money he was missing out on and how many vendors were out there bootlegging his work. It took only a week and a half to find out. The stores that had re-ordered copies of Ringo's CDs were reporting problems. They couldn't produce further sales. Out of 2,500 units that were delivered on consignment, 2,400 were collecting dust. The 2,500 other copies that Ringo had back at the inn didn't budge. The sting of the counterfeiters began to set in, and it affected Ringo's words and actions.

"The goddamned cable is acting up again. Shit!" Ringo pounded the TV with an angry fist, a half-empty bottle of Bacardi rum in his other hand.

"Want me to go talk to Kellogg?" Porsha asked.

"Bad idea. All I need to know is that pervert makes a move on you. It'll be his last."

"Wanna watch a video instead?"

"Seen 'em all," snapped Ringo, and he brought the bottle to his lips again. "Same ol' shit in 41E. Videos, cable, sex, fast food." Ringo let out a loud, obnoxious hiccup.

"Okay . . . Maybe my boo wants a nice back massage to help with some stress?"

"Stress? Does it look like I'm stressin'?" Ringo jerked his shoulder away from Porsha's attempt to soothe him. "A nigga just needs some breathin' room—shit. How come you chickenheads all say the same bullshit? Like that's the only word in your vocabulary. *Stressin'*. Like I ain't actin' normal."

"Baby?!"

"What!" Ringo roared at Porsha, wild and fiery-eyed. Porsha backed away, afraid to utter another word. She soon snatched up her purse and left the room, slamming the door behind her.

"And *I'm* supposed to be stressin'? You should look at ya'self. Shit—" Ringo gulped from the bottle again. "You don't see me slammin' doors and gettin' a attitude . . . and fuck you anyway! Post office bitch! Bridgeport ho! Who put this shit together? Me! That's who! All you know how to do is fuck and suck! I'm the big dog! I'm the one with the talent and guns!"

Before he could think, there it was . . . the gun was in his hand.

Chapter Eleven

It was an all-night trek, Ringo's journey from Bridgeport to Hartford. By car, the distance was only an hour, but Ringo was on foot. Sure, Kujo would've taken him, however everyone—including Porsha, Butter, and Sweets—had abandoned ship. They all knew that Ringo's sudden stardom was forged, and now that it was quickly melting away, they chose not to go down with him.

The only devoted supporter he had left was Tangi, who was about fifty or so feet behind Ringo, taking the walk with him.

"Ringo, stop! Don't do this! Things can work out . . . you'll see. Porsha was no good for you anyway, that bitch! I'll be your girl, Ringo. I can fuck and suck you just as good as she did. I can do it ten times *better*! Come on, Ringo, gimme a chance!"

"Shut up, Tangi, 'fore I turn around and shoot your young ass! You ain't even legal yet—plus, you done gave your pussy to every John in Bridgeport—what's up with the punk at WFMV? Huh? How many times you have to fuck him to get my record played, huh?"

"Ringo! How can you say these things? After all I did for you!"

"I told you, Tangi, shut the fuck up, or else I'm gonna shoot your ass—right after I finish off Solo and those I-Mix bastards!" Before long, Ringo was at the back door of Club Domino, waiting by Solo's Range Rover.

"Hey, Ringo! Long time, no see! I seen you in *The Source*! Man! You blew up!"

"Yeah. Now all I need is five thousand more CDs. Can you help with that?" Ringo didn't wait for a reply. He just capitalized on the stupid expression Solo had across his face. The 9 mm belonging to a certain dead check cashing proprietress was in Ringo's hand, pointed at Solo's forehead.

"Eat lead," barked Ringo. And he kept squeezing the trigger until the deejay's head spit red, white, and gray brain matter . . . until the clip of sixteen rounds was spent . . . until the bell rang inside of Ringo's head. The ringing that Ringo heard was not only in his mind but also filling 41E. *The telephone*. Ringo rose up from his couch, from his nightmare, to get the call.

"Hello," the rapper answered the phone, and looked over at his bed. *Tangi*. She was fast asleep. The clock radio read 9:30 A.M.

"Good morning. Is this Ringo?"

"Just about. Who wants to know?"

"This is Brooklyn Jones calling. I run the A and R department at PGD Records."

"Brooklyn *who*?" Ringo's vision was still fuzzy as he coped with a splitting headache. "And please stop yelling into the phone. My hearing works fine—so far."

"Uhh sorry. Cats call me Brooklyn, like the borough."

Ringo let the air out of his lungs in a miserable sigh.

"Okay, I, ahh, heard your work last night. A friend of mine at *The Source* . . ."

The good ol' Source *again.*

Ringo tried to recall the writer's name, but since Brooklyn mentioned it, he hadn't stopped running his mouth.

"I also see here that you got the thumbs-up mention in this week's *Hot Coco*."

"Hold up. Hot *what*?"

"*Hot Coco,* dude. As in the club magazine. I got it right here on my desk. Good photo too, if I do say so myself."

"Listen, ahh . . . *Brooklyn.*" The name sounded peculiar coming from Ringo's mouth. "I just woke up, and I really don't know about any thumbs-up in any *Hot Coco* magazine. But could you get to the part about why you calling?"

"Of course. Why not? I wanted to know if you've signed any deals yet. We'd like to get you on the PGD team."

"The PGD team," Ringo repeated with a bored tone to his voice.

"Sure, sonny. The *team*. I'm talkin' Magnum, Frenchi, Black Rain, the whole Murder Squad. I'm talkin' about adding you to our platinum lineup."

"Platinum lineup?" Ringo said, again with no emotion.

"Man, listen to me. Every one of our artists is either platinum or multiplatinum. They all get national exposure. BET, MTV, VH-1—and the biggest concert tour in the business."

"And you want me."

"Exactomundo, Ringo. We're lookin' for someone just like you—someone with a unique style. Plus, you're hot in Bridgeport. Those streets are *feelin'* you up there. Now, with a little money behind you . . . a name like PGD? Man, I'll have you *smokin'* a lot of these other rap artists. You'll chase 'em right off the map—"

Ringo cut in, "You know I'm independent. I have my own label."

"Okay, and that's all to the good. So we take your whole brand on board."

The word *brand* made Ringo think of Tide, Coke, Disney, and the Pillsbury Dough Boy.

"You'll still have your imprint, your name. The only thing we do is market and distribute you correctly. We've done it with Magnum already, and well, hell, we started out the same way until PGD came and swept us up."

"What about the profits I make? How's that work?"

"All I can say is mo' money, sonny. There's so much more land out here to conquer. Bridgeport? Okay, that's cool 'n' all, but you could have so much more going for you. Tell you what, why don't I come out to Bridgeport to see you? We'll do lunch, talk over some serious strategies."

"Strategies. Listen . . . sonny. Not for nothin', but I've turned down two major label deals already," Ringo lied. "And the bottom line is, I'm happy with where I'm going right now. It's only a matter of—"

Brooklyn cut in. "Why don't you gimme a chance, Ringo? At least, let's do lunch. Whaddaya say?"

"Gimme your number and let me get back to you," Ringo said with that finality in his tone. Afterward he dropped right back to sleep. Ten minutes later the phone rang again.

"*Damn.* Good morning," Ringo moaned, not at all in the mood to follow the phone etiquette that Porsha had learned and practiced.

"Hey, buddy. This is Clyde Hayes—everybody calls me Fathead though. Can I talk to the manager of a rapper by the name of Ringo?" Ringo was fed up with beating around the bush. It was no secret that he was the focus of most every call to come to this phone.

"Ringo speaking," he said unconsciously.

"Hey! Ringo!" The man on the phone was livelier than a dynamite fuse. "Wow, dude it's an honor to speak wit' ya. I wanted to discuss a possible exclusive booking agreement with our agency."

"What agency is this?" asked Ringo, as if he'd been solicited by twenty of them.

"I'm with William Walters. I handle most of the hip-hop rap acts on the east coast tip."

The east coast-tip. I really need to brush up on my music industry language.

Like Big Joe, Levi, Short Dog, Miracle, Ace Boon, Smoke, and the Cold Cash Brothas. There's dozens of 'em I could name. I could even fax you a roster if you want."

Fax? Man, I'm not ready for this shit. Where's Porsha when I need her?

Over the next few days similar calls came in from other record labels like Mo City, and magazines such as *City Life* and *Hot Coco* wanted exclusive interviews.

But the biggest call was from Lyons Films, interested in using Ringo's music for a movie sound track. The movie folks told

Ringo that they needed an answer within two days, explaining that it would be perfect timing to be included with the film project. Still, there was no word from Porsha.

Ringo went to the post office to speak with Momma Jo, and as usual, he also checked the wall of Most Wanted postings.

Whew.

"She hasn't been around for a few days, Ringo," said Momma Jo, reading Ringo's mind when he approached.

A few days. In other words, the day I barked at her she disappeared.

"I'm worried about her, Momma Jo. Did she at least call?"

"Nope. And she's *never* acted like this before. Maybe it's love," she marveled.

"Yeah. Uh-huh. You think it could be a family problem?"

"Well, her mom lives across town somewhere on Regina Street."

"Thank you, Momma Jo." And Ringo rushed out into the daylight. This was the first time he'd heard the Regina Street address. He'd been too busy with his own affairs—not devoting enough all-around attention to his new girlfriend. Ringo soon found Kujo and off they went to find Porsha.

"Regina Street, Kujo. And step on it."

When they got to Regina Street, Ringo felt himself desperate to get Porsha, just to talk to her face-to-face and satisfy his concerns about her well-being. He also wanted to apologize. Confronting whoever he ran into on Regina's sidewalks, Ringo asked stragglers if they knew Porsha or where she lived. It took a half hour of skeptical and even rude confrontations, but Ringo was finally pointed toward a two-story redbrick home with a tiny front yard where three stray cats of miscellaneous colors sat and watched everything that moved with a lack of interest. Ringo climbed the steps to the front porch and was spooked when a white woman opened the door.

"Sorry, I must have the wrong house," he said, and he turned to leave.

"You sure do, ya no-good nigga." The outburst made Ringo freeze in his tracks. But by the time he spun around the woman had slammed the door closed. He started to ignore it, but there was something about the woman's voice, how she expressed a fed-up attitude. And there was something else; her words had an edge to them, a sharp one that you had to grow up in the ghetto to recognize. It was a voice that an around-the-way girl would keep as her weapon.

How does she know who I am? Even if I was what she said, a no-good nigga, how would she know?

Ringo shook his head free of confusion and went to ring the doorbell again. And again. Without opening the door, the woman cried, "Whadda you want!"

"I want Porsha. Is this Porsha's house?"

"And it always will be, no matter what no-good mothafucka comes into her life."

Ringo felt the stab of her words and also got a better look at the woman this time. *Pretty, but a witch.*

"Can I talk to her?" Ringo asked, not allowing her words to penetrate his ego. The door swung open under the force of the angry woman—the pretty, angry white woman.

"Kinda late for that, ain't it?"

"Late for what? I don't get it."

"You mothafuckas never do."

There were but so many of her insults that Ringo would swallow.

"My daughter's down at the clinic gettin' rid of that bastard you put in her."

Daughter?

"You mean, you're her . . . The clinic? Gettin' rid of . . . Porsha's *pregnant*?! Oh no!" Ringo grabbed the woman's shoulders. "You gotta tell me where the clinic is! I gotta stop her! Please!"

Porsha's mother fought to free her shoulders from Ringo's restraint while snarling for him not to touch her.

"Please! You can't let her do this. I . . ." Ringo realized that the woman would be of no help. It was in her eyes—bitterness and pain. Some ugly past that was doing nothing but causing more pain now—as if she didn't mind that her daughter was experiencing some of the same misery.

Ringo swallowed the word *fuck*, and he shot down the steps for the Suburban.

Kujo knows where everything is.

"Kujo, where's the clinic? Take me there—fast." Kujo had to be breaking some kind of record in racing to downtown Bridgeport. The building that facilitated the clinics was massive, with four floors of business offices, including a storefront temporary employment agency and an office supply outlet. There was no sign or indication that there was an abortion clinic there.

Kujo said, "This is it. I *know* this is it. I brung some girls down here before. They go in that way." Kujo pointed to a lobby inside the building. It was manned by a security guard who immediately addressed Ringo.

"I'm sorry, sir. Unless you have an appointment, no visitors are permitted upstairs."

Upstairs. The clinic must be upstairs. But while Ringo was turned away, he noticed others—women, mainly—who passed by, entering the elevator cars without any identification badge or any questioning. It made Ringo assume that being stopped was his fault for appearing uncertain and out of place.

Then the guard explained, "It's not me, sir. We've had all kinds of security problems with threats and angry boyfriends—you name it."

And it dawned on Ringo: abortion clinic . . . of course. One of the world's biggest debates, the right to life. But never had the issue touched him until this very instant. What had been such a foreign issue in his life—something for other people to worry about—was now the foremost priority of his life. He could very well see the need for security, because right now, although he didn't show it, Ringo wanted to climb the walls. He wanted to stop time. Anything to keep Porsha from the inevitable.

"Maybe I'm in the wrong building," Ringo said out loud so that he could be overheard. The guard's phone rang.

Shit. This is life or death. I gotta do somethin'.

The guard stepped aside to answer the call. The elevator door was about to close. Ringo lunged for the elevator, just making it through the closing doors.

"Hey!" the guard shouted.

* * *

Ringo had no idea which floor the clinic was on. He found himself stuck with a choice of four floors, and already the car was moving toward the second floor, carrying with it a number of frightened passengers.

"Listen, I'm here to stop my girlfriend from killing our baby. Somebody please tell me what floor." Ringo smashed the side of his fist against the elevator's stop button and the car jerked to a standstill.

"Please! Somebody. What floor is the clinic on?" The five passengers squeezed up against the walls of the elevator, as far as they could get from this madman. One girl screamed.

"Look, I don't wanna hurt you—I don't wanna hurt *anyone*. I just . . . I didn't know she was pregnant. She never told me. . . . It was a stupid argument we had—I was drinking. Please! I need her. I want the baby. I know she'll want it too!" It was the Latina with the sharp nose, bedroom eyes, and long brown hair who spoke up.

"How do we know you're not an abuser—a woman-beater?"

"I've *never* beat Porsha. *Never*."

"And the baby, how do we know you'll be a good father?" The calm speech pattern of this woman was annoying but somehow authoritative as if she had the key, the solution to Ringo's dilemma.

"Well, I . . . I've never had children. This'll be the first. But he's my blood—how could I do anything but love him?"

"Him?" said another passenger, turning this into a tribunal of some kind. "How ya know it's not gonna be a girl?"

"I don't—I just . . ."

"Would ya' love her the same?"

"Of course! What is this? Come on, ladies!"

The Latina was satisfied.

"Third floor, hon. Calm down, I'll help you find her," she said, pressing the resume button to get the elevator car moving again. "I work there."

Others in the elevator breathed freely again, a couple still with some suspicion in their eyes, and yet they couldn't help but find themselves caught up in this man's soap opera. One of the women in the car was teary-eyed and dug into her purse for a tissue.

"Go get 'er, buddy," an older woman chirped, patting Ringo's back.

There was a lobby on the third floor where a receptionist sat behind a counter, talking on the phone, filing her nails, and chewing gum—all at the same time.

"Christine, I'll relieve you now. I know it's time for a smoke."

"How did you guess?" said Christine. And she said her farewell to the caller, took up her handbag, propped it on her lap, and searched for a cigarette. "Thanks, Lisa."

"Don't mention it," Lisa replied. Christine gave a quaint smile to Ringo as she passed by, wagging her ass through an employee entrance. No sooner had Lisa sat behind the counter then the phone rang.

"*That* would be our friend downstairs," said Lisa. She disconnected the call without a greeting, and then took the phone off the hook. Meanwhile, she checked through the appointment log. "I'd give you a couple minutes before the guard gets up here. Here she is. Porsha Lindsey is it?"

"Yes, yes."

"Okay. Looks like she's been here for a half hour. Go through the door; she's in the room farthest to the back. I can't take you back—I'd lose my job. But hurry." She pressed a buzzer.

"And good luck."

Ringo nodded his thanks and slid through the door that said NO ADMITTANCE WITHOUT APPOINTMENT. His heart thumping hard in his chest, Ringo's eyes wandered, soaking in the eerie atmosphere. His nose inhaled the too obvious sterile scent, likely camouflaging the death that hung in the air. There were fluorescent lights and everything was so clean, but Ringo wasn't fooled. He was sure that this was the welcome mat to hell. Things were a blur now as Ringo quickly moved toward his destination—the staff in their white uniforms, the women in flimsy robes, wheelchairs along one wall.

Ignoring the sights and sounds, trying not to succumb to the inquiries about who he was and where he was going, Ringo kept his pace.

She's in the room farthest to the back. The farther Ringo progressed, the noisier things got. He never looked back, yet he felt like a hunted deer. Room by room, Ringo called out for Porsha.

"Porsha! Porsha!"

"Ringo?" Porsha peeked out of a doorway. She was wearing one of those gowns. Ringo could see that she was mostly naked underneath the thin fabric.

"Porsha!" Ringo ran to her and they hugged in a shared moment of relief.

"How did you— Ringo!?"

Ringo hadn't come to talk. He swept Porsha off of her feet and turned to leave the same way he came in. At least half a dozen clinic staff members were posted in his way. But that was funny to Ringo, the idea that those people thought they could stop him.

"Now, I'm not here for trouble, but I swear I'll run you all over if you don't—"

"Put the woman down!" a man demanded.

"Maybe you didn't hear me; I'm leavin' here, and my girl's goin' with me."

Porsha pulled her face away from the crook of Ringo's neck.

"It's okay. Please let us go. I'll be fine."

"Are you sure, miss? We can call the police."

"No, please. I'm sure. Oh, Ringo. I prayed and prayed that you would come and stop me. I didn't know if I was making the right choice. I didn't know you cared," Porsha sobbed.

"Shhh shhh shhh—it's okay, boo. Don't fall apart on me. It's not your fault, it's mine," said Ringo as he hugged her closer, cradling her in his arms all the while. "I shouldn'ta went off on you like that. I chased you away when I should've held on to you when I needed you most. God, Porsha, a baby? We're gonna have a baby?" Ringo had to stop and wonder.

"Hey—you didn't . . ." Ringo's words broke off as he looked into Porsha's eyes with fright, fearing the worst.

Through her tears, Porsha said, "No, I didn't," and went back to burying her face against his neck. Facing the staff with greater determination, Ringo was overcome with relief as they parted and allowed him to pass. One of the nurses was in tears as well, while a couple of girls in robes hugged each other.

Lisa caught up with Ringo to hand him Porsha's belongings as he boarded the elevator.

"Good luck," she said to him and Porsha.

"Thanks," said Ringo. "Thanks for helping me save my future."

As one elevator door closed, another slid open, and the building security guard and a police officer stepped out.

"Where is he?" the guard woofed.

"Who?" asked Lisa in her best attempt at shock and amazement. And the two men pushed past her, splitting up to search the floor.

In the Suburban, Ringo and Porsha cuddled in the backseat while Kujo, happy as freed bird, rapped along with "Just Cause," the trucks' sound system drowning out any chance of eavesdropping.

"That was close," said Ringo.

"Too close," said Porsha. "Now I know what it feels like to be on death row."

"You got Momma Jo worried to death. And damn, your moms gave me the business."

The mention put Porsha on full alert.

"You saw my mother?"

"Did I? I'm glad she didn't have no gun, 'cause she'da blew my brains out."

"But how—"

"Never mind all that, Porsha. I have good news. PGD wants to give me a deal."

"But I thought you said no deals, that you were gonna stay independent."

"I know, I know. It's just . . . Porsha, they're talking so much money. And we've been struggling so much to grow—five CDs here, ten over there. It just feels like doing a big promotion could change things forever. They want two of my singles for some movie sound track—and get this, the movie they're talkin' about is called *Push*, same as my song."

"Really?"

"Really. And if that's not big enough, they wanna give me an apartment in New York where I can live closer to the action. On top of that there's two hundred grand they wanna shell out for an album and another hundred for the two singles. They say that money's comin' from the movie people, the sound track budget."

"Wow, Ringo. It's really happening," Porsha said, her eyes glistening. "I think I'm gonna faint." Porsha pretended to fall out, plopping herself back against the leather seat.

The mood was right, so Ringo didn't mind sharing something else.

"Mmm hmm. And it wouldn't be happening if it wasn't for a certain photographer from a certain local college, and of course there was that anonymous phone call to *The Source* magazine." Ringo spilled these revelations, faking a bout of naïveté, exaggerating with his eyeballs rolling back.

Porsha covered, saying, "You wouldn't hurt a pregnant girl, would ya?"

"No. But I might bite your nose off," said Ringo, attacking her with playful nibbles to her nose, cheeks, and neck. Her flimsy gown fell open, leaving her partially naked. Ringo stopped.

"What?" asked Porsha, as if she'd done something wrong. But Ringo was merely turning up the heat, taking a moment to look into her eyes, then easing down again for a sensual kiss and passionate fondling. Again, Ringo stopped.

"Kujo . . . *Kujo!*"

"Yeah, Boss?"

"We're not in a big rush to get back. Take the long way."

"You got it" was the reply.

And when Ringo faced Porsha again, she put her finger to his lips.

"Wanna know somethin'?"

"What? That your hair's a mess or that you're hardly wearing anything?"

Porsha smoothed her hand along Ringo's cheek.

"Nope. It's that you're gonna be a daddy in about eight months." Ringo worked his mouth around so that his face was practically palmed by Porsha's hand. He kissed every inch of it, even fitting his tongue in the gaps between her fingers.

"But guess what?" he took a moment to say. "You're gonna be a mommy *and* the manager of a big-time rap star."

And while Kujo took the long way back to State Street, Ringo made love to Porsha in the backseat. There was no looking over their shoulder, no hesitation, and no birth control. This was that next level, the big dive. This was uninhibited, liberated, and purposeful lovemaking. This was his way of committing himself.

When they arrived, Ringo flashed a devilish smile and asked Kujo to have the truck washed.

"Inside and out," Ringo told him. And they shared a silent laugh as Ringo carried his sleeping beauty into 41E.

Ringo didn't need to use his key since the door was snatched open from inside.

"Hey," Ringo said, keeping his voice low so Porsha wouldn't wake. "Look who I found."

"Oh. Um . . . hey—Porsha." Tangi wasn't the least bit surprised. She moved in to give her friend a fleeting kiss on the cheek, and Porsha warmed to a groggy consciousness.

"Hey, girrrl," Porsha managed to say.

"Good to have you back, 'cause *this* nigga was gettin' on my *last* nerves," said Tangi with a mock disgust directed toward Ringo.

However, Tangi was on the move, on some predetermined mission.

"Where you goin' in such a rush?" asked Ringo.

"Uhh . . . work," Tangi said, as if lightning struck her with the idea. "And I gotta get goin'—see ya."

"Hey! I thought we discussed this. We said you didn't *have* to work anymore. We—"

"Correction. *You* said that. Not me."

"Well, whatever. I thought we had plans."

"We do. I just . . . there's some loose ends I wanna tie up."

Ringo looked at Porsha. *Huh*?

"And besides, last I checked, you wasn't my daddy." Tangi flagged down Kujo before he pulled off.

Ringo felt he'd been punched.

"Oh, before I forget, there's some messages on the table—some movie studio guy or whatever. I'll see you later."

Tangi pulled the passenger door closed before Ringo could respond, and Kujo pulled off.

"Where to, Miss Tangi?"

"Take me down the block, Kujo."

"Your wish is my command," he said.

Porsha went to shower off the icky idea of aborting a baby, and immediately thereafter she transformed into the useful superwoman she had been just days earlier. There was a pride in her actions and hope in her attitude. She felt like taking on the world, but accepted the menial tasks of cleanup and of organizing Ringo's business affairs. Eventually, Porsha sorted through the small pile of messages. She wondered if these were the result of her contact at *The Source* and the CDs that she sent them by express mail.

"So you're definitely going ahead with the PGD deal?" asked Porsha.

"It sounds real good. I guess I'm gonna need to see some papers and hire a lawyer."

"Who is Brooklyn Jones?" she asked, noticing the name on more than one message slip.

"Some hyper dude, I'll tell you that much. But he really wants me with their company. He said Killer X liked my stuff and couldn't wait to meet me."

Killer X's name and likeness had been displayed countless times in many of the rap publications that Porsha subscribed to.

These magazines also helped her to become more familiar with other names and resources in the rap game, and she eventually had a long talk over the phone with an approachable woman named Cloe who gave Porsha many suggestions. She told her to stay well informed if she was to be a part of this business, and that meant studying trade publications such as *Billboard, BRE,*

Impact, Hits, The R&B Monitor, and *SoundScan* in order to understand the various charts and what kinds of songs were played and where. Cloe said that Porsha should at least be familiar with what the local radio stations were playing throughout the country.

"They tell you all that?"

"Every week," Cloe said. "College radio too."

That conversation with Cloe led Porsha to amass subscriptions, including newspapers, magazines, and newsletters. She had even convinced Ringo to invest in a computer so that she'd have direct access to the world by Internet and e-mail.

The computer was still in its box in the corner of the room—covered with a towel and used as a table for the time being.

But now that Porsha had officially returned to her role of part manager, part publicist, and part lover, she was ready to forge on at full blast. She was fueled by a greater passion than before, wanting to see Ringo—her baby's father—hit the big-time.

"Killer X. Didn't he sell, like, a gazillion CDs?"

"If you add up the last few albums," Ringo said, undressing to jump in the shower. "And yeah, I think he did over ten million albums. But we shouldn't get lost in the numbers, Porsha. All I wanna do is sell enough so me and mine can eat."

"Of course," said Porsha. *But I want you to sell enough so the world will know your name. They'll love you just like I do.* "Maybe his fans will buy your music like they buy his."

Ringo shrugged it off and stepped into the shower.

IT WAS during the discussion about the apartment in New York City that gunshots sounded. Not so loud as to sound like they came from next door, but enough to be concerned about. Ringo sprung out of the shower, no towel, no clothes.

"Baby!" Porsha was astonished, more so by the sight of her man streaking out of the bathroom naked than by the sound of gunshots.

Ringo didn't acknowledge Porsha; he was too busy checking through the rooms and rear windows. Then he went to reach between his bed mattresses.

The gun was missing.

Chapter Twelve

"Porsha . . . did—?" Ringo froze and his words cut off midway. She had gone to the window as he had to get a look outside.

"Huh? What'd you say, boo?"

"Nothin'. I was just thinkin' out loud. Hey—stay away from the window, babe. You gotta think for two people now." Ringo tugged at the oversized jersey Porsha had on—it was the only thing she had on.

"Don't you mean, for three? I got your back too, ya know." Ringo embraced Porsha with his still-wet body drying against the jersey. That he was naked like this, and how he held her, displayed a sense of urgency and worry.

"Baby, you shouldn't be so tight. Relax. Really. That was probably some of them immature boys we got around here, always bustin' shots in the air like they ain't got no sense. It's not bad like it used to be, like when a bunch of dealers used the inn as their headquarters."

But what's that got to do with my gun?

"By the way, is this your way of telling me you want some?" Porsha had her nose and lips burrowed against Ringo's bare chest and shoulder, an expression of desire in her eyes. However, Ringo's mind was elsewhere.

"Lemme go put somethin' on," he said, aware, but unconcerned, that Porsha was watching him from behind. In pants and a mesh top now, Ringo asked, "Porsha, when you were cleaning did you happen to check between the mattresses?"

"Ringo, why would I check there? It's not like we play *between* the mattresses—only on top."

Ringo shook his head, but not in response to Porsha's words. It was more of a frustrated reaction. A mental list of possibilities began to weigh on Ringo's mind.

Kujo?

Butter or Sweets?

Tangi!

"Do we have the phone number to The Last Kiss?"

"I don't. Maybe it's with Tangi's things."

Ringo looked by the bed where Tangi kept very few belongings, and fewer still since she was away.

"Ringo, are you gonna tell me what's goin' on? Or do I have to guess?"

Porsha's queries were beginning to irritate Ringo.

"Porsha, this is not the time for questions. Please. Can we maybe get some food? I'm starving."

Porsha sighed. *Oh well.*

"We eatin' out? Or in?"

"Whatever you say," said Ringo, still rummaging through Tangi's clothes.

For a time, Porsha stood and wondered what he was looking for; then she went to the phone to satisfy her craving.

"Hi, Mr. Su, this is Porsha over at the Inn. Yes, I'm good. We want some chicken and broccoli, egg foo young, an order of, and, baby? Ringo?" Porsha had her hand over the phone. Ringo turned to see Porsha near the window.

"Outside. Somethin' *did* happen out there." Ringo got up from his knees and came to the window while Porsha finished with Mr. Su.

"Yes, everything's fine, Mr. Su. No. That should be it. You know our address. We're waiting." Porsha hung up and joined Ringo at the window. There were police vehicles out in the parking lot and at least a dozen officers strolling back and forth between vehicles and residences. An ambulance made a noisy entry into the lot and two emergency workers got out to ready a stretcher. Flashing lights flickered everywhere.

"Whaddaya think happened?" asked Porsha.

"Whatever it is, there's a body involved."

An officer's voice barked over a megaphone then.

"THIS IS THE BRIDGEPORT POLICE DEPARTMENT! ALL RESIDENTS ARE ASKED TO REMAIN INDOORS UNTIL AN OFFICER INTERVIEWS EVERYONE. WE WILL DO OUR BEST TO MAKE THIS FAST, BUT AGAIN . . . ALL RESIDENTS ARE ASKED TO COOPERATE FULLY WITH OUR OFFICERS! WE ARE SORRY ABOUT THIS INCONVENIENCE!"

"What the *hell*? Tell me that five-o is *not* going door-to-door," said Ringo.

"I will, if that's what you wanna hear. But they always do this whenever somethin' serious goes on here—except I always watched from across the street. A girl got raped last year, and they did the same thing, door-to-door, like the rapist was somewhere hiding under a bed, then there were some drug busts, and it was door-to-door again. I think the police like to do this and they're harassing these people 'cause they're on welfare or housing assistance. They even search through people's stuff."

Ringo was dizzy with all the details—all of it news to him, making him full of concern.

"But *you* ain't gotta worry, boo. You're a *celebrity.* Half the police probably listen to rap music."

Ringo could see it now, Porsha holding up *The Source* magazine and saying, *See? My baby's father is a rap star. So don't harass us.*

Guessing that it'd be another ten minutes or so before the police reached 41E, Ringo began gathering things for a speedy escape.

"Keep an eye out and lemme know how far away they are."

"A few doors, maybe, Thirty-eight-E. But Ringo? What's?" Porsha seemed to have lost her voice and looked stunned by Ringo's erratic behavior. "Ringo, you're scaring me."

"Girl, this whole fuckin' State Street Motor Inn is scary. All this time I'm avoiding five-o, and here they come, right to my door."

"Avoidin' five-o?" Porsha had a confused look on her face.

Now Ringo reached down into the couch, where things like coins might find there way. "Look outside," instructed Ringo.

"I did," said Porsha. "They're—"

Ringo cut her short. "Look. Out. Side," he said with greater authority. And the moment she obeyed, he pulled out the enforcer, the gun that Brice had given him prior to the robbery. Once he stuffed the weapon behind his belt and pulled on a jacket, Ringo ran up behind Porsha. She was frightened, but continued looking out of the window.

"Listen, I gotta get out of here." He had his arms around her, kissing the back of her head. I can't explain it to you now. When they get to the door, answer it. If they ask, just you and Tangi live here. Tell 'em anything, just don't mention me."

Porsha made a face.

"Just do it," Ringo ordered. He kissed her closed lips. "I love you," he said in haste, thinking that the words would trigger some immediate devotion and duty. But there was no telling how Porsha took the words—the first time Ringo mentioned love—since her eyes were still closed, like she couldn't believe what was going on. Ringo never noticed the tear squeezing from her lids, too busy climbing through the window to the rear of the inn.

"Remember," Ringo said just before he disappeared. "Don't mention me. I don't exist."

Porsha could hear their voices through the door, even before they knocked.

"Okay, Zack. This is forty-one-E. Says here someone named Jenkins. Let's do it."

Then came the knock at the door.

When Porsha peeked through the peep hole in the door she saw four cops. One of the cops was still muttering, but it was loud enough for Porsha to hear each word.

"Fucking pity that Kellogg had to go like that—all these gypsies, tramps, and thieves livin' here—"

"Who is it?" Porsha finally answered the knock.

"Police. Open up, ma'am."

Porsha opened the door enough for a one-eyed view, and eventually all the way.

One of the cops cleared his throat. "We'd like to speak with you for a moment," he said, helping the door open wider with one hand. Meanwhile, he and the others were working to get a full view of 41E, as well as a head-to-toe view of Porsha.

"Are you alone?"

"Yes, I am." Porsha tried to get past the perverted staring. "What's happening outside?"

One cop nudged another, and that one said, "There's been a shooting. Are you a renter here?"

"I am."

"And your name?"

"Porsha. Porsha Lindsey," she said, folding her arms to interfere with their view.

One of the cops looked up from his clipboard. "Then who is Jenkins?" he asked.

"Oh, that would be Tangi."

"And where might she be?"

"She's at work."

"And where's work?"

Porsha began to feel herself part of an inquisition, as though she was the bad guy. She thought about how these cops harassed the State Street residents, and she became upset, although she didn't show it.

"Where my lover works is none of your business," said Porsha with a protective attitude.

"Your—I see. Well, Ms. Lindsey, do you mind if we have a look around?"

"Whatever," said Porsha, backing up to allow them access. "I was about to get dressed and I'm in a rush—hope you don't mind."

None of the officers disagreed with Porsha, who was already back near the bed. She had her back to them and pulled the jersey up over her head.

There was a silence in 41E to define the moment, and Porsha knew beyond a shadow of a doubt that four sets of eyeballs were glued to her naked body. She knew they'd be uncomfortable and that, for whatever Ringo's reason, she was buying time.

A two-way radio squawked loudly, and the volume was abruptly lowered as though some greater priority was at hand.

Porsha continued her little performance, turning slightly and making it seem unconscious.

"What're you all looking for, anyways?"

The instant Porsha faced them, heads whipped away fast enough for necks to snap. Two of the cops bumped into each other in their attempt to look busy. Another cop knocked over the clock radio and some papers from atop an empty milk crate, making a mess of things.

The man apparently in authority said, "I think, ahh, we're done here. If you hear of anything, Miss, I'll leave this card on the table . . ."

Porsha had her hands on her hips now, more or less posing with her full frontal showcase. The men punched and pushed one another, practically tripping to get out of 41E.

This had better be good, Ringo.

There was an alley behind the east wing of the State Street Inn. A five-foot fence cordoned off the walkway and on the other side was the State Street Baptist Church.

Oh, great. That's just what I need . . . to be saved.

It was much darker now, with the gray sky allowing enough gloom for Ringo to find his direction. At each end of the alley there were police emergency lights flashing and reflecting their laserlike rays, impressing a sense of crisis upon the vicinity. Ringo's heart drummed in his chest as if he were a marathon runner. And yet there was little room for running with both ends of the alleyway likely under police watch.

There was no other choice. Ringo climbed the fence, balanced there for a half-second, then jumped down onto the grassy yard of the church property. There were a few obstacles that were big and obvious—a shed for garden tools, a few trash cans, and a brick barbecue, which Ringo crouched behind, advancing farther and farther from the inn.

To his far right was State Street.

To his left, the farthest end of the church and the church driveway.

Ringo noticed a Dumpster in a corner, large enough so that he could use it to hurl himself over a second fence, perhaps into a backyard behind some house on the adjacent block.

He proceeded to duckwalk in that direction, along the side of the fence, and climbed the Dumpster like a prowler. When he jumped down he landed at an awkward angle and grunted when he hit the grass face-first.

A frightened shriek succeeded the fall, sounding something like a chimpanzee.

Ringo turned and found himself facing the nose of a gun, its metal glistening in the dim atmosphere.

Too out of breath to react and still trying to regain his focus, Ringo didn't budge.

"Ringo?"

"Tangi?"

"Ringo! Oh my God, *Ringo*," she gasped, dropping the gun and lunging at him. They both fell back onto the grass—Tangi in a frenzied relief, and Ringo flabbergasted, but happy to have survived the latest threat on his life.

"Tangi? What the hell are you doin' with this?" Ringo reached for the weapon. "And why are you back here?"

Tangi hugged Ringo and he felt her shiver.

"Oh *damn*. What happened?"

"I . . . shot him. Ringo, I shot the mothafucka."

"Ohhhh shit. Who? You shot who? Get down!" Ringo whispered and pulled Tangi to the grass.

A police car was passing by on Astor Place with its bright spotlight skating along the church wall, the fence, and Dumpster. When Ringo was sure the car had passed, he took ahold of Tangi's shoulders.

"I thought you were going to work? Tangi, what the fuck?!"

She seemed to shrivel before him and busted into a nasal-heavy cry.

"Shhh, shhh . . . it's gonna be all right. Easy. I got you . . .

easy." Ringo rocked Tangi in his arms and kept an eye out for five-o. After a time he asked, "Did anybody see you?"

"I don't . . . think so . . ." she answered with gut-wrenching sobs. "I—I'm—sorry I took your gun. I'm sorry. I don't wanna go to jail, Ringo." Tangi managed to utter the words, but she soon succumbed to her sobbing again, as though the worst were inevitable.

Rocking back and forth with her, Ringo said, "Don't worry, babe. You're not going anywhere." Ringo stuck the 9mm pistol in his pants pocket and sought Tangi's attention. "Is he . . . is Kellogg dead?"

"Ringo, blood was everywhere. A piece of his head fell off. *Oh God, Ringo, I killed him. I really killed him.*"

Ringo encouraged Tangi's silence and held her face with both hands. "Look at me Tangi. Don't ever repeat that. Don't ever tell anybody what happened back there. Put it out of your mind, you hear me?"

Tangi nodded.

"You're sure nobody saw you? I'm not gonna hear any stories about your mother later?"

Tangi wagged her head. "No. Momma wasn't there."

Ringo could see how Tangi became so vulnerable, so suddenly; she was like a little girl.

"I gotta get us away from here. You okay? Can you keep up with me?"

Tangi made a face—hardly the face of a killer.

"Nigga, I used to run track with Porsha."

"Well, excuse me," said Ringo. "Let's go. And stay down. We're gonna cross Astor and find a pay phone on Audubon."

Porsha was fully dressed now, pacing back and forth, looking through the window and checking out the scene in the parking lot—the body being taken away and different police in their two and three-man huddles—when the phone rang.

"Hey," she answered, expecting Ringo to be on the other end. "Yeah, they came and went. No, they didn't give me a hard time, but I probably—" Porsha snickered. "Never mind. It's nothin'; they're long gone. Down by forty-six-E now, probably buggin' the Brown family for information. Ringo, they said Kellogg was shot. Yeah, *really*." Porsha was at the window, still feeling like a prisoner, as she spoke with Ringo.

Five-o was definitely all up in the Brown's residence, and Porsha hated the sentiment she felt for them. It was just the cop's irritating idea in the back of her mind, how she practically lived here now, among people that, for the most part, didn't do so much as lift a finger to change their situation. Or rather, they became so comfortable with the taxpayers carrying them that there was no reason to change things. If it wasn't broke, why fix it?

"Tangi? Where'd you find her? I thought she—Ringo? You're down at No Man's Land?" Porsha stopped her pacing. And what was happening outside the window was no longer as important.

"*Whadda you mean, that's not important? Ringo! I wanna know what the*—" Porsha pulled the phone away from her ear, as if she'd been stunned by a strong electrical current. It was Ringo's shouting, commanding her to pay attention.

"Yes. I see the cell phone. Okay . . . *okay* . . . all the business papers—yes, I'll get 'em together, Kujo." Porsha sighed deeply. "Okay. See you around midnight I guess. All right already, I *promise*. Ringo? Whatever you're into, I just want you to know it doesn't matter. I still love you."

After the call, Ringo and Tangi found Kujo four blocks north of State Street at the Waverly Avenue car wash. Ringo's single "Push" was thumping so loud the ground vibrated halfway across the street.

As they got closer they heard Kujo reciting Ringo's lyrics by heart.

"*Lesson number one, the killers' creed*
Don't lose your mind in times of need
Never pull the trigger if the reason's greed
But when it's time to work, use grace and speed.
If you gotta save a life, don't buck—don't stall
just be the eye of the storm, deep breaths—that's all

Go hard, think fast, and if your back's against the wall
Don't waste no time, empty clips till they all fall . . ."

"Boss, *Tangi*, you scared the shit outta me," said Kujo, trying not to trip over the bucket and other cleaning supplies on the ground.

"Almost done, Kujo?"

"Just gotta finish the floor mats and—"

Ringo was already picking up the floor mats from the ground and tossing them back in the truck.

"Well, maybe I am finished," said Kujo, reading between the lines.

"Let's go," said Ringo. Tangi had loaded herself into the truck and slouched down in the backseat—her attempt to disappear.

Early the next morning, Ringo, Porsha, Tangi, Kujo, Butter, and Sweets piled into the Suburban and headed down I-95.

Fame and fortune was awaiting them just two hours away, in New York City.

Chapter Thirteen

NEW YORK CITY

"All right students, quiet down, please. Today marks part two of our look into the elements of evidence, or rather, what constitutes evidence." Professor Wilcox gestured for Justin to shut the door.

"If you wouldn't mind," he remarked.

"Ten-four, professor." Justin's gung-ho attitude provoked a few of his fellow students to either roll their eyes or suck their teeth.

"Teacher's pet," someone mumbled at the back of the lecture hall.

"Thank you, Justin. Now how about you, Janice? Yesterday we touched on a couple of these elements. Would you like to refresh our memories?"

"Well, you did mention something about hearsay . . ."

"Good girl. And what else. Ahh——Brenda? Any idea?"

"Witnesses and physical evidence."

"Oh, splendid. Some sharp young lawyers of tomorrow—I dare say that our courtrooms will be rich with estrogen. Should be a wake-up call for you young bucks who expect to skate through law school on a wing and a prayer. Yes indeed, when we investigate the areas of a crime, we must never dwell upon anything more than the evidence, since in a court of law, at least here in these United States, evidence is what a judge and jury must consider. Now, it would be tempting to consider every kind of motive as to why Harry shot Sally, or why Fred stole money from Barney." Wilcox's references drew some laughs. "But the bottom line is, we must abide by the standards of law. In other words, we've got to be most scientific. Witnesses. Hearsay. And as Brenda informed us—" Wilcox shifted his smiling eyes in Brenda's direction, somewhere among his class of thirty. "—we must consider *physical* evidence. Show of hands; somebody give me an example of evidence. Paul?"

"Fingerprints."

"Good, Paul. Maybe we'll balance out our courtrooms after all. Joe? How 'bout it?"

"Printed documents."

"Such as?" Wilcox meandered across the front of the lecture hall, hands behind his back, until he parked right underneath the framed portrait of Thurgood Marshall.

"Birth certificates. ID. Tax or expense records. Credit card receipts."

"Very, very good, Joe. I'm impressed. Anything else? LaShawn?"

"How about a confession?"

"Give me a little more on that, LaShawn."

"Well . . . like, the cops drag in a suspect and he gets all scared, and just tells everything."

"Informant!" someone in the back yelled, placing the blame on the tattletale as opposed to the wrongdoer.

"He repents!" added Gloria, with a voice that was louder than most others. Some chuckles followed. Wilcox smiled at Gloria.

"All right, students. Simmer down. Are there any other types of evidence? Anyone else? Yes, Justin?"

"What about videotapes, wiretaps. Internet e-mails?"

"Of course, Justin, and what about DNA? Hair samples?"

"Yes, professor, or even clothing, the reading off of a vehicle's mileage. Even blood," Justin replied.

Professor Wilcox chose not to challenge Justin, not now, especially knowing how Justin was one of his brightest students. To go on with this back and forth volley would cost precious time, maybe even his ego.

I like this kid. He's just like me.

"No sense in beating a dead horse," said Wilcox. "Ready your pen and paper, chaps . . ."

Justin Lewis—aka the teacher's star student—had been like this for so long, he tended to alienate himself from others around him, many times making his classmates sick with envy or jealousy.

And then there were the girls who conned him into doing their homework in grade school or seduced him to share his test answers in high school. Even now in his second year at John Jay School of Law, he had dates lined up with the very same girls that professors were preying on—girls like Toshi, who he was with the night before.

"I'm not sure this will help with you in the future, Toshi. You might pass in school but what about the bar? Don't you wanna be a lawyer?" he asked.

"Are you shittin' me? Justin, all I need to do is satisfy Daddy. He keeps payin' my car notes, my rent, three more years of those damned professors and I get my degree. Daddy gives up a down payment for my first house—you get the idea."

"Oh great. So I'm here thinking that you're gonna be the next woman to be a Supreme Court Justice . . ."

Toshi cackled until her eyes were wet at their corners. "You are so funny! A Supreme Court Justice!?" She laughed. Oh, my God. Justin, between you and me, I have the next fifteen years of my life planned—right down to the water bills—and *all of it* will be financed by Daddy. What more could I possibly need to do? Not including kissing the professor's ass, and yours. Now, could you help me with this statute of limitations nonsense so we can move on to this shit about evidence? You know Wilcox is gonna pull one of his pop-quiz bits."

Justin had to stop himself from daydreaming about last night, about girls in general, so he could focus on what Wilcox was saying. But with Toshi sitting right there in the next row, with her thigh showing intentionally, it wasn't easy. All he could think about was sex. To the left of him was another distraction:

Sandy. And he could damned well see past her charade too. She looked like this—the nerdy horn-rimmed glasses, the long skirt, and the meek demeanor—to curry sympathy. Those square-ass shoes and church clothes were basically for school only. Take them off, and the girl was a stone-cold freak. A wolf in sheep's clothing.

And just to think, if Toshi or Sandy ever found out about each other, Justin's murder might just be the focus of the next death penalty lecture—something for his classmates to really gossip about.

When the session was over and just about every iota of evidence was discussed, Justin went to the professor's office to speak to him alone, brotha to brotha.

"Justin. Why, this is a pleasant surprise . . ." *I'm your idol, boy.* "So, to what do I owe this visit?"

Justin took a seat, just as he would at home. A series of plaques dressed the wall.

"I kinda need your help on something, Professor."

"Oh? I'm flattered as usual. I swore you knew it all, Justin." It was a kindhearted jab, but a jab nonetheless. "How are things going with the internship? I bet it's exciting over there at the DA's office."

"Exciting. Wow. What an understatement. It's *crazy*. Murders. Robberies. Rapes. White collar. Blue collar. Organized crime. You name it, I'm lookin' at it every day. Never a dull moment."

"I envy you, young man. *We* never had the amount of activity in that office in my days as an intern. Did I tell you about my time there?"

"Yes. Yes you did, Professor." *So many times, I lost count.*

"It's not that I *want* to see so much crime in our city, son. It's just that you learn so much by being behind the scenes. You must be swimming in all things gritty."

"Believe me, I am. And well, that's really why I'm coming to you."

"Okay, hit me," said Wilcox.

"It's just a hunch, so I hope you won't think it's silly."

"Justin, just about everything in life is silly, except for birth and death. Those two are pretty serious. Something for a higher authority to address."

"Sure. Okay, well, see, at the DA's office there're so many people trying to earn a name for themselves, it's a dog-eat-dog environment. And you have to make a big bang to graduate, to excel."

"I follow you," said the professor.

"So, I was thinking. I have this, uh, big bang and I wanted to run it by you before I approach the district attorney."

"You've got me curious. I'm all ears."

"You're familiar with rap music, aren't you?"

"Justin, I'm more of a jazz man, myself. Joe Henderson, Ramsey Lewis, Miles. You know, *musicians*?" Wilcox was being sarcastic. "Other than that, I've heard of your Buster Brown, your Mack Daddy, and Doctor Ice. But that doesn't mean I'm a fan, just that I'm somewhat—how should I say? Old school.

Justin chuckled. "That's Busta Rhymes, Mack Ten, and Dr. Dre, Professor."

"Well, I might be a little dusty, but at least I was close."

"Getting back to my point, I kinda study rap music as a hobby, a second interest to fall back on in case law doesn't work out for me."

Now it was Wilcox chuckling. "That's a twist," he said. "To fall back onto rap music."

"It's a multibillion-dollar industry, sir. Nothing to take lightly."

"I guess not. So, how does rap music play a role in your question or your internship? I'm still trying to make the connection."

"There was a case some years ago out of California where a rapper was eventually convicted for a murder he and his friend committed five years earlier. I looked up some of the press on the case—stuff I found on the Internet and in the law library upstairs. The killers got away and the case was gathering dust for years. But one of the gunmen became a popular rapper and I guess he got big-headed and started bragging about his past, as if law enforcement didn't monitor urban music."

"Okay. I get it. There was an investigation, one thing led to another, and didn't you say he was convicted?"

"Not just the rapper, but his accomplice, too."

"Well then, that'd be more or less a confession, like we talked about in class today. So I still don't see—Wait a minute, you're not thinking of proposing a kind of rap music task force in the DA's office, are you, Justin? Now, *that* would be silly." Professor Wilcox arched one brow in suspicion.

"How so?" asked Justin.

"Well, you'd think that since your California rapper got convicted, the issue would be moot. I mean, what rapper is gonna be so *stupid* as to blab about his or her past crimes for all the world to record?" The professor took a stab at rapping:

"Boom-bap, my name is Wilcox
Boom-bap, I killed somebody,
Boom-bop, and here's my new CD,
Boom-bop, so come and get me . . ."

"Hey Professor, watch out. You might have a second career going—like you're a poet and you don't know it. "And I might even be a rapper, except I'm just too dapper."

Both the teacher and student shared a laugh.

"But lemme tell you what I have cookin'. In fact, Professor Wilcox, rappers do run their mouths today. A lot of times they do something called freestyling."

"Sounds like a swimming exercise."

"You could say it's swimming, except a rapper does it with his tongue; no life preserver. And many times, the rapper will be candid, meaning he'll spit rhymes from the top of his head, or, uhh, impromptu, if you can understand what I'm saying."

"I'm trying, trust me, I'm trying."

"It's just that for rappers to keep it real they have to rap about what they've experienced, adding to the spontaneous spit game—"

"Sounds disgusting," Wilcox interjected.

"It's just an expression. Like lawyers have legal jargon?"

"Yes."

"Rappers spit rhymes—a sort of coded language that only hip-hop heads would understand."

Wilcox nodded.

"Lemme give you an example. The other night I was listening to a rap song called "Come Get Me." It was a rap directed toward Jesus."

"*The* Jesus?"

"Exactly. And the kid had balls enough to say something like: *Thou shalt not kill, so I must a sinned. Hey Jesus, come cleanse me twice, so heaven lets me in.*"

Wilcox made a face, still deciphering the words.

"Don't you get it? You have to read between the lines."

"I suppose he's saying he killed twice."

"See, that's why you're the professor and I'm the student. That's *exactly* what he means."

"Okay, Justin, but what would you do next? Have the DA go hunt the rapper down? Ignore the first amendment's right to free speech? Maybe squeezing some kid until he deciphers a poem?"

Justin understood the complexities here and wagged his head, already anticipating the professor's objective viewpoint. He also had that closed-lipped smile, like he knew something his teacher didn't know.

"Or," Wilcox went on to say, "maybe there's more to this that you're not telling me."

Now Justin was nodding, his eyes glistening with promise behind his eyeglasses.

"What if I told you I could decode the rap, dig into the rapper's history . . ."

"And what—pull up roots? If you want my opinion, Justin, I'd call yours a long-shot fantasy, and I doubt that the DA would devote any serious resources to the idea."

Justin took a deep breath and removed his eyewear.

"What if I've *already* done the work? What if I've *already* investigated? What if I was so close that the, ahem, rapper-slash-suspect divulged his innermost secrets about his past, about maybe a *number* of murders?"

"*Whoa!* Justin, if I read your mind, as I often do, you are onto something hot—"

"*Smokin'* hot."

"Maybe so hot it's deadly. You needed my advice, did you? Well, you hear me out, young man—attention undivided. I want you to talk to your boss ASAP, because not only would you be protecting the public from harm; not only would you perhaps help heal—how many was it? Four?—families, but *your* life could even be in danger."

Justin wagged his head in defiance.

"There's no way."

"Well, just help *me* sleep better. Promise me you'll talk to your boss, okay?"

Justin nodded, but without sincere eye contact.

"Justin, was that an agreement?"

"Yes—okay, professor. I promise. I'll talk to the DA."

"First thing tomorrow?"

Justin sighed. "Yes, Professor."

There were three reasons why Justin was apprehensive about approaching his boss, Bill McDoogle, the city's most notorious district attorney since Rudolph Giuliani. Number (1) Justin hadn't even fully committed himself. *It's only a hunch, for God's sakes!*

Number (2) He knew that his involvement was so close to the muscle that he'd inevitably be called in to testify. Testifying would then expose him as a whistle blower, a supersleuth, or an informant—he just couldn't be certain which one.

And number (3) While Justin had one foot deep into the law, and behind-the-scenes access to the machinations of the justice system because of his internship, he also had a foot deep into the music industry. The parties. The women. The electricity of it all. It was all so exciting to him. It completed him with those liberal, controversial, most times leisurely and sometimes downright rebellious perspectives on life.

And making a move like this would set a fire that could spread so wide and entrap so many now-legitimate performers, that Justin would be known as a Judas. Sure, many rap songs boast about drug dealing, armed robberies, and yes, ruthless murders. But didn't all of that somehow get lost in the excitement? Weren't fans the world over so hypnotized by rappers, to the point where nipples hardened and hearts palpitated? To the point where the lyrics were irrelevant yet so memorable that they were accepted under the guise of "art" and "free speech"? To the point where so-called entertainers could magically walk that tightrope of mystery—that gray area between being considered a threat or a celebrity?

And since this was the majority's consciousness, to surrender to the infectious beats and the scathing lyrics, supported by massive record sales and numerous collaborations with the so-called role models of our communities, then wouldn't Justin be marked as the mole who undermined it all? Wouldn't he be seen as the one who pooped the party?

Above all, Justin wondered if he'd go down in history as the industry's biggest hater, recognized for the downfall of gold- and platinum-selling artists who claimed to have changed their ways, and were now on the right path and giving back, even while proudly flashing their rank and position among the criminal-minded. He wondered if he'd be seen as the opportunist who exposed it all just so that he, Justin Lewis, would come out as the hero. Indeed, there were reasons why he was holding back. And Diamond was one of them.

Justin had three jobs. One was being a full-time student. After school—and sometimes before, depending on the day of the week—Justin reported to work as an intern for the district attorney's office on Centre Street in downtown Manhattan.

Here, he performed duties that were similar to that of a paralegal, including bookkeeping, researching cases, and because he was considered trustworthy, Justin delivered important documents, including sealed evidence, from one office to another. There were hundreds of workers like Justin (or so it seemed) who flooded the floors of 101 Centre Street each day, and all of them performed the same or similar duties. All the bustle amid law books, the copy machines, and the building's Intranet made for a daily ritual, a web of scattered brains.

However, for those who were intricate pieces of this puzzle, there was a method to the madness. It was either one monstrous machine of justice, pressing on to no end, or else it was a mass of bodies, books, and bureaucracy—take your pick.

For eighteen months Justin also forged his own niche in the music industry. He started at Mo City Records, as an intern in the legal department. He worked beside corporate attorneys, who spent their days reviewing lyrics of songs, confirming copyrights, drawing up new recording contracts, and litigating others that had run afoul. Now and then there might be a public access TV show, a small-time gossip magazine, or even a radio personality who the attorneys had to sue (or merely threaten) for misuses of a performer's photo, name, or copyright.

After three months in the legal department, Justin easily changed focus. He joined the promotions team, distributing various forms of propaganda that were customary for each new project.

Where other labels might have a promotions department for different types of music—black music, alternative, pop, rock, and jazz—Mo City was focused only on black music. Justin quickly recognized the benefit of being dedicated to one formula where each artist, be it a singer or rapper, would go through the same routine, same channels, and sound relationships.

It was this sort of formula that could ensure maximum exposure in a market that had been carefully formed and thoroughly used over the years. And over the months, Justin had become quite familiar with it all.

There were the radio stations with their local, regional, and national reach. And now there was satellite radio to be serviced as well. There were the television shows, the video music programs, and the endless magazines in which the record company either invested piles of money or merely made their artists available for interviews or performances. It depended on that media outlet's impact and the number of impressions they were able to make on eyes and ears. Usually, if the performer and project was huge enough to break into BET's or MTV's rotation, then the demand was likely to be inbound, with the world knocking at Mo City's doors to get a piece of the celebrity light. That star power would be a resource for any magazine looking to be bought off of newsstands, and would even spur a rise in subscriptions.

For Mo City, it meant a cover story—the more magazine covers, the more visibility. Then there were the radio stations looking for increased Arbitron ratings, or television shows wanting more viewers.

Add to that race all of the tens of thousands of Internet Web sites that yearned for hits and the inbound desire increased enough to make a receptionist lose her mind.

However, Justin also learned that "the game" was a double-edged sword. When Mo City sought to break a new artist, or even an established artist with a mediocre project, the inbound interest was sometimes less than flattering if BET and MTV didn't catch on soon enough. Then breaking that new artist or promoting that lackluster project was usually an uphill battle. Some more advertising or a street team might be necessary. Or more promotion was in order, which was Justin's job.

"Here's the agenda for this week, people, listen up!" Kathy Moore was the woman with the heart-shaped face, the bubbly cheeks, and wide, encouraging eyes. And her body was sizeable enough to make two men happy at once, too much for just one.

But Justin didn't measure her as he would most other women. He didn't find himself attracted to her looks. Instead, Justin was magnetized by Kathy's charisma. He was captivated and excited by how Kathy maintained such energy. Project after project, Justin could be certain that Kathy was consistent in her work ethic.

"We're workin' four different projects this week, so zoom in here. I want us all to be focused on the label priorities. Last week was last week. It's my hope that we all did enough work that big numbers will show in the SoundScans, and by the way, Moreen? Kudos to you on securing Diamond for Rap City." Kathy started the staff of twenty-four in a big round of applause. "I think that's *really* unprecedented and highly rare to get an R&B artist on that show. So, good work.

Now this week we have two live events. One is, again, Diamond, who will be performing for a press-only event on Thursday night at S.O.B.s. She'll be doing a hundred percent of her show—live band and all. But *our* thing is to push that second single, 'Can't Swallow.'

"The flats and posters are in for the single, so we're gonna need a nice dress-up team to go into S.O.B.s and turn it into Diamond's paradise. Now, it's gonna be the usual in-store displays for Tahj's sophomore album. Plus, we have banners." Kathy reached down for a banner and held it up. It had bold red lettering on top of a glossy black background and it read: BOOGIE DOWN.

In smaller print the banner read: The 2nd album by hip-hop's neo-soul rapper. Album in stores Sept 4th.

There was also a sketch of the rapper.

"We need to be sure to get one of these to each of our mom-and-pop stores. Gotta represent for the little people! Now, Paco is coming to town tomorrow. He'll be doing light radio and TV only. But I found out about a little show his manager scheduled up in Portchester for Wednesday. It's a small club called Seven, but Paco's crowd is a friggin' *fellowship*—so they'll probably pack the place. I want a team up there to dress up. It's a slow night, so I shouldn't have a problem with volunteers, *should* I? Do I see a show of hands?"

Kathy waited.

"That's it? Just Moreen and Victor? Going once? Twice? All righty then. I happen to have, let's see . . . two, four, six tickets to the Knicks game. VIP."

A few more hands shot into the air.

"No, no. You snooze, you lose," said Victor, and he stepped up vigorously to receive the tickets from Kathy. "Thank you very much, Boss—happy to oblige."

A short wave of disgust spread through the office.

"Don't hate. Congratulate."

"That's enough, Victor. And the rest of you should learn a lesson here. These artists and these projects are our bread and butter at Mo City. And you should *all* want to raise your hands *whenever* it comes to contributing to the overall objectives. If not, then maybe you're just passing time here. Maybe Mo City isn't the place for you." A murmur came from the dozens of workers. "No, I'm serious. You all, this is our family. And that's how we need to do this. Together. As a family should. Now Victor, make Paco look good up there. Bring some CDs to give to the manager and DJ. Represent."

Moreen had approached Victor and now reached over his shoulder to slip the tickets from his breast pocket. He hardly knew they were missing until Moreen spoke.

"Yes, Kathy. We will represent," said Moreen, subtracting her half of the tickets. Victor playfully scowled at Moreen.

"*Finally*—people, Jabahri is doing the live broadcast this Saturday night for WBLS. Of course you know that's taking place at the Shadow, their weekly event. One thing though, people. Whoever heads to the Jabahri gig must—I repeat, *must*—arrive there before eleven. Last time we got there after midnight and the place was sold out, doors shut, and we had to do handouts on the sidewalk. We've got to be first-movers if were gonna take our artists to gold and platinum. Gotta be on top of our game, okay?"

Kathy arranged sign-up sheets on a desk for the interns to confirm their commitments.

"All my college interns, please make sure to sign up only for the events that you're sure you can make. I don't need phantoms at these events. We need *people power*. Any questions? Yes, Donna?"

"Did the Diamond hats and tees come in yet?"

"Got 'em right here. But take them only if you plan to make them work. This isn't bedroom gear here—not unless you'll be doing the nasty before a television audience." The office filled with laughter.

"Seriously, people. Our job is to expose these artists . . . to expose these projects. Yes, Justin?"

"Sorry I couldn't do the Paco campaign—school, you know."

"No problem, Justin. I understand perfectly."

"But I did wanna put my bid in for S.O.B.'s," Justin said.

"No problem. Step right up and sign on the dotted line."

Justin had been with Mo City Records for six months when he first met the singer, Diamond. He manufactured the brief encounter, where he'd "coincidentally" crossed her path.

"Excuse me. Hi. Ms. Diamond?"

"Oh, please hon. Just call me Diamond," she responded with amusement in her smile.

"Okay. And, ahh, you can *definitely* call me hon or Justin or whatever you want. As long as you call me." Justin realized only after the fact that his greeting was corny and he wished he could suck it back into his mouth.

Meanwhile, Diamond blushed and smiled with her head lowered and eyes looking away.

"Sorry, that was silly—"

"Nooo—it was *sweet*. Really." Diamond reached out to touch Justin's wrist. He was encouraged.

"I'm workin' your project and I just wanted to say I like your work. You have a beautiful voice."

"Thank you. And thanks for all your help."

It was an awkward moment that passed, with neither of them clear on what to say next. Diamond looked down the hall.

"Well, listen, um, I gotta keep it movin'." The way Diamond said that, wincing like she was afraid to upset him, made Justin's heart flutter.

"I know, I know. Duty calls. They're waitin' for you back there in John Nash's office. Break a leg."

"Ciao," Diamond said, cute finger wave included.

"*Mmm . . . yeah*," Justin muttered for his ears only. "Ciao."

From that day on it really didn't matter if he was a measly promotions person. It didn't matter that he wasn't being paid for this . . . that it only served as work experience for his resume. *Blah, blah, blah.* It just didn't matter. Diamond was damned fine. Her smile made Justin feel weightless and airheaded. He figured that these dizzy spells he was experiencing were the "butterflies" that folks talked about.

As scheduled, Justin was indeed at S.O.B.'s. looking and smelling as good as he knew how. He sat far away from the stage to watch Diamond's sound check for Thursday evening's show.

Posters had been taped and stapled throughout the club, decorating S.O.B.'s tropical atmosphere. CD covers were arranged in the shape of diamonds. There were banners that crisscrossed in front and behind one another behind the stage, as a backdrop for the show. There were softball-size diamonds—fake ones—at the center of each table, complete with a candle. And since S.O.B.'s was already designed to look like an indoor oasis, with a tree the size of a dinosaur that appeared to have grown out of the floor, the total effect was sensational for any new visitors—Diamond's fans.

Diamond rehearsed her thirty-minute set (part one of her two-part show) opening with her up-tempo, bass-heavy street banger "Be Advised." Then she jumped into "Smokin' Groove," "Conscious," and "More Love." She ended the set with the sexy smooth slow jam, "Inside of Me," the title of her album. There was a twenty-minute break, during which time she discussed sound and lights with the club's technicians; then she performed for another thirty minutes, singing her top-ten hit "Can't Swallow" and the follow-up third single to be released from her debut album, "All Up in My Milk."

Diamond's beautiful songbird voice sent chills through Justin, to the point that he'd swear she was singing to him exclusively.

After the sound check and rehearsal, Diamond went downstairs to be alone in her dressing room. Justin noticed that her close friend, Kianna, was left upstairs to talk things over with the singer's publicist. And so he waited patiently, using every second to plot his approach. He was determined to get some time alone with the singer but was all too familiar with how overprotective Kianna could be—mostly everyone at Mo City was also aware—following Diamond around like some blasted Siamese twin.

"Excuse me? Diamond?"

"Ohh, scared me there," she responded at an untroubled volume, and quickly pulled together the Fila sport jacket.

"Should I come back?" asked Justin. "I didn't mean to interrupt you." He noticed that Diamond hadn't been afforded much of a dressing room, and was almost embarrassed for her.

A slight funk hung in the air—*Diamond's?*—and on a chair was a sweat suit, the pink one she had on just moments earlier, still damp with perspiration. The Fila suit she had on now was plush as well, only it was an evergreen velour, and it made Diamond appear pampered and smug.

"No, no, no, please come in. I'm surprised my pit didn't take your leg off."

"Huh?" Justin missed her point.

"Oh—nothing. Just thinkin' out loud. You're with the label, right? Sorry, I'm not the best with names. So many new people comin' at me everyday. I gotta start some kind of memory course or somethin', *I swear*."

"I'm Justin, from promotions." He was more than glad for the opportunity to touch her again, and he moved closer to take her hand. It was a feeble handshake, and he would rather have kissed it.

"We only met once, and it was real brief . . ." *Too brief*.

"Up at Mo City—right. I remember."

"Oh, I can't ever forget it. You were going to meet with the big dog, John Nash . . . you were wearing tight jeans, a halter top—I think it was yellow—and that mini backpack . . . that one there." *I'll never forget that day*.

Diamond looked over at her bag, then back at Justin.

"Wow. Aren't *you* the observant one, Justin?"

Justin was so busy warming up to the store-room atmosphere, inhaling the spice of Diamond's flesh. This is where he wanted to be—wherever she was. Heaven.

"Actually, if you wanna know the truth, I've been looking forward to a couple of minutes alone with you."

"Okay," Diamond said, with a crooked smile and raised eyebrow. Her hair was down now, falling about her shoulders. She was seated on a cushioned stool that swiveled around so that she faced Justin.

"This isn't anything deep, is it? I mean, do we need a stenographer?"

Justin laughed under his breath. *Thank you for making this easier for me, beautiful*.

"No. No stenographer. No Justice of the Peace."

Diamond chuckled.

"I know you're a busy woman—I mean, I see your itinerary every week. L.A. last week, Atlanta the week before that . . . now you're doin' the northeast corridor with New York, Jersey, and Philly . . ."

"And next week I'm in Europe. Did you see *that*?" Diamond had that look, like she could be dreaming.

"Did I? Justin concealed his fret behind a simple congratulatory smile.

"You've got it goin' on, girl."

"Thank you."

"I just wondered if you ever have time for . . . well . . . socializing."

Another voice, sight unseen came from behind Justin.

"Hey I . . . excuse me . . ."

Jesus. It's the bitch from Hell.

Justin closed his eyes, praying for mercy from the god who supervised overprotective friends.

"Kianna, this is Justin. Justin . . . meet Kianna, *my mother*." Diamond pursed her lips and tasted a confused expression at her friend.

"Kianna, Justin is with Mo City. Promotions."

"Hmmm . . . I'm sure," said Kianna, taking in a full head-to-toe evaluation of Justin. "Sir, do you mind if we have a moment alone? Thank you."

"Oh, not at—well . . . Diamond, I—" Justin cleared his throat, however unnecessary.

"I guess I'll be out in the hall. I would like to finish—"

"Sure. We'll just be a minute," Diamond assured him, but spoke more to Kianna than to Justin. "*Won't* we?"

Justin excused himself past Kianna, careful not to make eye contact, lest she get wind of his bitterness. As someone once told him, a delay is not a denial. Justin hustled outside of the storeroom door, hungry for even a whisper. Thank God that the basement of S.O.B.'s wasn't exactly soundproof to accommodate Kianna, even though she tried to keep her voice down.

"Who is he?"

"He's . . . who he *is*. What're you gettin' all *crazy* about, Kianna?"

"Diamond, we talk about this all the time . . . about the people you let into your life."

"Okay, Miss Einstein—since you have all the answers—how am I supposed to know if he's good for me or not, if I don't get to know him first?"

"That's my—Wait a minute. Is *that* what this is? He's trying to get to know you? I thought you said he was from Mo City? *Promotions*, did you say? And, what—he's mixing work with pleasure? Sounds kinda sneaky, if you ask me. On-the-job harassment?"

"You're buggin', Ki."

"All that we've been through, Di? The first record deal . . . the accident? Rehabilitation? How those crumbs treated you afterward, and the shit in the courtroom? Now we get a new deal—the big money. And because I'm lookin' out for your best interest, *I gotta be buggin'*? You are fuckin'—my—head—up, Di. To the goddamned MAX!" There was a no-holds-barred volume.

The dressing room door was flung open and Kianna marched out, cutting her killer gaze at Justin. Before Justin could sigh in relief, Kianna whipped her body around and took a few steps back to the doorway.

Did she forget to stab Diamond?

"And we need to be out of here in ten minutes. There's a goddamned schedule to keep," Kianna snapped.

She rolled her eyes at Justin, as if to let him know that his efforts were a waste of time, and she strutted away with curves and attitude aplenty. Justin was humbled. He felt an urge to slap the woman; she couldn't be any older than he was—maybe nineteen or twenty, if that—and yet she was performing like she was someone's disciplinarian.

Fuck.

This was a strange, uncomfortable position to be in, to have to go back and face Diamond again, after such a scene. But, of course, he could just leave if he wanted to.

The first record deal? The accident? Rehabilitation? The shit in the courtroom?

Justin couldn't imagine what struggle this woman had been through. And she was so young!

The ideas made this a more difficult task. She wasn't merely a pretty girl who he was asking for a date. The dressing room's atmosphere was somewhat different now, having digressed from warm and intimate to cold and filled with an air of hostility. So much for silky smooth approaches, or for that matter, the element of surprise. Don Juan, unmasked.

"Jeez, Diamond. I—"

"Don't sweat her, hon—"

"Hon" again.

"The girl has issues. I love her to death, but she can get extreme sometimes, ya know?"

I guess, Justin thought.

"I suppose it comes with being best friends and going through this industry game."

"Well . . . after all of that, I feel weird saying this, but . . . if it is even possible, I'd like to see you," said Justin.

"*See* me?" Diamond put her palm over her mouth, hiding the expression there.

"Sure. See you . . . as in take you out and show you a good time, as in sharing a soda—two straws, one cup. You know . . . *experience* each other."

"Oh *shit*. No you did not just say *experience* each other."

"Oh yeah—I did. But I didn't mean it like . . . all that deep. Just dinner. A walk. Quiet time away from all this celebrity nonsense. I'd tell you my hopes and fears . . . you could tell me yours." Justin injected a decibel of bass in his voice and Diamond lost focus for a moment.

"If we're lucky, maybe we'll find things we have in common, or you could find out real quick that I'm a waste of time . . . but I promise you this: If you pass me up you could miss out on the best thing that ever happened to you. . . . Diamond? Are you there?"

Justin waved his hand, trying to get her attention, but she seemed a million miles away.

* * *

She was back in grade school, wearing a skirt and shoes—teased by other girls whose parents allowed them to wear jeans and sneakers.

She was in the school yard, grouped with a few other "skirts," while most other girls—the hip, cool, popular ones—were getting the attention of the best-looking boys.

She was in class, raising her hand to answer questions that nobody else chose to answer, and being pelted with spitballs, rubber bands, or bunched-up paper, labeled as the teacher's pet.

Diamond was elsewhere . . . the outcast in high school, the bookworm and Glee Club member. She knew too much.

She visited all of these places as yesterday's introvert who didn't know how to express herself . . . who didn't know how to say what she meant . . . who was alone most of the time.

"Mmm hmm . . . I'm here. I'm very much here.

I was just trying to see inside of you . . . trying to see what you're really after. 'Cause, let's face it . . . what tastes good and chocolatey on the outside ain't always have cherry filling on the inside," she quipped.

"Oh damn! Just peel my skin off, why don't you? Maybe they have a kitchen knife upstairs."

"I'm keepin' it real, Justin." His name felt interesting coming from her lips—like it was comfortable. Tasty.

"You're keepin' it real, and you just called me a predator—in a manner of speaking."

Hmmm . . . smart and good-looking too.

"My aunt Sara used to say, *First assume the worst, and only hope for the best*."

"I'm thinking I might like your aunt better than your, ahem . . . mother." He indicated Kianna.

Both of them chuckled, but it was Diamond who wondered if Justin saw more of her than met the eye.

Justin went on to say, "Not that I don't trust your aunt's good advice, but I really don't believe that—*assume the worst*. All that does is attract the mediocre results. And how successful would you be with this singing career if you took your aunt Sara's advice and only assumed the worst?"

"That's different."

"How?"

"My music or my voice could never let me down." Diamond reached for her handbag. "But there's something that's changed about me, Justin."

"What's that?"

"Today, I'm a woman who's an optimist. Otherwise, you wouldn't be here in this room right now. I would've asked Kianna to help me get rid of you."

Diamond let on a crooked smile.

"Hmmm . . . I don't know if that's good or bad," said Justin.

Diamond tilted her head some, then gave a snappy smile.

"Just look at it as your lifetime challenge."

"What's that?"

Diamond put her hand to Justin's cheek.

"Me," she said, hoping for a friend or fan as a worst-case scenario. She looked in her handbag and took out a tube of lipstick. She said, "Lemme see your hand."

Justin made a face, and Diamond got the idea he thought she was going to read his palm. She took off the cover from the lipstick.

Might as well freshen up.

She took out a mirror and wistfully glossed both lips. Then she wrote her number on Justin's palm. He turned squeamish.

"Here's my two-way number . . . humph . . . tickles?"

"Yeah. But maybe it's a good tickle."

"I gotta run," she said, working toward an exit.

"As usual," said Justin.

"You comin' tonight?" The way she said that, she knew, implied a number of suggestions.

Justin cleared his throat, and that was funny too.

"Ahh . . . yeah. Of course," he said breathlessly.

"Bringing a date?" she asked, ready to leave.

"An imaginary one," said Justin.

"Oh? Shoulda told me you were into ghosts. I woulda never

given you my digits. . . . Oh well, I suppose I'll have to beware of ghosts tonight, huh?"

"Every audience member is a potential Diamond fan. I guess that goes for the seen and unseen."

Diamond was amused, but she didn't say as much—not as much as her ass was saying as she walked away.

"*Ciao,*" she said.

Justin felt like a casualty as he stood there but couldn't help wondering what all was underneath that green velour sweat suit . . . wondering about the past five minutes, and if he had come any closer to finding out.

Later that night, Diamond dedicated "Inside of Me" to "my special friend in the audience."

Chapter Fourteen

Those were what Justin considered the good ol' days: indulging in that grunt work at Mo City, and then meeting Diamond, the love of his life . . . another important piece to the puzzle that was his ultimate purpose.

That was the issue that his father had pounded into his head: *You need to know what you want in life, Justin . . . you need to decide what your interests are and where you want to be. You need to think out the things you do and consider what it will mean in the long run. That's what your mother and I mean when we say, find your purpose*.

Naturally, as was the case with most young men, his father's message went in one ear and out of the other. It was a jewel of wisdom that fought the never-ending battle against the images swelling Justin's thoughts; images that were perpetuated by the television and magazines; images that had young men mastering another common practice: imitation.

The fortunate part of Justin's relationship with Diamond—singer or no singer—was that she kept him sharp. He had to be on his toes to compete for and to maintain her interest in him. That was reason enough to strive toward progress, to reach higher and to create substance in his life since anybody could merely exist.

Justin's second date with Diamond was an occasion where he had opportunity to see past the sunglasses and the studded leather outfits . . . past the cleavage that the world of entertainment (or the audience, anyway) demanded, and deep into her soul. He had the chance to peel away the shiny exterior and see

Diamond's pain and struggle—the essence that inevitably built her profound wit and healthy character. The date turned riveting when Diamond began to cry during their personal testimonies.

"I was shot," she told him with great hesitancy. And the *way* she said it was like she'd lost her mother . . . or like she couldn't have children, like something was irreversible or had been stolen and couldn't be replaced.

The revelation was startling for Justin, and he found it hard to believe that such a beautiful woman, with her beautiful skin and beautiful eyes and beautiful attitude, could experience such pain and trauma. As if such beauty (in Justin's eyes) was a form of immunity—a "pass" that might save her from such occurrences.

"God . . ." Justin gasped. "I can't even tell. The way you sway on stage . . . in your videos you're like a bird carried by a soft wind. Was it serious?" Justin asked this while he had that helpless look about him—his elbow on the dinner table and his chin in his palm.

"Serious enough for me to lose a recording contract . . . for me to be in the hospital for two months—"

"Not in that order, of course."

"No. I do value my health over my career—it's just that it all tends to mix into mashed potatoes in my head."

"Two months. Wow," said Justin, thinking of no immediate consolation.

"Oh—but, then there was the therapy afterward . . . I even had to learn to walk again. Took almost six months."

"Y-you are a walking *miracle*. I . . . I can't believe I'm sitting here talking with you right now. When did all this happen? Was it early on in your childhood?"

"Please. It was about two years ago. A robbery in Queens. There were gunmen . . . police . . . a big shootout. One of them grabbed me and took me hostage."

"Who?" Justin was immediately erect in his seat, enraged, at whom, he had no idea.

"I dunno who. One of the gunmen. But he had a mask on. Plus he got away."

"Got away? *How?*"

Diamond seemed to struggle with the recollections.

"They shot me, Justin."

"I know, I know. But the gunman just—"

"No. It was the *police*."

Justin stared at Diamond so hard that he began to see double . . . his vision became a blur.

Diamond explained it all even if it was against her conscious wishes. She spelled out the whole shebang, how she was in the middle of signing a major recording contract as Jesse Champagne—partly her real name—then left the Queens office, right next to where the armed robbery occurred . . .

"Just before I signed, I went to take a walk just to clear my mind, because everything was happening so fast, ya know?"

Justin had no idea.

"It's like my aunt Sara always told me . . ."

Her again.

"She said to always take a timeout . . . that I should follow my heart and never feel pressured. God, Justin, I just went for a walk . . ." The tears began streaming again, more uncontrollably this time. "How was I to know?"

Justin wanted to get up and go sit with Diamond, on her side of the table, but something told him that she needed this . . . that all of these emotions had been building up inside of her, starving to be aired out. Still, he didn't like seeing Diamond like this. It was counteractive to the joy that she generated.

"But look at you now, Diamond. You have an incredible recording career . . . you look healthy as I've ever seen any female vocalist. And people want you all over the globe—"

"Sometimes all that glitters isn't gold, Justin."

"Don't tell me . . . another Aunt Sara philosophy."

"But it's true. I had to fight my old record company in court. They didn't wanna go through with the deal we had on the table. Then they threatened to give me a bad name in the industry—said I'd never sell a record in my lifetime."

"I'm dying to know what happened in court. You sued the shit out of 'em, didn't you?"

Justin's legal mind was already in turbo drive, cranking out possible outcomes, solutions, and rewards . . . trying to piece the puzzle together even before Diamond explained it all.

"Mo City happened, that's what. Somehow Mr. Nash heard about me—maybe all the media reached him, thank God. And he stepped in, took over, really. He paid some expensive lawyers to sue the city of New York . . . and to sue my old record label. The city settled out of court. We won a lot of money—millions, only we haven't gotten it yet. It's a check's-in-the-mail kinda thing. But I was assured the money's comin'."

"What about the record people?"

"They're still puttin' up a fight, but the lawyers say they're about to settle too. I just want it to all be over with, to tell you the truth."

Justin reached across the table to smudge another tear from Diamond's cheek.

"Damn. You have been through a lot. I'm sorry to hear all of this—but then, I feel sort of privileged, too. Lemme ask you, Diamond . . . isn't there a bright side to this? The big album release? Your new home at Mo City?"

"Justin, my real name is Jesse. I was supposed to come out with my real name. But I can't even have my own name, Justin. There's so much legal stuff involved—plus all the pain to go with it. How sick is that, that I'm selling all of these records, doing all of these concerts, and I can't even do it in my own name? I can't even be a hundred percent proud of what I'm doing—like I'm just a brand name . . . a picture on some girl's CD cover."

"Now I know how Prince felt."

"Prince?" Diamond was too emotional to see his point.

"Yeah. The whole bit about signing a contract and the record company owning your name."

"Exactly. It's all this legal shit. And that's what I've been trying to tell you . . . underneath the pretty face, the makeup and fancy clothes, I'm plain ol' dysfunctional Jesse Chambers. Ya got it now?"

Now Justin did get up to sit by her side. He hugged her and spoke softly to her, rocking her in lullaby fashion. While Justin consoled his date he stared into the far reaches of the restaurant. The waitresses and diners and other activities were but a white screen on which Justin recalled some of those horrible details . . . the various newscasts covering the Queens Boulevard shootout . . . the aspiring singer who unluckily got caught up in harm's way . . . a cop with a sob story, how he was trying to save her life and how he was so sorry to have misjudged his shot. There was something cold and callous behind that cop's eyes. That was easy to remember.

There was the public outcry, so heavily focused on the four or five victims—four of them killed inside of the check cashing franchise—that the weight of the attention barely touched the injured singer. She hadn't been critically injured, was what they reported. But now Justin knew the entire story. He could see all that Diamond had endured and that she was a survivor.

Dinner for two turned out to be much much more than expected. They opened wounds and revisited Diamond's hurt. For her to even talk about it was a stretch.

But there was something about Justin. He appeared to be so understanding behind those eyeglasses. That disarming presence and that calculating mind made for an interesting look, or at least one that was new to her.

And Justin was bigger than the men Diamond previously dated. He had no obvious scars or annoying habits that she could see. He spoke intelligently but clearly had a degree of street smarts.

More than that, Diamond could see through to Justin's heart. Maybe he wasn't the movie star she dreamed about . . . maybe he wasn't the big willy in the industry . . . but for sure, Justin was a man with a good heart, a characteristic that screamed louder than any superficial idea like love at first sight.

Following dinner, Justin and Diamond took a stroll along a walkway that overlooked the East River. There was a delicate wind cooling them, soothing the two after such a drawn-out testimony.

Justin dropped his arm around Diamond as though it had been this way for years, or so it felt. And they said nothing, which in a way promised that there was so much more to come. So many more secrets—pleasing ones, hopefully—to learn and to reveal.

"Diamond, I don't know how you feel about me. I mean, we just meetin' and all if you think about it . . ."

"Don't forget S.O.B.'s. Doesn't that count?"

"As a date? With you on stage and me in the audience? With killer Kianna at standby?"

"Well, there *was* my dedication."

"Right, right. How could I forget? *To my special friend in the audience* . . ." Justin popped himself in the forehead with his open palm. "I should've known those lyrics were especially for me." Justin's head dropped down and he looked at Diamond in a cynical way.

Diamond got real timid all of a sudden, as if she now realized the full breadth of her dedication. "*Any*way . . . if I may be so forward, I just want us to grow like a tree, not like a flower or a weed. I want us to mean something."

"Why do I feel like I'm on the panel of a talk show and you're about to drop a bomb?"

Diamond stopped short during their stroll and the two faced each other for a moment of sincere discussion. "What? Now that I've exposed myself, now that I look like a handicap, you wanna back off?"

Justin put his hands on her shoulders.

"Hey . . . don't even take it there, Diamond. If you asked me to go home with you right now—I'll be honest—I'd jump at the opportunity. *Trust me*. But you showed me something tonight. Don't you get it? You showed something so real . . . so divine and so meaningful that I honestly don't wanna let you go . . ."

Justin lifted Diamond's chin with two fingers.

"Don't jump to conclusions," he said.

"So then, what were you getting at?"

"Just that . . . I'm not serious with anyone right now. I won't lie, I've been with one or two different women in the past months. But I keep it safe. That's number one. Number two, it was just for recreation, and that's why I'm suggesting we take this slow. 'Cause to me, being with you could be something bigger than a music career or any amount of money. Frankly, it could be bigger than everything that means anything to me."

Justin pulled Diamond in for a hug. Then he kissed her forehead. Her eyes welled up, asking for more, and he planted the sweetest, most sensual kiss he knew how to give on her lips.

A whirlwind of activity surrounded the album releases for Diamond's "Inside of Me," and her label mate Tahj's "Boogie Down." The hype was focused on luring music-lovers to their local music stores on the same day—Super Tuesday.

The big day had grown into a weekly ritual, thanks to the combined efforts of major and independent labels, as well as music stores and media outfits, which hammered Super Tuesday as a staple for fans.

For Mo City's artists, this was a great synergy, where the months of media hype and the marketing budgets for both recording artists fed a larger momentum, and now the rumor was out. The buzz around the music world was that the two releases together would easily top seven hundred thousand units sold within the first week—a big deal in terms of forecasting the success of the projects, especially with so many projects hungry for the same dollar.

The hysteria of Diamond's project was also a force in Justin's life. Classes at John Jay wouldn't begin again until September, so the timing of Super Tuesday (August 11) was just right for him. Diamond would be in town, available for in-store appearances, her debut on BET's *106 & Park*, and a walk-through at MTV's T.R.L.

To say the least, Diamond would be a busy bee. But Justin saw it as further access: an opportunity to put his all into this growing relationship.

First things first, Justin had to sacrifice his internship at Mo City in order to be with Diamond more often. If he didn't resign himself, he'd surely be let go on account of conflicts of interest.

More important to Justin was that he didn't intend to stand by so some Pierre in Paris or some chap in London could slip in and sweep Diamond from under his nose. Diamond's trip to Europe became an issue.

"You know I'm as poor as a bag lady these days. The label has been paying for everything," said Diamond regretfully.

"So?"

"Justin, you know they won't pay for me to have a friend come along. To Europe? That's already gotta be costin'—"

"Oh *damn*. You mean, you're not a millionaire yet? You can't pay my way? *What was I thinking?* Shit, I gotta go find me a new girl . . . maybe Kianna is available."

At first, Diamond was blown away by Justin's words. But then she heard him mention Kianna . . . a new girl? *They hate each other!* And the thought caused Diamond to laugh loud and hard. She could've rolled on the floor if Justin cracked another one like that.

"Diamond, I'm not rich either, but I have something saved in the bank. But who needs a car anyway? I still have two more years of school to finish."

"You mean, you're coming?!" Diamond spoke through a big wide smile, like a kid opening her favorite Christmas gift. And she threw herself into Justin's arms, ecstatic about having a travel partner.

"What *about* Kianna, now that I think about it?"

Diamond rolled her eyes at Justin's comment.

"Oh—you can *believe* she's gonna be a problem," she said. "But, please . . . let's cross that bridge when we get to it."

"I like that idea," said Justin. "Just like I like a thundercloud hangin' over my head."

Chapter Fifteen

NEWARK, NEW JERSEY

Just forty minutes southwest of New York, Newark was a city congested with hopes and dreams that for many were beyond reach.

For the most part upper-class living had disappeared, isolated to small suburban areas like Forrest Hills or Ivy Hill. Otherwise the majority of Newark's residents were middle-class merchants, blue-collar workers, and the disenfranchised, left to cohabitate in urban neighborhoods. These were depressed, neglected avenues, streets, and boulevards that were pockmarked with unsightly signs of blight, and scarred by murders, drugs, and homelessness. This was the likeliest environment for the rise of thug life, where the outlaw ruled and won, an atmosphere supporting a pattern of lawlessness that the community merely shrugged off in light of so much deep-seated municipal dysfunction.

Antoine "Brice" Samuels couldn't have rolled a better pair of dice when he arrived here two years ago. This spot was fertile ground for Brice, an out-of-towner who came to make a new name for himself. And he had all that he needed to make it work. There was the baby whop, that machine-gun pistol he kept strapped under his arm, he had $38,000, his take from the Just Right Check Exchange; and he called himself B-Money, which meant a clean slate and no ties to that mess back in Queens.

B-money had also created his own so-called crime squad,

known throughout Newark's underground as the B-boyz. And the B-boyz were always interested in new "talent."

"I'm tellin you, B, this kid ain't no fuckin' joke. He go harder than anybody we been workin' with."

"What that make me 'n' E.J.? We some cut?"

Mack made a face. "No, I ain't sayin' that, Outlaw. I'm just givin' my opinion. This mothafucka's heart is big as a battleship."

Outlaw and E.J. were seated in the front of B-Money's recently stolen and freshly painted Isuzu Rodeo, both of them sharing a doubtful expression.

"Well," said B-Money, slouched in the backseat like a tired passenger. "That remains to be seen. And I ain't tryin' to wait out here all night to witness this shit either."

"Don't worry, B . . . you got my word. I seen this kid work . . ."

A kid. That's exactly what I'm afraid of, thought B-Money.

"Hey—maybe this is it now. He's movin'."

Rabbit was focused on one thing: proving himself to Outlaw, and to B-Money, the leader of the B-boyz. Outlaw said that B-Money wanted to see his work before they even met. So this was it. This was where he would show them that he was ready, that he wanted to be down with their crew, a crew with the *illest* rep in Newark. The waiting was over. It was time to show and prove—*fast and furious, Rabbit.*

This was Broad Street, just a few blocks from City Hall, whose gilded dome and massive front staircase were still visible from blocks away. The clock outside of City Hall looked to be one of those old, dependable ones, also gilded, yet as tall as a tree. Its glowing white face read ten o'clock.

She was Mrs. Mollie Parr, the head bitch in charge at the McKenna Medical Center, just another executive cruising this major artery, trying to catch the green lights so she could get home to the hubby and the kids, and relieve the housekeeper. Not that Mollie was all bad, not that she deserved what was about to happen to her. She just had that way about her, a way of getting things done, balancing the Medical Center's expenses, making decisions about what to invest in and what programs to cut. It was her firm, no-nonsense approach that tended to mash other's toes, even if it wasn't intentional.

But then, doing this had become comfortable, and because she looked so comfortable, folks believed her—they figured she liked it.

Bitch.

Mollie changed the radio station from Jazz 106 to Power 95, in the mood for some up-tempo pop rock.

"La la la, la la la la . . . I just can't get you out of my head. Boy, your love is all that I think about . . ." Mollie even knew the words. For the mother of two pre-teen daughters who oversaw a staff of two hundred at the center, this was about as edgy as life got.

"OH MY GOD!" Mollie shrieked.

There was a young man, maybe Hispanic—she didn't have any idea—who had been hurrying across Broad Street. He tripped and fell right there in the center lane, right in front of her late-model, honey-flushed Lexus.

Mollie slammed her foot down on the brakes and braced herself. At the same time, the luxury car skidded to a long, dragged-out, rubber-burning halt.

Mollie was shaken, but also aware that there was no *thump*. She *couldn't* have run over the injured man.

Please, God, don't let it be!

With disheveled senses, Mollie was still able to put the Lex into park. Then she got out, almost stumbling from the realization—her feet touching the ground. Her hand to her chest, Mollie staggered alongside the car, afraid of what she might see out in front of the vehicle.

Please, God, please don't let him be dead. I promise, I'll never hurt another person's feelings. Ever.

The chills that crawled through Mollie's body were unlike any she'd ever experienced. But then her body jerked, rocking her with this new revelation. He was getting up onto his feet! As if he never fell at all!

Standing what must've been a full foot shorter than her, he now raised a gun, pointing it at her upper body. It was one of those palm-sized thingamabobs that Mollie had surely seen some detective, in some movie, stuff in his ankle holster.

"Lady, do y'self a fava. Lay down."

Shock overcame Mollie.

She couldn't move or speak, as if experiencing some stage fright, with all of Broad Street—asleep as it was—as her audience.

There had been no other traffic for blocks—and then there was. Two sets of headlights approached from about a block away at a cautious speed.

"Hey! I said, *lay the fuck down*!"

Mollie didn't budge, frozen stiff with fear and disbelief.

Another couple of stolen seconds passed.

"*Okay*. Be that way," said the gunman. He lowered his aim and squeezed off a round below her waist. The gunshot blast resounded for blocks.

The woman screamed, but it was somehow suffocated by the greater priority. Pain. A blotch of dark blood stained her lined slacks as she collapsed to the blacktop road.

"You vics neva listen," said Rabbit, stepping around her to hop in the driver's seat.

There were at least six or seven other vehicles now, all alive with headlights, idling engines, and drivers who were either unaware that a carjacking had just taken place, or they were coming to find out.

Rabbit saw it all as a blurred disturbance and threw the Lexus into gear, working the steering wheel until the car veered off like an underwater eel, wistful and slippery as it snaked around and between obstacles. He knew where the Rodeo was parked, and steered the vehicle in that direction, across two lanes and a median, then swinging a left turn off of Broad Street, headed for Drake Avenue.

Drake Avenue was a mile away from Broad Street, aligned with industrial properties and auto body shops that formed a long strip from I-95 to downtown Newark.

E.J. once established the beginnings of an auto repair shop here on Drake, however, the legit business that he labored to build wasn't nearly as lucrative as what B-Money had proposed so many months ago. Today, the repair shop was but another nameless, faceless building among so many others. Its large garage door was operated electronically, by remote control. Once the Rodeo and the Lexus crawled through the opening, the door eased down behind them, leaving an absence of light except for a glowing red EXIT sign to the rear of the garage.

Outlaw was the first to depart from the vehicles, and he stepped over to a wall panel. A second later, a wall that at first seemed stationary split open like sliding elevator doors. Rabbit quickly realized that this was a passage to an adjoining building, a warehouse where B-Money stockpiled the B-boyz' stolen fortune.

It was an amazing sight, like a cavernous jewelry box had been opened, with its contents glistening for their eyes only. But Rabbit knew better than to turn starstruck. He already felt lucky to get this far, to have proven himself to the most important of the crew.

This latest catch would make thirty such luxury vehicles that the B-boyz snatched by either carjacking or hotwiring. In addition to the car theft, the B-boyz hit a series of eighteen-wheelers, forcing them off of the road by tire blowout, then they'd hog-tie the driver until all of the goods—computers, televisions and other multimedia devices—were off-loaded.

Mack was twenty-six, a big-bodied Jersey boy with tattoos from four or five different prisons and half of his hair braided in cornrow fashion. The other half was left in a shabby afro. His part in the day-to-day scams and scores was to sell off the goods.

E.J., twenty-eight, was a lot shorter than the six-foot Mack. He had skin too colorless to be called black, and although his parents were both Puerto Rican, he denied his heritage. The color of E.J.'s short buzz-cut hair was carrot orange, but he didn't appreciate being called "Red." Meanwhile, E.J. had enough contacts in the import-export network that it was a cinch to unload luxury cars and trucks for top dollar.

Outlaw was born muscle-bound, or so it seemed, since he

never did a lick of exercising, with a monster forehead and beady, contempt-filled eyes that forever shifted, like he had a nervous condition. At twenty-five years of age, he still worked that diddy-bop walk that he started back in his teen years. But nobody who he befriended was real enough to say: *Why don't you walk straight, you phony mothafucka*? Even B-Money left it alone—better to let the guy *think* of himself as an "outlaw" so he could keep on playing his position as gunman, hijacker, and scout.

Spook, the pudgy white boy with the bald head and sideburns, had been left behind to keep watch over things. He was twenty-three, a dropout from the military, and had baby blue eyes and fangs for teeth.

And now there was Rabbit, who B-Money and crew considered still wet behind the ears, already symbolizing the worst of the lawless B-boyz.

"Whassup wit' him?" asked Rabbit. "He havin' a seizure or somethin'?"

"Nah," said Mack, the last to get his ass out of the Rodeo. "Tha's how a playa do. Every joint we snatch up he gotta snort a line of hype—cocaine—offa the hood. Tha's how a playa celebrate."

Rabbit stood there in wide-eyed disbelief while B-Money leaned over the Lexus, sucking up lines of cocaine into his nose, right off of the honey-colored hood.

Wow. He's like a vacuum wit' that shit.

"Come on, Rabbit . . ." Outlaw patted the young thug's shoulder. "B-Money wants us to go over a couple things wit' you. Looks like you're in."

Rabbit grinned from ear to ear. *Yes!*

"Holla at a playa, Mack!" It was a B-Money command that caught Mack off guard. He cocked his head back, stunned that he said it like that: *Holla at a playa.*

Those are my words, thought Mack. But he was soon flattered and all smiles to be acknowledged in such a way, the leader recognizing him as a "playa." Playas only recognized playas. Mack swaggered across the garage floor to confront B-Money.

"Whassup, B?"

B-Money was undergoing a fistful of responses to the cocaine he'd just snorted. His eyes were closed and his body turned tense, as though it were fighting possession by some unseen force. He cricked his neck and braced himself with his palms pressing down on the hood of the car. This went on for some time, and once B-Money shook himself free of the fire that enraptured him, he turned to Mack.

"You see the shit that young nigga did? He cold shot that bitch like it was his regular shit."

"Outlaw been sayin' that nigga go hard, B."

"That shit wasn't hard—that was some coward-ass shit he did. I bet he done that shit more times than he can count. That's why it look so easy." B-Money squeezed a loud snort in between his words.

"Ain't nothin' but a young fool, B. I bet if I take his ass out back and he don't have no pain—no gun—wit' him—"

"Nah . . . let that go, Mack. Sometimes we need a wild boy to balance shit out. Just in case, feel me?"

"Yo—whateva, B. It's your world and I'm just a squirrel." Mack was ready to agree with most any thought B-Money expressed.

"Plus, this baby oughta bring in twenty."

"For sho'," said Mack. But now B-Money had stepped back. Before Mack could blink an eye, his superior had that frightening machine pistol in hand.

"Turn around," said B-Money. "I need to see both your hands." But his words were unnecessary; Mack already had his hands suspended away from his body.

"Boss? What—what's this about?"

B-Money stepped forward with caution and reached under Mack's Windbreaker for the .44-caliber automatic he was known to keep in a side holster. He wedged the pistol in his waistband.

"Step away from the car now." The machine gun was level with Mack's chest now. Mack, the moving target.

"Boss. Please. Whatever this is about—"

"A playa ain't really got no worries if a playa ain't do nothin', do he?" said B-Money.

"Damn, Boss . . . this some kinda joke?

"Yeah, let's call it that. We'll call it . . . lemme see . . . how about we call it the ten-thousand-dollar joke. In other words, you . . . tell me . . . where my money is."

"What you talkin' 'bout, B?"

"That was part one of the joke, Mack. And you failed. Where you want the slug? The thigh? The calf? Or the arm?"

"B, *no*! *Please! Don't do this!!*"

B-Money pointed the baby Uzi at Mack's thigh.

"Okay! Okay! Please! I'll tell you. I'll tell you—just don't shoot. A playa just wanted a little somethin' for hisself, *tha's all . . .*"

"Hey, Mack. Calm down, playa. I understand. Really. Put your hands down, damn. Here . . ."

B-money handed Mack his .44. "And wipe that sweat from your face. A playa don't sweat like that."

"B, yo man, it was stupid, I shoulda neva tried that shit. I'll go home and get ya dough."

"Nah, Mack. I don't need it . . ." B-Money readied his Uzi once again. "But yo' momma will."

The echo from the machine-gun pistol sounded something like the false starts of an outboard motor as B-Money sprayed hot lead at Mack. The pistol coughed once, then again, and once more, riddling the Jersey boy's body with enough bullets to drop an entire football team.

Mack's body jerked and shook in spasms, spitting blood from its fresh holes before it plunged to the cement floor.

"Now . . . *you* holla at a playa, *playa*."

E.J., Outlaw, and Rabbit were back, guns drawn, trying to figure out what happened amid the haze of gun smoke in the air.

The storm also alerted Spook, who charged over from his post, shotgun in hand—back near the plush boudoir that B-Money installed at the rear of the building.

"Relax, fellas. Just some house cleaning. Wrap that scum up and toss 'im in the Lexus," said B. Then, to Rabbit specifically, he said, "You ain't the only crazy gunslinger, dawg." And B-Money flashed a twisted smile. Rabbit put his 9 mm back in his pocket, the feeling that he'd been outdone overcoming him.

"Now, I was impressed with your work on Broad Street, kid. Just watch how you act with that pain . . . we don't need no unnecessary heat on us."

Rabbit said nothing and yet it was a sufficient enough reply for the leader.

"Get rid of this—the car, the body, all of it. Chalk it up as a small loss . . . Outlaw, you follow the Lex—use the pickup. Make sure it goes down clean." B-Money executed a tricky dance step reminiscent of an old James Brown move, before he took a bow and sauntered off with Spook.

"So what's the deal, trooper?"

"Everythin' quiet, Boss. I think the girl is sleepin' unless the Uzi woke her."

"Neva that," said B-Money as he passed the assault weapon to Spook. "This crib has enough soundproofin' to keep me sleepin' through a nuclear blast." B-Money snickered. "But then again, if that happened, it wouldn't matter if I heard it or not, would it?" Now B-Money passed Spook his cell phone and two-way pager. No guns and no communications devices passed this door.

"Did you feed her?"

"Tried to. But she just kept cryin'. I think she's homesick," joked Spook, and the two of them laughed. B-Money unlocked his "chamber" and passed the keys to Spook.

"Can't forget these," B-money said.

"Wouldn't want my pet to try and escape on me."

"Right," said Spook with a crooked grin. Having Spook to sit by his bedroom door with that gas-operated 12-gauge across his lap was a better security measure than a burglar alarm, fire alarm, and Doberman pinscher all put together.

At six feet tall, with a biker's tattoo-ridden body, Spook had long since proven himself as the craziest white boy B-Money ever met. On command, Spook had blown a hole through a local drug dealer's chest when the dealer wouldn't come up with the cut owed to B-Money. It was a gruesome sight to see, a man with a hole in his torso the size of a boccie ball, but this was the life that B-Money chose. It's what made the B-boyz so notorious.

* * *

Inside of B-Money's chamber was a souped-up pimped-out luxury apartment. He could see Nadine sound asleep on his custom-made circular bed, still butt naked except for the spiked leather choker he had padlocked around her neck. It was a small padlock, but it kept the accessory in place—a reminder to Nadine that she was his sex toy . . . his slave.

Passing the bed, B-Money went about his ritual. In the corner of his suite he bent down on one knee, rolled a waist-high bookcase aside, and juggled the combinations of two safes that were positioned side by side.

The room was lit only by a weak glow of lamplight. However, even in pitch-black darkness, B could open his safe. To the right-hand safe, containing his cash, he added a small stack of hundred-dollar bills that he had stuffed in his jacket's inside pocket hours earlier. He shut that safe and didn't open the other, where he kept the kilos of cocaine. No need to go in there for now. He replaced the bookcase.

"Okay," B-Money gasped as he got back on his feet. He looked over at Nadine and marveled, deciding what he might do with her next.

He was feeling exceptionally unstoppable right now.

There was close to $300,000 in the safe. He had just extinguished a thief who thought he was a *playa*, and there was a new hot-shot on board—a new missionary to add to B-Money's vision. He was ruthless, too.

B-Money was also very buzzed from the coke in his system, and could think of no better way to release his aggression than with Nadine.

Wanting to fill his empty stomach some, B stepped over to a short refrigerator on top of which was a tray full of condiments and other ingredients he used from time to time.

On a whim, B shoveled two tablespoons of Maxwell House Coffee into an unwashed glass, two tablespoons of heavy cream, and two more of sugar. Then he chuckled at the idea of adding Heinz ketchup and Hellmann's mayonnaise to the drink.

"Fuck it," he told himself. And he squeezed equal parts into the glass, then he poured enough Guinness Stout to fill the glass the rest of the way.

There was another glass on the refrigerator, which he used to cover the first, and he shook the concoction rigorously till it foamed over. Three gulps went past B-Money's tongue, straight down his throat. Coke, Stout, coffee, and sugar now filled his system enough to keep his dick hard for hours.

"Wake up, girl," he said, flipping on his bright houselights and approaching the edge of the bed. "You look like you been cryin'."

Nadine had a hand over her eyes, offended by the bright light. There was a feminine grunt before she said, "When am I goin' home?"

"You didn't know? You *are* home."

"Be serious. I gave you what you want, now let me go. And let me have my clothes."

"I ain't done with you, sweet Nadine. Now tell me, why would I let go of such a good thing?"

Nadine sunk back down to the bed with both hands covering her face now.

"You're not gonna start cryin' again, are you? You know you like it here."

"You tricked me," she said.

"'Cause you *are* a trick," said B-Money.

"I . . . w-wanna go . . . h-home," she wept.

"Shut up! Shut—up!" B-Money had a handful of Nadine's hair in his fist now, twisting her face to the light.

"Don't I treat you good? Huh? You got all the toys you want—the big screen, the CDs, the DVDs . . . You can order whatever food you want. I even got a Jacuzzi back here—*damn*. I hate a snivelin' trick!" B-Money thrust her head back down to the bed and stood there looking frustrated.

"I wanna . . . go . . . home. Why are . . . you-hoo kee-heeping me here?" asked Nadine in utter distress.

Chapter Sixteen

She had turned her face away from him to suffocate her sobs with one of the bed pillows. A moment later she felt the bed give next to her, and he had his hand stroking her hair.

He said, "Look at you, girl . . . pretty black hair, perky breasts like a cheerleader . . . and your skin is like caramel, girl. Goes good with my silk sheets."

Nadine didn't whimper for him as he tried to get all Romeo on her. And she scrunched the sheets to her body, the only cover or clothing available since he took her clothes.

"Aww, Nadine . . . my pet—"

"I'm not your damned *pet*. And unlock this choker from my neck. I'm *not playin'* anymore."

"Oh? You thought this was a game? Is that what you thought? Shit—three weeks ago you were a cashier at Taco Bell. Look at you now. Nah, girl . . . this ain't no fuckin' game. This is reality. Your reality is that you are my prisoner . . . my sex toy . . . or anything *else* I wanna call you. That's the way it is."

Nadine boo-hooed in response to B-Money's proclamations. Three weeks had passed since she met this guy, since she had made the crucial mistake of saying yes to an afterwork ride. It was only the next morning that she woke up here, naked in the man's bed. There had been a bruise on her cheek and she felt drugged up. She had no idea what being drugged up was like, but she wasn't stupid. The man snorted up two lines of white powder in her presence, and he did that at least once a day.

Afterward she began to feel funny, too. And she realized that he was putting dope in her through oral sex.

The when and the how was a little blurry to her, but she remembered his head between her legs, then a stinging hot sensation in her pussy. It was an amazing feeling at first, when her heart would beat harder and faster than it ever had. And to think, she believed it was his work that was responsible . . . his masterful tongue.

After twenty-four hours of mischief, Nadine wanted to go home, but he told her she was his houseguest. Days passed by with no phone to call home, no clothes, and when B-Money was away, her screams went unanswered. The only relief was seeing this huge white man, who was polite when he came to ask her what she wanted to eat. Only, he wouldn't answer any other questions. And Nadine wasn't fool enough to try and run or attack him when he opened the door. He had that demonic look in his eyes and the big shotgun slung over his shoulder.

All Nadine could hope for was that the Taco Bell manager might contact her parents to ask why she wasn't coming to work. But then, that was another problem, since Nadine hadn't lived with her parents for a year. She had moved in—shacked up—with Terry Pough and *his* mom.

Will Terry come and find me?

Nadine didn't know what to think now. And the strange thing that had happened to her body and mind discouraged her from doing much more than crying. At least B-Money stopped putting dope in her pussy when she asked. But what about all the fucking and sucking he put her through? How much more of it could she take?

"Tell you what . . . you did a good job cleaning up my house, so I'll do you a favor . . ."

Cleaning up? I was looking for your guns, a cell phone, even a knife!

"You get to blow me," he said. Nadine turned to see B-Money cocking his head back, laughing wildly with his arms spread open wide like a damned swan.

Mothafucker, I wish I could blow you up!

"I'm not doin' it. I'm not doin' it anymore," said Nadine, pulling the sheets tighter to her body. B-Money laughed louder now.

"You are funny! Funny, funny, funny!" A moment later he snatched Nadine by the hair, positioned her, then slapped her repeatedly. She tried to block his assault, but it was no use. He was too strong, and she submitted, just like before.

Before she wouldn't say his name like he ordered . . . she wouldn't admit that she was his pet, his slave. There was the time she said no to cleaning his house, and no to fucking him like he wanted to be fucked. On more than one occasion she refused to suck his dick. She even tried being sluggish, tried being belligerent, tried to disobey and to fight him. Yet none of that did any good since all B-Money did was smack her or whip her with the leather belt, hard enough to give her bruises here and there.

And here she was again, back in that same hole, feeling like a battered side of beef.

She had no idea why she refused him and thought herself pretty dumb since it was only a blow job he wanted: nothing he hadn't made her do already. Satisfy the fiend and he'd let her be . . . He'd fall asleep and leave her alone. But these attacks were tugging at her pride, what little was left of it. And she felt she still had some fight left in her.

"Please," Nadine said, her face throbbing about both cheeks. "I'll do it. Just . . . don't hurt me anymore." She tearfully took him between her swollen lips and followed his instructions until his nasty-tasting semen spit down her throat.

B-Money wasn't finished with his "pet," as hyper as he was—so pumped up with chemicals. And for the next couple of hours he experimented with her like some life-size doll.

He bent and twisted her into awkward positions that allowed him maximum penetration. He pasted her face with semen and spit mucus on her, then instructed her to rub it in like lotion and to suck her own breast clean. When he was done treating her like his private sideshow freak, he ordered her into the adjoining foyer.

"Go lay in the Jacuzzi, ya slimy bitch. And don't come out till you're told. Hit the light, too."

B-Money lay spread-eagle and naked on top of soiled sheets. His erection wouldn't soften, as though it had a mind of its own.

After some masturbation, he reached for the remote control

and turned on his sixty-inch plasma screen up on the wall. There was a scan option that he pressed, and he watched the channels change one after another in five-second intervals.

This wouldn't last for long since he was so sleepy and satisfied from head to toe. His mind and body began to relax from his hour of adventure.

One image after the next, the TV screen flickered with various identities and brand names. Consumer products. Station identifications. Infomercials. More infomercials. Everybody was pitching something: every last image fighting for time inside of the viewer's mind, and using sex appeal (in one way or another) to do it. B-Money was mumbling, perhaps his way of counting sheep or talking himself to sleep.

"Dirty slut . . . wash that pussy if ya want, but leave that asshole for me. That's the next session . . . Ha ha ha ha haaaaooowweee." B-Money's voice drifted and carried and wavered like an out of control airplane. He was losing consciousness and his eyelids were dropping open and closed in time with the channel changes.

"Gotta get me a new bitch. A virgin. I'mma do like R. Kelly and get me a *young* bitch. Fresh meat . . . then I'mma make a video, too . . . shit . . . my face is already on them wanted posters . . . so what the fuck . . . I'll just be a most wanted, armed, robbin' pedophile. *And so what?* Long as I got money . . . long as I got my crew . . . who the fuck gonna touch me?"

CNN . . . MSNBC . . . CNBC . . . Animal Planet . . .

Cartoon Network . . . Comedy Central . . . Telemundo . . .

The channels went on changing automatically.

"Ain't nothin' on TV. . . . It's all bullshit. . . . They like them young girls, too . . . and I'm supposed to be the monster . . . mothafuck . . ."

C-Span . . . ESPN . . . ESPN . . . AMC . . . History Channel . . . Discovery Channel . . . MTV . . .

"Yo . . . *wassup, homie*? Long time, no see, dawg. Ha-haaa . . . you finally made it big-time, huh? BET. Mothafucka. Why don't cha holla at cha *boy*!"

A revelation erupted inside of B-Money that was so strong,

so electric, he was knocked into a full alert. He sat upright and shouted, fighting his body's lack of balance.

"OH SHIT! OH SHIT! I'M DREAMIN'! NO—I'M NOT DREAMIN'! OH FUCK! RINGO! GODDAMN, MOTHA-FUCK! MY BOY!"

He scrambled for the remote, losing it in the sheets, and eventually got the channels to quit changing. Then he switched back to BET. The *Uncut* video show was on, where a lot of up-and-coming artists got exposure despite the references to sex or violence in their videos.

"Shit! He made it! The mothafucka made it!!" B-Money was yelling at the top of his lungs as if they could hear him on the screen.

Then he realized he *did* have somebody to share the news with.

"Hey you! Ahhh . . . damn!" B-Money snapped his fingers wistfully, trying to recall his pet's real name.

"You! In the Jacuzzi! Hey—comeer! Quick!"

She took her time strolling out of the foyer, still dripping wet and with that discouraged expression on her face.

"Hey, *bitch*! You're drippin' on my goddamned carpet! Never mind—look . . . check out this video. I know you like that hip-hop shit. I know you wish you was one of them hip-hop ho's . . . see 'im? In the Cadillac truck! *Yeah man* . . . that's my dawg! *We grew up together*!"

The two watched the video with its volume pulsating in the boudoir, loud enough to rock a party crowd.

"That's my NIGGA!" Nadine's face didn't change, though she still recorded all of this—B-Money's yelling, the video on the screen, the music that accompanied it—with her eyes and ears, however involuntarily.

So what, asshole? She yawned. The video was coming to an end when a strobe light flickered over the door. *The white one*, thought B, knowing that the other one—the red strobe—would've meant Emergency.

B-Money lowered the volume of his surround-sound system, with his eyes still wanting to see more of Ringo.

"Go on back in the other room," he told Nadine. "Dry y'self

off—and while ya at it, fix your face. I might wanna take you out tonight."

Nadine's surprised expression made B-Money break out laughing.

"Get it? *Take you out? It was a joke, you bitch! Ha ha ha ha haaaa* . . . I made another funny joke, why ain't you laughin'?" Nadine's face hardened and she left the room. Spook poked his head in the suite.

"*Boss* . . ." Spook turned his head away. B-Money pulled a sheet around his waist.

"Okay, I'm decent. What is it?"

Spook faced him again. "They back. Everythin's kosher."

"Good. I'll be out in five. Listen for my buzz." Spook started to shut the door, then changed his mind.

"Oh . . . Boss?"

B-Money waited to hear what Spook had to say: It seemed important.

"The po-po found that girl's body. The *last* one."

"Oh . . . the Hannah trick. I kinda liked that white girl too, Spook. Hope you don't feel some type o' way 'cause o' that."

Spook still had half his body wedged in the doorway. He sucked his teeth and said, "Shit, Boss. I only fuck with black and Asian chicks—you know how I do."

"Just checkin' to make sure we on the same page, know what I'm sayin'?"

Spook smirked. "Aight. Five minutes, man."

"Gotcha." Spook locked the door again. B-Money looked back at the screen. There was a different video on—a different rap artist, and yet B-Money still saw Ringo.

Ringo the mothafucka really made it after all. Well, I'll be damned.

A commercial played.

"We gotta hook up, Ringo. Kick it a little, for old time's sake. You a rapper now . . . a real BET nigga. All blinged out with the whips and the dancin' chicks . . . you never know when you'll need a real gangsta to come and straighten somebody out for you. Ain't nobody fuckin' with my nigga, Ringo! *We made it, baby!* You got the fame and glory, and I got the underground . . . I got your back! This mothafucka is on LOCK! *We there, yo! We are motha fuckin' there!*"

B-Money was dressed and coming down from his high when he looked for Nadine. She was still soaking in the Jacuzzi.

"What happened?" asked B-Money. Nadine didn't answer, but she could've stabbed him with that vexation in her eyes.

"Ooooh . . . you get my dick hard when you look at me like that! Now listen . . . I'm being serious this time. I want you to dry off and get dressed. I'm takin' you out. We're gonna have our last meal together before I let you go home. Plus I want you to meet my rap buddy . . ."

Nadine could hardly care about any rapper. She squealed, delighted to know her captivity had come to an end.

"Wait a minute. You're lyin' to me again."

"Nope. I'm dead serious. I'm talkin' dead serious."

"Then, what about my clothes?"

"I got you, girl. Just dry off."

B-Money expressed his sincerity and Nadine fell for it. Then Spook and Rabbit escorted her to an old gray van out in the garage.

Thank God this is over. The second I'm free from these assholes, I'm reporting them to the police. That mothafucker is gonna fry for what he put me through!

"Damn, baby . . . you got it goin' on tonight," said one of the goons crouched in the back of the van. "Here, lemme give you a hand."

Nadine was absorbing the sights in the big warehouse—all the expensive vehicles, some of them glistening like new, others undergoing paint jobs. She hesitated initially, but the guy smiled politely while making the gentlemanly gesture, so she went ahead and accepted his help.

"Where do I sit?"

"Right here, boo."

Nadine remembered the guy who spoke up. He was the one they called Outlaw, with the big head and beady eyes. He was also the one who was with B-Money the evening she was persuaded to accept the ride home from work. And now he wanted her to sit on his knee.

"That's okay. I'll just stand," she said.

"Whatever. Ya betta hold on," he said.

Nadine grabbed hold of a cavity along the inside wall of the van as it eased out of the garage.

"Where's B-Money?"

"Behind us. In the pimp-mobile."

Nadine couldn't see too much through the van's rear windows; they were clouded with spray paint. She let out a disgruntled sigh.

"Where we goin'?"

"Don't ask so many questions," barked the driver. "I'm tryin' to concentrate on the road."

The van took a sudden turn and Nadine fell to the floor. The three goons laughed.

"Told you to h-hold on!" said whoever. Then came a loud laugh.

"Hey, wrap that ho up, man. Might as well before she fall out the back door or somethin'. That's all we need is the po-po catchin' us in the middle of this shit."

Nadine was getting negative signals—*as if they weren't already negative.*

"B-Money said we were goin' to dinner."

"Come on, Outlaw! Handle that shit."

"I wanna talk to B—"

Nadine didn't see it coming. The bottom of a boot slammed her in the hip and she was thrown into the metal wall of the van. She quickly fell to the floor, nearly unconscious.

She couldn't speak; there was no air in here. Her hair was grabbed so hard, her neck strained. Her arms were pulled back, and a foot or a knee pressed down on her back. A wide leather belt was strapped around her head, covering her mouth, fastened as a gag. Another belt bound her wrists, and a rope secured her ankles. All Nadine could do was whimper and whine.

B-Money followed the van through the open chain-link fence that cordoned off the deserted construction site. The Campo

Grande condo project had long been abandoned and it was just one location on a list of dozens where the B-boyz chose to play their late-night games.

B-Money thought back to the last late-night adventure—the Hannah trick—and how they let her run naked with her wrists bound behind her back and a gag in her mouth to keep her from screaming. Then they sicked Meathead, Mack's pit bull, on her.

It made him smile to recall how fast that white girl ran . . . maybe faster than an Olympian, like that Jones chick or even Flo Jo.

But when Meathead caught the girl—*damn*! He chomped on her body like she was tenderloin steak. Now it was Nadine who would be the victim. B-Money gave his boys the go-ahead to do with her what they wanted.

"All I wanna do is watch," B-Money had said before they left Drake Avenue. And that's what he was doing now, from the driver's seat of his pimp-mobile—the Isuzu Rodeo. Parked about ten feet away and blazing a stick of weed, B-Money reclined some and enjoyed the show.

Chapter Seventeen

MIDTOWN, NEW YORK CITY

This was everything that Ringo ever dreamed.

Before his rocket took off he read about the business in the various publications: There were the DVDs, the videos, and plenty of MTV-style behind-the-scences profiles with vivid footage of a pop star's day-to-day activities. And, of course, his big record deal automatically came equipped with an experienced staff who coached him through every step and procedure.

So Ringo was built and prepared for this. And besides, he had clout now as a certified platinum-selling rapper.

The day had finally come for Ringo's "Platinum party," where everyone who had anything to do with the project came out to celebrate the landmark achievement. There were so many people to meet that there was no way to keep track of who was responsible for what.

Ringo tried to categorize the people he met: There were those he felt were essential and others who weren't. Of those two groups, there were those he felt were phony and those who were genuine. He went with his gut feeling in each introduction. Publicists, marketing executives, promotions personnel, retail managers, booking agents, radio and television show programmers and personalities, magazine columnists, staff writers and publishers, club deejays, record pool operators, Internet moguls, photographers . . .

Opportunists and hucksters of every sort, and on and on and on . . . The reality of all the activity was that he was the driving force at the center of all the hoopla—the hallelujahs and the hip-hop hoorays—all because a million pieces wanted to jump for joy when he somehow released all the energy bottled up inside of him. But he also knew that he had to maintain his cool. He had to make it look as though this was not going to his head.

At the Palladium, where part one of his platinum celebration was staged, Ringo was congratulated by the majority of his label mates, as well as all of those "ultimate fans" and staff members who helped to put him in the spotlight.

"There's still a lot of work to do," Ringo announced amid whistles and impulsive cheers. "This celebratin' ain't gone to my head . . ."

He raised an open bottle of Alizé. "So let's make it another million!"

Ringo went on to shake hands and engage in small talk. There were so many people, like groupies, with instant smiles.

But it was part two of the celebration that Ringo most anticipated. All of his close friends and associates, the love of his life, his three heavies (who made sure that his immediate environment was secure), and of course Quentin, his baby boy, born just four days earlier.

They all mingled there in Ringo's Manhattan high-rise apartment, far from the phony handshakes and obligatory introductions. No jacks-of-all-trades passing business cards or wannabes warming up to him for photo opportunities.

Instead of the hype and pandemonium, this atmosphere was simply festive, with respectful volumes of cheer, music, and conversation. There were warm hugs for Ringo, and Porsha (the new mommy) was showing little Quentin to everybody like he was an unearthed treasure, or a fish in a tank.

Ringo had this giddy smile going all night, and Porsha even asked, "Did you smoke somethin' funny?" He adamantly denied it, but was too overwhelmed by everything to define his natural high for her. In the meantime, cigars were passed around to all the men in attendance: There was just so much to celebrate. Quentin's birth. Ringo's platinum status. And now that PGD and

Mo City had merged, there were so many other things in store—so much more promise for the future.

Porsha, however, couldn't have cared less about the reasons behind the cigars. She was unequivocal in her command: "Do not smoke those in my house," she announced. And she didn't allow it out on the balcony either. "Because I don't want anyone to even breathe tobacco around my child," she concluded, complete with a daring eyebrow.

Everyone agreed and abided by Porsha's house rules, and were more pleased than astonished at what kind of mother she would turn out to be.

While the private party stretched toward midnight, the buzz in varying circles was consistent:

". . . I can't wait for the premiere tomorrow. Did you hear that 'Push' isn't just the name of the movie? That's actually a guy's name . . . Push. Kinda has a ring to it, right?"

". . . I hear the opening credits are gonna appear while Ringo's song plays in the background . . ."

". . . You mean he did two cuts for the movie sound track? What's the other one?"

"Did you hear? His manager is getting all kinds of calls wanting Ringo for different collaborations . . ."

"Chuck, you never did explain to him about the whole merger deal . . . shouldn't he know where he fits in the whole puzzle?" Porsha asked Ringo's manager.

"Sure, Porsha, you're right. I'll tell you what . . . I was waiting for the right time—you know how busy we've all been . . . Ringo with all these promotional engagements, me doing all the contracts and agreements . . . you having the baby. Maybe now is the right time. Tell you what . . ."

Porsha took a deep breath at Chuck always saying, *Tell you what.*

"Ringo and I will sit and discuss it over lunch."

"When, Chuck?"

"Next week. I promise, next week."

Porsha raised an eyebrow to express how he had better not be lying.

"Lemme do this toast, sweetheart."

Chuck shuffled away from Porsha, exhaling with relief as he did, tapping a champagne glass with a fork. "Can I have everyone's attention, please? Gather 'round!"

Porsha went about her mommy business, cuddling Quentin while she fed him a mini-bottle of water. Tangi was sitting at the electronic grand piano by the window with a view of the Hudson River and Jersey shoreline. She tapped a keypad for the piano music to die off.

Brooklyn Jones was standing hear the piano as well, looking over Tangi's shoulder at the nifty device. Next to Brooklyn was his wife, quieting her chat with Jamie, Ringo's personal assistant. Lucy, the housekeeper, was playing waitress, unloading an empty champagne glass from Irwin Johnson, handing him an already refilled glass, and smiling at Kujo as she did. Darlene, Ringo's stylist, was munching on hors d'oeuvres while explaining some concepts she had for the forthcoming music video (Ringo's third) to Sylvia, a friend of J-Love's, Ringo's hype man when he did big stage shows.

"It's supposed to be finished in time so that there'll be saturation to support his Soul Train Award nomination for Best New Artist. 'Cause it all boils down to what viewers like—no matter what anyone says . . . hey, let's move closer. It looks like Chuck is gonna say something."

The doorbell chimed. Butter popped the collar of Sweets' tuxedo and dusted of a spec of lint, however imaginary.

"Your turn, Dapper Dan."

Sweets made a face in response to Butter going overboard as bodies crowded closer to Chuck, Ringo's manager.

Chuck waited to see who was at the door before he began. Most of the two dozen guests looked on curiously as Sweets skipped up from the sunken marble floor to the front entrance of the apartment. He pulled the door open in one sweeping motion. Chuck announced, "Fathead! I didn't think you'd make it. Come on in! You're just in time for the—"

Fathead wasn't alone.

"Hey! Big Joe! And Diamond? Is that you?"

The two celebrities behind Fathead were proud and humbled—in that order.

"Well, damn it, everybody. Give these two a round of applause! Welcome two of PGD's superstars of rap and song!"

Chuck stepped through the parted body of delighted faces to personally escort the new guests into the party.

A small entourage entered the apartment as well.

"You guys are just in time for our toast," Chuck continued, speaking loud enough to keep everyone's attention. Lucy was quick to approach with a tray of champagne for those joining the toast.

"Okay, people. Up with the bubbly! We've got a few big dogs in the house whom I'd be remiss—and out of a job!—not to mention . . ."

Laughter.

"If not for some of these cats, we might not be celebrating right now, so let me acknowledge them without further ado . . . We have the head of PGD's Black Music Department in the house—Mr. Brooklyn Jones. We also have the writer and critic who originally grew an interest in Ringo's music, enough to singlehandedly create a resounding popularity among industry moguls . . . Mr. Irwin Johnson. Sorry our hands are full, gentlemen. We'd love to applaud you, but a certain baby mama—I won't mention any names—" Laughter. "*—demanded* that only *her* baby's father—that would be Ringo—receive all the accolades this evening. So let's be serious for a moment. Ringo . . . you've done it. In a climate of whim and frenzy, you have carved out a niche that thousands of rappers can only dream of . . . a niche that all of us among you hope and pray will serve you and your new family for years to come. HERE'S TO RINGO! CHEERS!"

"CHEERS!" the crowd repeated.

Tangi programmed an up-tempo song by Mary J. Blige and the tone of the party kicked into high gear.

Ringo approached Diamond and kissed her cheek. Then he gave Big Joe a brief homeboy hug. He also shook hands with others who accompanied them. Big Joe was on the way to becoming a legend of the pimp-rap style—a heavyset version of the old-school rapper Snoop Dogg.

Diamond was one of Ringo's new label mates now that Mo City (her label) was merging with PGD (his label).

Before long, Diamond was holding and feeding baby Quentin. Irwin was taking notes from Fathead regarding his forthcoming studio production work.

Kianna, Diamond's friend, was kickin' it with Jamie, discussing a collaboration between Ringo and Diamond for a remix of "All Up in My Milk." The doorbell chimed again, though activities continued as though it hadn't.

"Your turn, buddy," Sweets said. He rolled his eyes at Butter popping his own collar.

Oh brother, thought Butter.

"Brooklyn, is there a way the label can increase the budget for the promotional appearances? I'm gonna need to bring a babysitter with us . . ."

"Baby, if you wasn't workin' for Ringo, I might have to make you my girl," Big Joe told Tangi.

Tangi was playful in her response. She said, "And you could probably get it, too—but I can only be with one daddy at a time."

Big Joe cocked his head back.

"Who yo' daddy?"

Tangi pointed to J-Love, who had been watching the two from across the dining room area. J-Love's jealous leer softened immediately into a proud gaze.

"Really, girl? I swore that you were J-Love's side jaunt, and that he was two-timing my girl Tangi. *Girrrl* . . . don't you know, after the party it was about to be on."

Sylvia had that crooked kitten's smile as she chuckled at Darlene's straightforward approach.

"No . . . I'm happily single and not *even* looking—*at men*, that is." Sylvia said that with a sultry head-to-toe appraisal of Darlene. She could see her naked.

"Oh," Darlene said breathlessly.

* * *

"I'm sorry, I don't think I know you. Do you have an invitation?" asked Butter at the front door.

"*Memories* is all the invitation I need. Now, if you'll *excuse* me, I need to see Ringo."

"Miss, this is a private affair. I'm afraid—"

"Excuse me! You *need* to back off of my body!"

Butter looked back over his shoulder, hoping Sweets might be alerted by this loudmouthed nuisance at the door. At the same time he grabbed ahold of the smaller woman, half-carrying, half-dragging her farther into the hall, toward the elevator.

"Take—your—hands off of me!"

She became a wild woman within seconds, trying to kick and scratch at Butter. He became more aggressive, wrestling her into a tight package with her arms harnessed at her sides, toting her horizontally into the elevator.

As Butter coped with the hysterical woman, Tangi made eyes at J-Love, Ringo's hype man . . . and Porsha pressed Brooklyn for more expense money, while Big Joe redirected his advances to Lucy, the housekeeper . . . and Diamond sang "Rock-a-bye Baby" to Quentin while Jamie went to see why the front door was still open . . . and Darlene warmed to Sylvia's advances, while Chuck made a cell phone call. In the meantime, the champagne poured, the piano entertained, and the future seemed more promising with each passing minute. On the surface, this was a happy time for Ringo and his extended family. But on the other hand, everything isn't always what it seems.

Chapter Eighteen

Jamie Horton was a charismatic woman who controlled or directed Ringo's every waking moment.

"You're gonna need a personal assistant," said Brooklyn the day that Ringo and his band of missionaries showed up, fresh from their Bridgeport exodus. And Porsha got into her feelings about him—*How's some white woman just gonna barge into our lives, Ringo*? But in the end it was Ringo's decision that won. Porsha was pregnant; Tangi wasn't prepared for this kind of thing, and there was too much at stake. *That's all there is to it*, Ringo had told her. The next thing he knew this aggressive chick—with long blond hair, seen-it-all eyes, and dancing water-balloon tits—marched through the door of his apartment, heels clicking against the floor and her ass outrageous enough to bring Porsha to a state of jealousy. At least, that's what Ringo saw in her eyes when she and Tangi shared a look.

"We're gonna need to set you up with a dream team, Ringo. I suggest Chuck Turner for your management. Darlene Askew is an excellent stylist—she can get your gear in order. And *ahh* . . . have you considered a housekeeper to help your—" Jamie had to lean in and lower her voice. Porsha was within hearing distance, and she didn't want to assume too much. "*Girlfriend or fiancée*?"

Ringo lowered his voice too. "I didn't pop the question yet."

"You two are really hittin' it off over there," Porsha said.

"Excuse me, Jamie. Lemme handle this." And Ringo went over to Porsha, all smiles, scooping Quentin from her arms. "The kitchen. *Now*."

* * *

Jamie had a background in publicity (for one record label) and artist management (for a popular boy group) as well, so she was equipped for this. Her trusty leatherbound organizer in tow, Jamie served as the glue that sealed the cracks and the hard-line authority that connected the dots of Ringo's life. She networked with everybody who was anybody in music, sports, and film, and didn't mind flaunting her sexuality to get things done.

Yes, there was a nice salary and a string of direction and the record label. But Jamie was compelled by something greater. Put simply, she loved this shit. The daily grind, the constant excitement . . . the power.

Ringo was maturing with great speed, no longer considered a local with petty priorities and small-time desires. He was twenty-one now, with a thorough understanding of his gift, his talent. He grew a commanding energy that successful movers and shakers often assume—the agenda, the fortitude, and the magnetism.

Artist or no artist, Ringo was focused. He kept a daily exercise routine, healthy eating habits, and an organized lifestyle. He knew how to speak intelligently whenever the occasion called for it, but he also kept it "gutter" if that's what the temperature required. He made sure Porsha was taken care of and spent quality time with Quentin whenever he took breaks from his national promotions.

Ringo essentially settled into a state of knowing—that certain confidence people have when they realize their worth, their value, and what exactly they want from life. It was a comfort zone that he could look forward to—knock on wood—every day he woke.

A week went by since the platinum celebrations, and since Chuck's promise to Porsha. It was about time for that conference, anyhow. Not by telephone, with the usual four- and five-way call. No, this gathering was for the few who mattered.

Ringo and Jamie sat side by side, across from Chuck Turner and Brooklyn Jones. The four of them were seated on individual sofas that semi-circled a short glass coffee table in a secluded corner of the Waldorf-Astoria Hotel's lobby. The street was bustling with activity just outside the window nearest them and there were other business discussions going on in other areas of the lobby.

"I don't see why we can't just run with this meeting and fill Mr. Lewis in when he gets here," said Brooklyn. "I'm two appointments behind schedule, and—" Brooklyn's eyes had been wandering, and when they settled on Jamie he changed his tune. "well . . . I have a lot of exciting things to share with you."

Chuck's body language said that he was in agreement, and then Jamie put her hand atop Ringo's wrist. It felt like a straightforward message, like they were all waiting for Ringo to say *Let's go.*

"A couple minutes more," said Ringo as he checked his two-way, then his pager. "I think I'm worth that, don't you?" He hoped he wasn't being too psychological, taking their collective intelligence for granted.

And who could argue? Take Ringo out of the equation and the others—all of them—would soon realize a tremendous deficit in the dividends he generated. Besides, this wasn't the same Ringo who signed his first major record deal two years ago. He wasn't about to be anyone's sucker.

If his friend and associate Justin was important at this level of negotiations, then so be it. They'd just have to wait.

"I liked the freestyle performance you did on *Rap City* last week," said Brooklyn, making use of the idle time. "I called three people to make sure they caught it, I was so excited. . . . I don't know why nobody's biting at the host—he's got a mean flow. He needs a deal. They repeat those shows, ya know."

Jones spit into his empty soda can again—a nasty brown goo that was the byproduct of his chewing tobacco—even as the negotiations were about to begin. "That means twice the exposure for us," he finally said.

Jamie attempted to lighten things up.

"We're gonna have a lotta fun with this next video. Who came up with the idea to involve four cities?"

"Hype's people. We saw the treatment and we immediately

knew it was a winner." Jamie wagged her head, but it was with an appreciative smile. *Blessings never cease.*

"Thereheis," blurted Ringo, combining three words to make just one. The others shifted their attention toward Justin, who now quickened his gait along the carpet.

"Sorry I'm late, people. Traffic was hell trying to cross town."

"Justin, you know Jamie and Chuck already . . . and *this* is the main man, Brooklyn Jones. Brooklyn, this is Justin Lewis."

"Good to meet you, Mr. Lewis. Okay . . . if you all don't mind I'd like to get this discussion underway." It sounded like too condescending a remark coming from Brooklyn, a shoo-in for a Harley Davidson rider who owned a suitcase full of heavy metal CDs.

Brooklyn projected that kind of image with his shoulder-length brown hair and the feathered earring hanging down on the left. The feather gave the effect of a green streak that peek-a-booed from within his dingy strands of hair. Jones also wore oversized clothing—a black blazer with the sleeves folded over and a green silk shirt with its collar opened enough to offer an unbecoming sight of bushy chest hair mixed with tattoos and a legion of gold chains. And the slacks matched the blazer, but they were cuffed up a bit too high so as to show his tube socks and high-top Converse basketball sneakers. Either that was a fashion statement or there was about to be a flood.

But even though Brooklyn's appearance had Ringo's belief systems confused, even though his high-pitched voice was something out of an annoying low-budget television comedy, even if he was no more than a hillbilly who chewed tobacco and spit into a cup every thirty seconds and didn't necessarily meet *GQ*'s fashion standards, that might all be overlooked when considering the man's wherewithal.

Behind the (dare one say) *unique* imagery was enough clout and power to squash those personal opinions. Brooklyn was one of the few who knew how to talk the talk, and to walk the walk, too.

Music industry insiders might argue that he indeed *was* "the walk."

* * *

The Source magazine placed Jones at number 19 on its power 100 list. VIBE's Juice issue placed him at number 12 on their list of 50, and XXL ranked him one of the industry's top 23 shot-callers in their Big Willie issue.

He had executive-produced eight of this year's thirty top-selling albums by artists including X, Big Joe, Christine, Luther, and the hot girl, Jennifer.

There were sound tracks that he put together for the motion pictures *Push* and *Sugar Daddy*, as well as a handful of singles that were currently in heavy rotation in the formats of R&B and hip-hop radio and pop radio, as well as five top 40 syndicated radio broadcasts.

Brooklyn Jones made hits, and the record spoke for itself.

"So . . . ," Jamie had warned, "When he speaks, forget about what he's wearing or what he looks like. Just listen and learn. And don't *ever* cross him."

And now, here he was in the flesh. The man who they called powerful . . . a big willy . . . a man with juice was sitting in front of Ringo.

"It's like this, Ringo. You're doing good. The big boys are happy about your work. And I don't mean they're crankin' your CD in their Lex's and Beemers—they couldn't care less. I'm talking about the product sales. Units are flyin' out of the mega-stores. That's all they care about. Now . . . there have been some changes during the past few weeks that I'm sure you heard about. I know you've been in and out of town, busy with your promo tour, so lemme lay the soup and nuts out for ya."

"The merger," guessed Ringo.

"Precisely. Mo City is a PGD group now. So there's a few things that are different . . ."

Brooklyn spit into the Pepsi can, and the syruplike drool strained the tolerance of those in his presence.

"Could you spell that out for him, B.J.?"

Ringo looked at Chuck for signs, hoping that last statement wasn't also calling him naive.

Chuck turned to Ringo with a tight-lipped grin to the side and eyes that said, *You need to know this.*

"Well, for one, the roster of headliners is bigger now. More superstars to handle. Our new philosophy is that the big names can handle their own since they have a devoted following that won't die out. All we'll need to do is keep their product consistent and fresh. Now . . . for new artists—take Diamond, for instance . . . or yourself—our strategy is to keep your product exciting. That means cutting-edge material. That means, taking risks . . ."

"What kinds of risks?" asked Jamie.

"Don't get me wrong, sweetheart. It's not like we've gotta make any dramatic changes. Ringo's image is good. It's hood. It's dangerous. It's straight from the mud. *Hey!* There's an idea. Straight from the mud. That sounds like a song title to me . . . *Anyway*, where was I? Oh. Before I make my suggestions, lemme tell you guys what the label has lined up during the course of the next quarter.

"First, we're gonna put Ringo in with more hot collabos. The ones we'll jump on immediately is you and Killer X, and also you and Diamond. I noticed that she hit it off well with your family at the party."

Ringo chuckled and peeked at Justin. "More like her and Quentin, my son. You oughta set up a collabo with *those* two."

Brooklyn had a poker-faced expression since the comment went way over his head.

"Okay. Now, with the remixes I wanna hit you with some concepts. Somethin' for you to chew on . . . with you and X, you both deliver that rawness . . . that straight-from-the-gutter image . . . only, for the collaboration I wanna see a sorta tag-team performance. We could call the song . . ."

Brooklyn put his hand to his chin, stoking his goatee as if the ideas were harbored within. ". . . Black and Blue. *Yeah*, that's it. You'll be that black shit, like a real urban, grimy street flow . . . you know, talk about how niggas act at night when the moon is full. An anything-goes attitude, feel me?" Ringo swallowed his shock, unsure of what might come out of this guy's mouth next.

"Then Killer X could do the blue end of things . . . like pain and violence . . . I'm talkin' blood and gore . . . how it's gonna feel to get your head cracked. You feel me? Real gutter . . .

"Now, as far as Diamond goes, we'll need a remix for 'All Up in My Milk.' We've approved a budget for a video with both of you, too. Did Chuck tell you? We wanna make it so they'll have to split that Best New Artist trophy down the middle. We want those *Soul Train* people to have conniptions trying to figure out whether it'll be you or Diamond." Brooklyn had that jaundiced tint about his teeth, a good-enough warning not to get in the line of fire when he spoke. Better to keep a certain distance.

"Now, there's something else I need to mention . . . we gotta cut down on all the mixtape appearances. You're hot property now, Ringo. And you'll get hotter with the merger . . . we don't want to hurt album sales by watering down your presence. Because, let's face it . . . that's what we're talking about here. That's what matters.

"It's gonna be a tremendous summer too . . . There's a national concert tour we're lookin' at—they're calling it One Hot Summer Night and there's gonna be four major headliners. We're working on a deal that can get you and Diamond a guarantee of thirty shows in thirty cities . . . Ringo was as still as stone. And he wondered if Justin was feeling any of this. He was afraid to look over at him.

"That's easily a quarter million cash in your pocket if you take away a fee of ten grand per show. The label gets none of that. We'll just be happy with the spillover into album sales as well as the big anticipation for your sophomore album . . ."

I know Justin heard that! If it's a quarter million for me, then Diamond's gotta be gettin' the same money.

It was obvious to Ringo that Brooklyn hadn't made the association between Justin and Diamond, how they were lovers. If he did, he would have given Justin greater regard. He wouldn't have looked past him as the nuisance-sidekick with a little law experience.

"Also, this summer there are twelve expos and conventions that will feature our artists. There's a stage show, a fan club tent, and a tie-in sponsorship with all of the Clear Channel stations, so it's a big deal. Especially at the *VIBE* and *Impact* seminars.

Now . . . are you ready for the big news?"

What, I didn't hear it already? Damn, thought Ringo.

"I got you a performance on . . . don't piss yourself now . . . ready for this? *The Tonight Show*! And The Source Awards! That's more television exposure than I could've ever bargained for, especially for a new artist. Album sales are gonna shoot *through the roof*!"

Ringo's heart was doing jumping jacks—he was sure of it.

"But hold on. Can you stand this?"

Ringo had to stop his leg from shaking.

"We're holding on, B.J. we're *holding on*!"

Jamie was quietly excited with her lips slightly parted.

"Now, you guys are the only ones to know this—and remember, you didn't hear this from me . . . The Grammy nominations are to be announced in a few weeks. And . . . *Ringo* is up for Best New Artist."

Ringo could feel the question boiling inside of Justin, even before he asked it.

"How about Diamond? Any inside stuff on her? asked Justin.

Ringo wanted to take a swing at Justin, thinking him selfish to interfere with *his* moment.

"Let's stay focused," said Ringo, keeping a respectful tone so as not to hurt Justin's ego. "So, does that mean we get a performance on that show too?"

"Bigger than that," said Jones. "Isner and I go back quite a few years, so there aren't too many secrets that we can keep from each other. But you must . . . no, on second thought, I can't tell you this. I can't—"

"*Aw*, come on, B.J.! How can you build me up like that just to drop me like a dead pigeon?" asked Chuck.

"Chuck, I can't. It could lead to scandal. . . .

"Okay, just put it this way . . . *somebody* is gonna win Best Rap Single this year. I can't say who, but—"

Brooklyn didn't get to say another word because Chuck jumped up from his seat.

"YES! JESUS CHRIST, YES!" It was praise even as it was trapped suppressed within his clenched teeth.

Ringo turned to Justin for clarity.

Is he sayin' what I think he's sayin?

Justin must have read his mind, because he leaned in to whisper a comment.

"Read between the lines, buddy. He's saying it in so many words . . . you got Best Rap Single."

Ringo sat back and ruminated on the idea.

What about the so-called votes? *The so-called tabulations I'm always hearing about by XYZ accounting firm*?

He wondered who was *really* pulling the strings on life's good fortunes . . . and was the "who" Ringo's guardian angel?

"Why, Brooklyn? Why all the hype about me? I'm a small-time rapper. Even Killer X is sellin' four and five million. Jay is doin' close to ten. I only now reached the million mark . . ."

"It's your potential to be an X or a Jay. That's what we're in the business to build, multiplatinum artists. We've got this game down to a science, kid. We know what sells, we know what doesn't. It all amounts to our money machine manufacturin' more money. That's how the big boys see you, Ringo. You may not represent a name or a living being to them, but you sure as hell represent numbers. And they're banking on that. Oh—and there's one other thing I neglected to tell you . . . They're laying out a second offer to you. They wanna exercise the option you gave them for your sophomore album . . . five hundred thou in advance—half up front, half upon delivery." Ringo finally let go of the breath he was holding. Jamie rubbed his back up and down the spine.

"You're not reading me, sir. What's the hook here? What did you mean by *changes*? You said earlier that we don't have to have *dramatic* changes. And from that I get the idea that there's gonna be some kinda change. I wanna know what that is. I ain't stupid, Brooklyn. You also said some other things . . . risks. You must have something in mind . . . Some—what'd you call it?—strategy? So I know there's some kinda price here." Ringo felt himself facing the ultimate big willy. It was an all-or-nothing encounter.

Jamie, Chuck, and Justin had the spooked look, like they were vegetating and merely reading Ringo's lips.

"Okay, I'll level with you. I wanna executive produce this album and the next four. I hire the producers for the tracks—no more small-time dudes like Deejay Solo—the bootlegger from Bridgeport. It's time to do things big, Ringo. Hundred, two hundred, and three hundred thou producers. I'm talkin' big names that guarantee platinum-selling work. If we get a group of them together on the same CD, it's a sure thing to do Nelly numbers . . . Eminem numbers.

Remember those two, and how they made history? How they raised the stakes? Well, we're gonna step to the plate with home-run product. And you're gonna have to be a lot more deadly with your rap. Even if you never did a crime . . . if you never killed anyone, you gotta act and pretend like you did. Even if you never shot a gun—and I'm not saying if you have or haven't—you're gonna have to juice up your lyrics some more. That hard shit is what people wanna hear. It's what's selling. If we gotta put you in the middle of a street battle or make up some phony police rap sheets . . . *whatever* . . . we need that real hard-core shit, kid. The question is *are you ready*? *Are you*?"

"What's wrong with what I'm puttin' out now? It was good enough to go platinum . . . to get me the nominations and the tours."

"Dude. Don't get too hung up on that stuff. Everything ain't always what it seems. Remember that. At PGD, we make 'em . . . and we break 'em. I could take you to my office and show you about a few dozen artists—rappers, singers, bands—doing nothing but collecting dust on my shelf. Just know for the record . . . shit don't happen on its own."

A heated argument tossed around in Ringo's head. It was the dollar signs and the fame on one side of the scratch line, the bruised ego and his conscience on the other.

Before Ringo said anything damaging, Chuck spoke up, as though he read the rapper's mind.

"Let me have a minute with Ringo, B.J. Please, come on, buddy . . ." Chuck patted Ringo's shoulder. "Take a breather," he told the rapper. Justin raised up from his seat, same as Ringo. Chuck stuck his hand up at the law student.

"Please . . . I need to be alone with him."

Ringo shrugged at Justin, like they were only pawns on a

board with many more power pieces overshadowing them. Ringo also looked at Jamie, and she winked as if to say he was doing the right thing.

There was an empty space not too far away that had the same multi-sofa arrangement around the same type table.

"Ringo, check this out," Chuck started to say even as they were still taking a seat. "And try to listen to what I'm saying with a clear mind. . . . I'm your manager. I wouldn't steer you wrong, because remember, I've gotta eat too. When you do well, so do I. When you don't . . . neither do I. So . . . I *need* you to do well. I *want* you to win . . . to make the right decisions.

This isn't about sellin' out; it's about you becoming successful. And sometimes decisions are hard to make. Sometimes, for the sake of success, you have to make bitter-tasting decisions. Everything can't be sweet like we want all the time. It's that simple. You make your choices in life, and you take the lumps to go with them. I like to say, if you gonna be true to the game, then stick to the game you got stuck in."

"Chuck, man, I don't like nobody dictatin' what I should say in my raps. You hear this dude? *Juice up the lyrics . . . we need real hard-core shit*. Where's this guy from anyway? He can't be from Brooklyn."

Chuck's response was spirited.

"Sometimes you can't be rich and righteous at the same time. You either want to make money, or you don't. And to make money on this level of the game, you have to feed the demand. Remember that . . . everything in life is about supply and demand."

Ringo deliberated over what was and wasn't sensible about Chuck's wisdom. Only, the words themselves seemed to be weighted down by the promise of money. It was something that couldn't be ignored.

"Damn, Chuck. That shit ain't me. These are *his* ideas, not the reason why I got in the game. Maybe he needs to start rappin'. Then he can kick any kind of lyrics he wants. He can cause whatever commotion he wants with whatever mud—*and what the fuck does he know about the mud*? And I swear, Chuck . . . if that white boy uses the word nigga again in my face, I'm gonna—"

"Ringo." Chuck extended a hand and vice-gripped Ringo's kneecap. "Lemme tell you somethin'. I'm your friend. I'm lookin' out for your best interests. I want you to remember your priorities . . . your family . . . your little baby boy. The music is just the means to an end, but the end is to feed your family. The end is your destiny . . . to live prosperously. Fuck what the lyrics say, kid. People are gonna listen to it for six months and they're gonna forget about it after six months and a day. The issue is that man over there is about to lay big money in your hands. Now . . . if you don't wanna do this . . . if you really and truly don't wanna do this, then it's fine by me. Your decision is my decision. Sure, I'll cry for a whole year, but I'm by your side. I just want you to understand one thing, Ringo: That man there? The freak with the yuck-mouth and the green feather earring? He just offered you a million-plus. That's a quarter-million from the summer tour, the five hundred thou for the second album . . . the sound tracks, a *Soul Train* performance and a Grammy. Ringo, this is where life separates the losers from the winners. All you need to do is go back over there and say yes."

Chuck got up and allowed Ringo to think alone. But the moment he did, Justin came over to take his seat.

Justin said, "*Wow*. That's a lotta cheese he just put up . . ."

But Ringo didn't listen to him. He was too deep in thought. He thought back to Queens Boulevard, where life seemed to begin for him . . . where things took that major shift, and where survival skills were necessary. He thought about his Bridgeport friends . . .

Mister, I don't know who you are or what drugs you sell, but you can't buy me. And I don't know what made you think I was for sale. . . . Ma holds it down. But when we go to the club it's me that gets most of the numbers. She might beat me out once in a while, but all the niggas say I'm hot like fire. . . . I'm really sorry, Ringo . . . You've been like a prince charming to Tangi . . . a hero . . .

Justin was still talking. "And just because they're laying out a quarter-million in advances doesn't mean squat. You'll still have to pay that back. You'll still have to recoup all of the expenses the label is paying for, and the money comes from record sales . . ."

But Justin may as well have been talking to the wall. Ringo was far away from Justin, the meeting in the Waldorf-Astoria's lobby, and he was even far away from New York City.

. . . Respect, respect . . . you definitely got the skills, dawg . . . I'm feelin' you. Yo, can't front . . . I got like four tracks that I can say fit your style. . . . You're fantastic . . . hot . . . like blazin'! Can I get your autograph? We can have two thousand CDs ready for you by Thursday. . . . A successful rapper needs a strong driver-slash-bodyguard by his side, don't he? . . . It's the money . . . I just wondered where it was all coming from . . . Bridgeport! Are you ready! It's no dream, baby. You must have pushed Bridgeport's button last night. Word of mouth gets around quick here . . .

Man, I don't need this bullshit. Tell the bitch the pussy wasn't worth shit anyway. AND you can kiss your airplay good-bye. . . . Ringo looked at Justin, but his lips were moving like in a silent movie. Whatever he was saying wasn't reaching Ringo. It was somehow being blocked by his own subliminal thoughts.

"And another thing," Justin said. "The money may add up to a million plus, but there are fees to consider, like your manager's ten percent, maybe the booking agents, and then you have your taxes to think about. You can't sleep on the taxes . . ."

. . . This is Irwin Johnson, staff writer and music critic here at The Source *magazine. . . . Sounds like you're doin' real good, Ringo. This makes what? Ten thousand CDs . . . Solo. He sell me many, many CD and tape. I pay cash, then I sell on street . . . please, I don't want trouble. . . . Cats call me Brooklyn, like the borough . . . We'd like to get you on the PGD team . . . we're lookin' for someone just like you. . . . This is Clyde Hayes—everybody calls me Fathead . . . I wanted to discuss a possible exclusive booking agreement with our agency . . .*

". . . But of course, this is all just my one opinion, Ringo. The truth is, you need to get your own entertainment lawyer—not just the guy who checked over your PGD agreement. And not a corporate suit or one of those tightwads that represent PGD. No, you need someone who is independent. Ringo, are you listening to me?"

"Huh? Uh, yeah. I hear you, Justin."

"I can't tell. It looks like you're daydreaming or somethin'."

. . . Porsha hasn't been around for a few days, Ringo. . . . She's never acted this way before. . . . Her mom lives across town on Regina Street. . . . My daughter's down at the clinic gettin' rid of that bastard you put in her. . . . Please! Somebody . . . what floor is the clinic on? Look, I don't wanna hurt you—I don't wanna hurt anyone . . . I didn't know she was pregnant . . .

Please! I need her . . . I want the baby. I know she'll want it too! Go get er, buddy. . . . Oh, Ringo. I prayed and prayed that you would come and stop me. . . . I didn't know you cared. . . . This is the Bridgeport *Police Department! All residents are asked to remain indoors . . . I shot him. Ringo, I shot the mothafucka . . .*

So many images blinked on and off in Ringo's mind, and with Justin in front of him, it was as if he was watching a split screen. On one side, Justin was consulting him, giving him a law student's sound advice, or at least the best he could think up. Meanwhile, beside Justin was a flashback—a quick time rewind of all the turning points that both guided him and offended him. Each scenario, good and bad, made him think about Porsha and his newborn son. He considered all of his past struggles, his brush with death and how he could've been the one who ended up dead instead of Cooksie. It was an uphill climb that brought him here.

Damn. A million dollars. I've never seen or touched that kind of money. And now this guy is throwing it my way and all I have to do is go back over there and say yes.

"Is this what you went through with Diamond?" Ringo asked. The question was directed at Justin, even though Ringo was looking across the way at Brooklyn, Chuck, and Jamie, who was urging Ringo with her eyes to get on with it.

"Well, I wasn't there in the beginning. So I can't exactly say what type of offers she got. I'm still learning every day. I can say that her situation is a lot different from yours.

"Mo City is a different family—but hey . . . I'm sure she had to face some big decisions just like you are now. I do know they've asked her for a few pop songs since the merger, so that she can attract a broader audience. It's crazy, really, this whole bit about crossing over and erasing the lines of separation. But Diamond is built for this. She's made for the big-time. Trust me."

The way Ringo heard that was: *Diamond is ready* . . . are you? But he didn't speak on it. There was too much else weighing down on him right now.

Chuck seemed relieved to see Ringo up on his feet, strolling back over to the meeting. It was as if his thoughts were being broadcasted: *Yes! I knew it! I just knew he'd go for it . . . This means a down payment on a new house . . . a new car . . . a bigger office. Yes!*

Ringo pursed his lips and tolerated the unseen judgment, however incorrect it was. In the meantime he went along with the newly created format. In other words, he signed away his soul.

"I knew that you might have legal questions for the more complex parts of the agreement."

Brooklyn raised his hand as he spoke. It was the sort of signal that one would exercise to summon a waiter.

Ringo turned to see two suited men—Justin knew them as tightwads—who were seated nearby. It never occurred to him that Brooklyn had his legal people on standby, or that he assumed his offer would be accepted without further delay.

"So it seemed prudent to have a lawyer on hand, ya know . . . just in case."

"You know what, Brooklyn? And this is real. I don't need any lawyer to help me with this. Wanna know why?"

Brooklyn swiveled his head some, curious about what Ringo meant.

"Because I can look you dead in the eyes"—Ringo did just that—"and I can say with all my heart . . . with every fiber of my being . . . so help you God, you will do the right thing by me."

Brooklyn rolled his eyes until they met with Chuck's, as if to ask, *What are we getting ourselves into?*

"Of course we will, Ringo. I wouldn't have it any other way," said Brooklyn.

On page after page, Ringo scribbled his signature, knowing that he was lending himself as a tool for the freak producer, Brooklyn Jones.

What he didn't know was that he was more than just a tool. From the very beginning, he was a target.

Chapter Nineteen

HITMAN STUDIOS, NYC

THE HIT PRODUCER, Jay Adams, was sitting beside Chet, his engineer, with the monstrous sixty-four-track Cyborg soundboard facing them. Its flashing indicator lights, slide buttons, dials, and meters were so sophisticated that you'd think it controlled a rocket about to be launched from somewhere nearby.

Walls of electronic devices and production equipment surrounded them, and where there was no expensive sound equipment, gray spongy foam filled in, insulating the control room so that the atmosphere had the snug effect of being shut inside of a jewelry box. Diamond was on the other side of the picture window in the soundbooth with its polished wood floor and a few upright microphones. There was a stool for her to sit on, but Diamond was up on her feet at the moment, taking instruction over the intercom system.

"We're gonna go for a second take, Di. From the bridge, okay? And let your voice carry on the part where you sing '*What can I look forward to?*' Let's do it."

Diamond gave "the Hitman" a thumbs-up and slipped the headphones back over her ears. The music started again and Diamond began to sing.

"I came dressed to kill
I've got dreams to fulfill . . .

What about you?
What can I look forward to?

This is my life at large
and it's a must that I take charge.
So what are you gonna do?
Do you even have a clue?

Diamond continued singing, but the music shut down in her earphones. The Hitman had all he needed. The intercom squawked again.

"That's hot, Diamond. Super hot. Take five, boo. Good job. We're gonna set up for Ringo now.

Ringo was in the next room over, a lounge that came complete with a multimedia center, a PlayStation, a table with an assortment of snacks, fruits, and a minifridge stocked with bottled water, soda, and juices. Next to the refreshment table were a couple of outdated coin-operated video games.

He was freestyling, with headphones snug over his ears, when Diamond stepped out of Studio 12. He wouldn't have recognized her if her name wasn't posted on the door—she was dressed in oversized gear and had on a fitted Red Sox baseball cap that shadowed most of her face. Those hoop earrings she wore caught his attention as well.

Ringo turned off his iPod and got up from the couch.

"You look surprised to see me," he said as he accepted the singer's hug.

"If you heard the horror stories—how guys show up late or don't show at all—you'd understand. I try to keep things on a professional level, ya know?"

"*Wait a minute*—" Ringo cut a look at Diamond, pulling his head back.

"I thought we were tighter than that. You were practically breastfeeding Quentin a couple weeks ago . . ."

Diamond had a strange look on her face. "Me?"

"Yeah, you. So how you gonna lay all those other rappers' faults on me? I thought we were *here*." Ringo gestured with his index and middle finger in a V formation, shifting them back and forth between them, so as to show an eye-to-eye understanding. His eyebrow also furrowed angrily.

"Sorry, *really*. I didn't mean—er, sorry I doubted you, Ringo. Don't be so serious, man."

Diamond seemed distressed, and that was all Ringo wanted.

"Psyche!" Ringo snapped, then broke into laughter.

Diamond put her hand to her breast.

"See . . . now you're gonna give me a heart attack before I reach twenty. You had me goin' there." Diamond playfully punched him.

"I dig it. I was actually lookin' forward to this. I haven't stepped in a studio in a while and I can appreciate a break from all the travelin'—in and out of hotels, dressing rooms, fast food joints. You know the deal."

"Do I? I not only know, but I feel your pain."

"I think they're ready for you inside," she said.

Diamond saw Ringo as not only a label mate that she'd do collaborations, concerts, and joint promotions with, but also as a friend. Porsha was so down-to-earth! And Quentin was so loveable that she wanted him as her own.

Kianna had been in the corner of the control room watching things from a quiet backseat perspective. And now she was entering the lounge to join Diamond and Ringo.

"Diamond! That was some work in there! And Hitman loves you—he wants you to sing some hooks for some other artist. I dunno . . . we'll talk about it later."

"Thanks, Kianna. You weren't playing backseat driver, were you?"

"Nooo, *Miss Thing*. I was on the phone handling *your* business. By the way, we're on for *Diary of a Diva*, and your mom wants you home for dinner on Sunday. Something about a family unity day? Oh, and . . ." Kianna moved closer, like she had a secret. "I wouldn't mind a few minutes alone with that engineer, Chet. He's kinda cute."

Diamond rolled her eyes and turned back to Ringo. *See what I have to put up with?*

"Ringo, any chance you'll let a starving songbird hear what you're gonna say in your rap?"

"It might be a little hard-core. You sure you don't wanna wait till I go in the booth with music 'n' all?"

Diamond sucked her teeth and hooked her head toward Kianna for support.

"You believe this knucklehead?" Diamond turned into a child, jumping at Ringo and taking what she could of his neck and head into a half-nelson.

Now, with Ringo giving in to her roughhousing, Diamond threatened him with her fist.

"If you don't kick it for me, we're gonna both punish you and leave you at the bottom of the East River . . . then I'm gonna get rid of Porsha and keep your son all to myself!"

Kianna was mortified. "Diamond!"

"Okay, okay! I give in . . . I'll do it, I'll do it! *Damn* . . . you sure you don't belong on the WWE and not in the music business?"

"You two are friggin' crazy!" hollered Kianna. Just then her cell phone rang. *"Reaally,"* she said, and stepped outside to answer the call in a less aggressive atmosphere.

Ringo finally got himself together and shrugged. *You asked for it.* Then he simulated a bouncy drumbeat with his lips.

Diamond stood by with her hands on her hips—it was less an authoritative stance and more of a model's pose.

"*Yeah, I'm in your milk, but more like in your mouth*
Don't get me twisted with them others goin' down
south; I ain't no drugstore cotton, and trick, I don't wear
chains. Ain't no Kool Aid runnin' through this nigga's
veins . . ."

Ringo stopped.

Diamond had been staring, even losing focus in the face of Ringo's hard-core lyrics.

"Why did you stop?" she asked.

Ringo wagged his head. "You ain't feelin this," he said. "I can do something less hard-core."

"Are you kidding? I loved it. Come on, Ringo . . . please, lemme hear some more."

He arched his brows and continued. Again he started to beat box.

"I'm the hardest, thuggest beast you ever met,
Just lookin' my way already got your stuff wet,
I'm not just up in your milk, but I'm packin' heat
got my nine on your tongue, my four-five in your seat

And don't think I just talk it, I sleep with the steel, like I
live with my past, with dreams you can feel
I'm like livin' with demons, in my head for years
Bodies droppin' all over, and windows droppin' teas

It's a stickup—Boom! And you better lay down or get
shot like that girl in the white suit, skin brown
The lead don't care 'bout you bein' drop-dead fine
'Cause for sho, you'll drop dead—wrong place . . . wrong
time.

Call me Ringo, the legend, I'mma take what I please
what's yours is mine, so get down on your knees
I'm here to get what you got, by any necessary means,
fuck around, and get wet up like them six stiffs in Queens.

I got that bang-bang, that buck-buck, the pop-pop, too,
I'm here to get your ching-ching, so don't make me go
boom-boom
There ain't no stoppin' if it's Diamond and me, 'cause—"

Kianna screamed from across the lobby.

"Oh shit." Ringo gasped.

Chet had come out of the control room just in time to catch Diamond before she fell to the floor.

Kianna was down near Diamond now, and the three helped the singer to the couch.

"*Damn*. What did I say?" mumbled Ringo.

Kianna smoothed her hand against Diamond's forehead and face, too disturbed to respond to Ringo. At the same time, Chet went back into the control room for the first-aid kit.

"Diamond? Diamond? Baby, don't do this to me," said Kianna, a tear traveling down her cheek.

"Wow," said Ringo, shaking his head. "This is crazy. Maybe she been working too hard. You think she's dehydrated?" Ringo wanted any excuse for it to be anybody's fault but his. "Imma get a wet towel," he said.

Chet returned with a smelling salt tablet. He cracked it and held it close to Diamond's nostrils. Diamond regained consciousness, frowning bitterly. She jerked away from the smelling salt. Kianna pushed Chet's hand away.

"Di," Kianna blurted. "God, what happened? Are you all right?"

It took a moment for Diamond to be herself again, for her to focus, but things eventually cleared up.

"Where—where is he? Where . . ." Diamond swung her head this way and that, with great fear in her eyes.

"Who? Who are you talking—"

"Ringo. That man—where is he?"

"He . . . he went for a towel. Diamond? What's wrong? What's going on?" Kianna asked.

"Get me out of here. Get me away—"

Kianna smacked Diamond's cheek. It was a riveting act that stopped everyone from breathing. Diamond put her hand to her cheek. She couldn't believe what her best friend had just done. Then, with her last bit of strength, Diamond grabbed Kianna's blouse. She could feel herself clutching the bra straps underneath. Diamond snarled like a seething beast.

"You . . . get . . . me . . . *out of here*!"

Kianna stuttered, suddenly corrected for all of her overdone guardianship. Meanwhile, Ringo returned, the hero, with the towel in hand.

"I got a—"

Diamond let out an exhaustive shriek. Get way! You get away from me!" she screamed, scrambling to get as far away from Ringo as possible.

Kianna was up on her feet. She put her palm up like a stop sign as she approached him. Then she took the towel and softly pushed him back, away from Diamond.

"Ringo, I don't know what's wrong with her. Maybe you scared her—I'm not sure. . . . Just give her some time. Let her clear her head. Please . . ."

Kianna ushered Ringo into an adjoining lounge outside of Studio 12, where they could be alone.

Kianna was still a bit shaken herself. She'd never seen Diamond faint like that. Then the hysteria. And never ever did she have to slap her like that. Kianna was beginning to think she was losing *her* mind.

"I thought she wanted hard-core?" Ringo offered his best plea. "I mean, I can change the lyrics. It ain't a problem. I just thought I could mix sex and violence—ya know, some real gully stuff."

"Maybe it was too gully—I don't know, Ringo. You work on it. I'll talk with her. Just give her some breathing room, okay? She might need to be alone . . . she's been through a lot.

Ringo shrugged.

Two days had passed since the incident at Hitman Studios. Justin decided to walk instead of taking a taxi or public transportation. He was on his way to Ringo's high-rise apartment, still unsure of how he'd do this . . . how he'd address this *situation* with the rapper.

He walked on, breathing in much-needed fresh air, the calm wind chilling him.

Fall was about to give way to the winter months, a reminder that snow tires and anti-freeze should be on standby, that street vendors better ready their heavy clothing, and the homeless would need to secure some form of shelter, be it a spot on a subway car, the vestibule of an automated teller machine, or a warm patch of sidewalk.

However none of that seemed to matter tonight. Tonight Justin's mind was a tossed salad of issues and concerns. Kianna had escorted a distraught Diamond back home the evening that she fainted. Justin had been working late at the district attorney's office, shepherding cases and zeroing in on the specific ones that were relevant for a pending trial. But when Kianna's phone call came, Justin broke away and raced uptown by taxi.

The moment Justin stepped through the door, Diamond rushed into his arms, crying, attempting to say all that she had on her mind in one breathless, panting outburst.

"I'm sure he had something to do with the robbery, Justin. If he didn't, then at least he knows the ones who did. He knows something! Justin, two of them got away! They were never caught!"

Diamond sobbed into Justin's collar, while Kianna went on to explain about Ringo's rap and the words he used.

"I was taking a phone call, but I told 'em to hold so I could hear. Ringo said some nonsense about demons in his head for years . . . bodies dropping years ago . . ."

Diamond eventually joined in.

"He mentioned a stickup, Justin. He . . . he said get shot like that girl in the white suit. Justin, he was talking about *me*! He even said something about six stiffs in Queens."

Justin played devil's advocate and asked how these statements were connected to Diamond's encounter—her getting shot.

"Don't you see, Justin?" Diamond asked. "*I* was that girl in the white suit. But the six stiffs . . . Justin, there were six people who were killed that day. Get it? Six stiffs?"

Diamond dug into Justin with an intense gaze, one he hadn't seen before. She was a frightened girl who had seen a ghost . . . a rape victim who had spotted her attacker.

"What if he happened to see this stuff on TV? And he just . . . took the concept and made it his own? Plenty of rappers do that . . . pretending to be something they're not."

"Justin!" she shouted. "Are you listening? I can feel it in my heart! In my *soul*!"

* * *

Justin was carrying those words with him even now as he strolled the sidewalks. He was an avenger, set out to pursue a hunch. And this was a strange feeling as well. After all, Ringo was a close friend now.

Justin and Diamond had become closer since the party. There was even a double-date, where Ringo and Porsha, and Justin and Diamond, had dinner together at The Shark Bar. They shared opinions about black radio with its vast universe of personalities. All had their cesspool of opinions and points of view, some more distorted than others. A few were way off center.

They all agreed on how exciting it was to be new in the business . . . how fortunate they both were—the rapper and the singer—to be platinum-selling artists when there were so many hoards of others who struggled daily for that same echelon of fame, of notoriety, of financial freedom. They even vowed to unify, to support one another's projects and to grow old in one another's company.

Justin recalled how clear the future looked from his standpoint, perhaps managing the legal affairs of both performers, overlooking their contracts and future business deals. Naturally, there'd be offspring who would join the family—other entertainers who would hold tight to the mission.

But now all of these possibilities were suddenly swept aside, no longer the priority. Now Justin took things a lot more personally. He had to become an investigator, suspecting everything, digging for the truth about the past.

So far, this was a long shot, but if Diamond was right . . . if Ringo *was* somehow involved, or even if he *knew* anyone involved, then he was no longer a friend. He was a friend of the enemy. Or worse, he *was* the enemy.

Justin arrived at Ringo's place, just thirteen blocks from where Diamond lived on West 43rd street. He was buzzed into the lobby, then rode one of four elevators to the nineteenth floor. He didn't need to knock since Ringo was waiting, standing outside of his door.

"Just . . ." Ringo sounded relieved, but Justin was more confused about Ringo using his nickname—Just. He wasn't sure he wanted to be that personal with him. "Thanks for comin' over. I didn't expect this," Ringo said.

"Don't mention it. You said it was important, so I came right over. What else are friends for?"

"Man . . ." Ringo took ahold of Justin's hand and shook it rigorously, even as he pulled him into the apartment.

"I didn't think you'd come over. I mean, I been callin' and callin' . . . I was startin' to feel guilty, like I assaulted your girl, the way y'all were avoiding me like the plague."

"Well, I been busy myself. And Diamond, well . . ."

"Listen. I don't know exactly what went down the other day, but you gotta give her my apologies, dawg. I mean, we didn't even get to do the remix. Plus, the label couldn't tell me jack. I'm in the dark about everything."

"Relax," said Justin. "Everything's gonna be fine."

Ringo made a face, expressing that he couldn't see how.

"Hey, Justin." Porsha swayed along the floor with Quentin in her arms. "How's Diamond? Ringo said she fainted."

Porsha . . . This is more complicated than I expected, Justin thought.

"She'll be fine. It's . . . it's just exhaustion, I imagine. You know, the promotional tour . . . in and out of hotel rooms, radio stations . . . jet lag. She's got pressure from every direction you can imagine." Justin did his best to cover up his ulterior motive. "But I'm sure you understand . . . I'm sure Ringo's goin' through the same things."

Ringo added, "And that's no lie. It's crazy, because I know I'm platinum, but I don't have that platinum money yet. Whatever I do get my hands on is like having M & Ms—melts in your mouth, not in your hands, if you know what I mean." Ringo rolled his eyes. "Gotta wait for checks, gotta get approvals and vouchers and turn in receipts. Meanwhile, I'm tryin' to get along with this per diem shit. I don't know why the label doesn't at least give me minimum wage so I can live. Hell, I already been payin' for a lot of stuff out of my own pocket. If I had to count on per diems to survive, I'd be starving and homeless," ranted Ringo.

"At least you'll have the limo rides and you can get into the clubs for free," Justin said, trying to inject some humor amid the obvious struggle.

Ringo fed into it, then said, "Even then, the bouncers wanna act like they don't know me—like they didn't just see my video on TV."

"Maybe they didn't," said Porsha.

"Right," Ringo said, tired of that excuse.

"I'm gonna put the baby to bed. You gonna be long?"

Justin answered for Ringo. "Not long, Porsha. Have a good night."

"You too, Justin. Give Diamond my best. And tell her I've been trying to reach her."

"Will do."

Porsha left the room with a warm smile, kissing Quentin's tiny hands and rubbing her nose into his tiny feet.

"You two get along great. Not a bit of stress."

"Don't let the pretty picture fool ya. Now Justin, let's have it," said Ringo, flopping down on a leather couch across from Justin. "What's the real deal? It was my lyrics, I know it. I'm not stupid. Was it too violent? Too much to handle?"

"Could be," Justin replied, not wanting to let on any more than need be. "The lyrics, plus all the other pressures." It was time for the pretending to begin.

"I knew it!" exclaimed Ringo, hammering his fist into the palm of the opposite hand.

"But that's just you, man. I was there at the meeting—did you forget? I know that's what they asked you for. So . . . I guess you gotta do you, so they say."

"Whew. At least somebody understands my side of things. I'm just givin' them what they asked for. Raw shit. I guess they want controversy . . .'cause controversy sells." Ringo wagged his head, perplexed by his dilemma. "Sometimes I don't think these record people make sense . . . they tell me don't bash gays or police, but then they let me spit lines about niggas doin' dirt, robbin', guns, and gangsta shit."

Justin turned his head down, shrugging his shoulders. "I'm not here to discuss ethics or moral issues with you, dude. Deal with that some other time. What did you rap about the other day that pushed Diamond over the edge? I mean what's so bad that she fainted?"

Ringo said he didn't know, then he repeated the rap he spit at Hitman Studios.

"Whoa. That's deep," said Justin. "But I guess that's what an artist has to do . . . shoot from the hip. Express what's in your heart, I mean . . ."

Justin's response was automatic, rolling unconsciously off of his tongue. But his thoughts were something else entirely. *Diamond and Kianna were right. Wow. The stickup, the girl in the white suit, six stiffs in Queens . . .*

"You must've lived some hard times to be so graphic . . . so detailed. I felt like I was watching a movie, putting images together with your words."

"Hard times is all I know, Just."

Tell me about 'em, Ringo. Make this easy for me.

"But this rap thing is like, boom, an avenue for me to get shit off my chest, ya feel me? I can vent. And now that Brooklyn is givin' me the figures . . . now that I have permission to go hard, that's better. It's like therapy for me."

"Yeah . . . uh-huh . . . You're gonna make a mint off of this, so you may as well get the most of it," said Justin.

"I still don't know what to do about Diamond. I mean, are we gonna do this? Or what?" asked Ringo.

"You know women . . . sometimes their emotions stir. Certain things go right to their heads."

Mmm hmm . . . Well, you know I'm ready to get back into the studio whenever she is. I can always adjust things—change a word here and there."

"I'll have to get back to you on that . . ."

"Mista Ringo? Maybe a drink for your guest before I go home?"

"No, Lucy. Thank you," said Justin. "I'm leaving soon."

"Okay. Good night, Mista Ringo and Mista Justin," said the housekeeper, bowing slightly on her way out of the apartment.

"I meant to bring that up the night we all went out to dinner," said Justin, his eyes following Lucy as she closed the door behind her.

"What's that?" asked Ringo.

"Your lifestyle . . . you rap about some heavy issues, Ringo. Things that are mostly about livin' hard, being without, and street survival.

But here you are . . . housekeeper, plush nineteenth-floor apartment, electronic grand piano and artwork on the walls. You're livin' like a king.

How do you do it? How do you keep the hard-core stage presence on one hand, but then come home to so much luxury? Don't you feel, well . . . like you're livin' a lie?"

"That's the game, Justin. I mean, now that I'm all caught up in the spider's web, I feel like just another Hollywood actor, gettin' into character for a movie shoot—only my movie shoots are every day. Plus . . . I've grown up a lot, Justin.

I'm not the same person I was two, three, or five years ago . . ."

Justin let Ringo carry on.

"If you wanna know the truth, there ain't no money in robbin', thuggin', and gang-bangin'. If you do get money, eventually it disappears and you gotta get more."

"Is that why so many rappers leave the hustle game and start up production companies? Every time I turn around there's a rapper talkin' about how he flipped this or stuck up that and turned his blood money into rap riches. Even clothing lines."

"Shit, it's the same way with tobacco," said Ringo, "and alcohol. Those used to be hustles that were outlawed. Then somebody with money and power—somebody like Uncle Sam—flipped the script. They figured, let's legalize and tax this stuff . . . make it legal and get paid forever. But instead of rapping about it, like we are, they advertise. Advertising is the same shit as rapping; it's about broadcasting the message and making people come to buy your product. Only, Seagram's and Philip Morris use billboards . . . and rap cats use the radio."

"What if . . . Did you ever worry about somebody makin' the association?"

"Whadda you mean? Association?"

"I mean . . . what if, say, the government decides to investigate where a rapper's money came from . . . how a rapper built his name and made a legitimate living? You know they have somethin' I learned in school called the RICO Act. The government uses it every time to take down organized crime, shutting down legitimate companies and confiscating homes, cars, money . . . What if they decided to come after you?"

"Then they'd have to deal with the consequences."

"What's that?"

Ringo laughed. "Just think about how much money the first moonshiner made—you know, way back when there was no Internet . . . no computers or cell phones. I bet if you do the research, you'll find that the good ol' boys made the law did it so that they could get rich. I'm not talking about the government. I'm talking about private businesses. As we speak, big *Fortune* five hundred companies are benefitting from the legalization of alcohol, of tobacco . . . shit, of slavery, Justin."

"Wow . . . I guess . . . if you put it that way . . ."

"So if they RICO a rapper, they better RICO a few other billion-dollar industries. In other words, if they make their bed, they better be ready to lie in it."

Justin's mind was sorting through complex scenerios and theories; subjects he'd likely talk to Professor Wilcox about. It was a hell-raising double standard too, the thought of prosecuting one industy and not the other. *Let's stay on the subject*, Justin told himself.

"Is there money in killing people? I mean, I'm just speculating, of course," Justin was cautious with his tone of voice and facial expressions—careful not to point the finger at Ringo.

"That depends. If it's intentional, like if someone owes you money or they hurt a person you love. Or it could be accidental. Sometimes things go wrong, but that wouldn't be intentional."

Was it intentional when you did it, Ringo? Justin couldn't find the nerve to express his thoughts directly.

Ringo went on to say, "The real money is about gettin' out of the life alive . . . makin' some kinda career out of what you know . . . your experiences."

"Damn, Ringo. You should be a preacher for the hip-hop community. Or at least a counselor. Lord knows a lot of rappers need counseling."

Ringo was amused by the idea. "The only cause I'm preachin' for is my own.

That's why I keep up on my readin', so I can be a step ahead in the game. But counseling? That's where you come in, Just. I need you."

"Whew. That's a relief. I mean, I wouldn't wanna be on your bad side and wind up like one of those stiffs in Queens you rapped about."

Ringo smirked, as if to banish a silly thought. Then he said, "Never that, son. What would I do without your good advice? Your good judgment? Stick by my side, Justin—"

What, as your partner in crime? Or your defense attorney? Justin thought.

"—and we can go all the way. Money ain't a thing, you feel me? Cars, trips to exotic places, big homes . . . The way I'm feelin', there's no limit. We can have it all. I'll be an institution one day, just like Run-DMC . . . or Master P, Def Jam or Roc-a-fella . . ."

Justin let Ringo carry on about his pipe dreams while he secretly did the math on his own, putting together the meanings and messages behind the words.

Sometimes things go wrong, Ringo had said. Diamond's rush to judgment wasn't far-fetched after all. *I'm sure he had something to do with the robbery, Justin. If he didn't, at least he knows the ones who did. He knows something!* Her words stirred in his head like tumbleweeds whirling about, like early warnings of an oncoming storm.

If Justin wasn't hearing things, Ringo had more or less served up a confession . . . a testimony that his rap lyrics helped him to unload some burden of truth. No, he didn't admit to killing anyone, but he didn't deny it either. And that was all Justin needed to approach Professor Wilcox for an educated opinion.

"In fact, Professor Wilcox, rappers do run their mouths today. A lot of times they do something called freestyling. . . . meaning he'll spit rhymes from the top of his head. Many times the rapper will be candid, for a rapper to keep it real they have to rap about what they experienced. It's a coded language . . . you have to read between the lines. I could decode the rap, dig into the rapper's history . . . What if I've already done the work. What if I already investigated? What if I was so close that the, ahem, rapper-slash-suspect divulged his innermost secrets . . . about his past . . . about, maybe, a number of murders?"

Justin laid out the particulars, from soup to nuts, and Professor Wilcox was clear in his response explaining to Justin, "Your life could be in danger . . . promise me you'll talk to your boss, the district attorney."

Chapter Twenty

The Beacon Theater had it all. Off-Broadway plays. Rock concerts. Classical and jazz concerts. Old-school soul. R&B and hip-hop.

Naturally, the younger, more impulsive crowds required more security, not only for the safety of those in attendance, but also to comply with the rules of the city.

Hip-hop, rap—whatever people chose to call it—was a form of entertainment that demanded increased security. Two or three times the usual amount of manpower would be on hand to squash fistfights, to wave metal detectors over patrons who entered the theater, and to control the crowd so that things would be as organized as possible.

The Hip-Hop to Fight Hunger Benefit, although an admirable event, was no different from any other affair. This was one of those gatherings that called for heavy security, despite its mission to raise money for the hungry and poverty-stricken. And this wasn't aid that was destined for any third-world nation, either. It was aid for lost souls right here on the streets of New York.

The sound check took place earlier in the afternoon, when most of the event's big names showed up to get a feel for the stage, to forge a temporary bond with sound and light engineers, to correspond with the stage manager and, if they were available, the event promoters as well.

Ringo was one of those performers who did show up on time for the sound check. He hadn't yet become so monstrous a celebrity that he could pass up such preparations with a simple wave of the hand, then "winging it" when it came time to perform. Also, this was Ringo's first big New York City performance since becoming established with his new record deal. Sure, the public had seen him spit his rhymes and his music video for "Just Cause" was in heavy rotation MTV-2 and BET, not to mention a few dozen regional shows, and four or five times that amount of local public access cable shows.

But there had not yet been a show—a live show—in New York.

So this was an important day for Ringo and for everyone else in his camp.

The old Suburban truck had been traded in for the newest version, a special edition of which there were only 100 in the world. What was so special about this model wasn't just the televisions built into the back of the headrest or the climate-controlled Gucci leather seats or the matching dashboard. It wasn't even the illuminated power-folding mirrors, the V-8 engine, or the intense Bose sound system.

"No," Kujo liked to explain. "This motha is also armored and tested to drive on flat tires in the face of a firing squad. It's ghetto fabulous, man! The exterior isn't just black—this is a special blend metallic midnight that had to be ordered. Plus, the interior looks like a suite at the Plaza Hotel—so white that you can hardly tell the seats from the floor. And the chrome wheels? The bulletproof tinted windows? Man! Don't just call this one ghetto fabulous, because it's also battle-ready.

Hey, you never know . . . things get kinda grimy out here in the streets. Especially for a popular rap star." To say that Kujo was excited about the truck he taxied Ringo around in would be a gross understatement.

Ringo's entourage spilled out of the Surburban, as well as from the two accompanying rental cars, until the group of them assembled on the sidewalk, right outside of the Beacon's backstage entrance on West 73rd Street. Tangi and Jamie were ahead of the others, both of them on cell phones, conducting business in relation to Ringo. J-Love, whose job was to join in on the chorus parts during Ringo's stage show, also doubled as an assistant to Jamie, Darlene, Chuck, Porsha, or to almost anyone else who might have use for him. He was an on-again off-again stage performer receiving part-time wages. There was also an additional man added to the Dream Team.

His name was Mel. He was armed and no stranger to protecting celebrities or politicians.

Mel stepped aside and maintained a wider view of the entourage while eight curvacious hip-hop dancers crowded the sidewalk. It seemed like everybody had baggage, be it an oversized sports bag, a wardrobe bag, or a shoulder bag.

Porsha had Quentin in her arms, adding an air of family involvement to the gathering, and Sylvia was there to help Porsha, with a carry-all over her shoulder, complete with an additional blanket, milk, and diapers.

Since this was only a sound check it was safe for Porsha and the baby. "But I don't want you there for the show," Ringo told Porsha. Even he was aware that things could become unruly at rap shows, so it was better to be safe than sorry.

A short white man with a head of layered red curls stood just inside of the backstage door with a clipboard and his own two-way radio, welcoming the entourage and informing them about the wheres and whens behind the sound check. He handed Jamie enough laminated All-Access passes for each member of Ringo's group to be worn around their necks, then he directed them to the dressing rooms. Once Jamie appraised things in the dressing rooms, she became loud.

"I specifically asked for everything on the rider to be in place by two," barked Jamie when she saw no bottled water, clean towels, fruits, vegetables, or the other accommodations that were customary for a performer's dressing room. And seconds later she was on the cell phone, dialing up the promoter's number, eager to chew him out for the inconvenience. Ringo saw Jamie's face turn angry and it reminded him of a show he'd done at the Indiana Black Expo. Things weren't in place and Jamie had a fit. All Ringo could even remember of the expo was so many black folks looking at Jamie like she'd lost her mind. And he didn't want a repeat performance.

"Jamie, don't trip on them people. We don't wanna act like no uppity niggas with attitudes. We got our own bottled water and towels. Plus, we can always send Butter or J-Love out for other shit."

"That's not the point, R . . ." Jamie had begun using the nickname R ever since the merger, when things grew so large in such a short period of time. "They're supposed to be ready for us. It's the principle that's important here. If they don't respect our needs now, word will spread that we're soft, and before you know it, every promoter will—"

There was a knock at the still-open dressing-room door.

"Room service!" announced a uniformed woman, pushing a cart loaded with the missing accommodations. At first sight, it looked like a miniature garden. Everyone's eyes reached out to the variety of fruits and vegetables. Sliced cantaloupe, watermelon, apples, pears, and oranges. The slices were set in many semicircles, built up as a foundation for the center arrangement: small hills of strawberries, seedless grapes, and cherries.

"Sorry I'm late," said the woman. "We're missing two waiters who got stuck—some big subway accident downtown. I'll have your cold cuts and water up here in a jiffy." Ringo and Jamie shared a compassionate expression.

"Ahh . . . miss? Please . . . take your time. We're not in any rush," said Jamie, already with her cell phone put away like some incriminating evidence. For the rest of Ringo's group, it was business as usual. There was a show to put on.

The evening's lineup was posted on the dressing-room wall with approximate times for performances.

The dancers were already dressed down in skimpy outfits, out on the stage adjusting their choreography, making the most of the space provided in order to make this latest platinum artist shine.

By two thirty that afternoon, Ringo and J-Love were on stage rehearsing "Just Cause" and "Push" with the dancers.

Jamie was in the empty auditorium, watching the stage from a distance, while at the same time tending to a handful of other concerns.

"Darlene, do you think you could put J-Love in a darker jersey? Like, maybe navy blue with gray lettering? I know I've seen one on him before."

"Don't you like red, Jamie?"

"I do," Jamie lied. "But the hype man isn't supposed to outshine the star. We're supposed to get some press coverage tonight. Change it." The stylist left Jamie's side, heading down the aisle to return backstage. Sylvia, J-Love's friend, passed Darlene from the opposite direction. The two exchanged an effeminate high five, more a coddling of hands than anything else.

Jamie noticed the show of affection and secretly scorned it.

"Jamie," Sylvia said, "were you able to get the extra tickets I requested? It's getting close to—"

"Not now. I thought you were helping Porsha with the baby? Because you are friggin' annoying me right now. Tickets are the last thing on my mind."

It was a dismissal—a hate-filled one—and Sylvia swung away, sulking as she did.

"Is it me? Or has the woman become somewhat extra annoying since she started eatin' Darlene's fur? Jesus." Jamie directed the comment toward Butter in the row just behind her. He shrugged.

Whatever. What do you know about women anyway? Jamie thought.

"What's the update on the girl?" Jamie asked after a brief huff and puff.

"No answer," said Butter.

Jamie put her hand to her forehead, a thinking gesture.

"Okay, Butter. Gimme your opinion. Do you think she'll go for the settlement?"

"Did somebody mention a settlement?"

"Oh, Brooklyn . . ." Jamie's hand shot to her chest. "Scared the shit outta me." Then, to Butter, she said, "We'll talk later. See if you can make any progress on that, would you?"

Brooklyn took the seat nearest Jamie.

"So what brings you here, B.J.? You know I have things under control."

Isn't this our boy's first New York appearance? I came to check out the show.

And by the way, I'm not buying the whole 'I have things under control' bit. Now, what's this about a settlement? And why is my office getting these crazy phone calls from some girl named Donia?" *Damn.*

"I was hoping it wouldn't some to that, B.J. I figured I could nip that in the bud before—"

"With a settlement, Jamie? Come on . . . is that something I'd do?"

"Yes, as a matter of fact, it is."

"Not in this case, doll. . . ." Brooklyn had a Coke bottle in one hand, only that wasn't soda that filled one-third of it. "Why didn't you just come to me in the first place? This one's a cinceh."

"How?"

Brooklyn spit into the bottle before responding.

Let the kid deal with his baby momma issues. Why go out of your way to protect him? A little drama never hurt a good promotion."

"I just—I figured it was too early for the controversy. And I didn't wanna stir things up before the awards shows."

Brooklyn wagged his head. "Fuck that. This plays right into our original plan, Jamie. Trust me. Just go on and let him deal with it . . . let the cards play themselves out. You'll see what I'm talkin' about."

While the two spoke, Ringo and company merged into the second song. Jamie sighed. "You're the wizard, B.J."

"I'm the truth, doll. Oh . . . let's see if we can't add a few more dancers to his stage performance," said Brooklyn, looking ahead. "Tits and ass never hurt SoundScan reports."

"Ahh . . . Mr. Moneybags . . . did I hear you mention a budget increase? You know extra girls means extra dough. Pussy don't come cheap."

"Depends on whose pussy it is, doesn't it? Last I checked there was a long list of wannabes waiting for a shot to ride this pony . . ."

Brooklyn eventually turned to Jamie and pinched her cheek. "Handle it without the extra budget. Promise 'em a shot in his next video. Do I need to explain this stuff to you?"

Jamie smirked. *Figures.*

"Do I?" Brooklyn pressed.

"I'll handle it, B.J."

"Good," he said. Then, before he turned to leave, he asked, "Did your friend join the game yet?"

"Tonight. After the show."

"See that? I knew you were the girl for the job . . . *Ciao*."

"Good-bye, B.J."

By 8 p.m. a little more than half the auditorium was filled. Plenty of patrons were still bustling outside in front of the theater, waiting for dates, waiting in line, or just waiting period, uninterested in the opening act—more interested in nosing around, surveying all the brown-skinned folk who assembled under the Beacon Theater marquee.

At 8:15 a host came to the stage and welcomed the early birds. Then he introduced Ringo as the first performer. There was unconvincing applause, however the loud familiar music encouraged the crowd's whims.

Even as people still negotiated their way to their seats in the darkened theater, they couldn't resist the energy up on stage. A series of spotlights targeted the dancers alone, all of them engaged in a boot-stomping fraternity dance. It went on for long enough to draw attention, even with no sign of Ringo.

At last, Ringo woofed his first line and an explosion was detonated at center stage. There was brilliant, blinding light, fiery sparks raining down, and a cloud of smoke.

While all of the fireworks erupted, the rapper appeared to shoot up from the stage floor, springing just a few feet in the air before landing on his feet. Then, as if that were an everyday maneuver, Ringo proceeded to perform for an unstoppable fifteen minutes.

When he was done, he barked "Hip-Hop to Fight Hunger!" into his wireless microphone. It was an obvious last-minute effort to show his concern, embracing the theme of the event.

The crowd's response was lackluster, at best.

"Goddamn," exclaimed Ringo, the instant he got offstage. "What the fuck they want me to do, drop my drawers?"

"You did good, babe. Fuck 'em," said Tangi, handing him a

face towel. Sweets and Mel were with her, and they escorted the rapper to his dressing room.

"Fuck!" Ringo paced back and forth like a misjudged boxer. "You think they could hear me all right? Too many dancers? What?"

Jamie eventually made it into the room, a smile on her face. "You killed 'em, R."

"What?! Jamie, I'm not for your sugarcoating right now. Were you even watching the show? Did you see the crowd? Dead as the crypt keeper."

"Ringo, what are you talkin' about? I was in the first row. You looked good. Especially the opening. Nobody was ready for that. They're still talkin' about it."

Ringo sucked his teeth, pulling off his jersey and toweling off his bare chest, then his underarms. All he could think about was getting out of the concert hall and back to what was comfortable, to where people could appreciate him.

"Don't take long," said Jamie. "I wanna bring you out to meet some fans."

Ringo made a face. *Yeah, probably two little girls who make a living out of collecting autographs.* Once he got himself togther, Ringo was accompanied by Jamie, Sweets, and Mel, winding their way through the corridor to where the stage door led to the auditorium. The second performer of the event was already on stage flipping his lyrics and pulling off magic tricks at the same time.

The moment Ringo stepped out into the auditorium a group of teenage girls clustered around the entrance. A few of them shivered as if experiencing anxiety attacks.

"Oh my God, oh my God!" one girl cried, and she pushed past the others. "Ringo, I love you so much. Your skills are just—oh my God."

Jamie stood aside to see this, snapping a few photos with her pocket camera. She then nodded at Sweets, a signal for him to let another girl past. That same girl forced her way past those closest to Ringo and more or less lunged into his arms, burying her face in the crook of his neck. Her praises were muffled, but were still understood.

Jamie snapped more photos as the girl jumped up and down inside of Ringo's embrace. When she had the shots she needed, Jamie signaled Sweets again to pull the fan away.

The disorder grew too much for the narrow passage and an usher asked that the activity be moved farther into the lobby area.

Ringo was escorted along the aisle and he managed to autograph a couple of CD covers along the way. In the lobby, he fulfilled another request, autographing a wrist, a girl's cleavage, and yet another girl's neck. Just a couple of young men stepped up to give homeboy hugs to Ringo, their way of giving "props" without weakening their hard images.

"Can you take my tape?" asked an aspiring rapper. "I'm tryin' to get put on like you was."

Ringo wasn't in a position to help other rappers right now; he was still busy trying to build his own career. But he took the tape anyhow, promising to listen to it and offering what he could in the way of encouragement.

After some more small talk, kisses on his cheeks, and autographs, Ringo headed back to the auditorium to catch one of his favorite old hip-hop performers. He got hyper, just like the rest of the crowd, when The Blastmaster came to the stage. There were no sexy dancers to accompany him . . . no special effects. Just the rawest lyrical delivery, coupled with bass-heavy music to move the crowd.

Ringo studied the rapper's delivery, his confidence, and his overall magnetism. There was rarely a curse word or a gratuitous reference to designer labels, drugs, or violence. And if any of those concepts were used it was done creatively, as a metaphor.

It was a bittersweet experience to watch this—the Blastmaster being such an obvious contradiction to himself. Ringo was a new artist, wet behind the ears in comparison. And his lyrical content was no match.

He got all this mad respect, Ringo told himself. *But at least I'm workin' with the big-money deals . . . the platinum sales, the movie sound tracks, and sexy chicks who want me to autograph their breasts.* These secret thoughts were the only means by which Ringo could make excuses for his place in the hip-hop game. *I guess it's different strokes for different folks,* he rationalized. But underneath it all, despite the money and pop status, he still couldn't help but realize the power of the legend. The voice. Ringo conceded to playing the cards he was dealt.

"We got the whips out back, Boss. you ready to be out?"

Whips. Ringo smiled to himself, recognizing how Butter was growing younger, even using younger, hipper terminologies in his everyday vocabulary. It seemed comical to hear Butter, who was in his forties with a slight pot belly and traces of gray in his hair, using words like *whips* (instead of *trucks* or *cars*), and *let's be out* (instead of *let's go*).

As a group, Ringo and company retired to the dressing room, collected their belongings, and headed for the backstage door at 74th Street.

"Hey, Ringo, can I get an autograph for my son?" asked the short redhead who first admitted the rapper to the concert hall earlier in the day.

Ringo was a little tired and anxious for the big dinner planned, but he obliged the doorman nonetheless.

Mel, Butter, and Sweets evaluated the mob scene outside and conversed among themselves as to how they'd handle things.

"Listen, Ringo . . . Jamie, we're gonna keep it moving once we get outside, all right." Mel announced it more as a directive than a request. Ringo nodded, feeling like the president again, ready to submit to any commands from his security team.

Mel spearheaded the entourage as they stepped out into the night. Butter and Sweets were to the left and right.

"Sorry, people . . . sorry, we gotta keep it movin' . . . No more autographs, sorry." Mel, Butter, and Sweets had their arms extended, blocking off access to the rapper, parting the mob, moving ahead toward the waiting vehicles.

"Well, well, well . . . if it ain't my main man!"

The voice was loud enough to capture Ringo's attention, and his eyes shifted to the brick wall exterior of the theater. There were four figures, all of them men under thirty, in dark leather or denim. All had on hats of some sort, making it difficult to get a full view of their faces.

At first sight, Ringo nodded, merely acknowledging the squad. Meanwhile, he kept up the pace in the direction of the waiting Surburban.

"Ohhh! So you don't remember a nigga now? It's like that? You just gonna ignore your ace-boon?!" It was the guy standing taller than the others.

"Ooooh, can I have an autograph? Oooh, please! I'm gonna be your baby momma, Ringo." A young female fan tried to get past Butter, but it was no use. Her begging fell on deaf ears.

Ringo mostly disregarded the fan, and his attention was once again with the shady characters by the wall. He was catching glimpses of them through the forest of bodies blocking his view. The guy that appeared to be taller was also standing on something . . . a box, maybe. Another had a bagged bottle in hand. A third was smoking.

A wall lamp overhead added to the distractions—fans waving and yelling Ringo's name, camera flashes—and especially with the entourage being encouraged to keep it moving.

There was an instant when Ringo caught a full-on view.

"Its me, muhfucka! Damn—what you poppin', stupid pills?" The words were supported with a semi-smile, the loud one somehow sure that Ringo wouldn't let him down.

"Hold up, Butter," said Ringo. "I need to holler at somebody."

Butter was confused. Mel was still moving onward, with Tangi, Jamie, and J-Love behind him. Ringo put a hand up, holding Sweets back.

"It's okay, Sweets . . . old friend of mine."

Sweets shrugged and nodded all at once while Ringo cut away from his pack and worked his way through bystanders and fans alike.

Brice.

It was as if a switch had been flipped, and Ringo was detoured from his mission, his rhythm, and suddenly sucked up into a series of homeboy-hugs and he-man handshakes.

"How the fuck I'mma forget a crazy nigga like you, Brice? Wassup!?"

"You, nigga! You wassup, all Hollywood 'n' shit, wit ya big-ass bodyguards—bitches screamin' ya name. I just about had a heart attack seein' you on TV. Damn . . . you done it big, dawg." Again, the two drew into a brief hug.

Ringo bowed his head some, but the pride was apparent in his slight grin.

"Can a nigga carry your bags? Shine ya shoes? Damn . . ."

Ringo smirked and said, "You still crazy as shit, Brice."

Brice put his arm around Ringo's shoulders and pulled him in, as the two turned away from the others.

"Yo, call me B-Money. That's what they call me now. You know I ain't tryin' to hold nothin' from the past. Nothin' to connect me, nah mean?"

"How 'bout just B?"

"Whatever, you rich muhfucka. You could call me B, C, D, E . . . whatever." Brice laughed. Butter, Sweets, and Mel stood between the crowd and the area where Ringo and his buddy stood.

"You all right?" Brice asked, now out of range of the others. "I mean, they ain't pimpin' you or nothin', are they?"

"Nah, man. Come on. You know me betta than that."

"Exactly."

"What? *What was that supposed to mean?*"

"Never mind, bro. You just let a nigga know if you need anything, you feel me? Anything . . . I got ya back."

Ringo said, "It's all good. I'm livin' good. Got a kid now . . . a steady girl. I'm in a fly-ass apartment downtown . . ."

"Yeah, yeah, yeah . . . whatever. Nigga, money ain't a thing to me, know what I'm sayin'? I done came up myself. You see my squad, don't you?"

Ringo looked over Brice's shoulder. Thugs 'R Us.

"I got my own damn syndicate, dawg. A muhfuckin' crime family."

Ringo digested the words, the images, and the meanings unspoken. Crime family. Syndicate.

"Yo . . . anybody get at you about that shit?" Brice asked, knowing that Ringo would understand exactly what he meant.

Ringo, on the other hand, was considering how "that shit" Brice asked about was Brice's fault in the first place. *The guns won't even be loaded. . . . Them people will be so scared shit-less that they'll hand it over—just like we say . . .* Ringo had relived those statements so many times since that fateful day. And now they were back in his head again, compliments of Antoine "Brice" Samuels.

"I ain't heard nothin'. You know I cut out the next day. I took my ass out of state to Connecticut."

"Psssh . . . lucky man. We real lucky. And Cooksie . . ." Cooksie's name was faint and distorted enough to sound chewed.

"I know," Ringo replied, unable to look Brice in the eyes. "Too bad what happened to 'im."

"You know they got my face on them Most Wanted posters in the post office."

Ringo thought about Momma Jo's place. She hadn't crossed his mind in what felt like a month of summers. "Yeah? Which one?"

"Which one? All of 'em, man."

"I thought you had your mask on?"

"Yo, I pulled that shit off. Bullets was flyin' everywhere and I was feelin' boxed in. I started blastin' everything and everybody. I ain't give a fuck if they seen me or not. But on the real—I think they went to that bitch's moms . . . remember, the one I offed? I can see her moms goin' crazy when she saw the news . . . the detectives . . . It don't take a rocket scientist to put the puzzle together, especially since I disappeared."

"Damn," said Ringo, looking over his shoulder, wondering how hot things were right this very second. "What if they see you out here?"

"It's cool. I'm a creature of the night now. I'm either fuckin' or sleepin' in the daytime . . . got a spot in Newark. And besides . . ." Brice lifted his shirt some to show Ringo the handle of his Uzi. The demonstration was hidden from anyone else's view, concealed under the flap of his leather jacket.

"Remember this? Dude, me and my boys is strapped like a muhfuckin' SEAL team. Ain't nobody in their right mind want it with me. And if they try, I ain't goin' down without takin' a mess o' Jakes with me."

Ringo's thoughts were still stuck somewhere between the

mention of Most Wanted posters and the sight of the Uzi tucked in Brice's waistband.

Man . . . if I saw my face on a Most Wanted poster I woulda never came back to New York.

"Yo . . . you think they got my face on them posters?" asked Ringo.

"Nah, man. Did you take off your mask? Did anyone see you?"

Ringo couldn't think of anyone who did. His mind wandered, recalling the standoff and the hostage he grabbed, a pretty girl in white who he used as a shield. Things were a blur from then on . . . the cop shot the girl . . . Ringo let her fall to the sidewalk and sprinted around a corner . . . the schoolyard.

"Nah . . . my mask was on the whole time. There's no way anybody made me."

"Well then, shit . . . you ain't got a goddamn thing to worry about. Just keep doin' you, nah mean?"

Ringo noticed one of Brice's buddies chattin' with a couple of autograph seekers. Then he and Butter locked eyes, exchanging a hundred different ideas.

"Yo, Brice, listen—"

"B-Money, man . . . it's B-Money, come on . . . don't blow my steeze."

"My bad. I forgot. B?"

Brice smiled. "Yeah?"

"I gotta split. Yo, let's exchange digits and hook up later," Ringo suggested.

"That's a bet," said Brice.

As Ringo stepped away from his homeboy the fanatics began hollering his name again.

Mel scooped Ringo in so that he was wedged in the center of his security squad. Along the way were more requests for autographs.

"Ringo, over here!" one girl shouted.

"Oh my God! I touched him," panted another girl.

"Sign my hand, Ringo! Ringo!"

And a number of hands reached out with various items—CD

cases, fliers, and photos. One hand in particular made it through, close enough to slap Ringo's chest. There was a small photo.

"Autograph this, you bastard."

Mel caught the invasion through the corner of his eye and he propelled himself into the flailing arms. He grabbed hold of the offender and carried her back toward a wall where a Dumpster was stationed.

"Let go of me!" she screamed.

A palm-corder, flash photos, and roving eyes captured the altercation—the kicking and screaming, and the way this woman was manhandled within seconds.

"Motherfucker, lemme go!" she cried, then let off a gut-wrenching scream.

Butter and Sweets were joined by Kujo, who had been watching over Tangi, Darlene, Sylvia, and Jamie in the truck.

"I'm good, I'm good," said Ringo, stopping the three-man rescue team before they could wrestle him to the Surburban.

But there was something else on Ringo's mind. He pushed his way through the herd of fans and tapped Mel on the back.

"Hold up, Mel. Lemme talk to her . . . please. I got this," Ringo said.

Mel expressed his aggravation, still holding the woman until she calmed. Inevitably, he released her, adjusted his clothing, and stepped aside.

"What's goin' on with you, Donia?"

She had to find herself, but when she did, she turned her eyes to Ringo. It was a surprised look.

"Me?" Donia had her hands on her hips now, and her eyes were bloodshot. "Why don't you ask your handlers, since they wanna try and keep a wall up . . . since they're tryin' to protect you from your past."

Ringo turned and saw they had an audience. He took Donia gently by the arm.

"Come on. Let's . . ."

Donia pulled her arm away, but Ringo insisted compassionately. "Would you just relax? I wanna talk to you in private," he said. Donia conceded.

Chapter Twenty-one

Jamie met with Donia that one time, the day after Ringo's private platinum party. It was her attempt to troubleshoot, to put a lid on the baby-momma drama before things got out of hand. There were fans to consider. There was Porsha, Ringo's steady girlfriend, to consider. Those concerns would affect Ringo's state of mind, and in the end hurt record sales.

But now Tangi had gone out of her mind, no contest for Donia, the woman scorned.

"No, wait, Tangi. She's no harm," said Jamie with a firm grip on Tangi's wrist.

"Fuck that, the girl's actin' a straight fool," Tangi vented. All four of Ringo's handlers, all of them women, were watching the mess from inside the truck—Ringo's mobile lap of luxury.

Jamie's grip tightened.

"Would you trust me? Please, Tangi. Believe me when I tell you, it's part of the bigger picture."

Tangi pursed her lips, having heard that story already, and she held her seat.

"I know one thing . . . the bitch betta not lay another hand on 'im. That's my word."

Jamie rolled her eyes, just another occasion she had to sit through. Another ghetto-fabulous moment. Meanwhile, she was anxious to see this play itself out. A little drama never hurt a good promotion, Brooklyn had said earlier in the day.

But Jamie knew all too well how outrageous these situations could become, how spiteful such bitter women could be. That's why it was her choice to pay this girl off . . . to commit her to silence by some concocted legal document, at least until Ringo could depend on a substantial fan base. She figured, more fan clubs on the Internet, more album sales, and more teeny-boppers with Ringo's name tattooed on them was the answer. Once that was the consistent pattern of activity, Jamie imagined Ringo would become that household name for millions, just as it had been for dozens of rappers before him.

By then, a baby here, a baby there woud be of no consequence: The revelations, instead of projecting Ringo as a deadbeat dad, would only help to empower his mojo. Then let the pieces fall where they may.

However, despite what Jamie had in mind, Brooklyn apparently saw things differently. The drama, according to him, might be what the doctor ordered. How so, Jamie hadn't the slightest idea. She followed orders, nevertheless.

"You guys, I'm gonna need a minute of privacy," said Ringo as he helped Donia into the truck. He didn't see the expression his ex-girlfriend cast on Jamie, that indignant leer.

"Ringo, it's fifty degrees outside. We supposed to freeze our asses off? For what?" Tangi's head rolled on her shoulders, challenging this strange woman's sudden importance over her.

Ringo huffed at this latest headache—five of his close friends all staring at Donia as though she were an alien.

It was during this stalemate that he looked at the photo in his hand, the one Donia slapped on his chest.

"That's your son." Donia's words evoked a chill within Ringo. Her once-dreamy eyes were now resentful.

"My . . ." He swallowed. ". . . son? But . . . how? When?" Ringo looked up, then back at the photo.

"The how part, you already know, Romeo. And the when? When you disappeared," said Donia, sharing her salty, slanted expression with Jamie and the others sitting in the rear seat with their mouths agape.

"How could you do this to me, Ringo? After all we've . . . I believed you," she labored to explain.

"Ahhhmmm . . . I believe we can wait with the dancers for a

few mintues," said Jamie. Tangi gripped harder on the cell phone in her hand. As if to read Tangi's mind, Jamie tugged at her to come along. "Ringo, take your time, but keep in mind that we're starving."

"I thought you'd never finish," said Tangi when Ringo was done. She was the first to leap back into the Surburban once the surprise visit was over with. "Now, if you don't mind . . . who's the girl? And when did you creep out on us to make a baby?"

The truck was in motion now, filled to capacity with Ringo's Dream Team.

"She's an ex, Tangi. It's not what you think. I wasn't creepin' on Porsha." Ringo cleared that up and came to lock eyes with Jamie. "And you . . . you and me gotta talk." Jamie had been on the phone, but she heard Ringo's every word.

Sylvia enjoyed this, Ringo's scolding gaze toward Jamie. Meanwhile, it was Darlene who was anxious to continue on with the evening's events.

"We have three after-parties," she said with a subtle disregard for the obvious issues that surfaced.

"The Kit Kat club, Chaz and Wilson's, and The China Club—that's if we have time. Lighten up everybody. There's nothin' that a little food and drink can't fix."

Nobody argued with Darlene.

Jamie got on the cell phone again to confirm reservations for Chaz & Wilson's. Darlene and Sylvia found things to talk about—the concert, the outfits worn by performers, and which would be the best after-party.

Ringo merely slumped back in the seat and allowed the different images to bunny-hop around in his mind—Brice and his "crime syndicate," Donia and a baby. Two years old?

Of course he's your son, Ringo. Who else was I fucking about three years ago?

Ringo found himself doing the math, counting backward by months and years. It was hard to see Donia as a liar . . . as one of those types who would use a child to spite him. And, of course, her mothering a child was entirely possible.

* * *

"B-Money, lemme introduce you to Christine and Hannah. "Girls, this is Ringo's Ace Boon . . . his brotha and manager. Might as well call 'im Mr. Money Bags," Outlaw snickered with his arms embracing both blushing rap fans. Both of them were shy.

"Really? You really know Ringo?"

"He's Ringo's brother, silly." One of the girls softly punched her friend, reaching across Outlaw to do so. "Of course he knows him," she said, buying Outlaw's lie.

"So wassup?" asked Brice. "Y'all tryin' to party? Wanna meet the rap superstar?" Both girls squealed in shameless agreement.

"Yo, B-Money, they got a couple friends, too. They out front."

To Outlaw alone, B-Money said, "Get 'em . . . load 'em up in the truck. Then, to the cute coffee-toned girl with the braids cascading down one side of her head, he said, "You can come with me." And he winked at her as well.

The B-boyz had themselves four instant and willing dates for the evening, a combination made possible by Ringo's popularity, and that these bad-boy types were seen in the rap star's company.

There was a buzz about an after-party at the Kit Kat Club, so the group of them went there. B-Money flashed his money roll, showing his willingness to pay everyone's admission, but one of the girls came clean about her age.

"I'm only sixteen," she told him in secret. "I don't have ID with me."

Rabbit and E.J. pretended to be annoyed, indicating how their night might now be cut short along with any potential meet-and-greet with Ringo.

B-Money said, "Don't sweat it, girls. Maybe we can go for some eats . . . have our own little party, and I can invite my brother to come by later."

The four girls beamed, feeding right into B-Money's tall tale. And the B-boyz put on a big show of it, treating Hannah, Golden, Christine, and Allison to some White Castle fast food.

"Where to now?" asked Christine, who appeared to be the

prettiest of the fanatics—that is, until B-Money got a good look at her friend, Allison.

Christine and Allison joined B-Money and Outlaw in his pimp-mobile, while Hannah and Golden were with E.J. and Rabbit in the white Chevy Blazer.

Christine took a long swig. She had just reached under B-Money's seat for the bottle, shook up its contents—the concoction of mayonnaise, ketchup, sugar, heavy cream, coffee, and Guinness Stout—and gulped at his so-called power drink.

"What's that?" asked Allison.

"Wanna try?" asked B-Money.

Allison shrugged and took the bottle. She sipped at it and a second later fought to get the Isuzu's window open.

Everybody, including Christine, choked back their laughter as Allison spit the mixture out into the night.

"So, where we goin'?" asked Christine again.

"A place Ringo and I stay at in Jersey. We call it the chamber."

"Whoa . . ." Allison's face changed from a sour and disagreeable frown to a hopeful, reassured smile. Outlaw patted and rubbed the girl's back, more to cop a feel than to allay her brief nausea. "You mean, Jersey, as in New Jersey?"

"It ain't nothing," assured Outlaw. "Just an hour down the pike."

"I never been outside of New York—not without my parents, anyways," admitted Allison.

B-Money said, "We're not gonna get y'all grounded, are we?" Then he snickered.

Christine seemed embarrassed at the idea and immediately replied, "No," sucking her teeth and rolling her eyes.

"We're all cool with it," said Allison from the backseat.

"Exactly," added Christine. "We all agreed earlier, if we run into Ringo, it's like, fuck school . . . fuck the parents. It's whatever goes." Christine reached back to share in a high five with Allison. B-Money looked up into the rear-view mirror, first to smile at Outlaw, and then to check on E.J. and Rabbit in the vehicle behind, wondering if they were having as much fun.

To pass time, B-Money whipped out his cell phone and called E.J. The phone was then passed back and forth among the

B-boyz and their guests. By midnight the girls had all submitted to blindfolds, a measure, said B-Money, to preserve the secrecy of Ringo's private crib.

"Okay, you can take 'em off now," announced Outlaw, his voice carrying inside the cavernous garage.

"Jeez!" drawled Hannah. "Yous all got a lotta cars. Which one is Ringo's?"

Rabbit took the liberty of responding. "Every last one of 'em . . . Just some of the fringe benefits that come with the rap game."

E.J. said, "Yup. Gotta have a whip for each day of the month. That's how we roll."

B-Money was eager to move things along, and his creative thinking led to an idea.

"Thing is, we have way too many cars and trucks for just one rapper . . . Any of you drive?"

"Me!" announced Golden.

Feeling challenged, Christine added, "Well, I have a learner's permit."

Allison bowed her head. Everybody already knew she was sixteen without any adult privileges.

"What about you, Hannah?"

Hannah had her hands in her pockets. She shrugged and wagged her head simultaneously.

"Maybe we could teach 'em to drive," suggested Rabbit.

E.J. tried to read Rabbit's mind. "Yeah," he said. "That's not . . . a bad idea. I'll teach Allison. Pick a car."

"And I can teach Hannah," said Outlaw, crooked smile included. "In the Bentley."

Rabbit said, "Since Golden already knows how to drive, maybe she could teach me a few things . . . in the Jaguar."

Golden looked at Rabbit with her unconsciously sultry eyes, and the three couples gravitated to their respective vehicles.

"Looks like that leaves you and me," said B-Money to Christine.

"But what can I do with a learner's permit?" she asked.

"Learn," he replied with an innocent tone, his arm around her neck, hand dangling close to her perky breast. They strolled in between various vehicles, toward the rear of the warehouse.

"Wassup, Spook?"

"Hey, Boss." Spook was quick to slide the shotgun out of sight.

"My friend here has a learner's permit, so . . . I'm gonna teach her a few things."

Spook was expressionless.

"Mind holdin' my cell phone? And, ahh . . . this." Christine gasped at the sight of the firearm.

"Oh, sorry. Didn't mean to frighten you, boo. Gotta protect the rap stars . . . you never know." Christine understood.

The door was shut tight once they were inside. The chamber was a little messy, but the lights were low, so it mattered little.

"Oooh . . . it's so . . . mysterious," said Christine.

"Yeah. Sit on the bed. Take your shoes off too."

"Wow . . . can't you, like, say please?"

Christine had her hands on her hips.

B-Money was en route to the corner for his routine check. But before he bent down to push the bookcase side, he answered Christine by merely casting his threatening gaze, a killer's naked eyes.

"Okay. God," she said. Then she sat on the edge of the bed, leaning over to remove her shoes.

B-Money slipped a stack of bills from his inside jacket pocket—a mere $20,000—and added it to his holdings. He shut the safe and turned around.

"What're you lookin' at?"

"I . . . sorry—God. Do you have to, like, talk to me so cruel?"

This was the part that made B-Money sigh—the grueling part of his relationships, how he had to break them in. There was no other way to do this. He couldn't befriend women by ordinary means, that whole boy-meets-girl routine, because then he'd have to trust her. A definite "no-no."

So he had to take what he wanted. He had to hold them captive. And when he was done, bored, tired, it was on to the next girl. Sixteen, eighteen, twenty-two . . . it didn't matter. Every one of them could be bought with some form of bait, be it cash or the illusion of generosity.

B-Money approached Christine, a compassionate grin across his lips. It was time to let her in on the reality here.

"I think I wanna go home," Christine pouted. And she bent over again, this time to put her shoes on.

B-Money grasped a handful of her long, brown hair.

"Owww! You're hurting me. Owww!"

He twisted her head so that her pretty white face was turned toward his heartless black one. Somehow, the idea occurred to him that he'd been here before—this exact scenario.

"I got news for you, pretty spoiled suburban bitch. You *are* home. From now on, I am your daddy. Now say that."

Christine struggled. "What?" she cried.

B-Money looked away. *Here we go.* He turned back to the girl and slapped her hard across the cheek. She couldn't get enough air out of her lungs to wail. Instead, there were these broken, openmouthed whimpers pushing out of her. Her pale skin also reddened under constant tears.

"Now . . . again. Who is your mothafuckin' daddy!"

94TH STREET, NYC

Ringo laughed uncontrollably as the comedian on stage talked about the pickup lines he used to get girls.

"These other chicks . . . the sassy ones? Man, they think they all that. Always got something smart to say to a muhfucka. She could be all ass out, breasts blinkin' atcha like searchlights . . . just beggin' to be picked up. So I step to her. 'Hey baby . . . you sure look pretty as a mug . . . How can a brotha get some play?' Then she gonna come up with the slick shit . . . 'Just stick your hand in your pants. Then you can get all the play you want.'

"See, that shit is cold-blooded. I mean, why y'all even go to the club if you ain't tryin' to meet nobody? Then, okay . . . I see this other chick. I'm talkin' about, ass like *Blam!* Breastises like *Pow! POW!* Eyes filled with lust and lips just juicy . . . ready for sucking! She's practically naked in some poom-poom shorts and one of them tied-off blouses. Pretty as fuck, too. But I don't say, 'Baby, you're pretty as fuck' . . . no! I say, 'Baby, you look good enough to eat.' And I figure she'd be ready to be my next meal, right next to the bowl of gravy, nah mean? Then she goes and says, 'And you look ugly enough to call the ASPCA.' Then she gonna just step off. What part of the game is that? Shit! Now, I may not be the handsomest muhfucka on the globe, but I definitely ain't as ugly as the next muhfucka to step to her. How she gonna take a mongoose-lookin' muhfucka over me? Damn! At least I got two eyeballs! Like I'm a scrub or somethin' . . ."

Chaz & Wilson's was jam-packed. A long line waited outside for people to leave before anyone could be admitted.

"Does this mean I'm forgiven?" asked Jamie, after a toast between the group. Tangi, Sylvia, and J-Love were sitting across from Ringo.

Ringo bit his bottom lip and cut his eyes at Jamie in some playful seething.

"I know. I heard you the first time. You'll break me in two and stuff me in a wood chipper."

Ringo let out a hiccup. "Yeah, that's what I'll do."

"Okay, okay. But what I wanna know is, what are you gonna do about her? Is she gonna be trouble? 'Cause that's what I'm here for, babe, to make life as comfortable as possible for you."

"What else can I do? I gotta step up, shit. I know it's my baby . . . my son." Ringo gulped down more Bacardi.

"What about Porsha?" Jamie asked.

Ringo took a breather before answering. "I guess she'll understand. She has to."

Tangi was reading lips and looking through Ringo, perhaps into the future and what it might have in store for him and Porsha, her best friend.

Ringo turned to the comedian again.

"And see, I was keepin' it all the way real, too. 'Cause—show of hands—how many women up in here like to get their pussy eaten? Come on . . . don't be shy . . . Now, ain't that a bitch! You tellin' me less than ten of you want a good lickin'? Goddamn . . . that means . . . one, two, three . . . fourteen . . . twenty, twenty-one . . . Man! There's over thirty women in here that don't want the coochie eaten? Am I dreamin'? Or y'all just stuck up like that? 'I don't want my personal business out there . . . That's for my man to know and you to find out . . .'

"See that, fellas? That's what we're missin' out here today, some cold freaks. I'm talkin' about a chick who ain't afraid to say she want her toes sucked . . . her ass licked . . . how the song go? Lick my neck, lick my back, lick my ass just like that! Man! Now, that there?

That's the freak of the week, straight up! You could put that 'Freak Like Me' singer together with some—what's the name of that old-head freak? Millie Jackson? Yeah. Put them two together, and it still don't add up to the lick-my-ass chick. Word! Ain't nothin' truer than a freak in the bed. As if there were great urgency.

"I'm serious! That shit is straight sexy. Now . . . some of you niggas out there ain't goin' for that, so be careful, ladies. You might catch y'self a beatdown talkin' to the wrong mothafucka like that . . . I can see it now . . . One of you timid chicks in here . . . You'll try that shit this weekend with candlelight, incense, both of you naked . . . a whole mess o' kissing and touchin' . . ." The comedian had his eyes closed and he went through the motions as if in the moment. He even altered his voice to sound like a woman's.

"And you'll suddenly get up the nerve to say it . . ." The comic mumbled an inaudible request into the mic.

" 'Huh baby? I didn't hear you . . .'

" 'I said, nigga, lick my ass . . . ' " The crowed hee-hawed. "And just when you had things all hot and heavy . . . just when you opened your timid-ass mouth . . . *Bam!* The nigga smacks the dog shit outta you. Then whadda you do? You start crying . . . and you end up with a stiff dick in your mouth . . . apologizing! The other half of you are dialing nine-one-one, yelling 'Domestic abuse, domestic abuse!'

"See, but I got the solution to all that . . . like the sayin' goes, baby, you need to drop that zero and get with this hero, word. 'Cause, a lotta dudes would eat that up! I'm serious . . . Okay, so I finally got this chick's digits, right . . . it was after a show. Don't knock the hustle, baby . . . and we talk on the phone for a week . . . yadda yadda yadda . . . After some of that silky talk I laid on her, she agrees to come over the crib. So, *bam* . . . I'm gettin' it all together. I stop at the supermarket. I spend some true playa's dough on a slammin' cuisine I'm about to lay out at home . . ." The comic went on with his story.

Ringo's vision was off, but he swore he caught Sylvia across the table, licking her upper lip in a sexual way. Next thing he knew, it was just he and Jamie sitting together, and across the way were Tangi and J-Love holding hands, making love to each other with their eyes alone.

"Ringo, I want you to meet a friend of mine. Audrey Pitts, meet Ringo, my boss. Ringo, this is Audrey, an old friend."

"Whassup?" said Ringo, his speech slurred some.

Audrey squeezed into the seat beside him.

Butter, Sweets, and Mel were in the next booth, close enough to still secure the rapper, but far enough away to afford him some privacy. The chicken wings, the comedy, and the joyful atmosphere inside of the restaurant made things seem relaxed. Not only that, but the customers here generally allowed the celebrities their space without constant attacks like requests for photos and autographs. Yet, it never failed. There were always one or two who ignored that respect, gloating the whole night long, fans and wannabes alike.

"I liked the show," said Audrey, with her wide, pretty brown eyes and hair pulled back in a bun.

"Thanks. Did you meet Tangi?"

Tangi displayed a dry, tight-lipped smile and the two engaged in a limp fingers-only handshake.

"So, Audrey handles publicity at Warner Brothers," said Jamie. "The jazz department, right, Audrey?"

"Mmm hmm. A small department, but I do my thing," she answered.

Ringo found himself absorbed in Audrey's good looks, looking directly at her when he wasn't focused on the stage. The comedian.

"So she's on her way to the crib, right? And I prepared these two juicy slabs of chicken, about to roast them on my George Foreman grill. And I decide, naw, fuck this. Lemme call this chick's cell phone and make double sure she's on her way. So I call her. She's in the car and says she's about twenty minutes away and that she had to stop at the gas station on the way. So I was amped—'cause how much interference could there be between the gas station and my crib? It was on like popcorn . . . I cut up all the veggies—ya know, like broccoli, garlic, onions, peppers, and tomatoes . . . I seasoned that joint with some Lawry's. That shit makes the worst meal taste good. So, okay, I'm doin' my thing. I even got some parsley to dress the plate when I serve it all up. Plus, I got a pot of white rice that I'mma lay the roasted chicken on. Man! I'm hungry just thinkin' about that meal. The meal to me is like a juicy pussy. Some of you in the audience know what I'm talkin' about—and y'all got that little nugget there that a nigga can just toy with . . . that he can twist his tongue around and around and around until it's all swollen, throbbing with life!"

Audrey was devoting more attention to Ringo than the comic, and he appreciated that.

"I listen to some jazz once in a while," said Ringo.

"I'm startin' to get into Coltrane and Miles, quiet as its kept."

"Good taste," said Audrey, sitting close enough for her hips to connect with his.

"You drinking, Audrey?"

"Sure, Jamie. Whatever you all are having." Tangi yawned for the second time, and Jamie took that as a signal. She turned around in her seat to address the other half of their entourage.

"Mel?"

He turned around. "Could you take Tangi and J-Love home?" Mel didn't respond. He merely finished his last few bites of food and got up to escort the two out of the establishment. "Check with me later," Jamie said.

Mel nodded while Tangi bent down to kiss Ringo's forehead.

"Don't be too long," said Tangi. "I promised Porsha I'd have you home by one."

Ringo nodded and his eyes followed Tangi from behind. It was hard to believe how far she had come, and how fast. It was much harder to believe that underneath the good looks, she was a killer. *My ride-or-die chick,* thought Ringo.

* * *

As the night progressed, Ringo found himself heavily influenced by the string of drinks he shared with Audrey, his new friend. The two of them giggled like it was just the two of them left in the world.

"You two look the sight," said Jamie.

"What the fuck," laughed Ringo, the miseries of his world swept under the rug. "Audrey says you only live once!" As Ringo made his proclamation, he and Audrey accidentally bumped heads.

Jamie cackled.

In the other world, the one swirling beyond their booth, a female vocalist stepped onto the stage in a glittery blue dress that revealed an abundance of bare flesh—the thighs, the cleavage, and most of her shoulders. Her diamond teardrop earrings twinkled as she sang a Phyllis Hyman classic.

"Meet me on the moon
soon as you please . . . .

While her voice fluttered like a bird in a soft wind, she flashed sensual glances at the audience, making everyone feel like a personal friend.

"Jamie, do you mind if I take my, ahem, jazz aficionado for a little dance?" Audrey never took her eyes off of Ringo.

"Chile, you know that man is practically married. Why don't you pick on somebody your own size?" Jamie made a strange face as she said this. And Audrey challenged that with her own.

"And that's just the problem these days. All kinds of lines and limits on life. Can we get past the fences, girl? Accept something exciting once in a while? Ringo doesn't mind, do you, Ringo?"

Ringo had that silly alcohol-induced smile across his face. His eyes were turned upward as he wagged his head, as if the answer to Audrey's question was up to God.

"See? I like a man who knows what he wants." And Audrey pulled Ringo out of the booth, leaving him no other choice but to go along with her wishes. Jamie rolled her eyes and went to join

Sweets and Butter in the next booth, the two of them chomping on chicken, with their eyes glued to the songstress.

"Well, excuuuuuse me!" Ringo testified as he stepped out of Chaz & Wilson's. Audrey held his arm as they looked ahead at the double-parked Mercedes stretch limosine. "This is you?"

"Every inch of it," Audrey said, with that particularly sexual overtone. "Well . . . you know what I mean. It's mine for the night."

Audrey walked arm-in-arm with the rapper, out from under the restaurant's canopy, and into the open door of the limo. She winked at the chauffeur just before he closed the door behind her.

"We goin' somewhere?" asked Ringo.

"Just to the moon," Audrey replied, chuckling. "Kidding, just jokes, baby. Actually . . . what I did wanna have is . . . a little toast."

Audrey reached for his-and-her glasses and gave them to Ringo to hold. Meanwhile, she pulled a bottle of champagne from its bucket of ice.

"Again? What're we toastin' now? We already toasted the sun and the moon . . ."

The cork popped and Audrey said, "Well, I guess that only leaves the stars!" Audrey had to keep Ringo from spilling his drink as she poured. "Ringo, you're gonna drop it."

"You think I"—*hiccup*—"had too much to drink?" His question was accompanied by a drunken laugh.

"Are you kiddin'? You're handlin' your drinks like a champ."

"Me? Whaddabout you?"

"It must be in my genes," was Audrey's reply. "My daddy was a heavy drinker."

Ringo uttered a belch as he said, "Then what does that make you?"

"I guess . . . heavy-er!" Audrey laughed so hard her drink spilled in Ringo's lap.

"Oh shit! I'm so sorry!"

"Fuck," Ringo said, assessing the damage.

"You wasted some expensive champagne there, woman."

"It doesn't have to be wasted," said Audrey, and she snuggled closer to Ringo so that her breasts brushed his arm.

"Huh?" Ringo washed down the misunderstanding with what was left in his glass. "Okay . . . can't spill any more now. It's all gone!"

Ringo wasn't even aware that Audrey had her face in his lap with her hand stroking and gripping his growing erection. Ringo thought he'd seen a ghost. *Is she . . . ?*

"I hope you don't think I'm moving too fast, Ringo. I just . . . couldn't stand . . . not . . . having you . . . in my mouth."

Dazed and flabbergasted, Ringo put up no fight even though his mind was going through psychological turmoil.

One side of his brain was saying, "No, you can't!" while the other shouted, "The fuck he can't! Handle your business, dawg! Who's gonna find out?"

Ringo found himself floating up and away from troubles . . . from mortality . . . from the earth. It was still dark for a time, but as he rose higher, the city of New York and its island of Manhattan began to form, illuminated only by a constellation of lights glowing below. They glowed, and as he ascended farther, they twinkled. Then they were distant stars that vanished, his view distracted only by passing clouds. The object Earth and its nations took shape. He was no more and no less than a satellite now, drifting in space. He could see the sun out beyond the earth. Other planets were farther away—the moon was behind him, close enough to be intimidating . . . big and heavy enough to make his own 150-pound body feel less than significant. In one night, Ringo's past had crept up from behind and smacked him in his head. And now, all was left to the consequences of earthly limitations.

He could see Brice down there with his B-boyz, the team of them hot-rodding along darkened streets, strong-arming the weaker humans, taking whatever resources they desired. He could see Brice shooting those who were uncooperative—the cashier, his inside girl at the Just Right robbery. Brice, the gangster.

Farther along, Ringo's aerial view zeroed in on Donia, his ex-girlfriend.

"Ringo! Come for me, Ringo!" She was screaming out to him from her hospital bed . . . the bed was right in the middle of the street where the shootout was ongoing. Donia had a hospital gown on and her legs were up in stirrups.

"Push, miss! Push! Harder!" ordered a nurse standing between Donia's legs with her rubber-gloved hand inside of the womb. "Push!" Donia screamed and cursed. A doctor stood nearby, arms folded.

"Ringo, you muthafucka! Don't leave me here with the pings—those striking sounds from the bullets flying back and forth. There could've been fifty cops down there, all tiny like toy soldiers, all of them shooting at the pretty girl in white.

There was the loudest scream now. Then a flushing sound. It was the baby. The newborn shot out of Donia's cavity, blood and all, and it got away. The baby began to float, like Ringo did! The baby somehow chased him, still attached to its umbilical cord and the gory sac at the end. The baby's cry got louder as it came closer. Donia was still far away, exhausted on the hospital table—the shootout still progressing around and about her.

All Ringo could do was try and swim away, a laborious task, with only space and time to carry him through the images both repulsive and outrageous.

Something cold and clammy woke Ringo.

The daylight was too much to accept at once. His hand shielding his eyes from the intruding sun, Ringo tried to lift himself up from the comfortable support beneath him. But he couldn't move so easily. It seemed as though the weight of the world held him down on the bed. Not only the burden of the hangover, but Audrey's naked body was laying on top of him. Her legs were parted so that her gluey folds pressed snug against Ringo's leg. Her hand cupped his scrotum and her face was nestled close to the pit of his arm.

What did I do? How did—awwww, fuck!

Chapter Twenty-two

NEWARK, NEW JERSEY

This was what B-Money proposed: "Groupie Heaven," he called it, as if it were an actual place.

E.J. and Allison were in the silver Porsche with its exterior shining so brilliantly it could've doubled as a mirror.

"Come on, don't be such a baby," E.J. told the sixteen-year-old, encouraging her to go ahead and take a toke off the cigarette. This wasn't your average cigarette, since Rabbit and Outlaw had these specially "fixed" for occasions such as these. The tobacco had been emptied, mixed with cocaine, and then replaced.

"You're not afraid of a little cigarette, are you?" E.J. teased Allison, as if to say that she wasn't mature enough for such involvements and she might be wasting his time. He'd used these persuasive tactics in the past, but tonight had been different. This was starstruck pussy. The best kind. "This is the grown-up thing to do, girl. One puff won't hurt you. Plus, you know Ringo smokes, don't ya?"

"Really?"

"Psssh . . . are you kiddin'? He swears by it. And on some real? He won't wanna meet you if you can't get with this. But if he do see you—plus with your good looks? Girl, you're about to be in his next video."

"What?" Allison cocked her head back. "Stop lyin'."

"Babe, if I'm lyin', I'll give you my gold Jesus piece . . ." E.J. lifted the chain and pendant from around his neck. "Matter fact, here, you can wear it now, just to show you I'm serious."

He draped the gold around Allison's neck. She swooned, sucked in by E.J.'s gift of gab. Allison had stars in her eyes, with a mess of false hopes to cloud her judgment.

"Wow," Allison said some time later. "I feel so numb. Like I'm on a cloud."

E.J. grinned his snide grin and felt around inside of her short-shorts, fiddling with her soft pubic hairs. Her tube top was already pulled up to reveal her pointed breasts.

"It's your world, baby. Just let it happen. Go with the flow," said E.J. "Go ahead, take another pull, boo." He passed her the last of the fixed cigarette, she sucked on it like a true amateur and choked. Some of the smoke swirled from her nostrils as she held her breath.

"That's right . . . hold it in baby . . ."

She was holding.

"Now swallow like you have a mouth full of strawberry ice cream." She did. "One bad bitch," exclaimed E.J.

"Who? Me?" Allison put her hand to her bare breasts as she asked this. Allison, the angel. E.J. laughed.

Then he said, "Now come hit me off again."

"Okay," she said in a silly singsong voice. "But remember, I wanna save some for Ringo."

"Don't worry. There's plenty of you to go around." E.J. was already directing her head to meet his exposed penis. His hand grasped a selfish amount of her auburn locks and helped her to slide up and down over his bone-hard erection.

It was the idea of this girl, this absolute stranger, smoking and sucking by his instruction, that gave E.J. a thrill. It was a bigger thrill than even crime and money.

Just then, there was a knock at the Porsche windshield. It took a second to snap out of the spell, but E.J. soon realized B-Money was standing there.

E.J. pulled Allison's head back.

"What's the matter?" she asked.

But E.J. didn't respond, having already zipped up, and now he was stepping out of the car.

"Wassup, B?"

"I got a slight problem," he said. Then he stepped away from the Porsche, back toward the chamber. E.J. gestured for Allison to stay put, and he followed the leader.

A moment later they arrived in the chamber.

"Oh shit. What happened?"

"Things got a little . . . rough. She had some kind of fit—maybe some kind of health problem. Who cares what happened? The bitch stopped breathin'. That's the bottom line."

Both men stood at the entrance to the suite looking at Christine sprawled out on the bed with blood trickling down from the corner of her mouth.

Spook returned now. "I got us some plastic for the body," he said.

"You know what this means, don't you?" said B-Money. "We can't let any of 'em go home."

"Whoa," said E.J., digesting the reality behind B-Money's words. Then he turned to look back across the warehouse where the Porsche was parked. The car door was open.

Allison!

The teenager had gotten out of the Porsche and was standing partially naked, with her hand cupping her mouth and her eyes stretched to capacity.

She was close enough to see this little problem. And now she was backing up, away from the three men.

"Get that girl, man," B-Money ordered. "Before—"

"Nononono Christiiine! Ohmigod! Hannah! Golden!" Allison screamed again. Then she broke into a confused sprint, running awkwardly as Spook and E.J. scattered to catch her by any means necessary.

"As I was saying . . . before things get out of hand. Shit," B-Money said to himself.

B-Money went to inform Rabbit, who had occupied the Jaguar.

"What's goin' on, B-Money?" Rabbit was departing from the Jag even as B-Money approached. At the same time he fiddled with his pants.

Inside the Jaguar, the girl was naked, as far as B-Money

could see. Her face was red with embarrassment. Now she was turning this way and that to get a look at what was happening—what all the excitement was about.

"We had a little problem in the back," said B. "But it's nothing we can't handle. Just make sure you keep that one in check. The last thing we need is—"

"Christine! God help us! Hannah! Golden! It's Christine! They killed her!"

"Stay in the car. Hey!" Rabbit demanded. "Stay in the goddamned car!"

Golden, wearing her Adam and Eve outfit, disregarded Rabbit and worked up an uncertain trot in the direction of the screams.

Even before Outlaw realized what was happening, Hannah sprung out of the Bentley. She still had on her denim poom-poom shorts, but no top. She went to Golden's side and they jumped up and down erratically, afraid for their lives.

B-Money went to retrieve his Uzi and fired it at the ceiling and catwalk high above.

"Now, I'mma say this one time! And one time only! I want every one of you bitches to come to me right now! And I mean, right now!" Whimpers could be heard in the distance. "Don't make me have to find your asses. It won't be pretty!"

It took a few minutes of threats—threats of violence. But one by one the groupies emerged from the far reaches of the warehouse.

"Now, where the fuck did you think you were going? No clothes . . . no way home . . . You can't get out of this place unless I let you out. So you're wastin' your time running. Now call your little Latina friend out here . . . before I start shooting again. And this time, it won't be up in the air that I'm aiming."

The two girls held onto each other, crying with fear. One of them whined. "G-G-Golden? Come on out . . ."

"That's the best you can do?" asked B-Money and he squeezed off a round into the air. Both girls screamed, grabbing each other even tighter. "Now call that jalapeño again—like your lives depend on it. 'Cause they do," B-Money sneered.

Both girls cried out for their friend. Rabbit, Spook, and E.J. all had weapons in hand, standing beside B-Money.

"Got her, boss," announced Outlaw, emerging from a blinding-yellow Dodge Viper. He had Golden's hair in his grip, tugging and twisting her along. Out in the open, it became obvious that she was Golden, both in name and in appearance, as they could see from her pubic area.

"See, fellas? They're stubborn up until they have no other choice," said B-Money. "Get her over near her friends."

Hannah, Golden, and Allison huddled, all of them half naked.

"On your knees. Now!" barked B-Money.

One girl whimpered, but her words were clear enough to recognize. "They killed Christine." And the sobbing escalated as the girls lowered themselves.

"Now, see? You're looking at things all ass backwards. . . . What happened to your friend was an accident. That's all it was. But now . . . if I let you all go home, you'd go and tell everybody I killed her, wouldn't you?"

"Nonono . . . please. We won't say a thing," Allison pleaded.

"We promise," exclaimed Hannah.

"And I guess the same goes for you, too, huh? Huh, my little jalapeño?"

"He's gonna kill us, Golden. He knows he—"

Shut up, you!" B-Money swung the nose of the Uzi toward the bigmouth. Then he gestured to Rabbit.

The girls were holding hands now, forming a sudden prayer group, with broken sobs and wails.

"You know what has to be done," B-Money said in a hushed voice. "But it's gotta be smart. *No* stupid shit. We can't afford to leave a trace—our DNA is all over these tricks."

"Don't worry, Boss. We know what to do."

"Good." B-Money slipped the Desert Eagle .45-calliber from his waistband. He pulled back the slide on the weapon to arm it, then placed it in Rabbit's hand. The transaction was made out of sight from the groupies. "Handle this."

MANHATTAN

Ringo's first thought was to call Butter or Sweets for his rescue. But Jamie showed up before he could make the call.

Audrey, the guilty party, had just gotten up from the bed—her bed—and barely faced Ringo when she slithered off to the shower. The instant was a reminder that this woman was a perfect stranger. He hardly remembered her name, for godsakes.

Ringo hunted around for his clothes, feeling like a domestic pet forced into some foreign environment—the jungle.

It was only when he stood up straight, his boxer drawers in hand, that he noticed Jamie standing at the threshold of the jungle. She had the nerve to make that *tsk tsk tsk* sound with her tongue.

"And here I thought of you as the faithful daddy," she said, clearly ashamed of Ringo.

"Where'd you come from?"

"Baby, I'm everywhere. Now put some clothes on. Ours is a business relationship, buddy. And right now you're way out of line." Jamie's arms were folded and she had this scandalous look in her eyes.

Ringo had to ask himself, *Do I even know you?*

"You look a mess," she went on to say as Ringo scrambled for his clothes. Avoiding a reasonable reply was easy. Especially now that she'd seen him fully naked.

"I feel a mess," Ringo said.

"Take your time. I took care of home—called Porsha . . . gave her a great excuse."

Ringo made a face. "One we haven't used before?"

"Of course. Come on, man. That's my job, I told you—to look out for you. So get it in your mind that Brooklyn needed you to rush over to Hitman's place for a last-minute fix on a remix."

"What remix?"

"Does it matter? Use your imagination, playboy. . . ." Jamie took a moment to investigate Ringo's body parts and the soiled bedding. "You seem to have used it last night."

Ringo was about to jump on her ass for that answer. But she had already spun away, calling for her friend as she did. Feeling defeated and wanting to vanish, Ringo mumbled, "It's your fault." Then he held his forehead.

A cry echoed from another room: "He was an animal!" It was a joyful proclamation.

"Shit," Ringo grunted.

Things were quiet in the Suburban as it glided back up toward midtown. Rush hour was just about done with, leaving the taxi cabs to battle for dominance among the many delivery trucks and buses.

"I changed your itinerary some so that you could spend some quality time with Porsha and Quentin today. You could use it."

Ringo was too exhausted and too knee-deep in guilt to dish Jamie an answer. Instead, he steered his cockiest gaze to her.

"Hey, don't give me any shit. I'm not the one that was—how'd she put it?—an animal. You should've seen the glow on her face when she saw me this morning. Wow. What I wouldn't give to have had a camera . . . You never cease to amaze me, Ringo. Just one thing, though. You can play all you want with the fishies, but you've always gotta take care of home."

Ringo was still at odds with the throbbing in his head, dizzied by the passing activities along the city streets. Somehow, he knew he had been satisfied with his choices, but it was as if there was a strong aroma—maybe wood burning—and he could smell none of it due to a stuffy nose.

After all he'd been through . . . after growing so fast and making so much progress, he'd compromised it all within the space of a few hours.

Good thing Jamie's here today to help. And, wow, she handled this so naturally, like she's done this a dozen times before!

Ringo sighed with relief.

"I also got a strange call this morning—I mean, after all that's happened . . . Justin called to say Diamond is ready to finish the remix. He says it's okay to use the rap she heard. He emphasized that exact rap, and said the grimier, the more detailed, the better for the project."

"Huh?"

"Hey, don't beat me in the head. I'm only the messenger. And he said he'd holla at you later. Humph . . . holla. Everybody wants to be Tupac."

It was another dose of relief, and some weight seemed to lift off of Ringo's shoulders. Justin and Diamond. He had been wondering about them for nearly two weeks.

"Also, Brooklyn wants you to stop by the office later to meet Clive Andrews, the label president. Now, that's big."

"Why me?" was the only thing Ringo could think to say.

"It's not just you, bighead. All of the label's artists will be there. Just a meet-and-greet for the staff . . . hobnobbing with the new employees, people who will be making their living selling your face to America."

"Well, shit . . . I gotta clean up." Ringo started to straighten up in his seat, but Jamie stopped him with a hand against his chest.

"That's exactly why I made the schedule changes. Relax."

"What time?"

"Four."

"All the label artists?" Ringo wanted to be sure.

"All of 'em! Then we have an in-store in Jersey, dinner with . . ." Jamie's rundown of the evening's itinerary a blur by now.

Diamond, Ringo thought. *Maybe I can apologize to her.*

The truck was parked outside of Ringo's place now. Before he disembarked, Jamie said, "And next time you pull that without lettin' me know, I'm gonna feed you to the sharks . . . literally.

DISTRICT ATTORNEY'S OFFICE, NYC

"Thanks for coming in, Lewis. I've been thinking about the hunch you told me about . . . your little scenario. And to be honest with you . . . we did a little pre-investigation to see if this would be doable. We even had to ask a couple of teenagers to do some interpretation party—you know like they say in the entertainment world . . ."

As if you know, thought Justin.

"Anyway . . . I have some photos here. Something interesting, actually." McDoogle pushed a folder across the conference table so that it conveniently skidded to a parked position in front of Justin.

It made Justin nervous to know that his hunch had turned into something more serious, something that warranted expenditures and manpower.

Justin opened the folder as if a bomb might explode.

"The one on the left has been on the Most Wanted list for almost two years now. He was identified as one of the gunmen who robbed the Just Right, a check cashing outlet on Queens Boulevard. It was two summers ago, but the file is still on the grill with NYPD. You see . . . there were six casualties involved, four of them employees. It was very messy . . ."

Justin shifted the photos aside, one after another. The first photo that McDoogle referred to was one that had been taken outdoors when it was dark.

Thugs.

They were exchanging buddy handshakes and man hugs with Ringo. Ringo stood out the most in sportswear similar to that worn in another photo—Ringo performing on stage with dancers, lights, and a sidekick, who Justin knew to be the hype man, J-Love.

"He goes by the name of Brice. He's got a number of aliases, actually. But his birth name is Antoine Samuels. He's got a rap sheet about ten feet long . . . juvie time, a few short terms at Rikers . . . troublemaker since he was little. We pulled school files and looked for known associates." The DA fixed a sincere grimace across his face.

"Lewis . . . we want this Antoine Brice Samuels real bad. He's got a lot of people frustrated. Detectives, F.B.I., the chief of police caught most of the heat, since a girl was shot by an officer—a mistake they say. But two of the gunmen got away with more than a hundred grand. We know Brice is one of them. It's not clear who his partner was, since there was a mask over his eyes. One of those Halloween masquerade jobs. But now when we take into account these lyrics—the ones you mentioned to me last week about six stiffs in Queens—your hunch becomes more like a newsflash, Lewis. I think we're onto something here. No, I should rephrase that. I *know* we're onto something here."

Justin further reviewed the photos. One showed the group of Brice's associates.

"Oh, we couldn't ID the other characters. Not yet," added McDoogle.

Another photo showed two teenage girls. There were photos of various vehicles, some with out-of-state plates.

"Some of these plates turned out to be dummies from out of state. If one of those vehicles happened to be pulled over on a routine traffic stop, there'd be no way to get detailed info—not unless we held the driver for questioning. Then . . ."

Justin was only hearing portions of the DA's explanations, too consumed with curiosity.

Why is he telling me all of this? Justin thought. He began to feel a strange burden.

"But besides that, we believe these guys have some kind of monster cash flow to be pushing such expensive vehicles. Either that or they're stolen."

"What's with the concert photos?" asked Justin.

"It's about Ringo. This guy . . . he intrigues me, Lewis. Not because he performs or makes music and videos. It's his cocky attitude. His bold way of doing things. Now, I know this is supposed to be entertainment, but perhaps you can help me here . . . Here he is, rapping about gunslinging and dead bodies in Queens . . . in front of, what? Maybe a million or so people—that's what platinum implies, doesn't it? One million sold."

"More or less," Justin said.

"See? I know my stuff," said McDoogle jokingly. "So, what then? Is this Ringo laughing in our faces? And he's got the nerve to come out in the open, to more or less admit that he knows and associates with robbery-homicide suspects? Someone who we know was a part of creating those six stiffs in Queens?"

"Too much of a coincidence," said Justin.

"Of course it is, son. Too much of everything."

"Bill?" Another attorney, Ruby Webber, stuck her head in the door. "I found something more on the rapper."

"Come on in, Ruby. You know Justin Lewis, one of our interns from John Jay."

"Yes, I think we've come across each other once or twice," said Ruby, stepping up beside McDoogle.

"Let's see what you've got."

"It's the press kit for the rapper," said Ruby. "It comes complete with a bio."

"Bio?"

"That's short for biography," Justin added, demonstrating his inside knowledge on the music industry.

"Basically, just background about an artist—but beware. In a lot of cases the information is contrived.

Even exaggerated."

"But I can get an idea of his past? Let's see," McDoogle said, digging into the black-and-white print. "Says here he's from Bridgeport, Connecticut."

"And I checked that," said Ruby. "He performed at a few local clubs and a store owner or two seem to like him, but I couldn't get a handle on his birth name, or his family's residence. But then—"

"Where were these taken?"

"At the Beacon Theater the afternoon before the show. Same as the others."

"Okay," McDoogle said, reviewing the photos.

"They call this the sound check—a rehearsal, really. And she's Porsha Lindsey; I'm guessing she's a girlfriend, so I did some checking on her. Her last known address is Two Forty-one Regina Street—also Bridgeport—"

"Is that her newborn she's holding?"

"Seems to be. And this . . . could be her nanny. So my guess is this could be—"

Justin intervened. "It is. Porsha is Ringo's girlfriend and that's his son, Quentin. They live in the city now."

"Well then, that solves half of my problem. So then the calls I put in oughta be informative. I'm checking for the parents' names on the birth certificate."

"Good thinking," said McDoogle.

"At least all the photo-taking wasn't done in vain," said Ruby.

"You took these pictures yourself?"

"Had to. No additional manpower that day. Plus, it was sort of spur of the moment. So I just grabbed a Minolta and one of the press passes we got from the mayor's office, and voilà, the Beacon management gave me full access."

Ruby had her long brown hair twisted into a single braid that was pinned up at the crown of her head, revealing her sharp facial features. She never asknowledged the impressed expressions of McDoogle or Justin.

"Well, before you ask, I've already contacted reliable sources to check on who the father is. Now . . . this girl here? This is Tangi Stokes, also from Bridgeport. That info was a cinch because apparently, a lot of what this rapper buys or leases is in her name. Porsha, his girlfriend, also handles different business concerns for Ringo. Tangi's just eighteen, Porsha is a little older, and already they're knee-deep in bank accounts, credit cards, cell phone and two-way pager accounts. Tangi's got a place in the same building as Ringo and Porsha. I'm assuming now that Porsha lives with Ringo but the super says Tangi's practically living at both residences. You figure that one—"

Justin cut in. "She's been doing a lot of the business management since Porsha had the baby. They also have a housekeeper, her name is Lucy, and the nanny is Sylvia."

"You think they're managing more than just the rapper?"

"It's just his personal business as far as I know. The woman in this photo . . . that's Jamie Horton, his personal assistant. But cumulatively these women handle his life. Appointments, interviews . . . They make sure that cleaning and food and bills are all taken care of. All of his conveniences," said Justin.

"Conveniences? Jeez, Justin . . . I'm a heartbeat from going to the record company myself. Is this how all the rappers are living? Like kings and queens? All because they know how to run their mouths?"

Justin's facial expression suggested that it was a probability.

"All I can speak on is what I know," said Justin. And Ringo is a close enough—" He almost said "friend" "—acquaintance, that I've gotten to know his lifestyle."

Ruby jumped back in. "But there was something I needed to add about Tangi Stokes. She had been a resident at the State Street Motor Inn, a welfare motel more or less, back in Bridgeport. Porsha, I found out, worked across the street at the local post office, which I'm told also doubles as a convenience store."

McDoogle hadn't yet caught on to Ruby's connection.

"What I'm getting at is, about a year ago, there was a homocide at the inn. It was the same time that Tangi, Porsha, and a resident named Greg Jenkins disappeared. There was a police report and Porsha had been interviewed, but she wasn't a suspect."

"Greg Jenkins would be. He happened to be working with their crew? Did we do a search?" asked McDoogle.

"On a hunch, I checked. There are twelve men named Greg Jenkins in Connecticut, but none of them live in Bridgeport. So I was thinking . . . this is just theory, of course . . ." said Ruby.

"Of course it is. We'd have nothing if we didn't have theories. And we only get convictions from theories that we sell to juries. So, shoot. Theory on."

"What if . . ." Ruby bit her lower lip and turned her head so that she faced a wall of law books containing the many cases, trial transcripts, and court decisions that she'd studied over the years.

"What if the Jenkins name was a fabrication . . . an alias? What if Ringo is Greg Jenkins and we've been barking up the wrong tree? Maybe Ringo is just as dangerous—if not more so—than our Most Wanted man. What if Ringo took a sabbatical, changed his name from whoever he really is, forged a new identity . . . a new start . . . ?"

"Ohhh . . . I'm getting the picture now," said McDoogle. "He drops off the face of the earth, then emerges two years later—alekazam, presto chango, hello, world! I'm Ringo, the rapper."

"Exactly."

"So . . . while he's hiding at this State Street Motor Inn, he meets Porsha and Tangi—probably something freaky keeping them together—and Porsha has a baby."

"And his rap career happens to shoot through the roof," added Justin.

Ruby said, "And maybe he can only make it big with his rap thing if he does it in New York. . . ."

"So he returns," said McDoogle. "Figuring that the trail grew cold on the Just Right job."

"And he's back in business," said Justin.

"Doing bigger and better than ever," said McDoogle.

"Not so fast," said Ruby. "The inn keeper in Bridgeport? The homocide? That's still an unsolved mystery. The locals out there aren't calling Porsha and Tangi suspects, but I kind of get the idea that they'd like to interview them . . . again."

"Hmmm . . . maybe our rapper was smack-dab in the middle of that party, too," said McDoogle.

"I smell an investigation," said Justin.

"I smell an indictment."

"Not yet, Ruby. There's more work to do. We need somebody to ID Ringo for the Bridgeport killing, or the Just Right job before we turn up the heat. We also need more links between Ringo and Antoine—what's his nickname? Brice."

Well, what exactly is their relationship? This could turn out to be nothing more than a photo opportunity. But then . . . since Ringo's out there on BET and going around the country running his mouth, we should at least be able to get some recordings . . . build up a file. Let's get him wired up like a marionette . . . see if we can't get some more intimate details from him. Maybe a more defined admission on the Just Right case or the Bridgeport homicide."

"What about Brice? We should be able to go in and sweep him off the street like that." Ruby snapped her fingers for emphasis. "All we need to do is keep a tail on—"

McDoogle wagged his head. "No, Ruby. Brice looks like only half the show . . ." McDoogle poked at Ringo's photo now. Then he grinded his forefinger like a spike. "I could be off here, but if I'm right, this could turn out to be the granddaddy of all snags. What if this guy's rap career is just a front for ongoing organized criminal activities? This could be the straw that broke the camel's back, even opening doors and launching investigations into all of these other rappers we've been getting complaints about. . . .

"I have enough information here to set up a task force. We'll get the necessary funding, sufficient manpower, and all the proper clearances for wiretaps, warrants, whatever. Lewis . . ." McDoogle handled Justin's shoulder as a speaker would a lectern. "If you can get closer to Ringo, if you can fish out the truth—no drunken confessions—then we will have something here. Operation Bigmouth we'll call it. And we'll inevitably design a routine to take down every thug-turned-rapper who took the shortcut to the top. Every rapper with a grimy past will be a target. We'll force them all to face their own music. If they wanna be bigmouths, if they wanna brag and boast about their criminal histories, then I think they should answer for it. We'll put together a good enough argument for a congressman to propose a statute that'll make the Son of Sam Law look like a board game. If not, these rappers will continue to send a message to our children that crime does pay."

Chapter Twenty-three

NEWARK, NEW JERSEY

Club Zanzibar's huge dance hall had a consistent weekly following. But tonight was beyond anything the club normally experienced.

Uncle Luke was in from Miami, promoting his annual Freak Show, a night that promised raunchy stage shows that would be videotaped for his exclusive Pay-Per-View cable specials. His name attracted legions of young women, both exotic and home grown, all of whom became uninhibited once they became part of the freak show atmosphere. Normal for this event was a girl on her knees, doggie style, with her butt cheeks clapping for a sea of lust-filled men, or else she'd be on her back, legs kicked up in V formation while she pulled her thong aside for a dollar's worth of peek-a-boo.

Working-class men, business owners, and an infinite number of so-called playas, ballers, and pimps—both genuine and phony—tipped the best looking, most aggressive, and even the shyest amateurs. Whatever the thrill of the moment was, whatever was most exciting, attracted the most money.

Outside of the club, the parking lot as well as every side street was bumper-to-bumper with expensive cars. If the vehicle wasn't expensive then many times the domestic brands stashed something valuable.

"But tonight? No bullshit, I'm tryin' to snatch up the expensive joints. At least twenty of 'em. So let's keep on our toes, and watch out for the heroes. I'm tryin' to make money, not spill blood."

"Yo B—the cat with his hat on straight? He ain't with us . . ." Rabbit was pointing toward one of three parking attendants. "The other two said he was a stiff—his moms is some type of big deal at City Hall, so he's on the straight 'n' narrow."

B-Money pursed his lips and his face tightened, as if considering a solution. "What about the others?"

"They're down. I had 'em flip their hats backward so we could tell one from the other. Plus they worked it out so their third man handles the far end of the lot."

"Level with me, Rabbit. Is the stiff gonna be a problem?"

"I offered them dudes enough money to make sure he wasn't a problem. But I think we should stay on this side of the club. Cars is cars," said Rabbit.

"Yeah," muttered B-Money, and he secretly vowed to keep an eye on the stiff.

The time had come to get moving and the B-boyz took their places. Outlaw, Rabbit, and E.J. stood at various intervals in the parking lot, where most of the expensive whips were kept. Meanwhile, B-Money sat on the hood of his Isuzu Rodeo. He had a series of remote devices in hand, those tiny black plastic thingamajigs that drivers keep on their keychains that they press to arm and disarm car alarms.

The remote controls B-Money had, however, were specially designed by an electronics expert to serve as a "universal" remote, not unlike the ones made for the television. Essentially, B-Money was equipped with enough remote signals to communicate with any number of vehicles.

From his post, B-Money could see most of the lot. There were still clubgoers pulling in, then hurrying into the club entrance, hoping to make it before the event was sold out.

It was a good guess that once inside patrons would be fascinated enough to stay put, out of the way. *I want twenty whips tonight* thought B-Money. Upon pressing the remote, bleeps sounded from near and far and the B-boyz went to work.

The thieves were unafraid, thrusting their lock drills into the keyholes and then into the ignition to free the steering wheels. In less than ten seconds—their routine time frame—the vehicles were hot-wired and the engines fired up.

The seconds ticked by and one by one the whips eased out of their parking spaces and crawled toward the exit.

An operation as big as Zanzibar required the use of a nearby garage that was away from mainstream traffic but also near enough for the B-boyz to shoot back around the corner for another snatch.

The plan went smoothly for the first twelve vehicles: two Mercedes sedans, a Lincoln Navigator, two BMWs, a Cadillac Deville, a Range Rover, two Lexus GS 500s, one Sleek Chevrolet Corvette, a $200,000 Aston Martin, and a Chevy Suburban.

Behind the no-bullshit expression, B-Money smiled at how successful the night had already been, well worth the payoffs—the valets and the rental of the garage a few blocks away.

When Ringo mentioned a "boys night out" in New Jersey, Justin knew he couldn't pass it up for the world. But as the night unfolded, he minded how much deeper he was getting involved in this so-called investigation.

There were a few hours' notice before Justin was to be picked up by Kujo, Ringo's driver. So detectives Blair and Dobson (McDoogle Operation Bigmouth operatives) got the go-ahead and wired Justin up to tape the rapper.

"Don't cross the line," McDoogle warned.

"The main thing, Justin, is to relax. Try to ignore the funny feeling on your chest and act as naturally as you normally would. We'll be close by."

"That's right," Dobson confirmed, standing behind Blair, while he affixed the tape to the wire. "Worst-case scenario is we'll perform a phony bust . . . somehow we'll get you out of there."

Somehow? Justin thought nervously.

The buzzer sounded. It was Diamond's penthouse and Justin had been housesitting while she was in L.A. performing on *The Tonight Show.*

"Okay, Justin. We're outta here. By the time you go down in the elevator we'll be in the car. We can do a mic test then."

"And good luck," added Dobson.

Luck? Why should I need luck?

An hour later, Justin had that so-far-so-good feeling as he sat side-by-side with Ringo.

Sweets was at home. "I want you to stay with Sylvia and Porsha," Ringo had told him earlier. "Sweets, they're having their little girl function at the crib. Make sure the stripper they hired—yeah, I know all about it—make sure he leaves immediately after his l'il show is over, if you know what I mean. I don't wan't any nonsense spillin' over into Quentin's bedroom."

And Kujo was at the entrance to the VIP area. "Kujo," Ringo had ordered, "I'm not asking you, I'm telling you . . . come on in the club. Would you rather worry more about that damned truck or me, your boss?"

In the meantime, there was a girl-girl-girl show entertaining the VIP area, right there on the carpet in front of them. Waitresses with WELCOME TO MY HOUSE scripted in white on their ripped black T-shirts stopped by the table now and again to serve drinks and snacks.

Ringo had learned his lesson about drinking too much Bacardi Rum, then one mistake leading to the next. He chose to drink Pepsi.

Johnell, the owner of Zanzibar, soon came to join Ringo's group, praising the rapper again on his performance two months earlier.

"And what about the gal who climbed up on the stage to show her tits? Was that fascinating or what?

"I thought she was gonna attack me," said Ringo, remembering the time. "But my people were right there, thank God."

"That doesn't happen too many times at Zanzibar. We've never had any attacks on the entertainers who come here—and we've had some pretty big names." Johnell hushed his voice some. "So did you let her do ya?"

Ringo's laugh was from the throat. "Are you kiddin'? I'm practically married! My woman would beat my ass," proclaimed Ringo. Then he flashed a cynical expression at Johnell.

J-Love tossed a handful of crumpled dollars on the carpet, oh so close to the three girls who formed a steamy human chain on the floor.

Johnell slapped Ringo's shoulder, cackling, "I knew it! Good for you, man. I'll tell ya, you gotta live it up while you're young and popular, dude. Get all the pussy you can . . . it's good for your ego . . ."

Is that so? thought Ringo.

". . . Keeps you creative, know what I mean? Only, you gotta watch out for the big A, ya know what I mean?"

"The big A?" Ringo asked Mr. Talkative while the girls on the floor licked and ate one another.

"AIDS, dude. Gotta be careful."

Still looking and still in disbelief, Ringo said, "Always."

He took another sip of his Pepsi, hoping to escape the conversation.

"So what next? Any chance we can get you back here to do another show? You were extremely hot. And I hate dealing with those blood-sucking booking agents. Nothin' but middlemen."

Ohhhhh . . . so that's *why he invited us out here!* Ringo realized. *Come along with Uncle Luke and me, Ringo . . . bring your friends—the night's on me!*

"That's the thing, Johnell . . ."

One of the girls on the floor was on her back now, another was on top of her, the two of them in a missionary position while the third girl ate the two of them separately and all at once. The third girl kept winking at Ringo, then she'd apply greater attention to the deed.

"They get me gigs all over the world, not just in Jersey. Them people put me in Switzerland, Morocco, Holland. I don't know the clubs and promoters, the good ones who are gonna follow through on their commitments. So the booking agents make sure my money is right, my rider and all the transportation . . ."

Again, the girl on the floor winked, then back to the smut.

"They uhhh—whew . . . Where was I?"

"The booking agents."

"Right, right. They got my back, know what I'm sayin'? I

can't do them wrong if they doin' the right thing by me. Why? You having problems with Fathead at William Walters?"

"Aw . . . I get the runaround sometimes. I call to ask about a date when you'll be available, they put me on hold or say they'll call back. Sometimes I feel like I'm standing in line for hand-me-downs," said Johnell as he waved off an employee trying to summon him to the phone.

"I dunno, Johnell. That don't sound like Fathead. The dude is a deal-maker, night and day. But you gotta remember . . . the agent deals with promoters and clubs from all over the world. Maybe I can put the good word in for you. I'll have my people call your people, you have your people call my people. Either way, we'll get the job done. Cool?"

"Would you? I'd appreciate that."

"Consider it done. Just call my girl Tangi and have her remind me."

"Want me to jot that down for you? In case you forget?" asked Justin.

"Thanks, dawg. You think of everything," Ringo said.

Justin winked at Johnell to give assurance.

"Let 'em in, Kujo . . . it's cool," said Johnell. Kujo understood the club owner despite the volumes of music that filled the establishment, and he unhooked the velvet rope to allow three more women into the VIP area. They all appeared to be twenty-something and had been vying for Ringo's attention for a while now. Once inside the ropes they were all smiles, sitting on each of the rapper's thighs, while the alternate girl snapped photos. Suddenly Ringo was suffocated by sex—the sequined micro-mini dresses, cleavage aplenty, open-toe heels. And still there were the others on the floor. Justin noticed one woman whispering in Ringo's ear and then sticking her tongue in and out of it. *No shame*, he told himself. And at the same time he couldn't help his erection.

"Hey, girls . . . meet my buddy, Justin. He's my manager," Ringo lied. And that's J-Love, my hype man. But go easy on him—too much excitement and he busts in his pants."

A photo was snapped as one girl changed places and the

other went to sit with J-Love, kissing his cheek and brushing his arm with a partially exposed breast.

When the picture-taking was done, the third fan sat on Justin's lap.

Johnell expressed his satisfaction with an earnest smile and went to take his phone call, leaving Ringo and friends with the three hotties.

"So, how can a girl get with a true playa like you?" asked the vixen in Justin's ear. It was more than a pass and his erection throbbed now.

"Sorry, babe . . . I got a girl back home."

Whispering all the more, she said. "Don't worry, she'd never find out. You gonna let a hungry girl down?"

Justin let out a deep breath but couldn't rid himself of the exciting inferences.

Eventually, the vixen sucked her teeth and called Justin a party pooper.

Dobson and Blair are having a ball right now . . . I know it.

Johnell brought Uncle Luke back and introduced him to Ringo. He left them alone to talk about the politics of the music industry and how everything sounded so much alike.

"A lot of times today it takes something outrageous to make a name for yourself. That's how we did our thing, 'cause sex definitely sells . . ."

The discussion moved quickly from subject to subject, with the old-school rap icon dishing advice and leaving his unshakeable impression.

One thing led to another and Ringo agreed to be videotaped for Luke's Pay-Per-View special. The cameras were soon focused on the VIP lounge, the girls who sat with Ringo and the girl-girl-girl activity on the floor. This, to someone arrested by his couch, was considered real TV. Luke began passing out money to the girls who had just come to join Ringo, and dresses started to come off. One girl, with a black ponytail and wheat-colored skin did a partial somersault right there in front of him. She then twisted herself around in such a way that her bare feet and calves ended up hooked around the rapper's neck.

Ringo got a kick out of Uncle Luke giving a sportscaster's

play-by-play account before the roving cameras. With a thong as her only clothing, the girl simulated oral sex on Ringo, although he was fully clothed.

The two other girls were not as conservative as their friend. The two of them stripped for Ringo and afterward they pulled his shirt off. Next came the licking and nibbling at his upper body, collarbone, and neck, leaving very little flesh unsatisfied.

A chorus of *ooh*s and *ahh*s encouraged the action, with a camera crew zooming in for the most captivating footage. Soon the VIP area transformed into a money pit, with the girls on the floor as well as the others making a meal out of Ringo, creating an exciting spectacle.

Justin chose to stand off to the side, along with Mel, Butter, and Kujo, amazed at how abruptly this all escalated. So amazing was the action that Justin forgot all about the wire he wore and the detectives who were nearby in an unmarked car.

"Okay, okay," said Ringo. "Y'all got me all hot and excited. Let's get out of here."

"Wait a— Ringo, they're coming with us?" asked Justin.

"Why not? You think I'm gonna leave things like this? I'm ready to back off, dawg."

Justin made a face, then leaned in to whisper, "What about Porsha?"

"What about her? You only live once, Justin . . ."

Ringo's words seeped into Justin's conscience for all of two seconds. Then he blurted out, "Psyche!" Ringo laughed hard and engaged in a playful chokehold.

"Relax, Justin. I'm just gonna make sure they get home safe. We'll stop to get some food and I'll let J-Love keep in touch with them—maybe throw 'em in the next video."

Justin was relieved to hear this, although he didn't know why he cared.

Kujo stepped away before the others, finding his way through the many congregated onlookers, in order to reach the club's main entrance. Ringo and his bodyguards weren't far behind Kujo, forging their way through autograph seekers and others who reached out just to touch a star. The three women in his company only made for a convenient spectacle, through their nameless bodies of energy. No thoughts, just smiles, curves, and reflections of lust.

Johnell shook hands with Ringo as the gang made their way through the vestibule with its stand-alone metal detector and portal windows for the cashier and coat check.

An invisible force seemed to shove Kujo through the entry. For an instant it appeared as though he might tackle Butter.

"It's gone."

"What's gone?" asked Ringo even though the comment wasn't directed at him.

Clearly flabbergasted, Butter said, "The truck."

Ringo twisted his lips. "Man, stop buggin'. You probably forgot where you parked it."

"I'm tellin' you."

Their movements escalated now, more urgency in their eyes . . . more pep in their steps.

Justin found himself in an odd position, knowing that there were police officers outside in the immediate vicinity. And if they didn't have something do with this sudden development than did they at least witness anything?

The women in Ringo's entourage were beginning to take this personally. "You mean they stole your truck?

How dare they!? I have a car. Let's track 'em down. They couldn't be far, could they?"

Mel shook his head. This wasn't right. Kujo should've been outside with the truck. His job was to secure their transportation, not the VIP area at somebody else's dance club.

Ringo didn't feel as destroyed as he might have during leaner times, yet he did suffer the stab of inconvenience. He cursed before grousing, "That truck is custom! Over a hundred grand went into that. Nah, Butter has to be wrong."

Johnell and a couple of staff members emerged from the club, joining the group out in front.

"There must be some mistake," said Johnell as he gestured for a valet to come forth.

"That's what I said," added Ringo.

I saw a Suburban leave the lot about ten minutes ago," said one of their parking attendants. The other two merely struggled.

"We didn't see anything," said another. "Nothin' strange anyway."

"Matter fact, there was a Suburban. A white one, right? It just left the lot. But . . . I thought everything was kosher. No alarms went off . . ."

The mixed comments led to nowhere, the obvious confusion arising from the choices—vehicles were parked either by self-service or valet, with no accounting for the entire inventory.

Off on their own, Butter and Mel stalked the parking lot searching beyond the empty space where the Suburban had been.

"Oh my God!" The cry came from one of Ringo's thrill-seeking VIP guests. Her friends couldn't contain her ranting about car payments, her personal belongings, and a diamond ring she had left in the CD caddy of her burgundy BMW.

"Bobby put in a call to the police," said Johnell. "And you three . . . Jesus!" It was suddenly impossible to place blame on anyone in particular.

To Ringo, Johnell said, "I'm truly sorry about this, man. We're gonna get your truck back. You got my word . . . even if I gottta buy you another one."

This was a reaction that B-Money expected, only not so soon. The Zanzibar parking lot was busier now, with a couple of folks venting about their missing vehicles.

He ignored the cries in an effort to disassociate himself from the personal loss. After all, this was business—nothing personal.

With a sigh, B-Money hopped down from his seat on the hood of his truck where he had been overseeing the entire operation. His cell phone buzzed.

E.J. was on the other end of the phone call.

"We'll just have to be satisfied with twelve," said B-Money into the cell phone. "Whatever you do, don't come back over here. This spot is gonna be hot like— Oh shit! Nah. Nothin'—I thought I just saw . . ." B-Money sounded as though he'd lost his voice. "I'll be damned. That's . . . Yo, E.J., roll a few of them muhfuckas to home base. I'll get back atcha . . . Yeah, everything's aight. Holla." B-Money shut his cell phone, content that his instructions would be followed exactly.

"Yo, homes . . . you see anybody get in a Sub?"

Ringo was coming right at him.

B-Money would rather have avoided this confrontation under the circumstances. But he thought twice about it. *I can't duck him—too late. Besides, what's the big deal? As much dirt as we did together.*

"Brice?" Ringo's eyes widened with awareness. He was separated to some extent from the others—the club staff, a bouncer or two, a few hysterical women—all of them stirred up about the missing vehicles.

"Shhh . . . easy, man. Remember, B-Money's the name."

"Oh. Yeah. Wassup? What you doin' out here?"

This was almost funny. *Don't tell me*, thought B-Money. *Not the black Suburban!* He recalled their run-in at the Beacon Theater and the truck Ringo eventually zipped away in. He didn't make the association earlier, this being so far away from New York City, Ringo's new hometown. But now it was clear: The B-boyz had snatched Ringo's truck!

"You wouldn't believe me if I told you," B-Money answered.

"Try me," said Ringo, clearly sensing that this might have something to do with the missing truck.

"I'm stealing cars," B-Money said with the beginnings of a hearty laugh. "And trucks," he blabbed with no sign of remorse.

Ringo's face hardened with misunderstanding but then warmed into his own laugh.

"You mean . . . you?" Ringo asked, pointing at his old friend, hardly able to get the words out. "You took the . . . Suburban?" Ringo laughed hard enough for tears to form at the corners of his eyes.

"Shhh . . . it's a secret," hissed B-Money. Then aloud he said, "But not anymore!"

And the laughing commenced for some time, as if they were two drunken bums.

Ringo said, "Hold on," and without notice he trotted back to where Johnell and Justin were mixed in among the others.

"What the hell was so funny over there?" asked Justin. "Who was that?"

"Cool it, Justin. Everything is gonna be okay." A line of livery cabs was waiting in a designated area and Ringo raised his hand to signal one of them. "Do me a favor, would you, Justin?" Ringo waved a second taxi over, still speaking as he did. "We're gonna call it a night. And . . . would you mind taking these girls wherever they wanna go?"

Ringo's request left Justin frozen.

Butter, Mel, and Kujo were just behind Justin. The girl with the missing BMW was with them.

"Boo, lemme holla at you for a minute?" Ringo asked.

There was some relief about her as she approached Ringo. He reached out to caress her tear-stained cheek, as though he were about to solve all of her life's ills.

"I'm gonna get your car back," he said to her.

"Huh? Really? But—"

Ringo's thumb shifted from her cheek to her lips to hush her. Others were watching.

"Really and trust me, it'll be the same as you left it. . . ."

Ringo's smooth confidence hypnotized the young woman and she listened closely, a patient under his influence. "There's just one thing I'm gonna need from you."

"Anything, Ringo."

"Here's a hundred dollars. I need you to get in this taxi. I'll pay the fare—wherever you want him to take you. Gimme your address and I'll see to it your car is cleaned, waxed, and parked in front of your house by morning."

Her sequined dress intact, her hair ruffled and her eyeliner running, the young woman stood before Ringo, her newfound authority figure, and she his humble servant. She looked up into his eyes wanting so much to be part of his secure world by whatever means. And then a more pressing concern seemed to wash over her. Words began to seep from her lips. "But . . . what about my girls?"

"Uh . . . yeah. No problem, baby . . ." Was the best response Ringo could come up with, blurting out answers while his mind was elsewhere—Brice waiting for him, and all these sets of eyes targeting him.

"You, your friends . . . whatever."

Sirens sounded in the distance.

Gotta get movin'.

"Sweetie, if you help me out, I promise you, you'll be a happy woman when you wake up tomorrow."

"I will?"

Ringo waved to get Butter's attention.

"You will . . . Butter, take down this woman's address and phone numbers . . ."

"What about my name? Don't you need that, too?"

"Right—of course. What was your name again?"

"Tanya. But my girls call me Nay-Nay."

"Okay . . . ," said Ringo, failing to see the importance of the additional details. "Good . . . ahh, listen—"

The sirens cried closer now.

Brice started his truck.

Ringo kissed Nay-Nay's cheek for assurance. "I really need to leave so I can help you, Nay-Nay. Fellas, I'll call you later. Use the taxis. I'm rollin' with my buddy. Can't explain now."

Mel stepped forward and applied a firm grip to Ringo's shoulder. "Everything all right?"

"Mel, I'm good. Trust me here. Break out—and no talkin' to Five-O. I already know where the truck is . . ." Ringo slapped two hundred-dollar bills in Mel's palm. "This should take care of the taxis. And make sure the girls get wherever they wanna go."

Ringo the troubleshooter.

Mel was stumped. This was so not the way things were supposed to be. His job was to secure this guy. But Ringo was the boss.

Chapter Twenty-four

"I guess this is what they call a coincidence," sad B-Money, carefully watching his rear and sideview mirrors as the truck eased out of Zanzibar's parking lot.

"More like irony," said Ringo.

Or fate.

The Isuzu dipped left, gliding eastward on Randolph, then took a right turn, southeast on Lincoln, a residential block. They followed Lincoln for a time, then shot across Waverly and Edison.

Ringo jumped in his seat when B-Money steered the truck down a one-way street.

"Sometimes I gotta take precautions in my line of business," said B-Money.

Ringo held tight onto the dashboard as the vehicle hooked a sharp right turn, contradicting all manner of traffic laws and forcing Ringo against the passenger-side window.

"Of course," Ringo managed to say.

" 'Cause you never know when you're bein' followed," said B-Money.

Once he was satisfied that there was no tail, the drive was smoother. This was an extended route but as far as B-Money was concerned, it was a safe one. Drake Avenue was mere blocks away.

Happy to be physically and mentally intact, Ringo still felt as though he was daydreaming. There was the rough ride . . . the smooth ride . . . the Jeep crawling onto an industrial street, then into a garage . . . a large wall parting, revealing a sort of inner sanctum, something mysterious and underground until finally there were all of these cars and trucks glistening underneath miserable lighting.

"Welcome to my house," said B-Money. Ringo remained speechless. Only now did he come to know the larger picture, a picture so many worlds away from the man he once knew.

B-Money could already see the newest additions—the whips that had been snatched from the club were still lined up along the wall, an inventory of sorts that would go through a number of transitions before they could be resold.

"Damn, that's a pretty sight," he said when Rabbit, E.J., and Outlaw came to receive their leader.

"We could've picked up a few more, but . . ."

"But what?" asked B-Money. By encouraging E.J. to explain he was also saying *It's okay to talk in front of our visitor.*

"I don't think you understand," said E.J. "Things got a little serious in the past hour—"

B-Money shrugged. "E.J., listen to me. Better yet, this goes for all of you. This here dude? This is like my brother. I don't have no secrets from him. And what's mine is his. So whatever you have to say, go on . . . you can say it in front of him, too."

E.J., Rabbit, and Outlaw all looked at one another with doubt-filled eyes. Hesitantly, E.J. conceded. He strolled over to the Lincoln Navigator, the last in the line of stolen vehicles, and pulled open the rear hatch. Inside there were three men either seated or lying on their sides.

"What'd y'all do? Go fishin'?"

Rabbit offered the explanation. "After you told E.J. to call it off, I came to back you up . . ."

"Huh?"

"Well, I thought somethin' funny was goin' down. I figured I'd just make sure you were safe, ya know? But then I saw some crazy shit goin' down . . . a taxi was pullin' out of the parking lot, loaded with jokers. Next thing I know the taxi stopped cold in the middle of the street. A dude got out and the cab left. Dude ran up the block some. I followed him . . ."

E.J. was frustrated with the dragged-out story and intervened. "B, the bottom line is we got us three cops in the truck. They were out near the club in an unmarked joint, watchin' everything."

Outlaw added his two cents. "Rabbit's one crazy muthafucka, B. He went and stepped to them fools on his own, guns and everything . . ."

"I didn't know they was five-O," said Rabbit. "They looked like they was schemin' on us."

"By the time we showed up it was too late," said E.J. "They already saw Rabbit's face. Plus, if we let 'em go we might have the whole New Jersey police force down here. We didn't have no choice."

B-Money looked back at the inside of the Navigator at the three men, all of them with their wrists and ankles bound by wire or leather belts.

"And look at this," said Outlaw, showing an electronic device. "One of 'em was wearin' a wire." B-Money mashed his palms against his face as if to try and erase it. After that he stepped over to the wall and laid his hands against it. For a time it appeared he might slam his head against the cinderblock, but all he did was press his forehead to the wall.

Cops . . . a wire tap . . . What is this shit? thought Ringo.

"Wait a minute," Ringo said, snapping out of his own daze. He approached the Navigator, unable to believe his eyes. *Justin? A cop?!*

Ringo was at a crossroads here. How would it look if these dudes knew Justin and he were—

"Ringo, isn't he . . . ?" B-Money looked closer at the youngest of the catch. "Ain't that the dude who was outside the club with you?"

Ringo was on the spot. He calculated his responses. *Yes, he's my personal advisor. . . . We have dinner together all the time. . . . Our women are close friends too! Jesus, Justin! You're a cop?*

"Yeah," said Ringo, locking his eyes with Justin's.

Justin was gagged and motionless, a heap of helpless flesh laying in the truck. "But I thought he worked for the club. Guess I was wrong."

And without hesitating, Ringo turned away, desensitized, as

though Justin was expendable and didn't matter on the grand scale of things.

"Shut the door, E.J. I gotta figure this out. . . . Outlaw, you and Spook take a look outside . . . secure my fuckin' house. Make sure we don't have any unwelcome visitors out there."

To Rabbit, B-Money said, "Don't worry, kid. You did good. Now keep an eye on these pigs. Make sure they don't get loose. It's gonna be question and answer time shortly."

B-Money directed E.J. to make certain corrections regarding the Suburban. "It needs to be in mint condition," said B-Money switching his somewhat apologetic grin in Ringo's direction. "Seems we made a slight mistake." While those instructions were carried out, B-Money took Ringo to the rear of the building.

"Well . . . here she is. It's not much, but it's been home for almost two years. Bedroom . . . entertainment center. No kitchen but I got a bedroom and a Jacuzzi in back. If I wanna eat I send somebody out; I alternate between Chinese, Italian, West Indian, and McDonald's." B-Money shrugged at this point. "What am I gonna do? They got my face all over the country. I feel like a damn vampire—can't go out in the daytime. I'm a fucking prisoner, Ringo. But shit, it beats doin' a bid behind the wall with no pussy, no scores . . . Fuck that. I'll take my underground penthouse over the prison yard any day."

Ringo chuckled some as he said, "I know exactly what you're goin' through. In Bridgeport—"

"Don't get me wrong," interrupted B-Money, not as interested in Ringo's story. "I'm not cryin', 'cause a nigga gets his thrills up in this joint for real. Trust that." B-Money was also busy mixing his soupy drink.

Ringo watched this and said, "What the hell?"

"Don't knock it till you try it, troop. This keeps me lubricated. The coffee . . . that keeps me up. The Guinness Stout hits my bloodstream . . . that rush, ya know? And shit, I just happen to get off on the cream and sugar. The ketchup just makes the stuff look like blood. Thick, slimy blood. And I love it." B-Money took a single swig. "Want some? I'm tellin' you it'll change your life." B-Money raised the glass in a toast.

"Hell fuckin' no. I swear, you done gone off the deep end, bro."

"Whatever," he said, and he gulped the rest of the goo down. "Works for me." He let out an obnoxious belch. Now he snorted what he called a scarface and the reponse that followed was total nonsense.

"Ahhhh . . . now . . . I'm God!" Ringo was offered a line and he quickly passed. "You was always a killjoy, Ringo. I remember you used to beg your moms to let you come out to play."

"I see that shit you just took is getting to your head, B." But Ringo said this only in light of the bittersweet past. B-Money's comment was more of a blow than a fond memory about the good ol' days. "And maybe it was a good thing I stayed in the house. Otherwise, I would be where brother Rah-Rah is right now." Rah-Rah was buried somewhere in Queensbridge Cemetery.

"What you say, nigga? You bringin' up Rah-Rah? Homey, I ain't the one singin' and dancin', runnin' my mouth all on BET 'n' shit. Talking about shit I did. That's my shit, nigga. You ain't nothin' but a bamboozled Hollywood nigga now. Plus, I don't believe you got the nerve to say some shit about my brotha. The only reason he dead is 'cause you couldn't come. We needed the extra man, nigga . . . you and your talent shows . . ."

Ringo quickly realized that he'd opened a can of worms, with all of those haunting ugly memories crawling out of hiding. Rah-Rah's death had become street legend—how he was shot during a holdup on Guy R. Brewer Boulevard. To add to the loss, Brice shot the store owner who killed his brother. And if that wasn't enough, the store owner's daughter went to the wake with a sawed-off shotgun, hopped up onto the casket, and blasted the head off of Rah-Rah's corpse, killing him a second time.

All of those images were suddenly exhumed to be relived if merely by the memories alone. And it was now that Ringo noticed Brice's bitterness. This wasn't B-Money who was angry, it was Brice who was drugged up, spitting words out faster than the thoughts that belied them. It was all coming out, the dirty laundry.

"Nigga shoots one person and thinks he's gangsta," said Brice, referring to the Just Right proprietress.

"Brice, I saved your fuckin' life! That woman was about to blow your brains out."

"Well, lemme look up from a grave, a nigga who was proud—who kept it real—instead of watchin' MTV, seein' you and yo' shiny jewelry, fakin' like you me. Nigga, you could neva be me! I am hip-hop, nigga—you . . . all you do is rap. I don't care how many times you go platinum, you'll neva live this shit like a real nigga!"

"You? You hip-hop? Nigga, if you supposed to be hip-hop, then I don't ever wanna be you. Never!" Ringo took a spinning gaze at B-Money's everyday reality, his "underground penthouse." Then he mumbled, "Loser."

That did it.

B-Money charged at Ringo, no different than a football linebacker would or Hip-Hop attacking Rap. They both fell back onto the circular bed. Hip-Hop popped Rap with a right cross to the cheek. The blow knocked the rapper's head into the pillows. He lay there beneath Hip-Hop. However, split-second timing was the rapper's advantage. He grabbed one of the pillows and thrust it up into Hip-Hop's face, then he flipped him onto his side. They scrambled, both of them struggling for the advantage. Rap shot a blow at Hip-Hop's gut, then another to the ribs.

The two rolled off of the bed and swung at each other, as best as they could in horizontal positions about the floor, cursing all the while as the worst of enemies would.

Rap got into an upright position and threw a left hook that caught Hip-Hop across the jaw. He then attempted to get up on his feet, but Hip-Hop kicked him as he was thrust into the table with the microwave and various accoutrements. All of it toppled to the floor.

Now B-Money was on his feet and the two charged at each other like wild rams. Their heads butted and a bloody gash formed above Ringo's right eye. But the pain only made Ringo angrier. With renewed energy, he pummeled B-Money with unanswered blows to the body, then one to the jaw. B-Money was hurled back against his giant video screen, unhurt still, and laughing.

Ringo went again.

B-Money used the rope-a-dope act, challenging Ringo to hit harder.

"Hahahahaa . . . you need some of my power drink, soft-ass Hollywood nigga!"

Ringo unleashed a fierce hook to the jaw. Another.

Still, B-Money laughed unaffected by the ass-whipping he was taking. Ringo slowed his attack.

"Come on. Knock me out, y' gangsta rapper . . . What happened? Ya run out of gas? Shit, you been gassin' niggas on TV and radio . . . Ain't you got no more for your homeboy?"

Winded, Ringo said, "You . . . are . . . fucked . . . up."

"All my life, homey. All my life."

Both of them slid down to take a seat on the floor and had to find the humility to face each other's wounds, mental and physical. Ringo put a hand to his gash, only causing it to sting more.

"I guess that makes two of us," admitted Ringo.

B-Money's face knotted up. "How could you be fucked up? You're rich now. You ain't gotta bang no more. You're famous—you said it yo'self. You livin' good, got a kid now . . . a girl in a fly-ass apartment . . . You got everything a man needs."

Ringo let that settle. Everything a man needs. "That sounds good, B. But the real deal is I'm goin' through growin' pains. I'm travelin', meetin' people . . . white cats who swear they ghetto, black cats who forgot where they came from . . . sometimes I even forget who I am, where I came from. It's all growin' pains, dawg. Damn, B, can you believe I'mma be in the next Soul Train Awards? Me . . . on *Soul Train*. That shit is like a dream come true. But there isn't a minute that goes by that I don't think about being the next washed-up rapper with nothin' to show for it but some words and music on a few plastic disks. And another thing—"

Just then the door was kicked in, with Spook and Rabbit behind it, guns pointed.

Neither B-Money nor Ringo budged. "Shit! Sorry, Boss. We

thought you—uh—you okay?" Spook and Rabbit lowered their weapons.

"Oh, us? We were just havin' a nice quiet conversation. Things got a little . . ." B-Money used his shirt to wipe blood from his cheek and lower lip. He was spitting blood as well.

". . . out of hand. We homies, man. What you think, we was fightin'?"

"I . . . uhh . . . well."

"I know one thing; we're doin' a lot better than my door you just broke. You coulda just knocked. It was unlocked, meat-head."

"My bad, Boss. I just thought . . . I'll fix it right away," said Spook, sharing a strange expression with Rabbit. Then the two pulled the door closed as best they could.

"As I was saying, B, I know I'm putting on a show. I know it's not all real, 'cause like they say, gangstas don't advertise what they do. So, I'm no better than Bozo the Clown. But what else am I gonna do in life? Sweep streets? Wash windows? Rob folks?

Shit, B . . . if you only knew how many little boys came up to me, talkin' about 'I wanna be like you.' Then I get the older dudes braggin' about what blocks they held down, the guns they busted, and how they gettin' big money. Man! I swear I don't know how I made it this far, 'cause the way I see it? The way this game is designed, very few people are gonna get to where I got."

Ringo's revelations were enough for the two of them to dwell on.

"Yo, I didn't know you was livin' like that."

"I'm livin' a lie, dawg. Do you know I ain't even spoke to my pop since all of this happened? And I never got to visit Cook-sie's grave—if you wanna talk about what's fucked up, *that's* fucked up. And, yo . . . you remember Donia?"

"The chick from Linden Avenue?"

"Right. Well, she springs up outta nowhere talkin' about a two-year-old son I got."

"What?"

"You can say that again."

"She givin' you problems?"

"Nah. We talked. Plus, I met the . . . I met my son for the first time last week. He has my eyes and nose, B."

"At least you know your kids. If I got any, I never met 'em."

Ringo wagged his head. "It's just a lotta shit, B. I just gotta play my cards the best I can. You feel me?"

"Listen, man . . . I was outta line to scream on you like that. The truth is I envy you. I'd give anything to be in your shoes every day. You got the rock now, and you gotta take your best shot. I know what I said, but . . . maybe I'm just jealous. The real is you rappin' me. You like my other half—the half that has a name and a face. You was always the one tryin' to be something in life. So I can't fault you for the choices you made in the past. Whatever happened, happened. And since we on some keep-it-real shit, thanks for savin' my life, man. If it wasn't for you, I'd be buried beside Cooksie right now. Word . . ."

Ringo was reminded about the botched robbery and the lady about to fill Brice with lead.

"But you was probably meant for that rap shit, Ringo. For real. You gotta keep it up. You gotta keep growin' . . . for all us cats that's trapped."

For long minutes nothing was said. And then B-Money remembered his unfinished business out in the garage.

Chapter Twenty-five

"Pull 'em out," ordered B-Money. Spook, E.J., and Rabbit dragged the bodies from the Navigator. At the same time Outlaw came from the front garage.

"It's all good outside, Boss. Ain't nobody followed you or nothin'."

"Good. Help get these pigs to the middle of the floor . . . near the drain, 'cause I got a feelin' blood's gonna spill. E.J., find me some wire cutters."

With his hand on Ringo's shoulder, B-Money crossed the floor to a sink. Underneath was a pair of yellow rubber gloves. "This move I'm about to make might get messy. But I figure, maybe you could take notes . . . this could be your next single. You could call it 'Punishment.' Check out the lyrics: Wire cutters in the hand . . . five-O's fingers in the can!"

B-Money crowed, amusing mostly himself.

Wirecutters? Fingers?

For the first time, Ringo was concerned about Justin.

Dobson couldn't believe the bad luck he was having, and all because he listened to Blair, his partner. *If he told you to jump off a bridge, you'd do that too?* It was a saying his pop always used when he did the wrong things, following his friend's lead—peer pressure. And now that old saying was haunting him worse than a broken Bette Midler record, that nasal cry drifting through the air ad nauseam.

Following Justin, their intern turned deputy investigator, into New Jersey was considered extra, an activity that was above and beyond the call of duty. Especially since they were out of their jurisdiction and such an option required a call to New Jersey authorities, if only to notify them.

But Blair was convincing. "Hell, Dobbs, this is nothin' but a simple tail and tap," was what he'd said. "We'll just fall back, record what we can to support Operation Bigmouth, and we go home. Why do we need state troopers for that? Besides . . . all they're good for is profiling. . . ."

That was the general idea.

But now, all Dobson could think about was his wife of four years and Becky, their three-year-old daughter. The thugs grabbed Dobson's collar and pulled him from the back of the Lincoln Navigator, leaving his legs to drop to the cement floor with a thud that was felt mostly in his knees.

Left laying at the center of what appeared to be a garage or warehouse, Dobson realized that the DA's hunch was right. Evidence of crime was everywhere: luxury vehicles—some undergoing paint jobs, others sparkling new as if fresh off the showroom floor—and stacks of boxes branded with electronic giants Magnavox, Sony, and Panasonic.

Somehow the fluke—Justin leading these crooks to their unmarked car—put them at the center of this criminal organization. Maybe it was a small crime family, but a lucrative one nonetheless. And this would be their headquarters. So far, Dobson counted six of them.

One of them, obviously, was Ringo. Another was Brice; of that he was sure. Dobson noticed at least half of the six had automatic or semi-automatic weapons in clear view.

Now they were dragging Blair and Justin from the truck to the floor, according to Brice's instructions. The leader.

"Okay, gents, Jakes, pigs—whatever they call you . . . I'm gonna start by saying I hope this is a case of mistaken identity, and that you all just happen to be the wrong pigs in the wrong place at the wrong time. For your sake." B-Money stretched the second rubber glove onto his hand, then he crouched to address each prisoner individually. "But somethin' tells me . . . that ain't the case. So! We're gonna play a little game. See, when I did my last skid bid upstate— Thanks, E.J., for the wire cutters.

"There was this book I read . . . it was called *The Last Kingpin* . . . my fuckin' bible, for real. A vicious joint, too, the way them Columbians handled their business. I don't know how they sleep at night. Anyway I learned some amazing interrogation techniques from that book. Now, I know I don't look like the average bookworm, but cats was tellin' me, 'Yo, B, you gotta read this.' So me bein' that next-level nigga, I said okay. And maaan . . . I ain't been the same since. See . . ." B-Money was down on one knee now, with a head nod to one of his cohorts—the white one.

Ringo perceived things as a backseat driver would, but in his heart there was a heavier burden, that of an accomplice to the car stealing, the kidnapping, and now the torture he was about to witness. The one who B-Money introduced as Spook went to weigh his foot on the bound wrists of the white cop, provoking a grunt. B-Money flashed an evil smile and snatched the rag from the cop's mouth, then he went on with his show.

"They take the finger . . . right here past the knuckle. I prefer the pinkie myself. Then they fit the wire cutters over it like this . . ."

Ringo's heart bumped against his inner chest.

"Fuck you," the cop said.

"Oh yeah, a tough guy, huh?" B-Money gritted his lips together and squeezed. Ringo couldn't control his body's own reactions—the way his rectum shut tight as a fist, how his penis stiffened, his belly ached and his throat swallowed at nothing.

"No, fuck you!" growled B-Money. The cop was left to roll about on the floor, his body twisting and contorting as though trapped in a straight jacket. His wrists remained tied behind his back as he shouted obscenities at his tormentor. B-Money seemed to enjoy this, standing over his victim and inhaling the fruits of his actions. Ringo was shaking now, although he wouldn't show it. He could feel the blades cutting into the skin and snapping the bone. He actually did it. . . . He could imagine the brushfire swooshing through the guy's body, vaporizing any sense of control as he yelled, calling B-Money every obscene name in the book . . . He was blinded for a moment by the red, orange, and yellow flashing before his eyes, the blood spraying continuously as the cop struggled for sanity, instinctively squeezing the wound, lessening the loss of blood and maybe the searing pain as well. Now the guy peed himself.

"See what happens when we invite company over? They don't know how to act. Shut the fuck up, PIG! Matter fact—"

B-Money stepped over to the short one he called Rabbit. He took the gun from his waistband. He approached the grieving cop. "This is for every nigga you shot in the back!"

A bullet discharged into the cop's neck. "And for niggas you harassed!"

Another bullet, this one to the torso. "Police brutality!" A bullet to the abdomen and one in the hip. B-Money took two steps and held the pistol over the cop's head. "Fuck it. Take another one for the niggas you called nigger!"

He squeezed off three shots, bloodying the man's face beyond recognition. And as if that wasn't enough to satisfy him, he swung his arm up in the air and threw the gun at the body with the force of a major league pitcher.

Ringo's eyes fell on the corpse, then the amputated pinkie, at least part of it, laying in its own growing pond of fresh blood. He couldn't tell if it was him spinning where he stood or if it was everything and everybody around him. To keep from falling, he leaned against the Jaguar.

"Sorry you had to see that, Ringo. But you gotta admit . . ." B-Money yucked it up and wagged his head. "Ain't nobody keepin' it real as me!"

B-Money wasn't finished. He switched his attention to the second cop and grabbed him by the neck. He pulled the oil rag from his mouth. "See that? Huh? See what his big mouth got him? It got him dead."

The cop was thrusted back to the floor and B-Money checked him for a wallet. "Oh . . . okay, Mr. Grover W. Dobson." The wallet was held up as if to show the rest of the gang the photo ID inside. "His name is Grover, y'all. What'd your people do—name you after the Muppet or the jazz musician?"

His voice trembling, Dobson replied proudly, "I was named after Wingfoot, the warrior."

"Wingfoot? What—you're a fuckin' Indian?"

"Seminole warrior," said Dobson.

"Well, damn. A real live native. Well, my Indian friend, what are you doin' here? And who you work for?"

Dobson hesitated.

"Name, rank, and serial number." B-Money sighed as if to tell himself, *Here we go again.* Then he turned Dobson over for access to his hands for another finger-snipping session. "Shit!" B-Money snatched open Dobson's hand and produced a cell phone. "Did anybody think to check these fucks before you brought 'em here? Goddamnit! The mothafucka's got a cell phone! How stupid can—" B-Money cut his ranting short to notice that the cell phone was on. It was in the midst of a call!

He put it to his ear, then looked at it as the source of his rage. Then like he did the gun, B-Money threw the cell phone to the floor, where it smashed into so many pieces. "I oughta bust a cap in your ass right now! Fuck!" B-Money kicked Dobson in the side. He was about to do it again, but E.J. stopped him. "B-Money, what if he called for backup?"

"What if?! Moron, of course he called for backup! Spook, Rabbit, outside . . . E.J., Outlaw, get up to the roof. Ringo, if you give a fuck about anything besides your own ass, you'll watch my back."

B-Money took up the Desert Eagle, bloody from when it hit the dead cop. He slapped the gun in Ringo's palm. "Keep an eye on these pigs."

This was the first time Ringo had held a gun in a while. He had a mind to reject it, but then he also thought about the last person to reject B-Money's requests—the one laying dead on the floor—and the idea caused him to hold the gun more affirmatively.

B-Money went to grab his money and drugs, leaving Ringo with Justin and the two detectives—the living and the dead. In the distance B-Money shouted reminders. "Hold me down, Ringo . . . I know you got my back . . ."

"Ringo," said Dobson.

"Shut up. Don't say shit."

"You're not a killer, Ringo. You're not like he is. Don't throw your life away. Don't—"

Ringo went to grab Detective Dobson. This didn't quiet him.

"Don't do this to your son."

Ringo's breathing stopped, self-controlled. "What'd you say?"

"Quentin. He needs you in his life. This isn't you . . . I don't know how you got tangled up in his mess. But so far I don't see you as an accessory."

Justin's mouth was still gagged and he was struggling to join this conversation.

"Ringo, whatever you might've gotten into in the past has nothing to do with what just went down. Your buddy back there, he just killed a cop. He's up to his neck in kidnapping, grand theft auto, and probably a dozen other felony charges."

The words hit Ringo hard. *So far I don't see you as an accessory,* and he had to drag Quentin into this.

But he *was* a part of this. *Quentin. He needs you in his life.* And siding with his homeboy would jeopardize that.

"Put the gun down and help us, Ringo. For godsakes!" he said with a great urgency but still aware that the ringleader wasn't far away. Sirens.

B-Money emerged from his suite with a sports bag over his shoulder and an Uzi strapped over the other. He stopped in his tracks to get a sense of the looming threat as if he could smell how far away the sirens were. A second later he was in motion again, climbing the stairs that were against the wall, leading up to a catwalk and the roof.

"Hold me down, Ringo!" shouted B-Money before disappearing through a doorway.

Ringo wondered to what extent he meant. Was he supposed to stand here and wait for the police to come barreling in?

"That's our backup, Ringo. Don't be foolish. There's no way out of this," said Dobson. Justin wagged his head, more or less agreeing with the detective. Then he and Ringo locked eyes.

B-Money joined E.J. and Outlaw in the spectacular aerial view of Newark's skyline, as well as that maze of streets surrounding Drake Ave. Farther up Drake, a line of emergency lights speedily approached. A number of police vehicles had already arrived and others were just now skidding to screeching halts down below.

"They look like a swarm of white beetles," said E.J., finding some humor in the building tension. "And they're sealing the block off," said Outlaw. The dark of night seemed to suppot all of the electricity below, providing a perfect backdrop for the ongoing activity. There was the stream of headlights, the searchlights skating about, spinning and reflecting off of any thing and everything. And yet, despite all of that they could never be prepared enough for what was about to go down. "In a minute they'll have choppers in here," guessed B-Money. "But that ain't gonna stop us," he said as he whipped the Uzi from his shoulder. Outlaw smiled, likely anticipating a battle. E.J. shrugged, readying his weapon as well. "Empty on 'em," ordered B-Money. "And hit everything movin'!"

It was like he had just answered their prayers. The three of them opened fire on the posse of law enforcement. E.J. worked with a 9 mm Uzi submachine gun, shaking in harmony with its vibrations, spraying hot lead as if watering a lawn, the empty casings dropping there by his feet. Outlaw had the pump action 12-gauge shotgun, causing more hysteria with its fearful blasts than anything else, especially from this distance of thirty some feet. His Uzi firing hails of bullets, B-Money seemed to make the most out of this, shouting, "You can't fuck with us, pigs!" And, "That's right, back that ass up!"

There was barely any return fire as the assault continued. Some vehicles backed away and out of range, others were abandoned as police dove for cover. Spook and Rabbit were shooting at the police as well, first from windows down on a catwalk, and then they joined the others on the roof. After a time, B-Money called for cease-fire. "Hold up!" It was more obvious than a snowman standing tall in a sweltering July heat wave. "I must be dreaming," snapped B-Money. The white Suburban, Ringo's truck, had smashed through the garage door and now raced down Drake Avenue. B-Money didn't know what to make of it. More bizarre was that the police were firing at the truck as it sped toward them, crashing through their road block. From the roof it all looked like a video game that had gotten out of hand.

Shaking the surprise from his senses, B-Money was ready for his next move. Ringo had provided a perfect diversion. "This is it. This is our break. We go our escape route—roof to roof all the way to Gabriel Street. The mustang should be right where we left it." He reloaded his Uzi with a full clip. "This spot is history. Shit!" B-Money vented.

"But all those cars," E.J. appealed.

"Don't remind me. We'll just have to take it as a loss. Let's go." B-Money started to lead the others from the roof, but he stopped and suddenly turned around.

"What's up, B?"

"I forgot somethin', he said and he took the 12-gauge from Outlaw casually, as if receiving a pool cue.

As soon as B-Money took the shotgun, it discharged a blast. To the others it appeared unintentional.

"Oops . . . Damn, was it loaded?" he asked, wincing. But the others immediately saw that this was a mistake. The blast was directed right at Rabbit's midsection, sending him back to the ledge of the roof. A hole the size of a softball was still smoking right where a stopwatch might hang. Without hesitation B-Money reached down to grab Rabbit by the feet and he tossed him over. "Hell of a job that you did, Rabbit. Real good work," said B-Money. Then he led the rush from roof to roof, just the four of them now, like some victim's football squad determined to reach the end zone.

Chapter Twenty-six

MANHATTAN

"Tangi, you ever see Ringo with another woman? And if you did, would you ever tell me?"

Tangi's eyes burned with astonishment as she stood there, her back to Porsha. She had been reaching for a diaper from the walk-in closet, but now she froze, wondering what Porsha knew. "Tangi, I'm talkin' to you."

"Girl, you are straight trippin'. I mean straight trippin'." Tangi hustled up the nerve to finally turn and face Porsha. "How you gonna go there at a time like this? Y'all got a son together. And regardless, Ringo ain't done nothin' but love your yellow ass on the regular. You trippin'." Tangi turned again, finally retrieving a diaper. "Tangi, I'm not trippin'. I'm gettin' a funny feeling, that's all. Am I allowed?"

"No," affirmed Tangi, pushing Porsha aside so she could change Quentin herself. "I better do this, 'cause the way your brain is tickin' right now, you might put it on his head instead of his ass."

Porsha stepped back and folded her arms. "Tangi, we haven't had sex in almost four weeks." Tangi kept herself occupied, wincing at the odor. *Whew-ee, you stink, boy.* "Well, you know Ringo, boo. He's a busy man. Face it . . . you married a superstar."

"Marriage. Ha. Don't make me laugh," said Porsha.

"Well, you are practically married . . ."

"Shut up, Tangi."

Tangi did surrender to Porsha's sweet and sour expression. At the same time she hoped that the subject changed. No such luck.

"Well? If you did know anything, would you tell me? Or would you be more loyal to him?"

Hold me down at home, Tangi. Ringo's words were there at the forefront of her thoughts, forcing an unanticipated psychological conflict on her. Thinking fast, Tangi said, "Baby, I'll do you one better. I'd kill the bitch he was fuckin'!"

Porsha choked, her head flying back and her eyes feeling as if they'd inflated in their sockets. She'd never seen this side of Tangi, so hard-core. But then, Porsha had a lot to learn. Softening her attitude some, Tangi said, "Well shit, girl . . . you and I go back like green eggs and ham, like Humpty Dumpty. What you expect from me?"

"I don't expect you to go that far."

Her head knocking back and forth on her neck, Tangi said, "Well, wouldn't you do the same for me?" Porsha took too long to respond. "Well, ain't that a bitch. Like you gotta think about it . . ." Tangi was done with the diaper. She nudged little Quentin's nose with hers, lifted him from his crib, and handed him over. "Just for the record, Porsha, we gotta have each other's backs. Otherwise what kind of best friends are we?"

"Yeah, but to kill somebody?"

"Bugle by my side for you, right hand high for you," said Tangi, quoting a Lil' Kim rap, a determined screwface showing she meant business.

"I love it when you get all ghetto like that, Tangi." Porsha chuckled. "But God help J-Love if he ever crosses you."

"You can say that again."

"I just hope Ringo's not cheatin', Tangi. You don't have no idea how much I love that man."

"Want me to investigate?"

Porsha thought about it. "I'm afraid to say yes—but yes!"

Tangi laughed at her friend and put her cheek to Porsha's in a show of affection. The sight of Porsha and her child prompted

Tangi to stop laughing. First she felt pride, then concern over the insight of fate.

SOME 3,000 FEET ABOVEGROUND

"Okay, Di, you've been quiet as a mouse for pratically the entire flight. Plus, you know I don't mind keepin' it real with you." Kianna took a second to consider what she'd say. "Your performance was kinda green last night. Don't get me wrong, you gave a good show—for them, that is. But for me? Honey chile, I've seen a lot better. The Palace in L.A., the Hard Rock in Montreux, House of Blues in Atlanta . . . what about the Copa? And I have videotape for that show, in case you want me to cry, Kianna."

"Diamond? What's wrong? Tell me what's goin' on in that skull of yours. That's the one place I want an all-access pass for." Diamond began counting her fingers on one hand. "What're you doin'?"

"Counting the roles you play in my life. Lemme see . . . we have mommy, daddy, you're my personal assistant, my manager . . ."

"No. Justin's already doin' that job," said Kianna with a hint of sarcasm.

Diamond flashed a cinical tight-lipped smile. Then she said, "What about therapist? Can anyone but you claim that role?"

"Can't a sista care? And stop deviating from the subject. We were talking about you." Kianna gave Diamond a friendly punch. "What's up? Penny for your thoughts."

"I got a funny feeling, Kianna. Something like butterflies but more on the queasy side."

"Ohhh my God!" Kianna gushed. "Tell me you are not pregnant. Tell me, Diamond. I'll kill him! I swear!"

Kianna's eruption attracted attention from other first-class travelers. Anything close to a disruption made people nervous these days.

"I'm not pregnant, Ki." Diamond's voice was intentionally hush-hush, an attempt to control the temperature of the conversation. People who were watching Kianna released whatever anxiety that developed through an exasperated exhale.

"It's something else entirely. Like a feeling about the future. Ever have one of those? What are they called?"

"Premonitions, and yes, I have had them. But usually it's something I knew was coming anyway."

"How do you mean?"

"Like for instance, something you could've avoided or projected. So it's part premonition, part sixth sense, and part cause and effect."

"Whoa. You're getting scientific on me, Ki. It's about forecasting, the kindergarten version?"

"It's about forecasting your heart. Like it says in your song . . . my dad once told me that we were designed to survive. Like what we go through when we get the flu . . . we get a fever and that's a warning that we're sick. Our body needs something, usually water. Then our body goes into survival mode, sweating, coughing up phlegm. That's our body's way of getting rid of the foreign elements that got us the flu in the first place. So like I said we're designed to survive, to know and cope with life's challenges."

"Okay. That makes sense. It's a little deep but I understand it."

"What do you think I should do when we're stuck in a hotel room or long flights?"

"Boo, I read. So, what you're going through, the mood swings you might be having? Remember that we're given certain tools at birth. All of us are. We have brains to think with and we have senses to feel with and even antibodies to fight off germs. We have it all. So if something is indicating danger then listen to it. Take it as a warning or as guidance to protect you from something or somebody."

"Okay," Diamond replied, somehow unsure of how she'd do that. The announcement filtered out of the airplane's P.A. system informing passengers to buckle up.

"Di?"

"Hmmm?"

"You're daydreaming, fantasizing or something. Seat belts, babe. And that's not to say you can't finish telling me what's on your mind."

Diamond fixed her seat belt and reached to open the valve for some fresh air. The plane would be descending shortly. "The week before last?"

"Uh-huh?"

"When we were supposed to go to the meeting with the label execs and I said I was sick."

"You weren't really sick. I already know, Diamond. Sometimes I think I read you better than I read myself."

"Okay, now ask me why I said I was sick."

Kianna looked up toward the roof of the plane. "I give up. Why, Diamond? Why did you play sick?"

"I can't face Ringo. I'm afraid I'll break down again."

"You're shittin' me, Di. You're still feeling some type of way about him?"

"That's where the premonition comes in, Kianna. Remember Queens Boulevard?"

"How can I forget? Wasn't I the one in the hospital with you, like twenty-four seven?"

"Don't think I'm crazy, Ki, but the guy who grabbed me? I think that was him."

"You are shitting me," said Kianna as the cabin angled downward. "How ever did you draw this conclusion? Didn't you . . . didn't the newspaper and the police say the man had on a mask? That they couldn't ID him?"

"Yeah, but . . ."

"Di, when they flashed a police sketch on *America's Most Wanted* like two hundred people called in. None of them was right. So how in the world could you ID him? Are your butterflies tellin' you this?"

"Don't make fun of me, Kianna. This is serious. It's something deeper."

"Like?"

"My heart. In my heart I know it was him." Her ears popped as the airplane descended into LaGuardia. She hated this part of the trip even more than all of the new precautions at the airports, the way this vacuum overcame her, making her feel helpless under the intangible force of the plane.

A series of awkward facial expressions and jaw movements got Kianna's ears to pop and her senses back to some kind of normalcy. In the meantime, while the 747 landed, she told herself to revisit the Ringo issue as soon as she set foot on solid ground.

Chapter Twenty-seven

NEWARK, NEW JERSEY

Ringo may as well have been facing a firing squad, or maybe this was suicide. Either way it was nothing close to what the cop told him. "Just smash right through the garage door. We'll be safe once we're behind police lines." But there was nothing further from the truth. Ringo never challenged the idea and he never thought to ask, *How will they know it's us?* After all, the detective was the authority under the cicumstances. Ringo the fool listened to Dobson. But the instant that the Suburban made it through the garage door, destroying it, they were met with a blizzard of gunfire. To think that he was escaping the threat of violence was an ass-backward mistake. But that was an afterthought. Too late to turn back. Bullets of every caliber pelted the exterior of the Suburban as Ringo whipped the vehicle away from the driveway of B-Money's home. The truck was weighed down with four bodies, one of them a corpse, but was still able to muster the horsepower to charge at the barrier of squad cars. Ringo had no choice, he simply prayed that he got his money's worth when adding so many preventive options when customizing and arming the Suburban.

"You plan on stopping?" asked Dobson, afraid to look.

"Why? So your buddies can kill me?" Ringo floored the accelerator and was thrown around like a cowboy holding onto a wild steer. Only this wasn't a rodeo, it was a so-so driver barreling through, crashing into squad cars under heavy gunfire.

"Shit!" The tires gave one by one, but the blowouts didn't stop the speedy escape. Ringo couldn't understand it, however he continued pushing the truck dispute to the flat lines.

"What is this thing, a tank?" asked Dobson, lifting himself from the floor. He looked back at the blitz of emergency lights and teams of dumbfounded, outsmarted police officers.

"It's armored," said Ringo. "A good thing too since I went and listened to you." Ringo checked his rear-view mirrors. One of them showed the reflection of Justin. Five-O.

"Can we get to a hospital?" asked Dobson.

"A hospital? Wake up, Dobbs. Your man needs a morgue. Plus, I don't even know where the fuck we are!" hollered Ringo. Although the attack had tapered off, Ringo's insides were ring-a-linging like an overworked pinball machine. In his mind he was still frustrated, entrapped, and afraid. "And any minute more of your friends will be chasin' us."

"You gotta stop, Ringo. I can—"

"I'm through listenin' to you. You almost got me killed just now! Shut the fuck up and let me think!" Ringo slammed the steering wheel as he yelled. "You better not say one goddamned word! Not one!" All Ringo could see was hot lava when he saw Justin . . . Justin at dinner . . . Justin holding Quentin . . . Justin at his business meetings. *Stick by my side, Justin. What would I do without your good advice? Your good judgment?* Just to see his face made Ringo sick to his stomach.

Justin felt worse than uncomfortable, to have been discovered with the detectives outside of Zanzibar and then kidnapped by some half-assed thugs and exposed as the insider. It was worse than he dreamed. He wondered if there were any excuses that he could come up with. But he dismissed the possibilties when he remembered the recording device they had found. The wire that had been taped to his chest.

Jesus, of all the dumb luck. The boys night out . . . this under-cover shit is finished. K.O.

"The hospital! Where's the nearest hospital?" shouted Dobson at the first late-night wanderer they could find. Sirens screamed in the distance. The pedestrian gave directions, though apprehensively. Ringo had slowed just enough for Dobson to communicate with the stranger, but when he heard what he needed he took off again, flooring the accelerator.

"Cut a left," instructed Dobson. And there it was, a big blue sign with a block letter *H* on it.

Ringo had a better idea. Instead of taking the turn at the corner he cut through the corner gas station, leaving attendants and patrons equally horrified as he careened through a narrow passage. Two police cruisers shot out of nowhere like the result of a radio call for help and they attempted to keep up with the Suburban. But the confusion that Ringo left—like the Toyota that now blocked the passage behind him—forced one of the cruisers to skid and slam into a gas pump. There was a second or two when anxiety was in control, sending panicked customers and a gas attendant leaping from their cars for cover. *Boom.* One compact car was tossed twenty feet or more. Another vehicle was kicked into a column, bringing that towering metal pavilion crashing down on top of everything below. The blast also set off a bright, blinding heat that mushroomed into the air and the surrounding streets, forcing traffic to a standstill. At once all of the violence left squad cars to spin out of control. Ringo looked over the back of his shoulder, half stunned, half excited by the explosion. A rush of energy pushed through him and he gunned ahead, wondering when the next police vehicle would pop up in his path. The hospital was two blocks away. A glow illuminated the atmosphere where Ringo presumed the hospital was located, and he instinctively cut a sharp right turn into some corporate property parking lot. The Suburban smashed the gate nose first and swerved toward a grassy embankment, hopping a slight hill and slope until it broke through a fence on the opposite end.

"Here's your stop. And watch the closing doors."

"That's it? You're just gonna leave us here with a body?"

"Look, hospital's over there. Holland Tunnel's over there. Guess which way I'm goin'."

Justin couldn't see what Dobson was arguing about. They'd barely escaped torture or worse death. And now they had a chance to walk away.

"Roll out!" ordered Ringo.

Dobson said, "Help me, Justin." They pulled Blair from the truck in time so that it wouldn't drag them off as it raced away. Justin couldn't help but wonder how far Ringo could get with an army of New Jersey police hunting for a white Suburban with tinted windows, rolling on half-filled tires. "What the hell are you waitin' for? Someone to take your picture? Help me get him to the hospital."

Justin looked down at Detective Blair with his inflamed head wounds and bloody flesh. He wanted to puke as he helped carry the dead body but there was just so much going through his mind keeping it occupied. The past two hours of terror, guns, and stolen cars. The thugs, the cold-hearted murder. This was far from his routine day as a law student; it was more like a lifetime of thrills and fear compressed into a night-long nightmare.

Justin tossed and turned in the hospital bed. His eyes opened to the harsh light and it was as if he was being stabbed in his eyeballs. Someone was standing over them. B-Money, Ringo, Rabbit, and a couple of others. Justin's body jerked around uncontrollably. Then someone's hands were holding him down. "Oh God, no! Don't kill me!" he yelled. Someone was stabbing him, this time for real. He let out a bellowing cry. The pain.

Someone—a female—was speaking. "He's going through it," she said in an echo.

Now a male voice. "Give him six CCs. That oughta smooth him out. Better keep him strapped down too; we don't want him to hurt himself."

Another male voice—Dobson? "What's the deal, Doc? Why's he actin' up like this?"

"Trauma. Shock. A little of both. Whatever calamities he experienced in the past few hours have taxed him. He's lucky he hasn't gone into a coma."

Justin's body relaxed again and he felt his mind, his thoughts, melt back into nothingness.

Bill McDoogle called for a three-car escort and six additional men. Then the group of them broke records speeding through the Lincoln Tunnel and down the New Jersey Turnpike to get to Newark General Hospital. Detective Dobson had placed the emergency call to the DA, woke him up, actually, informing him about the foiled investigation and how things literally blew up in their faces. McDoogle might've simply turned over in his bed, perhaps addressing these issues in the morning when he was really awake. Except Dobson mentioned Blair's severed pinkie. And nothing could wake McDoogle faster. He cut the call short and put emergency calls in to the police commissioner and the mayor. Those two subsequently contacted authorities in New Jersey. Newark General soon became a magnet for any available officer in the area. It didn't matter that Detective Dobson was from New York. There was enough outrage stirring about the torture to upset law enforcement at large. "This is gonna be a madhouse," exclaimed McDoogle as his three-car escort worked its way onto the hospital lawn, about the only other area left near the E.R. entrance. "What is this, a police convention? And how the hell did the press get here so quick?" McDoogle led his support team across the lawn to the entrance of the emergency room. An officer was posted outside of the sliding glass doors and he immediately stepped aside to allow entry. "I'm Bill McDoogle, district attorney, here to see Detective Dobson." They were in front of a reception desk.

"Just down the hall to the left," the attendant said, as if she'd uttered the same directions a dozen or so times.

The emergency room lobby, its corridors, and the waiting room were abuzz with police officers who were both in and out of uniform. Those in plainclothes had their badges exposed—hooked on their belts or draped around their necks like medallions. One such man accompanied McDoogle into the immediate area. He had more firearms than a well-stocked gun shop might keep. And every pistol-packing officer also carried the burden of this occasion, hungry to be the one to catch the beast who did this to a cop.

"Good news, Doc?" "I'm sorry, you are?" McDoogle presented his identification. "Oh okay, well, Detective Blair is gonna be fine, except for the pinkie I'm afraid. A nice hatchet job they did to it, but nobody has been able to produce the severed digit, so I don't believe we'll be in time to reattach it. Time is of the essence in these cases . . ."

"How is he?"

"He's in stable condition. He's a trooper, this detective. Half the victims of these types of wounds either pass out or go into shock. Like the other patient . . ."

"Other patient?" asked McDoogle.

"Sir," Detective Dobson interrupted as he approached.

"Dobson, what happened to you?"

"The sling is just a precaution, nothing is broken. Truth is I didn't even know I was injured. Then I went through a minor checkup and they said it was fractured—just the wrist though."

McDoogle blinked his eyes wider, relieved that both of his men were doing okay, all things considered. "Well, at least I can breathe easier," said McDoogle. "There's no counting how many times the job calls for visits like these."

"Uh, sir? Didn't they tell you about Justin?"

"As in my intern? Justin Lewis?"

"Yes, sir. He was with us."

Dobson didn't have to say much more before the DA demanded to see Justin. The doctor followed and gave a diagnosis along the way.

In the intensive care unit the group of them stood alongside Justin. "He's pretty drugged up right now so you won't be able to communicate with him. But I believe he'll recuperate back to normal health. It's the anxiety he's dealing with, perhaps witnessing the torture, the bit with the finger. This kind of thing happens."

"How long will he be like this?"

"Right now he's going through a sort of thawing out period. That's the way it gets. There's a bout of madness as a result of the intense fear. According to the detective here our friend may have sensed some impending doom. So in my experience this sort of thing is more or less a reaction. The palpitations, the dizziness, and the spasms. I'm most certain that he's been having flashbacks."

"Doc, is this something related to his current state of health? Or is it specific to the events of tonight?"

"I can stand here all morning and speculate without the patient's medical records in hand, but unless you have any reason to believe Mr. Lewis has a history of repressed unresolved childhood experiences or some other psychological disorder, I'm gonna guess that a bit of rest will get this man in tune again."

"So he's gonna be okay."

"That's my best guess. Now, if you gentlemen will allow the patient some peace."

Out in the hallway McDoogle faced Dobson. "What happened out there?"

With a sense of guilt, Dobson said, "It was crazy, sir. That's the only way to explain it. We were at least a few hundred feet away, Justin wore a wire and we sat in an unmarked car monitoring everything. He was with the rapper and everything was going smoothly. Then before we knew it, we find ourselves witnessing a vehicle heist. And it looked like our man Brice was overseeing it all. He and the rapper somehow double up because the white Suburban, the one belonging to Ringo? Brice stole it. I don't think he knew it was Ringo's. So those two drive off, then Justin comes out of the clear blue, jumps in with us, and we're about to tail Ringo and Brice. Then *bam*, we get ambushed. Some other guy, one of Brice's people, shows up with a gun. We have no choice but to surrender." Dobson went on about being tied up, the hideout on Drake Avenue, and the torture. "It was right after they cut Blair's finger off. He was doin' a whole lot of yelling and blood was everywhere and Brice was about to shoot him. That's when Justin seemed to lose it. I could see it in his eyes, how he was there but not really there, if you know what I mean. The guy looked like a zombie, a vegetable."

"Well, the main thing is you're all alive. I just wish you had called someone for backup. At least call the locals. I mean, what if one of you had gotten killed? What if Brice did shoot one of you? Do you know how much I'd have to deal with? Putting an intern out there in the line of fire? They'd have my neck, Dobson."

"Sorry, sir."

"No excuses, Dobson. Did we get anything on tape?"

"A lot of loud music and laughing. But even if we had gotten something, they grabbed our recorder when they ambushed us. What they didn't see is the cell phone in my back pocket. Thank God. That's how I called 911, and of course there's the Global Positioning Satellite that probably pinpointed our location. Thank God for technology, sir. This Brice is bigger that we pictured. He's swimming in crime, assault weapons, probably—no, definitely drugs."

"Was the rapper involved?"

"You're not gonna believe this, sir. Ringo was the one who rescued us."

"Rescued? But I thought he and Brice . . . ?"

"You had to be there, sir. If you were you might wanna see this guy get a medal of honor."

"What the . . . ?"

McDoogle had to contain himself. "Never mind. Just give me a full report, Dobson."

Just then Ruby Webber, the assistant DA who had gone out on her own pre-investigation, snapping photos at the Beacon Theater and checking into the background of Ringo's tagalongs, came behind the powwow of men.

"Sir, I wonder if the detectives saw any sign of the girls."

"Girls?"

"Yes, of course. How could I forget. Dobson, it seems like we have another problem. Christine Lieberman, Senator Lieberman's seventeen-year-old daughter? She and her friends, four of them all together, were in New York attending the concert at the Beacon Theater."

Ruby pulled out a folder with photos. "The girls in these photos. Here they are mingling with the rapper and again with Brice."

She pointed out the four faces as she showed Dobson. "These four girls have been missing ever since that night. The parents initially thought they left on some school trip, only they never returned home. These pictures, as far as we can tell, were the last time they were seen," said Ruby. McDoogle asked, "Are you sure you didn't notice any sign of the girls? Maybe at the club you went to?"

"Sir, we never stepped foot in the club, but Justin did. Still, that place was nowhere that you would find these girls."

"How do you know if you didn't go inside?"

"Trust me, sir. It was an altogether different crowd. Like mixing fish and whipped cream."

"I see. Well, I'd better get somebody from Newark PD on this. Let me know when Lewis is alive and kickin'. I have a trial first thing tomorrow."

"Gotcha."

"And by the way, I want you to meet a few people." McDoogle led Dobson to the team of enforcement who joined him for the trip. "This is Adams, Stevens, Armstrong, Knight, and this young woman is Shonna King, a private investigator. She's independent. Just keep her updated."

"Oh." Dobson was confused for a moment. "Does this mean the budget has been approved for the task force?" He had to make himself turn his attention away from Shonna.

"So far. We'll see how things go. Let's just pray for Justin's full recovery so we can catch these bastards. And you all should go ahead and get acquainted because after we drop this group of hoods, there're a number of others who we're targeting. All right, that's it for me. Let's take these guys down and find the senator's girl."

Chapter Twenty-eight

Ringo was beside himself during the ride back to New York. He made it out of Newark and into the tunnel without being stopped, but he figured it was a fluke or an oversight. So much the better.

Along the way he wondered if and how he might be considered an accessory to his homey's evils. There was that and there was also the once-upon-a-time to think about. The skeletons in his closet. What was it the cop said?

Ringo, whatever you might've gotten into in the past has nothing to do with what just went down. Your buddy just cut off a cop's finger.

And then Ringo set his eyes on Justin. Justin, who looked as though he'd visited the Twilight Zone. But for the moment, there were other concerns. *Am I a fugitive? Are they at my crib?*

Once he reached 43rd Street, Ringo decided to park farther down the block, away from his address. For now he was a little paranoid about all the possibilities taking shape in his mind.

He entered the building through the garage and climbed nineteen flights so as not to be surprised by a posse of police detectives who might be awaiting him by the elevator doors, the typical way up to his apartment. Winded, Ringo eased the door open on the nineteenth floor, peeking and listening.

It was four in the morning, so anything out of the ordinary would be obvious.

"Listen. I'd love to discuss this more, but honestly I've made up my mind. This makes two times that procedure has been ignored: once at the Beacon Theater and last night at Zanzibar.

There's no third chances with me. I've been through this before—celebrities and their arrogance, their egos. They think they can do what they want when they want and have absolutely no respect for the service I provide. I'm a professional, Jamie. You know that."

"Mel, it can't be that bad. And Ringo isn't as irresponsible as you say. He knows better."

"The hell he does. Jamie, I've been this man's Siamese twin for the better part of a month now. The promotional tour, radio shows, the music conferences, and do I need to bring up Chaz and Wilson's? I think you get my drift. It only takes one incident, Jamie. One. I know you've heard the horror stories, the star gets into trouble because he's in the wrong place at the wrong time, words are exchanged, one thing leads to another, and *bang*. The shit hits the fan. And who do you think has to answer for it? Whose reputation is at stake? And who has the most to lose? Me, that's who. And I'm not havin' it."

Ringo got a good enough look to know Mel was easing away from Jamie. He had reached the elevator doors by now and Jamie circled around to stop him with her back to the doors.

Mel wasn't deterred. He reached around her to press the button with its arrow facing down.

"Can't you make this one exception, Mel? For me? You know these hokey-pokes that he has with him are for the birds. And the only way this can be a winning team is with winning players."

"Save the sales pitch. I'm not stickin' my neck out for this guy. He's hard-headed."

Ringo showed himself as the doors parted.

"Let'm go, Jamie. I wish you luck, Mel."

"Back atcha."

Inside the elevator Mel shrugged at Jamie and the doors closed.

"What happened here?" asked Jamie, the question directed toward no one in particular. She blew steam as she marched after Ringo, down the hall and into the open door of 196.

"Okay, what went down in Jersey? Because Mel wouldn't tell me."

"It's a long story, Jamie. How'd the pajama party go? Where's wifey?"

"The girls finally called it a night about an hour ago. I stayed to help Porsha clean up, and then Mel pages me. Now do you mind tellin' me?"

"In the morning. Right now I'm bushed. You have no idea what kind of night I had."

"I thought I heard Ringo." Porsha was barefoot, her hair still frazzled from a shower, and a T-shirt draped down to her thighs. "You had us worried, boo. When Mel came back without you we didn't know what to think."

"Well, I'm here now," he said, pulling Porsha in for a hug, his hands full of her ass. Nobody realized that Jamie had picked up the phone.

"He's here," said Jamie and she hung up. A moment later, Butter and Sweets ambled through the door.

"See?" said Butter to Sweets. "Told you he was all right." Then to Ringo, he said, "Yo, Mel was trippin', Ringo. Ramblin' about bein' a professional bodyguard and whatnot."

"Fuck Mel. For real. We didn't start with Mel, did we?"

"The truck?"

"One block over. In front of the Blue Velvet. That's where it's parked."

"My man," said Butter, and Ringo clasped hands with his two loyal soldiers.

"You gonna tell us what the hell went down in Jersey?" asked Sweets.

"Tomorrow. But right now a brotha needs some space. A little family time, if you don't mind." Ringo handed over the key to the Suburban, and Butter immediately recognized it wasn't the same key.

"Don't ask," said Ringo, reading his mind. When the front door closed behind the two, Ringo amused himself thinking how surprised they'd be to find blood in the truck and the tires flat.

"You have fun? How was your boys night out?"

Ringo scrunched his face. "Maybe not as exciting as yours, you and your exotic male dancer."

"We canceled him, Ringo. I couldn't go through with it. You know you're the only stripper I need."

For the first time in what felt like weeks, Ringo got his hug on.

"Where ya goin'?"

"Some personal hygiene. A nice hot shower. A quick snack, and—"

Porsha put her hands on her hips.

"And hopefully some dessert," said Ringo with a suggestive grin.

Porsha took Ringo's chin in her hands and kissed his nose.

"I was beginning to feel neglected."

Ringo attempted to comfort her with another hug.

"We'll just have to see what we can do about that," said Ringo.

The two brought in the dawn with a passion that surpassed any sense of space or time, a passion that left both lovers in their own states of nothingness. Another kind of coma.

If Justin was sick right now it was the kind of sick that was absolute bliss. He had not a care in the world. The dope that the doctors ordered had him feeling pretty nice right now, where before he opened his eyes he was moonwalking in forward motion. Instead of backsliding through the frightening encounters, he was floating ahead, experiencing joy and prosperity. There was Diamond mothering their two children, a boy and a girl. They lived in a gated community with a million-dollar home and a small army of servants.

There were no threats, no problems, and no worries. Everything came to them in abundant measure and life never looked more colorful.

Kianna's face appeared. Reality check. Justin opened his eyes to a graceful morning sun ray leaking through the blinds. He was still at the hospital, still feeling nice, floating with that warm satisfied smile in his mind, although his face hadn't changed the slightest bit. When he did budge, an alarm sounded. It wasn't a loud alarm, just a *ding-ding-ding* or maybe he was imagining that, too. *Is anything real here?*

"Justin."

It was Dobson's voice, although it seemed somehow separated from him . . . somehow preceding the movement of his lips. *I'm seeing things.*

Justin's senses were better aligned now, or at least better than before. No villains with fangs and horns and fire in their eyes. Nobody was out to get him or threatening to kill him.

A sigh of relief made Justin aware of the sterile aroma. There was the IV drip attached to his wrist, and the requisite lifesaving digital machinery at his bedside. *Am I alive?*

Justin tested things. He wiggled his toes, then his fingers.

A nurse rushed through the door and it might've shook him except everything was too nice. The world was okay. But then, of course, that nurse could have been a fire-breathing dragon and according to Justin, the world would still be okay.

"Did he move?" the nurse asked.

"I heard the beeps. He must've. Justin?"

"In the flesh . . . I think."

"O-ho, man. Yeah! Can you . . . can you move?"

"I'm afraid to try. What happened? Did I get shot? Do I have all my limbs?"

"The doctor said it was some sorta anxiety thing. Somethin' to do with the shock . . . You feeling okay?"

"I guess," said Justin, but then he noticed the restraints. "Why am I tied down?"

"Oh. Ahh . . . nurse, could you?"

"Let me just get a doctor. Hold tight, Mr. Lewis."

The nurse scurried out of the room. Dobson sucked his teeth and started unfastening straps.

"This is silly. If you're okay, you're okay. Why keep you tied down?"

"Whoa," Justin said. "Man . . . I feel nice."

Dobson rushed to his aid. "Easy, Justin, they put some kinda dope in you."

"Is that why I feel like a balloon?"

Eventually he was sitting in an upright position. The doctor came in and explained all kinds of complex medical opinions. But that was all so irrelevant, considering that Justin was feeling as though he had to learn how to use things again—his lips, his voice, and his limbs.

"It's like I've been sleeping for a few years. What day is it? What century?"

Dobson ordered some solid food for both he and Justin. He also filled in the gaps, those blanks that still remained from the late-night hours. The weight of the world was returning. The concerns, responsibilities, and burdens were gradually returning to Justin's shoulders.

Ringo, Brice, Diamond.

"I knew it was too good to be true."

"What?" asked Dobson.

"Oh nothing. So then, this task force . . . they're taking over? I'm out of the loop?"

Dobson made a face as if his stomach was queasy.

"So that is it. I initiate the whole get-the-rapper effort. I dig into the project as an inside man, deceiving people, befriending Ringo and his band of supporters . . . then I get exposed as a Judas."

"But Justin, wasn't that exactly what you expected? I'm saying . . . in the end, wasn't that gonna be the reality? That you'd be recognized as one of us? The good guys? And perhaps you'd earn some kind of justice for Diamond? The woman you love?"

"Except for almost being killed. Dobson, I put my life on the line. How can the DA just kick me to the side like this?"

"Justin, he is the DA. He doesn't necessarily need your approval to do his job."

"Oh, so go ahead and kick a man who's down already. Shit, Dobson. You're blowin' my high . . ."

"Maybe you're looking at this the wrong way, Justin. I don't think that McDoogle had anything more in mind than your well-being. You should've seen him earlier. He rushed over from Manhattan—not even . . . it was Long Island, where he lives. And the minute he found out you were hospitalized he demanded to see you. He even forgot about Detective Blair, which is why he came over in the first place. I think you should relax, get your clean bill of health, and I'm sure he'll have some role you can fill in the task force."

"You'll talk to him?"

"All three of us will," said Detective Blair, surprising the two. Justin thought he'd seen a ghost.

"Where'd you come from? I thought they had you on some heavy pain relievers?" said Dobson.

Blair's hand was wrapped like a giant Q-tip, but his injury didn't break his spirit.

"I'm okay. We were just talking about you."

"I hope it was the good stuff."

"It's all good. And guess what? You're just in time to listen to my great idea," said Justin.

Dobson and Blair shared a doubtful look.

The task force wasted no time in their hunt for Brice and his cohorts. McDoogle also made it clear that the investigation was still ongoing and that grand theft auto wasn't the only charge he intended to bring against the crew. However, time was of the essence now with the senator's daughter missing.

If it was a choice between waiting to substantiate organized crime charges and rescuing the girls, the latter would have to become the greater priority. And the DA would redirect his efforts, perhaps including the federal government in a series of kidnapping charges. In that event it would be difficult to drag the rapper in without some concrete evidence.

"See what you can come up with," McDoogle told the group. "Start with the hideout they used on—what was that? Drake Avenue?"

And that's where the group of them were nosing around at four in the morning. The DA had called ahead to see that the Newark PD was informed and that his investigation would work seamlessly with theirs in a joint effort.

"If you ask me, the place is a tell-tale house of mayhem," explained the lieutenant on duty at the Drake Avenue address. "Sure, there's a shitload of cars and trucks, household electronics, and the like, but then there's this sort of swanky bedroom in the back. . . . There's gotta be eight million stories back there. Sound proofing, mood lighting, psychedelic fabric on the walls. I don't mind you guys takin' a look around, but please observe the usual preliminary measures—rubber gloves and that kinda jazz. It's real sensitive back there."

An officer handed out surgical gloves.

When Adams, Stevens, Armstrong, Knight, and Shonna King approached the rear of the garage there were already more than a dozen or so law enforcement personnel scattered throughout. But things seemed twice as crowded in the bedroom the lieutenant had warned them about.

Forensic specialists were dusting for prints. Police photographers snapped and flashed the camera relentlessly. One officer circled the boudoir with a video camera.

Of course the safes were empty, indicating the hasty escape. And, as Dobson had suggested, there were traces of cocaine everywhere.

"Look at this, Stevens." Knight pointed out a number of drawers that were opened underneath the bed with the contents draped over the edges for further viewing. Handcuffs, chains, shackles, and leather restraints. There were gags, blindfolds, and rope. Leather masks, a whip, nipple clamps, a bondage manual, and even a rubber stopper with a tail designed with synthetic hair.

"Jesus," said Armstrong. "What the hell do you s'pose that's for?"

Shonna King explained how it was a prop used in S&M circles. And she wasn't stingy with the details.

"They plug it in a person's ass so they'll look like horses," she said.

"What kind of woman would allow that?"

"Hmm . . . How about the men who use it?"

Shonna's comment quieted half the room.

Besides the sex toys there were the knives, daggers, and a larger tempered-steel Shogun model with a gold handle.

"What the fuck could that be for?"

"Whatever it was for involved blood . . . You mind?" One of the forensic specialists took the sword from Adams. "We're taking this in for further examination. Evidence, ya know." There was a slick smile with the interaction.

"Watch your step, sir. There's a bloodstain on the carpet—

the bed too . . . You really should be careful. This is a crime scene, y'know."

A bit frustrated, Knight and Armstrong wandered into the adjoining room where a jacuzzi was stationed. A photographer was angling his camera to get the best shot of a blood-soaked towel on the ledge.

Farther ahead in the bathroom, another photographer was standing over a sink.

"What the hell is that?"

"Well . . ." The photographer pulled the camera from his eye to respond. "Looks like a partial breast if you ask me."

Knight turned a funny look toward Armstrong, unsure if the officer was kidding.

"Except . . . right here? It looks like teeth marks where the nipple had been bitten off."

Armstrong made a face now, noticing how ants were crawling about the flesh and blood.

"Let's get out of here."

"I'm with you."

Diamond bent over to kiss Justin's forehead, allowing him to continue sleeping. He seemed so peaceful. So at ease.

She looked over at the digital clock. Twelve noon. *Why aren't you at school?* she wondered. Then she smiled, thinking that he was probably watching her on TV last night. *And you waited for me to come home . . . aw booby.* Assumptions. She was so proud of Justin, so happy to have agreed with him that they were meant to be together. She with all of her sour grapes. He with his straight and narrow way of life. It was a long flight and she could use a little unwinding right now.

A shower. A V-8 juice.

Diamond began to come out of her clothes. When she was fully naked she peeked down at the scar—that and the memories were all that she carried as reminders of the nightmare on Queens Boulevard and the cop that shot her.

She wished that Justin would open his eyes right now so that he could take a real good look at her—not while in the heat of passion, and not in any snazzy outfit on stage.

Look at me now, Justin, and tell me that you'll love me forever . . . even if I can't give you children.

A tear rolled down Diamond's cheek and made it as far as her breast, dissipating before reaching her erect nipple.

The shower helped to soothe her, somehow washing away her anguish.

Conveniently she peed where she stood—after all it was all going to the same place, the dirty water and the urine—and it stimulated her enough that she played with herself. She slid her fore and middle fingers in, out, and around her most sensitive folds, folds she imagined under Justin's soft tongue . . . folds she imagined him penetrating. She got to thinking about their love . . . their happiness . . . her total satisfaction.

"Diamond?"

Her body was convulsing when she heard his voice.

He was on top of her, gliding in and out of her, making her that total woman. Her breathing was hyper.

"Justin!" She cried out his name and it came out as if she were thanking God for some miracle.

"Diamond?" It wasn't a dream! He was there in the bathroom. And now his head peeked into the shower stall.

Diamond shrieked and her body jerked simultaneously. Here she was finally experiencing orgasm and Justin appeared out of nowhere, scaring the living shit out of her.

She wanted to collapse, but he reached in to hold her upright.

"You okay?"

Exhausted, relieved, frustrated and lost between the world of fantasy and reality, Diamond grabbed onto Justin, throwing herself at him with her wet body, climbing out of the shower stall, and sobbing onto his shoulder.

"What's wrong now?"

"Nothing . . . noth—" She allowed her emotions to pour out, explaining nothing but expressing everything.

The two of them showered together with not a sexual thought between them and afterward they laid in bed naked, holding each other.

* * *

Before the day was out, Justin went to see McDoogle face-to-face. He needed to convince him of his intentions and tell him that he was the best man for the job.

"Good to see you're well again, Lewis. We need to talk."

"Okay," the DA put down his eyeglasses.

"I've gone through a lot to make this case, sir. And I came to affirm my determination."

"Oh?"

"Yes. If I'm not mistaken, you're pressed for time."

"Always, Lewis." McDoogle looked down at his messy desk.

"Well, no . . . I'm speaking about the girls. The senator's daughter."

"Oh . . . oh, sure. Of course. That reminds me. I need to call my task force for an update."

"I've just spoken to Dobson. He says the status is the same. No strong leads . . . Sir, I'd like to finish what I started. I want to help catch these guys."

"Out of the question. I won't allow it."

"Sir, if I can just explain."

"Explain away. But I won't allow you to put your life in danger. This crew is full of maniacs. They're on the loose, armed and dangerous."

"Okay. But Ringo isn't running with them."

"It looks like he's pretty close to it."

"Looks are deceiving. But let's assume he is. That just makes our job easier. I think I can convince him to help us. This guy has a heart—I've seen it."

Justin thought about the happenings on Drake Street and Ringo's response to the violent ordeal.

The phone rang.

"Just a minute, Lewis. DA's office, McDoogle speaking. . . . Oh, yes . . . hello, Senator. Um . . . would you be so kind as to hold for one minute?" McDoogle covered the mouth piece. "Give me a few minutes, would you?"

Justin left the DA's office and perched himself on the receptionist's desk. This was how it was in the off hours. Quiet as a yard of polyester. He could even overhear some of the conversation in the next room. And the longer he was on the line, and the more McDoogle struggled to pacify the senator, the broader Justin's smile became.

Here I come, Ringo.

The following morning, Justin woke before Diamond did. He prepared a full-course meal with scrambled egg whites with freshly sliced tomatoes, cheddar cheese shavings, and miniature steamed broccoli spears. Instead of V-8 juice, he concocted a fruit drink with oranges, grapefruit, melon, strawberries, and apples, all of which were blended into a juice minus the unwanted pulp.

For effect, Diamond's breakfast was served to her in bed, her tray dressed with rose petals, while Justin relaxed there with her, marveling at the diva's slightest movements.

"If you don't quit with that, I'm gonna fling a tomato at you."

On the tray beside her food was a tiny model of Miles Davis, a gift that Justin had given Diamond, and for the eighth time he wound it up to play "Someday My Prince Will Come," the short version.

"I thought you liked Miles."

"Yeah, but please . . . didn't anybody ever tell you too much of a good thing can kill you?"

They both got a kick out of that; then things turned serious.

"If that was the case then I could die today, 'cause I can't get enough of you," said Justin.

"Oh no, you didn't!" Diamond gushed with wide-eyed excitement. "Did I ever tell you how incredibly corny you are?"

"I can think of a few occasions."

"And did I then tell you how much I love the corny side of you?" Diamond curled her forefinger, virtually pulling Justin closer.

She kissed him with closed lips, as sensually as she could manage with food still in her mouth.

Justin's tongue pushed past her lips, indulging in a deep nutritious kiss.

"Mmmm . . . you are soooo sexy," muttered Diamond.

"Corny . . . sexy . . . daring." He kissed her between each word. "You know I love you, don't you, Diamond?"

"And I love you too, Mr. Lewis."

Justin allowed her to eat some more before he continued on. This wouldn't be easy to explain.

"We're getting close, Di."

"Close? To what?"

"Close to catching him. I'm almost a hundred percent sure you're right. I think Ringo had something to do with . . . well, that day." Justin realized how sensitive Diamond was about the past, and he wasn't looking for another of her crying spells.

She was looking down at her empty plate now, and Justin took the tray and set it on the floor beside the bed. Afterward he scooted up to her side. "You okay?"

Diamond nodded.

"I'm telling you this because the stakes are a little higher now."

Diamond looked up to Justin with subtle wonder.

"Things got a little dangerous the other night, and well . . . it's uncertain just where or how things will go if I go see him again."

"Who?"

"Ringo. Diamond, this thing is getting a bit unpredictable, to the point that lives are at stake.

"Can't they just arrest him? Why do you have to go?"

"Because it's really too complicated to get into. I just wanted you to know how close we are. I was hoping to make you feel better about the whole thing." *Without mentioning fingers, guns, etc.*

"Well, I don't. Not if you get hurt. Isn't there an easier way?"

Justin could've pulled out right here. He could've agreed with Diamond and taken the path of least resistance. Except, he'd already committed himself. In his mind, there was a target. And in his heart, there was a drive to go after that target.

"No, Diamond. There isn't."

"Thank you," Justin told the building's doorman. He flashed his credentials for this visit, a way of keeping this out in the open, figuring that more exposure would insure less danger. And it was somewhat amusing how the employee's badge—a simple laminated ID that was necessary to water the plants in the district attorney's offices—conveyed such authority. But Justin also knew that it was his will that directed the doorman to step aside and allow him access. "And please, no phone calls," said Justin as he entered one of the elevator cars. "I'd appreciate it."

He didn't expect his wishes to be obeyed.

On the nineteenth floor, Justin knocked on Ringo's apartment door, anticipating a cold shoulder or that the rapper might just ignore him altogether.

But Justin was determined. He was even willing to camp out. He'd come prepared with a copy of *Essence*—his attempt to keep up with Diamond—and was ready for the long haul.

"I know you're in there, Ringo. I'm not gonna disappear. I'm not leaving until I talk to you."

Again, Justin pounded on the door. He did his best to be respectful of the neighbors, but there were lives at stake, concerns that were way more important than any quality of life standards.

"Open up, Ringo! We need to talk! You can make this difficult or easy. Your choice!"

Justin slumped down to take a seat on the carpet and began flipping through *Essence*. Too much commotion and someone might call the police; that would really cause his plan to backfire.

The magazine's table of contents hadn't yet come up when the door eased open. To Justin's surprise, Porsha stood there in a red satin robe that reached halfway down her thighs and clung to her body enough to hint at her curves. There was no makeup and her hair was having a bad day, but the woman was never more beautiful. In that second of digestion, Justin wondered how in the world Ringo ended up with someone so priceless. Then his eyes rested on Quentin, who was cooing in Porsha's arms.

"Is that you, Justin?" Porsha was squinting as though she had been rudely awakened.

"Oh. Sorry, Porsha." Justin got up from the floor. "Is Ringo around?"

"He left a while ago, I think. He said something about the tire shop. Maybe he'll be back soon. Why don't you come in?"

Wow, she doesn't know.

"Uhhh . . . sure," he said.

"I don't know who was louder—you or the baby." Porsha led the way across the sunken living room. "Where is everybody?" she asked Justin, rocking Quentin affectionately. "I must've been knocked out."

Justin had to refresh his thoughts . . . had to remind himself why he'd come here in the first place. It was these sudden realities hitting him all at once: his friendship with Porsha and how she so readily accepted him in her home . . . the images of motherhood, the essence of family. Ringo's family. Before his eyes—that concept of family that Ringo was beginning to build—was something that Justin wanted with Diamond if she'd only step away from her stage name for a while . . . long enough to work on something more important, something that would transcend their mere mortal existence. Like making a baby.

"Well I'm ahh, glad to have been your human alarm clock," Justin said with a slight guilt preceding his complete smile.

"You want coffee? A slice of apple pie?"

Justin smirked, remembering the double date that he and Ringo took the women on. The four of them had apple pie and coffee while they talked for hours.

"I'm good, really. I just came to speak with Ringo."

"Oh. Business?"

"You could say that."

"Oooh . . . Quentin." Porsha casted a playful scowl at her baby. Then she said, "Excuse me. Have a seat, God. Don't look so uncomfortable. You're family . . . just make yourself at home." And Porsha slithered away, barefoot and intent on her motherly duties, scrunching her nose all the while.

Justin mumbled to himself, "Hmmmph. Make myself at home. Wait'll Ringo gets back . . . fireworks in October."

Justin took the liberty of strolling around the living room. He'd done this before—checking out the gold and platinum plaques, some for singles, others for entire albums, the canceled check for Ringo's first big advance. But now, after having been through the violent storm the night before last, after the emotional turmoil that he saw behind Diamond's eyes, these plaques and photos seemed so trivial. Nothing but worthless plastic and egotistical propaganda. A waste of good wall space.

"Hey, Porsha?" Justin called out so that she'd hear him from the next room.

"Yeah?"

Justin was studying a group photo now. He recognized at least five of the eight individuals: Porsha, Tangi, Butter, Sweets, and of course Ringo.

Meanwhile, he recalled Ruby's rundown. *This girl is Porsha Lindsey, formerly a resident of Bridgeport. Lived with her mom . . .*

Justin assumed the photo had been taken in Bridgeport. And then he looked closer and noticed the edge of an outdoor sign. There were the last two letters of two words; TE and ET. The other word on the sign was visible in its entirety: INN. Then Justin figured it out.

State Street Inn.

Justin was conversing with Porsha now, even if his mind was shifting back and forth through time.

"Where's your friend Tangi? Doesn't she help you with the baby?"

Ruby's words again: *Tangi Stokes, also from Bridgeport. Tangi's almost eighteen . . . Porsha's almost a year older . . . As far as we know, Tangi is Porsha's best friend . . .*

Porsha answered Justin now. "Oh, you know . . . her and J-Love . . . they're in deep."

"You think that's love? Or convenience?"

Porsha's laughter could be heard throughout the residence. Then she answered, "Maybe a little of both."

"If I haven't told you already, you and Ringo really do have an interesting lifestyle."

"We tryin' to keep it together, ya know? It's sometimes hard with him always away."

Justin could've sympathized with Porsha, knowing how he went through much of the same with Diamond.

However this wasn't that kind of conversation. Porsha didn't realize it, but Justin was working right now.

Justin, the investigator.

"But you know . . . the funny thing is, Ringo has this rough and tough image he projects in his music . . . in his videos. Nothing but violence and rage."

Porsha was quick to respond as if she'd defended other men many times before.

"And it might've been a lot more violent if it wasn't for B.E.T. and MTV censoring things. There's some kind of standard they have now concerning violence and the excessive exposure of female flesh. Especially when it comes to boobies and badonkadonks."

"Badonkadonks?" Justin had heard the term before, of course. But it sounded funny coming fom Porsha.

"You better not be laughin' at me in there."

"Me? Never!"

"But seriously, Justin, why is it that when white folks make all kinds of violent, sadistic movies, with bodies droppin' all over the place it's all good . . . all hunky-dory. But the minute you put a black face in the mix . . . the minute we start spittin' fire, they gonna start all kinds of mess. And our own people are just as much to blame. Imagine them startin' up some hip-hop police. What is that about? I hate it when folks with power twist things in their favor. Black, white, or whatever."

"But Porsha, I was just amazed by Ringo's particular angle on things." Justin wasn't interested in the whole double standard issue that Porsha was leading into. Sure she had a valid opinion on the subject, remarks that have been voiced for years, as far as Justin could recall—but his concern was about Ringo and his past.

"How in the world he does it, I'll never know."

"Does what, Justin?" Porsha peeked in for a moment.

"How he can go out and do music, shows, videos, putting on this persona of the fearsome rapper, but then he comes home to this luxury . . . I mean, Ringo is like a living breathing oxymoron. You've got a grand-prize piano in your home for goodness sakes. Now what thug is gonna have that? Not to mention a stable household with a family."

"Imagine that?" said Porsha. "And I don't even have to take him to court for child support or domestic abuse. But ya know the press wouldn't put those ideas out there."

"Yeah. God forbid," replied Justin.

"But you know what? That's an accomplishment, Justin. To be able to maintain like we do. No, I'm not his wife, but I might as well be. One day, when his schedule permits, maybe before the next album . . . But . . . do you know what I'm saying? Every time I open up some magazine or newspaper, or when I hear the gossip wags like that book— Did you read that? *Baby Momma Drama*?"

"No. Can't say I have."

"Well, in a nutshell, one form of ignorance leads to another. Priorities and goals are either twisted, tossed aside, or they're not there at all. Then, before you know it, the violence and destruction become the main priorities."

"It's a sick cycle, I know," said Justin.

But again, he felt Porsha leading the conversation where she wanted.

"Funny you mention violence and destruction, Porsha, because, even though Ringo raps about those kinds of things, there doesn't seem to be any of it in his life."

"That's because this is show biz, Justin. People need to lighten up and remember that sometimes. Give a brotha a chance to do his own thing . . . his own realities, know what I mean? The videos that rappers make are just short versions of what Hollywood makes. Music is just the vehicle. Some will stay with the music and rap on. But the others? Look at Will Smith, Busta Rhymes, and DMX. Big thing a gwon."

"But Ringo is definitely no Will Smith. They're like day and night . . ." Justin imagined that Will Smith was squeaky-clean enough to shoot for the presidency.

"Different backgrounds, I guess."

Justin lit up at the sound of Porsha's latest words. He flashed a deceitful grin.

Backgrounds? Ahhhh . . . paydirt!

They had traveled down Baby Momma Drama Lane, turned down Violence In Music Street, and cut across the courtyard of black-white disparity as it related to censorship. And now, finally, Justin had her right where he wanted her.

"You think Ringo's background is as violent as his raps? I mean, the killing, robbing and gang bangin'? Where do you think he draws from?"

"I really can't say, Justin. When I met him, it was like we started this new life together. For both of us, the past was the past. It was a sort of pact we had."

"Do you ever worry about the past catching up with him? To where it maybe threatens your future? Your . . . interesting lifestyle?"

"Not really . . ." Porsha's voice was closer now, until she emerged from the next room, a freshly diapered Quentin in her arms. "What are you getting at, Justin? Why all this talk about Ringo's background? You writing a book?"

Justin inhaled and exhaled.

"Porsha . . . maybe you and I should sit down and talk."

Chapter Twenty-nine

That excuse about tires was just that: an excuse. The truth was, his pager was vibrating wildly and constantly while he was in bed. Each time he checked it there was a different number, all of them unfamiliar, until he eventually had to shut the device off, vowing to have its number changed at his earliest convenience.

He tried to put it out of his mind and turned over to embrace Porsha once more.

Probably one of those groupies from God knows-when. Unable to erase the curiosity, Ringo searched his mind's filing cabinet to try and match a number with a face or name.

But then, there was Porsha's naked body next to him, oh-so-close to his nose. The aroma of flesh mixed with the sheets pulled at his senses. If there was anything to get a tight grip on his mind, it was her essence—a force wherein he could surrender himself. And the power of this was overwhelming enough so that there was nothing more important in the world.

The two-way pager began chirping, and only his most important friends and associates had that number. So, Ringo let out an exhausted sigh and checked the display on the device: *It's me. Audrey. Need to see you ASAP.* And she left her number, one of those unfamiliar ones that was also left on his pager earlier.

For a time, Ringo had no idea who Audrey was, or how in the world she'd gotten his two-way number. As far as he was concerned, whoever she was, it was a non-issue. Nothing, if you asked him, was gonna drag him out of his warm bed on this chilly October night.

He shut off the two-way and went back to cuddling Porsha, appeased by her body heat and the purr from her lips.

Minutes later, Ringo's cell phone rang.

Shit! Leave me the fuck alone.

But now that he thought about it, there were only three people who had his cell phone number, and one of them was in bed with him. Tangi was another. And Jamie. Ringo was as comfortable as velvet right now and a bit drowsy to boot.

I'm not answering it.

Porsha moaned, obviously annoyed by the electronic beeps attacking their ears. There was also the baby to think about.

All right! All right already! Jesus!

Frustrated, Ringo grabbed the cell phone and took it into the bathroom.

"This better be important," he said in his groggy voice.

"Listen, lover. I'm sorry to bother you, but you've been a pain in the butt to get ahold of."

"Huh? Who is this?"

"Audrey. I'm outside, and I need to see you right now."

"What the—Audrey? Audrey who?"

"Audrey who? Audrey WHO!? You have the nerve to run that game on me? Negro, don't make me get black with you, 'cause we can both be ignorant."

"I'm afraid you have the wrong number."

"That's not what you said when you stuck your dick inside of me. Now, don't make me come up there!"

The line went dead.

Ringo didn't bother disconnecting or shutting off the phone. He simply dropped it into the toilet and went back to the bedroom . . . back to holding Porsha. He was safe again, isolated from the world in every way.

Her bare back snuggled up against him, and her curves fit with exactness along his chest, stomach, and groin. Ringo assumed that Porsha felt the same, that this was their Heaven on Earth.

* * *

. . . . .

. . . man . . .

Audrey . . . don't make me get black with you . . .

. . . . . That's not what you said when . . .

. . . . Don't make me come up there!

The words began to play tricks with his memory. The images came to life on the walls of his consciousness.

Again, feeling more grief than ever before, Ringo huffed.

Audrey . . . the woman from Chaz and Wilson's . . . Jamie's friend.

Drama.

"I'm pregnant."

"You're what!"

"You heard me, and I don't speak Portuguese," said Audrey with a salty attitude.

The two were in Audrey's emerald green sports car, and Ringo's first thought when he stepped out from his building's front lobby was: *How can she afford something like this?*

Jamie's introduction began to haunt his thoughts.

This is Audrey Pitts, an old friend . . . Audrey handles publicity at Warner Brothers . . . the jazz department.

And Ringo remembered being attracted to the woman's wide, pretty brown eyes, her girlish giggle, and how she knew so much about this entertainment game.

"But . . . we used a rubber," Ringo recalled.

"Did we?" she replied, maybe intentionally inviting doubt. She directed the car onto the service road that ran alongside the West Side Highway and parked facing an expansive view of the Hudson River.

"Are you sure?" asked Ringo, trying to find any way he could to escape this mess, even if it meant considering every back door.

"You wanna come and meet the doctor?"

Ringo didn't like the way Audrey said that, with her smart-aleck flavoring. "He's got plenty of pamphlets on the finer points of maternity. There's one on how to be a good father, too. I got you one."

Ringo made a face, still in denial about the damned news.

"You must be smoking something. You not thinking about keeping it, are you?"

"I'm already two months' pregnant, Mr. Suck My Dick Bitch. Or don't you remember that? Chaz and Wilson's . . . the blow job in the limo . . . my apartment?"

"You . . ." Ringo stopped to purse his lips together. "You didn't answer the question, woman," he said, digging into her with his steel-eyed gaze.

"Yes, yessss, Ringo. I'm having your baby," she answered, both sincerely and excitedly.

He closed his eyes and fumed.

Jesus Christ!

Just when he'd satisfied one issue with his ex-girlfriend Donia . . . just when he had escaped death, bullets, and possible arrest, here came the storm again.

And the words echoed in his head now: Donia. *Autograph this, you bastard! . . . That's your son. How can you do this to me, Ringo? . . . Of course he's your son, Ringo. Who else was I fucking about three years ago?*

And now, it seemed as though life was repeating itself, and Audrey's attitude about it all further compounded an already difficult situation.

. . . I've even got his name figured out. We'll call him Duncan—that's if it's a boy—and we'll call her Desiree if it's a girl. I always liked that name . . . Her words were going in one ear and out the other. He was still stuck on Audrey's first words: *I'm having your baby . . .* It was worse than the Liberty Bell's thunderous gong, with his head trapped up under its shell. It was such a trite statement and yet it was powerful enough to fill a canyon.

Funny, Ringo thought, *the sex didn't seem to match with this mighty relation. How stupid can I be?* And Ringo thought of that saying: *Stop thinking with your head and use your brain.*

Those routine maternity visits were coming back to him

now, how he escorted Porsha to the Bridgeport Clinic, and then, because of the sudden financial freedom, to a private physician in Manhattan. He coped with her cravings and the kicking that the unborn Quentin was doing down in her belly, and he provided all manner of assurances: *No Porsha, you're not ugly. You're the most beautiful sight a man could see. You're bringing my seed into the world!* Then, of course, Ringo had to come through with the pizza, the strawberry shortcake, and the all-important mint-chip ice cream. And that was just the Monday menu.

Whether it was three in the afternoon or three in the morning—if Porsha asked for it, Porsha got it.

Fortunately, for Ringo's budding rap career, he was able to afford to answer Porsha's every whim. He even set it up so that there were fresh flowers delivered each morning of her third trimester.

He'd done it all. Ringo, the phenomenal man, soon to be Ringo, the first-time daddy.

But no, that wasn't his first child since Donia surfaced with the shocking news. And now this. When it rains, it pours.

Audrey's announcement, even if she was in fact pregnant, was looked upon in a much different light. After all, she was just a fuck. A fleeting thrill . . . a plastic sleeve in which he could unload his anxieties. And no, he didn't love her.

"I can't believe it, because our child is about to come into this world. He or she is gonna have your eyes, my nose, and our combined talents."

"Talents? What talents do you have? Besides tricking me into sex?" Ringo opened the passenger-side door and got out. He needed breathing room.

"Bastard. Listen, I'm not gonna go chasin' after you. . . . I'm not one of your little die-hard fans or a chickenhead groupie with your name tattooed on my ass. I'm a grown woman about to be the mother of your child. So start treating me like it. Don't do me dirty, Ringo," Audrey shouted from the passenger-side window she lowered. " 'Cause you don't wanna see my evil side."

I already have, he determined.

"I need time to think," Ringo told himself. But Audrey had wheeled the car around, onto a bicycle path and past the off-limits sign. *Jesus! Can I ever get rid of you?*

"I don't have that kind of time. I have needs and responsibilities . . . for me and your child. So what's it gonna be, playa? Are we working this out? Or do we become enemies? You need to decide, and you need to decide now."

Still strolling side-by-side with the car, Ringo envisioned himself across the river, on the New Jersey side . . . He was standing there looking across the water where two people were arguing underneath the New York City skyline—they were plugged into each other once upon a time, but were now at odds over the idea of committing to eighteen years of responsibility, the consequences for having engaged in a moment of lust.

With all of his might, Ringo wished that the reflection he saw was not himself.

He was back in the passenger's seat now.

"I'm sure we can work this out, Audrey."

"Now you're talkin'."

"On one condition."

She seemed to soften . . . to listen closely.

"This has to be kept between you and me."

"That's fine."

Even to Ringo the woman appeared to be backed into a corner, agreeing with him against her wishes.

"And another thing . . . don't think this means booty calls or dating. I have a woman at home. A son, too. And I don't want this to mess that up."

"Whatever you say. Besides, I don't need no man to give me headaches. Just handle your B.I. and it'll be all good."

Ringo breathed a little easier. Maybe this would work out after all.

"So what do you need?"

"You can start with a hundred, and we'll go from there."

Ringo withheld a satisfied grin and reached into his pocket. *Money ain't a thing, baby.*

"No problem . . . just keep your word," he said as he peeled off a number of bills from his money roll. "As a matter of fact . . . here . . . take a couple more. Three hundred should handle those late-night cravings." Ringo's smile was a twist between compassionate and condescending. It was how he was feeling at the moment: in control.

"Ahem . . . what's this? Audrey's head shifted back and forth on her neck.

"It ain't peanuts, girl. That's three C-notes."

Audrey laughed. "Negro, please. Don't play with me. I want a hundred, as in a hundred thousand."

After the shock registered on his face, Ringo exploded into a riotous laughter.

"You gotta be outta your goddamned mind, trick. A hundred thousand? Your pussy ain't made of diamonds."

"You can do it in installments, Ringo. I'm not trying to cut your arms off. And I know you can afford it. Don't you have a concert tour coming up?"

"Oh! So that's the point. You're counting my money, is that it?"

Audrey held her ground, ready to debate this with her last breaths. But Ringo was already up and out of the car again. This time, it was for good.

It would be quite a trek back to Broadway, where he would flag down a taxi, but it was no matter, he had plenty to think about.

"So that's the way you wanna do this?" she shouted.

" 'Cause I swear, Ringo, if you walk away now, don't come back cryin' the baby daddy blues later."

Ringo was far enough away for his voice to carry.

"Fuck you," was his reply.

Audrey was a woman scorned.

It took her less than five minutes to reach Jamie's apartment, which wasn't far from her own.

"Brooklyn, listen . . . Audrey's just getting here. I'll see how things went and I'll get back to you. Okay, you too." Jamie hung up the phone and listened for Audrey's first words.

Audrey's actions might've said it all. She tossed her keys on the demilune—that walnut table in the entrance hall of the apartment.

"Shit! I thought you said this was gonna be easy."

"Maybe it would have been back when we first set it up. But you gotta figure the boy is getting wiser with each passing day. All the people he has to meet . . . the interviews and the traveling. Plus, you know he reads a lot. So don't think this is our average street thug. He's not."

"Yeah, now he's a smart-ass street thug."

"But one with money. Don't forget that . . . So what happened, anyway?"

"You want the three-hour movie? Or the half-hour sitcom?"

"Just gimme the bottom line," said Jamie as she stretched a pair of leather driving gloves over her hands.

"He told me to go fuck myself."

"That bad, huh?"

"I even gave him the option to pay me installments of twenty grand."

"And?" Jamie clenched her hands to tighten the fit of the gloves.

"And? Girl, don't you know that asshole got out of my car and left me by the Westside Highway? Somethin' told me this wasn't a walk in the park. Fuck."

Jamie looked back at the phone, imagining it as a living, breathing being, one that might be eavesdropping on their conversation. "Oh."

"He says to do what needs to be done and do it now. He's ready to move with plan B. I don't know how, but he says that—"

Jamie was close enough to Audrey to reach out and slap her across the face. The smack caused Audrey to twirl so that she almost fell off balance.

"Record sales should go through the roof."

Audrey put her hand to her cheek and immediately felt it throbbing. She looked at Jamie, her best friend.

"Jamie!? Why'd you—?"

Audrey's astonishment was cut short by a second smack. It was harder and connected with the opposite cheek.

The blow threw Audrey and she fell against the back of the faded green upholstered couch.

"No sense in delaying this, Audrey. You already knew the deal."

Jamie took hold of Audrey's hair, unconcerned with the grief and tears, and she spun her around, pushing her to the floor. She then kicked her in the ass.

Audrey shrieked in pain.

"We have to . . . stick . . . with the . . . plan!"

Again with the kicks. Another to the forearm. Now Jamie mashed her sole against Audrey's face.

"Trust me, boo . . . this hurts me . . . more than it does you!"

Jamie reached out to punch Audrey about the face until she had obvious bruises and a football for an eye. When Audrey was semi-conscious, Jamie squeezed her eyes closed and grimaced.

"You should be black and blue in no time . . . I'll give Brooklyn a call and fill him in."

When Brooklyn was on the line, Jaime said, "It's done . . . She's real busted up, nut."

Jamie bent down and put her hand over Audrey's breast.

"Her heart is still beating. In a few minutes I'll call the police and rush her over to the hospital. . . . Well, thank you. I was hoping to make you proud." Jamie hung up and went to shower. She had a long day ahead of her.

5 A.M.

Ringo expected that Porsha would wake up to handle the five o'clock feeding. If not, hopefully Lucy would come in time to handle it.

Quentin was almost fourteen months old now, so he could eat the Stage 3 food that Beechnut made. But Porsha also fed the baby slivers of this and that. It wouldn't be long before Quentin could eat three squares along with Mommy, with maybe a snack here and there.

What Ringo didn't expect, especially at this time of day was another man's voice in his home. And then, when he got close enough beside his teary-eyed woman, Ringo lost his sanity. "What the—?!"

Ringo didn't utter another word. He couldn't. He was too involved just now, charging after Justin . . . literally diving over the sectional couch to get his hands on him. Justin succumbed to the impact, falling under Ringo's force until the two of them tumbled to the floor, with the couch overturned and a table lamp toppled.

Ringo was close to unleashing a flurry of punches, but Justin had help he hadn't counted on.

"Ringo, stop. Stop it!" Porsha pulled at Ringo's arms.

Now Quentin was awake and crying.

Ringo pressed on, trying to get Justin into a headlock. "What's going on here!?" Tangi had just come through the door with J-Love right behind her.

The two hurried across the living room to break up the melee, finally helping to pry Ringo off of Justin.

"I told you I didn't wanna see you again! What the fuck are you doing in my mothafuckin' house?"

"Stop it, Ringo! Just stop it!" Porsha shouted and pulled, shouted and pulled.

Porsha, Tangi, and J-Love finally curbed Ringo's rage.

"What's going on here?" asked Tangi, her face flushed from the struggle. Meanwhile, J-Love stood between Ringo and Justin so that they wouldn't bump heads again.

Justin fixed his clothes.

"I thought we were friends here." Tangi said.

"He ain't no goddamn friend, Tangi. He's a cop."

Tangi turned to Justin and her head rocked back as if she'd just smelled something awful.

"He's not a cop, Ringo," said Porsha.

"I'm not a cop, Ringo."

"Well shit, you might as well be. And Porsha, how do you know what he is? You have no idea."

Ringo had a flash—Justin on the couch with Porsha—and he charged at him with renewed vigor. This time, Justin had to back away to keep out of harm's way.

"Ringo, sit down!"

Now it was Ringo rocking his head back, shooting looks of utter disbelief at Porsha. He wanted to know who in the hell she thought she was, talking to him like that.

Porsha lunged toward Quentin, who had nearly fallen off the couch. She caught him in time, pulled him to her breast lovingly, and cast an angry gaze at Ringo. *This is your fault,* she was saying with her eyes as she hushed Quentin and rocked him with motherly love.

The sight of Porsha and child was a greater authority at the moment, and Ringo settled himself, swallowing his ego and planting his behind back on the couch.

Justin was exhausted himself, relieved that Ringo had let it go—even if he had not set it aside—and he sat on the floor.

"Ringo, I came because—"

Porsha cut in. "Justin, wait a minute. Please I need to do this. . . . Tangi, would you—?"

Porsha didn't need to complete her request, because Tangi read her mind and swept the toddler out of Porsha's hands.

Sitting beside Ringo now, with her hand on his knee, Porsha regrouped and tried to do this as delicately as possible. She asked Tangi and J-Love to leave her with Ringo and Justin. *And yes,* she expressed with her eyes, *I can handle this.*

"Ringo. Let me finish what I have to say. . . . I just had a long talk with Justin. He told me about the other night."

"He told you his version."

"Please. Let me say what I have to say. . . . He also told me about somebody, a friend of yours named Brice. Honey, Justin isn't a cop. He works as an intern at the district attorney's office. Ringo he says his boss is targeting you—and other rappers too. He told me about a hunch . . . a hunch that Diamond had about you. She happened to get caught up in a holdup some years back . . . She thinks that's you."

Ringo started to stand up. "I don't have to listen to this."

Porsha pulled him back into his seat.

"No. You do have to listen to this. Ringo, Diamond was there. . . . She was grabbed by one of the gunmen."

Ringo's head was spinning. It was only Porsha and Justin in

his presence, but it felt like they represented a world of attention—all of it focused on him, the defendant up on the stand.

"Ringo." It was difficult for Porsha to say what was on her mind, but somehow she went ahead and spit it out. "She thinks it was you who grabbed her. Now, I don't know if it's true or not, and neither does Justin for that matter . . ."

Ringo was dizzy with the images zipping through his conciousness.

"Diamond is . . . well, she's got her whole life ahead of her."

"A few psychological issues," Justin added. "But she is fine otherwise." Justin bowed out and allowed Porsha to continue.

"Ringo, Justin's not here to come after you. It was only a coincidence that he and Diamond are in a relationship and that they both came to know you. Small world, I guess. But whether it was you or not, back in Queens . . . it doesn't matter now. He says there's no proof that you were involved."

"She's right, Ringo. There's not a bit of proof."

"So then why are we discussing this?"

"It's about Brice," said Justin. "He's a madman. A lunatic—and I'm not talkin' about cutting off that detective's finger, either."

"This involves some of your fans, Ringo," Porsha added.

"My fans?"

Just then, a loud knock interrupted the conversation, except it sounded like a hammer hitting the door.

"I'll get it," Tangi cried out. "I'm comin', dawg!"

Tangi didn't even check to see who it was before she pulled open the door.

When the door opened Ringo, Porsha, Tangi, Justin, J-Love, and Quentin were staring in disbelief at three uniformed officers, all of them with unfriendly, ready-for-anything poise.

"Is there a James Valentine here, otherwise known as Ringo?"

Minutes later, Ringo was in handcuffs, arrested for assault and battery. And besides that, said a wise-ass cop, he might also be facing attempted murder charges.

* * *

"You're just gonna sit there?"

"I told you, Justin. We don't have anything to do with this. This is his own doing. He's gonna have to deal with it," said Detective Dobson. Detective Blair, bandaged hand and all, sat quietly watching the activity across the street—the police, Ringo being led away from his apartment building in cuffs, then tucked into one of the many police vehicles.

"But how can we get help now if he's in jail? What about the senator's daughter?"

"Justin, relax. My high school teacher? The one I told you had the expert memory?"

Justin put on an *oh brother* expression.

"Well, besides all the stuff he taught us about Darwin, Orwell and Freud, I never forgot this one quote he always hit us with . . . he said it was the Serenity Prayer. It goes like this: God, grant me the patience to cope with the things I cannot change, the courage to change the things I can, and the wisdom to know the difference."

Justin for the umpteenth time, asked himself why Indians—this one in particular—seemed to be so much more grounded that others. It made him feel like such a mere earthling.

"We need to contact McDoogle. Let 'im know about the latest developments," said Blair.

Porsha called Jamie before leaving to follow up on Ringo. She seemed to be the major troubleshooter since the beginning of Ringo's platinum status. "Try and relax, Porsha. I'm sure there's a mistake here. I'll have a lawyer get on it as soon as possible. A good one, too. And we'll get your man bailed out of there before you can clap your hands . . ."

Jamie hung up and laughed. It was one thing to sit and plan something, but to watch it play out so perfectly was better than sex . . . better than a monster orgasm.

" 'Try and relax,' ahh ha ha haa! I simply slay myself. Oh God—I am a riot!" What Jamie said she'd do couldn't have been further from the truth.

First, she had to stop by the hospital to see Audrey. Hopefully the reporters would show up in time. And of course she'd have to update Brooklyn.

Ringo was the last priority on her agenda.

ST. JUDE HOSPIAL, NYC

The hospital room had been flooded with flowers since Jamie's visit earlier that morning. It was the least that Brooklyn Jones could do considering the sacrifices Audrey had made—seducing Ringo, the confrontation about her pregnancy, becoming the willing victim of an assault . . . and now she was laying in a hospital bed, heavily sedated, with her face bandaged from ear to ear. How much more could a woman give of herself?

"Sorry if we went a little overboard, girlfriend."

Jamie mentioning "we" was supposed to be some sort of plea that this was so much larger a project and that so many other people were grateful to Audrey for her part in this. "But it had to play out that way. If we had told you, you might've chickened out—and then where would we be? We had to stick with the plan . . . you understand, don't you?" Jamie did a bunch of explaining, exercising her best effort to allay the doubts and guilt in her own mind. But Audrey wasn't responding. She couldn't, as numb as she was with pain relievers. Jamie may as well have been talking to a slab of well-seasoned steak. She was unfeeling, motionless, and pathetic with disability.

"And besides girl, it was you who agreed to plan B, so don't even look at me like that . . . By the way . . . he's been locked up so everything is going as expected." A nurse walked in to check Audrey's temperature, so Jamie had to change her tune.

"Yeah, uhh . . . it's such a shame that jerk did this to you, honey. I hope they catch him and hang him . . .

"I'm going over to see him now . . . to do my part. Trust me, this is gonna be worth every bit of your pain. Next thing you know, you'll be laying on a beach full of hundred-dollar bills . . ."

Before Jamie reached the 33rd Precinct station, before the call to the lawyer, she made her press calls.

"This is anonymous, baby, but I'm a neighbor of Ms. Audrey

Pitts . . . yes the pretty girl who was hospitalized tonight. . . . Well, I overheard some things.

"Hey, Curtis. You don't know me, but I'm a close friend of Ringo, the rapper who was arrested for attempted murder . . . What? Whaddaya mean, you don't know about it? Well, I'm sorry, I really shouldn't be calling you then.

"Yes . . . MTV? Who handles the news regarding the attempted murder charges on Ringo? You know, the rapper who recently went platinum? Sure . . . I'll hold."

By noontime the media frenzy was off and running. MTV news, "Where you hear it first," called Ringo's encounter an alleged "fit of rage," that took the rapper-groupie myth to the next level. They also side barrowed the story with a history of other rappers gone bad, compounding the credibility of the allegation. There was also video footage of Audrey before the bandages, as she was escorted by gurney into the emergency room. Clips from Ringo's music videos—showing the most fearsome expressions that were available—were merged in with the news feature.

The story grew legs and wings. *E! News, Entertainment Tonight, Access Hollywood,* along with every gossip peddler on black radio stations broadcasted varying versions of the incident, all of them using video and audio clips to engage and entertain audiences.

It would be a matter of weeks before the story hit newspapers. And a matter of weeks before it hit the nation's rockpile of rap publications.

"I just wish this shit wasn't so domestic," said Brooklyn about the arrest phone call from Jamie. He was in his midtown office with its walls full of platinum plaques, joint photos, and promotional posters that were rotated or switched according to which artist happened to be present.

The merger between PGD and Mo City secured this plush executive office for Brooklyn, and the view from the fortieth floor wasn't bad either. It was a place in the world that was considered godly and all powerful, if not by Brooklyn and those that kissed his ass all day, then by just about any wannabe who sought a record deal.

"But what's the difference, Brooklyn? Gang bangin', the thug life, mistreating women . . . isn't that all sort of the same mess? Doesn't it all fall into the same category? Troublemaker? Mischief?"

"It depends, Jamie. You gotta remember that I've been studying this."

Brooklyn spit his tobacco juice into a coffee mug, then continued with his almighty declarations.

"I've been in this game for a long time. So I've seen how the media sells the latest newsflashes. Sometimes these things can pull at the public's consciousness and other times it passes them by like a runaway bus. But then you never really know because domestic shit can make a man shine—look at the history books. Remember Dr. Dre? How he slapped the shit out of a woman? Dee Barnes? In the end what did it do but help his career? Made him look like a true pimp."

"Or a true coward," said Jamie.

"Well, pick whatever side you want. The incident turned out to be just what the public appreciated. He even boasted about it in a later record . . . and if that doesn't convince you, then look at the former president." Brooklyn was flipping channels with a remote while speaking.

"Of Mo City?"

"No. Of the United States. He took advantage of his position and influence to stick it to that intern—whassername?"

"Lewinsky, Monica Lewinsky, B.K. Even I know about that story, with the semen on the dress, so on and so forth."

"Okay. Well then you can probably agree with me that his misdeeds turned out to work in his favor. The man made blow jobs popular. Hell, they talked about the stuff on every TV and radio format around the globe. And sure, he had a team of publicists to help him through it. But you had to see the polls. The ladies saw him as a mack and the men idolized him as a king on the throne."

"Okay, Mr. Media, then how do you think things will work for Ringo? He's not Dr. Dre, and he definitely ain't no president of the United States."

"It's hard to tell. He might not be large enough to curry public favor—and then again, he might not be large enough to arouse any interest at all. It's probably best that we get some other dirt ready . . . feed this monster. Do we have anything else on him? Something we could tie in with the assault?"

"B.K., they're gonna try the boy on attempted murder charges. Shouldn't that be enough?"

"Oh, Jamie, you know how these cases go. The DA usually stacks up as many charges as he can just to try and get a defendant to buckle. There's no way any attempted murder charge is gonna hold up. We need more. There must be something—lyrics can't be all untrue."

"I dunno, B.K. I can look into it, but really, I've been glued to this kid for a long time. The promo tour, the backstage meet and greets, and even in his home. If you ask me, he's squeaky clean and the lyrics are all made up. But . . . I'll check into it. I'll find something even if we have to make it up."

"Well, get it together, babe. I wanna secure this joker as a brand name by any means necessary. I want him to be a household thug that people are so afraid of that they'll feel they have to buy his product—anything to satisfy their curiosity and allay their fears. Because we know enough about the game to recognize that rappers with problems equal media attention and when you think dollars and cents, that's free publicity in my book."

"Okay, B.K. . . . you've talked my ears off as usual.
I'm just now arriving outside of the police station.
We'll talk."

"Hey! Hold on. What about the girl? The one with the child."

"Donia."

"Yeah, her. Maybe we can set her loose . . . maybe encourage her to spit fire on the six o'clock news. Maybe we can paint this kid as a baby dropper, then teenage girls all over the country will be lining up to get a piece of Chief Beatemup and his mighty tomahawk."

"BK, he's owning up to that. It won't work."

"It's just a thought. We gotta make lemonade out of this lemon. Otherwise we'll get no more mileage out of it."

"Good-bye, B.K.," Jamie said and hung up.

* * *

If there was one thing that Porsha was familiar with it was critics. As Ringo's meteoric rise progressed she too felt the punches and stabs that reporters and writers and radio personalities inflicted.

In the beginning she thought she could control it or at least make a difference. She'd call any newspaper, magazine, or radio station to defend her man. But it seemed the more she did, the more they came at him. They adored him, but it was the bashing that stood out most.

"His lyrics are offensive and violent."

"He has no respect for our women or our race."

"His posse raps about the same old mess: crime, bars, clubs, chicks, and Cristal."

Porsha went from fed up to frustrated to afraid that her man's career would diminish. But Jamie and Tangi were around to keep her from losing her mind. And eventually, Porsha stopped reading and listening altogether. It was easy enough to devote her energy to Quentin.

Just when she thought she had the passenger seat paranoia licked, the latest events in Ringo's life were broadcast on TV screen.

There was the relationship between Ringo and Audrey, detailed from soup to nuts. There were photos of the two laughing it up in close company at Chaz & Wilson's. There were snapshots of the two as they got into a limousine that same night. And then the whopper: Audrey had apparently announced her pregnancy to a few of her close friends, two of whom were conveniently available for comments to news reporters.

"I can remember how happy she was when she found out she was pregnant with her first child. She couldn't wait to show Ringo love by taking care of their child. Even if she had to keep it a secret. Now, I can't even say if she'll be able to go through with the childbirth . . . he beat her so . . . so bad. He's so cruel, a beast."

Porsha was as still as a sidewalk. This was all video and audio trickery. It had to be. Theirs was such a tight relationship. He was such a good father. But now, Porsha didn't know what to believe. There was an instant that she wanted to take one of the irons near the fireplace and throw it at the TV, the cause for all the stress and anxiety. But before she budged there was another photo. Another women with a baby in her arms. Porsha scrambled for the remote control to raise the volume, because she thought she was hearing things.

". . . The rapper's ex-girlfriend couldn't be reached for comment, but close friends say that the two had a similar encounter where there was an alleged altercation after the Hip-Hop to Fight Hunger benefit concert just a couple of months ago."

Porsha had had enough. She was in tears now, rocking Quentin in her arms, the movement and his warmth helping to keep her sane. She cut the power off on the TV and closed her eyes . . . rocking . . . rocking . . .

Ringo's face . . . their family photo . . . the luxury surrounding her . . . Ringo's face again . . .

Just hours earlier she was snuggled against her man, feeling secure and in love. There was no greater feeling.

And now there was betrayal and fire and pain entering her secure world.

Another woman? Two other women? One with a baby and another with one on the way?

As the tears streamed down her face, Porsha wondered what other lies and deceit were hidden and waiting to drop. She could've dealt with a lot of things. Groupies she was used to. So what if they lined up after shows to suck him to oblivion. That meant nothing. *But a baby?*

Right under my nose!? I'm at home taking care of our child, and you're out there making more of them?

"He's living a triple life, Tangi! I can't believe this shit! What a fool I've been! An absolutely stupid fool!" Porsha thrust Quentin into Tangi's arms and stormed into the bedroom. Tangi kissed Quentin, answering his "mama" with soft caresses. Lucy came over at Tangi's gesture and took Quentin. His short choppy steps were noisy against the wood floor.

"We'll go next door to Miss Tangi's place. Come on, Q. Come with Lucy."

"Mama."

From the bedroom, Porsha's voice cried out, "We were just talkin' about this! It's like . . ." Porsha was back in the living room again, suitcase in hand. She shook it as she spoke, then made a pivot to go back into the bedroom. ". . . my heart could forecast this before it happened . . ."

Tangi took a deep breath and followed Porsha. She found her rummaging through closets now.

"Shit! I know I have another suitcase around here somewhere."

"Porsha."

"What?" Porsha swung around with her red eyes squinting. Tangi put her hands up, palms forward, and didn't say another word. She turned to leave the room. "Wait." Porsha had a sudden change of heart. "I'm sorry, Tangi. I didn't mean to blow up at you . . . Oh my God! You're like my sister! Tangi, what's happening?" Porsha melted to the floor and Tangi raced to cushion her fall.

"You don't have to apologize. Say what you want—you wanna blame me for not stopping it before it got to this point? For not keeping an eye on him? Go on. Please, it's my fault."

Porsha wailed. "No, no, no, it's not your fault. If anything, it's my fault . . . I should've seen it coming . . . How ignorant can I be?"

Tangi pulled Porsha ever closer and shared in the wetness of her tears.

"I could've forgiven him for anything, Tangi. An STD, a quickie with a groupie . . . but, Tangi, he's got a kid with another." Porsha sobbed and struggled to breathe all at once.

"It's all right. Let it out, Porsha. Let it out. Tangi looked toward the wall—practically through the wall—seeing Ringo's fans attacking him with all kinds of questions.

Why are you doing this? she thought.

"I need to go home, Tangi. I need to get away from all of this."

"Porsha, what are you saying? You helped to make all of this happen. This has become your life, like it has for me. This is your home."

"I don't need it, Tangi. This life . . . the music, the radio, the parties and limos and money . . . he can have it all. I don't want nothin' from him. Nothin'. I'll go as I came, with the clothes on my back . . . and my child."

"What about me, Porsha? How could you just leave me? I'm your best friend."

"You're still my best friend, Tangi. And you know what? I don't expect you to leave with me."

"Oh hell no, I'm—"

"Tangi, listen. I don't want you to leave. Your life has changed so much because of this. There's a whole world out here for you. A whole lot of opportunities. Go for yours, girl. Pimp this game for everything you can get. Just don't put all your eggs in one basket . . . like I did."

Porsha packed a few things and paged Kujo. When he arrived, Porsha wasted no time. Her motor was running and nothing could change her mind.

"So that's it?" asked Tangi. "What about Ringo?"

"Huh? No you didn't ask me that. That man . . . he's got more than enough people, hangers-on and whatnot to get out of this, Tangi. The last person he needs is me, 'cause I'd be the one tryin' to bury him."

Porsha handed Kujo her suitcase and hugged Tangi. "We'll stay in touch. Don't worry about me. I'll be at my mom's."

From there Porsha went next door to retrieve Quentin and she had Kujo drive her back to Connecticut. Back in time.

A story that earns the media's push, whether it's about some feel-good feature or if its inflamed with terror, oftentimes spreads like a virus. And the more fear that comes embedded within the story's walls, the more highly contagious it is, the more attention it's given. People have been groomed to enjoy the concept of terror, where they don't mind watching or hearing about it, so long as it doesn't affect them directly. It's why spectators squeeze into seats and arenas to watch boxing—nothing more than cockfights disguised as sports events. Such stories may be graphic or entertaining enough to fill a minute's worth of radio time, or possibly three minutes of TV time. But as much as one media outlet feeds the next, that same story can grow legs, reaching the majority of the country—and the world—within record time.

And so, news being as ubiquitous as the air we breathe, everyone became aware of Ringo's overnight dilemma.

Chapter Thirty

The arrest was so early in the wee hours of the morning that there was plenty of time for him to be processed, fingerprinted, photographed, booked, and questioned—and still appear before a judge so that he avoided the storage facilities which contained and detained people under the worst conditions, sometimes for extended stays.

The wheels of justice turning as they did, Jamie was about to catch a glimpse of Ringo as he was led out of the stationhouse, taking the "perp walk" amid flash photos and aggressive reporters, until he was helped into a waiting police transport. Ringo (the notorious) was being taken to city court where he'd face Judge Shane.

Jonas Walker was somewhat notorious himself, with a name that stood out when it came to celebrity trials and tribulations. His trademark appearance was camera ready—the yellow crew cut, the green eyes, and the pinstripe suits made him colorful in anyone's book.

But his fashion and style were not to be confused with his work in the courtroom, where he was one of the toastmasters of the trade—a salesman right down the line, to the core.

Jonas was also for sale to the highest bidder, which made justice, including all of its rules and procedures, nothing more than a money machine with which he filled his bank accounts. No more, no less.

"Your Honor, I'd like to present our motion for bail at this time," announced Walker, his nasal voice carrying from the front to the rear of the busy courtroom, a dull and gloomy atmosphere of reporters and spectators, all of whom seemed out of place and humbled by the monetary display staged before them.

Ringo was still wearing the clothes he was arrested in—the baggy jeans, the throwback Sixers jersey, and Phat Farm sneakers fresh out of the box—as he stood with hands cuffed behind his back, accepting the occasion with passive, composed poise.

This is stupid and you all have been tricked.

This was the way Ringo chose to look at this—as a pratical joke, with him as the possum. And underneath his cavalier manner he had been doing one of two things since the knock at his door; he either bubbled with rage like a disturbed can of soda about to explode or he did what he was doing now, laughing down deep in his stomach.

Things were happening faster than he could keep up with—like a blitz of one full day squeezed into six or so hours. He didn't even ask about the Walker dude or who hired him. He just assumed his people, Jamie and Chuck—Ringo's personal assistant and business manager, respectively—sat a few rows back. Butter and Sweets were there as well.

"Just one moment, Mr. Walker . . ." The judge was bending to listen to the court clerk. "Is that so?" The words were overheard despite Judge Shane's hand covering the microphone.

"I'm sorry, Mr. Walker. We're all quite aware of who you are, but we don't seem to have you noted as the attorney of record for this defendant."

"There must be some mistake, Your Honor. I have been retained by the defendant's friends and family."

"Pardon me." It was a female's voice—it had the most captivating authority to it, such as a teacher might wield to control a classroom of students—and she was moving effortlessly toward the front of the courtroom. "There's no mistake here . . . I am the defendant's attorney of record."

"And you are?"

"Madelyn Young, Your Honor. I'm with Stern, Myers, Gregory, and Boskey," she said, more or less intoxicating the courtroom with her shapely full figure, packaged to the nines in a sky blue pantsuit and a yellow scarf around her neck, fixed so that it ruffled then neatly disappeared somewhere down in her cleavage. Somewhere.

Madelyn greeted Walker with a pert smile and immediately leaned to whisper into Ringo's ear. Meanwhile the judge and clerk both checked court documents for confirmation.

"Yes . . . indeed you are, Ms. Young. Well, Mr. Valentine. I see you are quite the popular one this morning to have two defense attorneys here on your behalf."

Again, Madelyn Young whispered to Ringo. "Ms. Young is my attorney for these proceedings, Your Honor."

"See . . . well, that wasn't too painful." The judge turned to the district attorney's table, and then to Jonas Walker. "I suppose that means you're excused, sir."

Walker swung his head around to address Jamie with a strange expression, then he gathered his things from the defense table, mumbling to himself about not having time for this nonsense.

Jamie rose from her seat to follow Walker from the courtroom.

"Alrighty then."

"Your Honor, I'd like to start by asking that the distrcit attorney provide me with a copy of the formal charges and the evidence in this matter, and a list of witnesses to be called forth in this case. Finally I'd like to make an application for bail at some point during these proceedings."

While the legal mumbo jumbo carried on, Ringo couldn't help wondering what was up with Jamie going after the lawyer like she did.

Did I do the right thing?

But he also felt himself being handled with expert care by this woman who seemed so in control over everyone within the earshot of her voice. The proceedings took less than ten minutes to reach the argument regarding Ringo's bail. "As far as your motion for bail . . . I'm certain that the district attorney has something to say regarding that. Mr. McDoogle?"

"Thank you, Your Honor. We have reason to believe that the defendant, Mr. Valentine, is a danger to society. He is not a stable resident of this city, having moved here from Bridgeport,

Conneticut, as recently as two years ago. He travels frequently, enjoys the freedom of international travel and"—the DA reviewed a printed document—"it shows here that during the past year alone Mr. Valentine has traveled to Nigeria, Aruba, the Netherlands, Brazil, Europe—"

"We get the message, Mr. McDoogle."

"Yes, well, we're simply arguing that Mr. Valentine is a certain flight risk. Most important, our office is intent on raising the charges from second-degree assault to attempted murder."

A wave of conversation swept through the courtroom, forcing the judge to bang his gavel. "I'll have quiet in my courtroom. Silence. Please elaborate on your intentions, Mr. McDoogle."

"We have been conducting an ongoing investigation, Your Honor, with respect to the defendant's involvement with a number of shootings that go back as far as two and three years ago. Two years ago there was a shooting—a homicide, actually—that took place in the same area where the defendant resided. Prior to that, there was a robbery and homicide in Queens. This latest assault merely tips the scale in showing that this young man is a danger to society—not just ours, but to others around the world as well . . ."

Ringo was awash with recollections; Porsha mentioning earlier: *Diamond was out there the day of the holdup. She was grabbed by one of the gunmen . . .*

"Do we have any concrete proof to support these claims, Mr. McDoogle?"

McDoogle riffled through his notes and made small talk with his assistant. He also looked back to scan the courtroom, as if some help would appear for him as it did for the defendant when Madelyn Young entered.

"No, Your Honor. We're still investigating these—"

"Still investigating? Your integrity is at stake here, counselor, and I'm afraid I've known you too long. You aren't the kind to rely on phantoms. So I will limit you to the current charges of assault."

"Yes, Your Honor."

Madelyn Young concealed a smile, but also relayed her confidence with a look toward Ringo.

Don't worry, kiddo. The cards are stacked in your favor.

Ms. Walker? Can you respond to the claims of your client's residence and the issue of alleged flight risk at this time?"

"Your Honor . . . I, uh . . . I'm going to need a few minutes with my client before I can prepare an appropriate defense, on account of my having just met—"

"Say no more. Fifteen-minute recess." The judge smacked his gavel and breezed away through a side door.

"I d-don't know what to say, Mrs. Young." Ringo stuttered some as he and his lawyer stood just outside of the courthouse entrance. "They were tryin' to fry me in there . . ."

"That's Ms. Young. And a simple 'thank you' would be okay."

"Well then, thank you a thousand times. You saved my life."

"Excuse me—Ringo? Can I get a quick quote for *Double XL*?"

"Sorry," said Madelyn, not giving Ringo an opportunity to respond. "Like we said inside, no comment at this time. Now please . . . I need to be alone with my client."

As the reporter drifted away, Ringo followed him with his eyes. Up until now he had always been told to respect the press and that their attention equaled record sales. But she had sent at least a dozen on their way.

"And you've gotta maintain the same answer no matter what, Mr. Valentine."

"Ringo. Please, call me Ringo, Ms. Young."

"Well, Ringo, do not let these reporters ruin your chances in the courtroom. God forbid there had to be a trial by jury and the press was able to manipulate their opinions by twisting your statements around. It's best to say nothing at all right now . . ." The attorney was shaking her finger in a subtle but firm way. Madelyn Young, the disciplinarian. "Promise me?"

"No problem."

The attorney cast a skeptical eye on Ringo.

"Ringo?"

"All right, I promise."

"Cross your heart?"

He was amused by the way she said this, as though that would be a most binding gesture, and that any violation might be punishable by death.

Ringo chuckled. "Cross . . . my . . . heart. You satisfied?"

"I'll be satisfied when I get you clear of this mess. I'd like to see you in my office next week. Here's my card. My home number is scribbled on the back. Don't lose it."

"I won't."

"Meanwhile, there's a car waiting for you."

Ms. Young's hand swayed like a wand, and Ringo looked down the broad staircase, past the sidewalk. A glistening stretch limousine waited, double-parked in the street, with a uniformed chauffeur posted there like its Siamese twin. Just before Ringo stepped in the car he looked back over his shoulder. She was still up there at the top of the steps. She nodded reassuringly before Ringo slid inside the car.

The interior of the limo was soft leather with a bar and television. Sitting in the middle of it all was Brice.

Chapter Thirty-one

The rapper was no less shaken than a man facing a firing squad. At the same time his brain worked through a series of possibilities, as if they were complex math problems.

A voice revived Ringo from his clouded thoughts.

"Good to have you back, son."

There's a car waiting for you . . .

"You hired Ms. Young?"

Brice was cavalier about it. He relaxed in his seat as he took a swallow from an open bottle of champagne. He then passed Ringo the bottle, still without responding.

This was a test, Ringo realized. To drink from the same bottle would be a testiment to his solidarity and commitment. If he turned the bottle away it would be disrespectful. And there was no telling how his homey would respond.

Ringo didn't hesitate. He took the bottle and threw down a mouthful.

"What'd you think? Lawyers just drop out of the sky?"

"Oh. Shoot, I didn't know where she came from. I know she saved my ass though."

"I wish I could say it was a big deal, but it really wasn't. The woman's good. I know a few people who talked about her. All I had to figure out was how to get her for the job . . ."

"So? How'd you do it? I'm sure you didn't just step up to her office in broad daylight."

"You're right. I feel funny now, seeing all these people in the streets. All this exposure . . . If it wasn't for the tinted window and the shades, I'd be naked."

"Well . . . thanks for the lawyer."

"You can thank your girl, too."

"Porsha?"

"Donia!"

"Huh?"

"Son, I seen you and her go at it that night at the Beacon. It took me a minute, but then I remembered her face from those photos you used to show me—the ones from your different talent shows, man . . . I didn't know you and her had a kid."

"Funny. I didn't either, until that night."

"Well, I had a talk with Shorty . . . I had to calm her down a lot. Plus, she told me about—who is this white woman that's workin' for you? Some bitch named Jane? Janie?"

"You mean, Jamie."

"Yeah, her. Check that bitch, son. She was meetin' with Shorty, talkin' about payin' her to stay away from you . . . sayin' shit like your public image was important—that kinda mess.

Ringo disregarded that.

"But what does she have to do with this?"

"She was my front man. I had her picked up and she went to see the lawyer lady . . . paid the woman enough money to buy a car, I swear."

"She paid?"

"Yeah, but not with her money, y'damn fool. It was my bread. She was the one to finesse it . . . y'know claimin' she scratched up the cheese from this friend, that uncle. You know what I'm sayin'. 'Cause, you can't just go in and drop all that cash these days without havin' some kinda legit source—otherwise them lawyers kick you out their office. Especially the good lawyers."

Ringo felt himself flooded with irrelevant information again.

"Well then . . ." Ringo drank from the bottle once more and handed it back to Brice. "Thanks to her too. Man, they tried to cook me like roast chicken in there."

"Don't sweat it, son. Besides, I feel like I owe you."

"Owe me?"

"Shit, that diversion you pulled off on Drake was just the thing. Did you see how many Jakes they had out there? We would've been at war all night tryin' to get 'em offa us. You did yo' thing, dawg. For real. That's the kinda soldiers I fucks with. Go hard."

"Uh . . . yeah. Right . . ."

He thinks it was a diversion?!

"I'm surprised you made it out alive."

"Me? Man, when I heard all the shootin' I thought you were done. There was only one thing to do, nah mean?"

"And you did the right thing, too. Here's to crime and freedom," said Brice, lifting the bottle for another gulp.

"To crime?" asked Ringo.

"And freedom," answered Brice. "Me . . . and you. Shit, crime pays, son. Look at us. You went and bought you a shortcut into fame, And me? Shit, I make more money in a goddamn hour than Jake makes in a year. And that's on a good day." Brice arched over to knock at the window that divided the passengers from the chauffeurs.

"Vick, take us to Chelsea." And the window rose again.

"What's in Chelsea?" asked Ringo.

"That's my new spot. My posse is over there now gettin' shit in order."

"But I thought you wanted to stay out of New York?"

"I did. But I figure my picture's in every post office around the country. If they ain't found me by now, they ain't gonna find me. We just gotta watch our backs better, nah mean? No more mess like Zanzibar . . .

We? Just gotta watch our *backs?*

"I been away too long, son. And it ain't like I ain't been comin' through the city. Long as I keep my ass out of the daylight, the night belongs to me. . . ."

"What about your spot in Jersey?"

"Fuck Jersey. It was a good spot. I made a few hundred Gs. But the way I look at it, I raped that town and now it's time to move on to bigger and better things . . ."

Brice pulled out a compact aluminum case the size of a business card. He opened it and laid it on his knee. This all looked to be a routine—the preparation of cocaine into two thin lines . . . the miniature straw and how he held a finger to one nostril while leaning over to snort up the coke with the other nostril.

"So I got me an industrial joint down on Thirteenth Street, between Hudson and East Fourth . . . used to be a big printing press there . . ." Brice went through a series of snorts, wiping his wrist against his coke-dusted nose, then sucking the residue from his wrist.

"Brice—"

"B, remember? You supposed to call me B."

"Well, you need to know somethin'. These people ain't no joke. They're still lookin' for you. They know you're doin' cars, drugs, and I heard 'em say somethin' about Queens . . . Dude, they're closer than we think. Don't you think you're playin' it kinda close, comin' to the courthouse? What if we're bein' followed right now?"

"Scared money don't make money, son. I almost died a whole lotta times to get this far. So as far as I'm concerned I'm God, son. Remember Queens? How that lady almost busted me off until you blew her wig back? Yo, that right there? That changed my life. That made me invincible."

"I guess you were just built to be the outlaw, B. Me? I'd count my money and run."

"Then that's the difference between you and me. I lay it down for real, and you . . . you entertain. As long as you don't get the two twisted. Just play your position. Feel me?"

Ringo's response was a partial shrug.

"And speakin' of layin' it down, what's all this about an assault? You? Beatin' up a woman? That don't sound like you at all."

"Seriously, B . . . I did not touch that woman."

Brice looked at Ringo sideways. "You ain't gotta hide nothin' from me, son. I seen the *Daily News*. Them photos don't lie."

"Listen to me . . . you know I don't get down like that—"

"I know, I know. You wasn't doin' nothin' but jugglin' chickenheads since we was young bucks. Women and talent shows—that was you."

"Good. Then you of all people gotta believe me . . . we

fucked. We used protection too. So I don't know how she's supposed to be pregnant. Then like two months later she show up talkin' all this mess. Plus, she tried to extort me."

"Then you broke her neck. I like this already."

"Nonononono . . . that's what I'm sayin'. After she tried to blackmail me for a hundred Gs I told her to go fuck herself."

"A hundred Gs? Her pussy made of gold?"

"No, diamonds," Ringo lied. "It's a con—can't you see it? She's settin' me up. Got herself pregnant, and now she's trying to get paid."

"What about the beatdown?"

"I already told you. That's exactly how it went down. Next thing I know, Five-O is at my door at two and three in the morning."

Brice studied Ringo.

"So, what'd the lawyer say?"

"She's gonna give her best defense. That's what she said. But this woman—Audrey's her name. Did you see her face?"

"Son, I'm sayin', she look like she been gang-raped. They got you lookin' like a caveman."

"But it's all made up. Lies."

It was the moment of truth.

Then Brice asked, "So what you need me to do?"

"You? Man, it's not you—it's her. I want her to leave me alone. She needs to drop all this craziness."

"Say no more. From now on we don't discuss Audrey."

The limousine crawled down Hudson, then onto 13th Street. A worker in a hard hat and coveralls was standing outside, as if waiting specifically for the car.

A metal gate raised enough to allow them to drive underneath.

"I think the nine-eleven shit put the printer out of business," said Brice. "I got a lease for dirt cheap . . . for the price of an office space I got, like, thirty thousand square feet."

Ringo didn't realize the overall benefit of Brice's explanation, but it sounded good.

One of Brice's associates shuffled up to the limo and Ringo overheard the conversation.

"Yo, B, we got a lot of new heads in here—they're with the construction company. You might wanna take the steps."

"Gotcha. E.J. you know Ringo. Ringo, E.J."

"Wassup."

"Peace."

"Call me up in the office if you need me," said Brice. Ringo tagged behind as Brice led the way up to the offices. There were thick glass double doors at the top of the steps. An impression of the company name—Centipede Press—was still on the wall where block letters were removed. A number of plaques had apparently been removed as well. There were two dead indoor trees and the lobby had a dusty sense about it. Inside another set of double doors was a carpeted reception area, empty work stations, and a broken water cooler. The atmosphere was filthy enough to taste. The two eventually entered a large executive office, barren except for the new or like-new upholstered furniture.

"It ain't much, but we're a work in progress. I should have this place in tip-top shape in no time," said Brice as he lifted the lid from a cooler.

Ringo witnessed this once before: the whole routine of the coffee, liquor, mayonnaise, ketchup . . . and some sugar. It made his jaw tighten just to see Brice throw this concoction together.

". . . Plus, I got enough dough to build a damn indoor amusement park . . . sit down, bruh, relax."

"You know . . . I can't be too long, B . . . there's a whole mess of stuff I need to take care of. I'm even scheduled for a show—"

"A show?! Nigga, slow your roll. Your ass might still be in jail if it wasn't for me. You forgot so soon?"

Ringo wised up to the idea. Brice was right. His freedom was a blessing. To hell with that other shit. *I got all the time in the world.*

"Now, lemme tell you why I got you here. I'm plannin' a little underground party. In two weeks—as soon as we got this place lookin' like paradise. It's gonna be private, too, on some real upscale tip . . ."

Brice downed his nasty juice and belched.

". . . I'm invitin' a couple dozen dudes—nobody you know. Just . . . personal friends. I'm also . . ." He handed Ringo a few photos. "Gonna have a whole harum of fly bitches. I'm talkin' fly. No hoodrats. Straight dime pieces."

"Sounds like a baller's bash, like they do in Atlantic City and Vegas. I been to a couple of 'em." Ringo examined the photos and handed them back.

"My man. So we're on the same page.

'Cause that's what I need from you. I need you to come through with a couple of your celebrity friends."

Ringo shrugged. "Whatever. That ain't no thing. You want me to spit a few verses? Hype it up?"

"Nah. Jokers ain't comin' out to hear anotha dude rap. They comin' for the bitches . . . I'm sellin' sex—know what I'm sayin'? I want you to cohost the joint with me, and I want one of your label mates, that trick Diamond, to entertain us."

Ringo let out an "ehhh" and put his hand to his head.

"No-h-h-h-ho. No way, hell no. Brice, I mean, B—I didn't tell you. That girl you talkin' about? Diamond? It must be a small world because she was out there that day on Queens Boulevard. The day of the robbery."

"So? What's that mean?"

"So?? Yo, son! This girl is the one I grabbed . . . the one the cop shot to try 'n' get at me. And somethin' else . . ."

Ringo realized that he'd talked himself into a mess. There's no way he could mention Diamond and Justin and how there was—or had been—a relationship between them.

"What?" said Brice, encouraging Ringo to spit it all out.

"She . . . she might've ID'ed me as the one who grabbed her."

"How could she know that? You said you had a mask on. It coulda been me that grabbed her. Plus, it's my face on the wanted posters, not yours."

Ringo stuttered, saying, "It . . . m-might be my voice . . ."

"Huh?"

"No—I'm serious. One day we were in the studio together workin' on a remix for her song."

"So?"

There he goes with the "So" again.

"B, the woman fainted. She just fell out right there on the floor. When she came to, she didn't want to see me . . . didn't want to be around me. Man—ain't no way we can be in the same place at the same time. That girl would flip out. Word."

"That shit gotta be a joke. The girl is a big-time singer, ain't she? I seen them videos with her pretty ass . . . the short braids, them juicy lips . . . and man! She got a body on her that's nothin' but boom-boom-boom!

Ringo didn't want to go against Brice's wishes, but in this case . . .

"Can't do it."

"I'll tell you what. I already told my people she was gonna be there, so that's what it's gonna be. I keep my word. No, listen . . . hear me out. If you can help, good. If not, fuck it. There's more than one way to skin a cat."

The determination on Brice's face—the way he winked at Ringo, sent a chill down his spine. Was this dude serious? Did he not know how popular Diamond was? Concerts with twenty thousand and thirty thousand fans, trips back and forth across the globe, interviews, TV . . . *Shit! That girl's performing at the Grammys. She's on the cover of* Essence *next month. Who does he think he's foolin'—me?*

"Sorry, I can't help you on that, B. I'll definitely get you some other people. Maybe Big Joe . . ."

Ringo considered his relationship with Brooklyn Jones, who had worked with Britney, Jennifer, and Luther. He also thought of Clyde "Fathead" Hayes, his booking agent at the William Walters agency, who had access to Levi, Miracle, and other platinum artists.

"Maybe I could get Frenchi or Jabahri . . . they're on my label too. A little alternative for ballers, but I think—"

"Nigga, please," said Brice, sucking his teeth. "You can name any of them bitches you want . . . my people want that freak, Diamond."

Ringo decided to leave the subject alone. *Let him figure it out for himself. Ain't no way he's gonna get Diamond in here.*

Then he remembered something his pop used to repeat: "Sometimes you can't tell people the truth. They gotta learn it on their own. They might get their feelings hurt, but they'll never forget you told 'em first."

The memory got Ringo to thinking about his pop. He suddenly missed him very much.

"So, listen," said Ringo, wanting to get the hell out of this underworld hideout—the second one in as many weeks. "If I get back home I can get on top of this. At least I can get a head start, nah mean?"

Brice swallowed the last drops of his gooey drink, and he stared at Ringo for some time, virtually studying him.

"You're right. No sense in me holding you prisoner . . ." For a second, time seemed to freeze Brice in motion. Then, out of nowhere, he let out a deep belly laugh. "Lemme show you the exact spot where the party's goin' down," Brice told Ringo as they went for the door.

The route that Brice took was dark except for lights that were strung about, illuminating work areas with busy tables full of maps, tools, and other construction materials. In distant areas there were disabled forklifts, printing machine parts, and massive rolls of paper—things that Ringo assumed were left by the defunct Centipede Press.

"Watch your step. Nails 'n' shit."

Brice and Ringo strolled along a catwalk that was above the workers and mostly out of sight.

Another of the B-boyz approached who Ringo recalled by face only.

"Wassup?" said Brice.

"Spook is back from Philly. I inventoried everything. He even got the AKs you asked for," he said. "Wassup, Ringo?" Ringo nodded, still unsure of his name.

"They wanted a little more dough, but it was worth it. You'll see."

"Did you test any of it?"

"Yeah, but we left a mess down there in the basement."

Brice made a face.

"While you were out—no construction people around—we practiced shootin' rats. I hit about twelve of them myself. E.J. got four, that no shootin' muhfucka . . . and Spook, man, that dude crazy."

"What happened?"

"Man, that white boy chased down one o' them rats with his bare hands, broke its neck, and swallowed that shit."

Ringo's abdominal muscles tightened.

"You right. We might need to get that boy's head checked. I don't know anybody who likes to eat flesh like he does." Brice said this with an awkward sense of pride, glad to have Spook on his team. In the meantime they headed down to the basement.

"Think you can handle this, Ringo? Or is this gonna be too gully for you?"

Ringo resented the implication, and he knotted his face—a response that said *Are you kidding?*

Through a metal door, they proceeded down a case of sturdy wooden steps. A single low-watt lightbulb illuminated the way to some degree and there were others hanging from a high ceiling, more visible as the two descended toward ground level.

The room immediately reminded Ringo of Club Underground, even without the laser lights, the mirrored walls, or the monstrous sound system.

"Whew . . . this is gonna be a lotta work, B. You sure you'll be ready in two weeks?"

"Funny thing about money, Ringo. Enough cash can make a tree grow overnight."

Ringo knew that to be true, especially seeing how fast things moved once he signed his recording contract. People were willing to bend over backward to satisfy his every whim.

"I guess I'm impressed, then. 'Cause if this is gonna be anything like your penthouse suite, then I can already see it."

"You been to a lotta clubs. Lemme get your opinion . . . Where do you think I should put the stage?"

"I saw this spot in Chicago. Dope dope dope. They had the stage right in the middle of the club. It could rise, rotate, and all while performers did their show."

"I never thought of that. I might go with it."

"And along the back walls you could have cocktail tables, booths—ya know, the intimate stuff. And in front of those spots . . . lower so they won't block anybody's view, you could put in some theater-style seating."

"Damn. You ever think about goin' in the business? Nightclubs? Maybe if your rap career don't work out."

"It's already workin' out, B."

"Yeah, but . . . just in case. Let's say you get shot in the throat and you can't speak no more. What then?"

"Me gettin' shot in the throat is like the Earth crashin' into the moon—it ain't gonna happen, B."

"Don't think that way, Ringo. I hate to see you thinkin' you invincible, and then . . . *bang*."

Look who's talkin', Ringo thought.

"Yeah, yeah. But you know what I mean." "Anybody can catch a bullet these days," said Brice.

Ringo let that comment lay flat. He didn't answer it.

"I'm ready to cut out. Oh, and don't forget to have mirrors on all the surrounding walls. It makes the room look twice as big," said Ringo, as he and Brice climbed the steps. Ringo secretly wondered if Brice would be able to get permits for the construction in time for his deadline. But then he laughed to himself. *Of course . . . he doesn't need permits. He's God.*

It wasn't twelve hours earlier that Bill McDoogle sat at a bar in Central Islip, a strong Long Island iced tea in front of him, and his brother Don at his side. The two were carrying on about the investigation and its various directions. But it was Don that ended the conversation. He said, "By the looks of things, there's some kinda Nigger Heaven behind that rap stuff. Them boys can hoot and holler and make all the racket they want, and people—their own people—just keep financin' that shit. Imagine that . . . I gotta get underneath cars every day, grease and soot under my nails, up my nose, but some wise-ass from off the corner slings drugs and guns and then makes a million dollars by runnin' his mouth."

"Donny, I can't stand to sit around and watch you get pissy

drunk and listen to you carry on like this. Where'd this attitude come from?"

"Hard times. Didn't y'know? Oh, I forgot—you're the DA now . . . a big-wig makin' moolah . . ."

"That's it. I'm done here. This should take care of the tab . . . Jimmy? Hey, I've got a big day tommorrow. Gotta run. Could you see that this numbskull gets home safe?"

"You got it, Bill. Have a good one."

"Thanks. And you . . . get your head together before it's too late."

McDoogle ruffled his brother's already unmanageable hair and left the bar. He could still hear his brother crying out behind him, "You just lock them niggers up!"

Those words had been with him all night. And it made him wonder if what he was doing was or wasn't a byproduct of the racism that underlay his childhood . . . his upbringing. They said that his would be the last generation of bigots, and that most of them have died off or changed their thinking with the changing times.

But then, they—that all-powerful, all-knowing "they"—said a lot of things.

The emergency meeting McDoogle called for was early enough so that he'd still be in time for various crowd appearances: the arraignment for a double homicide, a sentencing hearing for a three-strikes offender, and in the afternoon there was a bail hearing for the son of a reputed Mafia don in trouble once again.

"Okay, let's get this conference cooking—we can't wait for her all morning. I've got court in exactly twenty-five minutes. Armstrong, please be so kind as to fill in Ms. King when she arrives."

Armstrong rolled his eyes.

"In the meantime . . ."

The group of law enforcement officers, including the detectives and Justin Lewis, gathered in the DA's office, all of them having been briefed regarding the bail hearing for Ringo and his subsequent release. All of the events having weighed in favor of the rapper only angered McDoogle. And he wanted Ringo, Brice, and their riffraff friends locked up more now than ever before.

"Operation Bigmouth is not going well, fellas. We're choking on all of this information, all this fine investigative work, and yet we have Christine Lieberman being held against her will. She's being raped. Or worse, she's already dead. In any event, the pressure is on. We have to go after this Brice—how did Malcolm X say it?—by any means necessary. And I mean that. Whatever we have to do, whoever we have to use . . . Our time is up! We're at the end of our rope and about to fall into a sea of dog shit . . ." McDoogle wiped his brow—the combination of the anxiety and the alcohol from the night before.

"Justin, my friend, you've come this close"—McDoogle spaced his thumb and pointer fingers inches apart—"but, unfortunately not close enough.

We need to get ahold of this fool—*these* fools. For godsakes! Think of Christine as your own daughter!" McDoogle slammed his fist on the desk hard enough to shake the paperweight—a personalized plastic doll (a gift from his brother) with a head that seemed detached, bouncing, boinging, and wagging on some hidden spring.

"Now, how would you treat this? Do you comprehend the urgency here? Dobson, you're the top cop on this manhunt. I'm not the cop, so what's the next step?"

Dobson issued instructions much like a high school basketball coach—that "let's get down to business" approach.

"Okay. Adams and Stevens will be working on the Queens perspective. He's gotta have some family somewhere. Check school records—before he dropped out. Plus, don't forget the late-night hangouts. There's a rack of 'em out on Farmers Boulevard, Linden Avenue, and Merrick. But concentrate on some of those go-go bars, too—Gordon's, Dreams, Johnny Tay's. Do a dragnet approach—plenty of photos flashing in dancers' faces. Shake that borough up till people are ready to drop dimes on their moms and dads, if you know what I mean . . . and don't sleep on clothing boutiques and barbershops. The guy seems to lean toward the slick look, so maybe . . ."

"What about the S and M stuff?"

"Good point, Adams. Check out those shops where they sell that mess. Any lead we can get . . . Armstrong and Knight, you both will join me in some around-the-clock surveillance on the rapper. Somehow, I get the feeling that he'll wind up in his friend's company again. When he does, we'll be right there to bag 'im' . . . . We'll use two-ways, we'll plant electronic tracers on his trucks, on his associates' vehicles. We need to treat this like a life-or-death mission."

"What about Justin?" asked McDoogle, more or less accepting him as a staple of the operation.

"Something not so dangerous, if you don't mind."

"Already have an assignment for you, Justin. See if you can find out which of his friends or associates hired the expensive lawyer. We already know it wasn't him, and his closest people weren't even aware of the sudden change in attorneys. Also . . . can you work on getting us into the next celebrity event without getting noticed? Ruby did a helluva job with the whole press-pass bit at the Beacon. But I feel that may be too much for more than one person . . . I figure we can always show badges and crash the party, but then everyone's gonna know about us. However . . . as guests, it'll be a secret. We'll be able to surprise this guy if he shows his face."

The phone rang and McDoogle excused himself. He had expressed to his secretary that he wasn't to be interrupted unless it was urgent.

"McDoogle."

Shonna King was projected as "the girl most likely to" in her high school yearbook, only no one was quite sure of what she was most likely to do. Not even her. And here she was, just nine years later, at age twenty-seven, with her own practice—Shonna King, private eye. It was those blasted Leslie McGowan novels that got her here. Oh sure, the woman's niche was mentioning food on every other page some way, somehow. But Shonna saw past that and took things to another level. The Bachelor's degree, the necessary licenses . . . the gun. And Shonna's niche . . . her calling?

Shonna was a black woman with chestnut brown skin and a thousand-watt smile to complement her penetrating eyes. Not to mention that she had the body of a debutante, and at age twenty-seven, she didn't look a day older than seventeen. A wholesome, naive seventeen-year-old, if she so chose.

These were the kind of attributes—her edge—that impressed McDoogle. It was why and how she came to address him on a first-name basis.

"Bill, it's me."

"Calling to say why you're late," McDoogle assumed.

"Uh-uh. I'm outside of an industrial building on Thirteenth Street—just off of Hudson, down in the Chelsea section of the Village . . ."

For years Shonna had been doing small jobs for the DA—ever since she tracked down a bail-jumper for him. Saved him from a heap of bad publicity, too. Shonna King, the bounty hunter.

"Okay. And?"

"Bill, I've been here for two days now—ever since your boy was released on bail. He came here that afternoon and left an hour later by chauffeured limo. I decided to stay here on Thirteenth."

"Okay . . . maybe you'd like to fill me in some more, because I'm not reading between the lines."

"I can't be sure, but I'm thinking our boy Brice is here. I just can't be sure."

"Christ, can't anybody be sure of anything around here, just once?"

"I can tell you this . . . there's a lot of activity here. Some ongoing construction, as far as I can tell. Thing is . . . it's all indoors. When trucks pull in, the door opens and closes. I never get to see more than that."

"Great. And that's all I need this morning . . . another hunch. I suppose you want a search warrant now based on this hunch."

"It would be nice."

"No, Shonna. It would be my career. Don't you know the press, the ACLU, and every other community group in Chelsea—not to mention gay rights people—would wring my neck if I approved something like that? Getting the judge to go with it might work, but what happens if you're wrong?"

"And if I'm right?"

"Would you bet your life on it?"

Shonna thought about it, then said, "Gimme a little while and I'll get back to you. I just might take you up on that."

"Take me up on what? I didn't make a bet with you."

"No. But I have a feeling you'll learn to trust in a woman's intuition after I come up with somethin' concrete."

"I'll hold my breath and cross my fingers." The two disconnected.

Chapter Thirty-two

Ringo tried to reach friends and associates for a week, but nobody was returning his calls. Not even Brooklyn Jones, who had until now treated Ringo like his star athlete.

"Can I speak to him, Margaret? Please. I've left ten messages. At least."

"I'm sorry, sir, but Mr. Jones is in meetings all day."

"Margaret, it's me. What's all this sir stuff? Just the other day I was Ringo. Just the other day you'd transfer me without question. Meeting or no meeting. Even if he was at lunch, you'd put me through to his cell phone. This is crazy."

"I'm sorry, sir. May I take another message?"

Sir again . . . messages . . . arghh.

"Never mind," Ringo said, and he hung up. His speed dial was also set to reach Chuck Turner, his manager. This would be the fifteenth time he tried him.

"Chuck? *Chuck?* Chuck, answer me, man." Ringo was sure he heard someone pick up the receiver over the voice recorder.

"Don't hang up on me, man."

"What's up, kid? I'm busy."

Finally.

"What's up? You're busy? Man, this ain't no punk you talkin' to—this is Ringo, mothafucka. What the fuck is goin' on around here? Why can't I get through to anybody? Plus, I gotta get smart-mouthed by my manager? Supposed to be my manager. What happened to me bein' your platinum rapper? Did I lose my shine all of a sudden?"

"Calm down, Ringo. Please. Let me level with you once and

for all. *Billboard* came out this morning. Both your songs fell at least twenty places on both the singles and radio airplay charts. And you disappeared all together from the album charts. You ready to hear the news about SoundScan report?"

"Not good. The album went from eighty thousand to twenty-two hundred. Next week . . . and I'm merely forecasting . . . you'll be lucky if you sell more than a dozen."

"Shit, Chuck, don't tell me this is all because of this girl, Audrey. You gotta be kiddin'."

"I'd be lying to you if I said anything else, kid. Truth is, for whatever reason, the record-buying public has shut you down. Domestic abuse issues are suddenly a no-no since that NBA player was found guilty last month. And that's the way it goes. The public's conscience—your audience especially—is very fickle, Ringo. Very much here today and gone tomorrow. Funny thing is . . ."

Ringo listened quietly.

". . . or perhaps it's not so funny, but five weeks ago? Slapping a woman around was the 'in' thing. Remember that Jesse Stringer show? The one with the pimp who wrote the book *Smack 'Em Down*? He had twenty women up on the stage saying he was their god and that they fantasized about being bitch slapped. Ringo, I swear, you should see the press on this guy. Books sold out all over the place. And probably half of Jesse Stringer's viewers were the ones who bought your album and made it top ten—just so they could have something created by a tough guy. You were their tough guy, Ringo. And now? Guess what? No *106 and Park*. No Grammy. No nothin'."

"That's crazy, Chuck." Veins were showing in Ringo's neck.

"I know, Ringo. I know. And trust me, it hurts me a lot more than it does you. Remember, I'm the one who makes ten percent. I don't make the big bucks like you do. But then, that's how this monster works. Like I said, here today, gone tomorrow. Maybe it wasn't such a good idea for you to hit that girl. By the looks of things, she's connected."

Ringo slammed down the phone hard enough to smash the glass table on which it was sitting.

"What the hell is everybody thinking?"

It was all closing in on him. Porsha left town with Quentin. Mel jumped ship. Jamie was nowhere to be found. The hell if he knew where Tangi, Butter, and Sweets were.

Even when he called his bank, Ringo got the cold shoulder. He was put on hold for fifteen minutes.

"Joe! Thank you, Jesus. Can I get a balance please? This is—"

"I know who it is. Hold on," said the banker with what sounded like a salty attitude.

When he came back on the line and said eighteen thousand and change, Ringo felt as though all of the wind was knocked out of him. He couldn't speak. His expenses for one month added up to $18,000. Besides that, he had only the things he'd purchased—part of living up to the image of "ghetto fabulous," what his fans expected of him. A few platinum medallions, chains, watches, and maybe a thirty-thousand-dollar wardrobe. if he liquidated the chains.

"Is there something else, sir? I have a client with me."

Sir, again.

"Of course you do," said Ringo. "No. There's nothing else."

"Then good day, sir." And Joe, who recently bragged about how he purchased Ringo's CDs for one family member or another, hung up without another word.

It was evident, more than ever before, that Ringo was at the center of a quiet storm. All these fair-weather friends were bowing out, dodging him, and weren't even genuine enough to discuss their feelings with him.

He was about to throw the cell phone across the living room, but he looked up to find Tangi standing there in the doorway. He was too aggravated to be startled.

"Oh. Are you turning your back on me too?"

"Baby, we gotta talk."

"Yeah, we can talk. But first tell me where everybody went. Where's Butter . . . Sweets? Where the hell is Jamie? And the goddamn housekeeper!"

Tangi was cautious, but she approached Ringo and put a hand on his shoulder.

"Ringo, I was the one who told everybody to give you some

space. You went buck wild when you got back. I've never seen you like that—drinkin' and yellin' and throwin' things. All this time I've known you I never feared for my life like I did when you went off . . ."

"Wh-what day is it?" Ringo asked, thinking he'd lost his mind.

"It's Monday. I've been checkin' on you here and there . . . peeked in on you Friday night and even Wednesday. I hope you were'nt takin' drugs, Ringo."

Ringo put his hand over his face. A moment of reflection.

It was this past Monday that he was with Brice in Chelsea.

Here . . . take one of these to calm your nerves . . .

And Ringo remembered the champagne.

"I . . . I think I did," Ringo told Tangi. "An Ecstasy pill . . . supposed to settle my nerves or somethin'."

"You okay now?"

"Frustrated? Yes. Okay? Hardly. You can't imagine the shit I'm goin' through right now."

They were sitting on the couch now, Tangi turned toward him with a leg tucked under her seat.

"Ringo, please tell me you didn't do what they say . . . about that woman bein' pregnant by you . . . and you beatin' her up."

"If there was ever a time I would put my hands on a woman, it would be that one. That . . . bitch Audrey is a lyin' sack of shit. Tangi, the night that you went home—remember Chaz and Wilsons? After the Beacon Theater show? I ain't gonna lie to you—I got wasted off of a bottle of Bacardi rum. Just happy about shit, y'know? And Jamie introduced me to her friend . . . next thing I know, me and Audrey are all hugged up like the best of friends. Then we're in a limo and she's got her head in my lap. We went to her place . . . and when I woke up, I thought I was dreamin'. I couldn't believe I went to bed with that woman. A stranger. There was no love. No feelings. I can't even remember gettin' off."

"So you did get her pregnant."

"That's what she came to tell me two months later. Popped up out of nowhere. Plus, she wants a hundred thousand dollars. I told her to fuck off, and the next thing I know the cops pick me up. I swear, Tangi . . . on everything that I love, I never touched that woman. If anyone can believe me, it's you. You and me got history like a tomato got seeds." Ringo twisted his pointer finger and middle finger around each other—a vine. "And that's no shit. If I beat that woman I would've told you—no bullshit."

Tangi looked into Ringo's eyes.

"What about the other girl, Ringo. Donia?"

"Yes. I used to go with a girl named Donia. Yes, I know she had my son. But that was all news to me . . . of course I have to take care of my responsibilities. I gave her money and promised I'd visit and get to know my child. But Tangi, that was all before I met Porsha. What I have with Porsha is serious. It's like a dream come true. I love that woman."

Tangi nodded, finally with a better understanding of things.

"Porsha asked about you."

"She did? Where is she?"

"At her mother's—and you know I'm not supposed to tell you that."

"Mmm . . . and her mother loves hatin' me. I can see her now . . . holding Quentin, kissin' him . . . tellin' my son he ain't got no father."

"They're safe, Ringo. That's all that matters. But right now? I'm feelin' some type of way about this bitch, Audrey."

"Ouch. Easy, Tangi. It's all gonna work out when the truth hits the light. You know what they say: The naked truth will beat a well-dressed lie any day."

"Fuck her and the sewer she climbed out of." Ringo smiled for the first time in a long time.

My ride-or-die bitch, he thought affectionately.

"What about Butter, Sweets, and Kujo?"

"They're next door. Ringo, it wasn't like we weren't here to protect you. We were just—" "I gotcha. Sorry I acted up. Shit was just gettin' to me, y' know?"

Tangi nodded.

"But you just watch a pro turn things around," said Ringo. And he pinched Tangi's cheek. "And keep bein' you, Tangi, 'cause I know you got my back a hundred percent."

"A hundred and fifty percent," proclaimed Tangi, raising her hand in the air as if to take a solemn oath.

The gang of Ringo's close associates were together again, with him presiding over them like a politician. There was Butter, Sweets, Kujo, Tangi, and even Lucy and J-Love. Something told Ringo not to call on Jamie, and he followed his heart.

"I gotta make something clear to you guys . . . First of all, I'm being set up. I never beat up that woman—at least, not the way she says . . ."

The second half of his statement was an inside joke, since the group already knew Ringo had sex with Audrey.

"Secondly, I need you all to have a little faith in me. I've done some dirt in the past, and maybe this is just life gettin' back at me. But, whatever the case, I'm gonna win in the end. The truth will set me free. My life depends on it. The lives of my sons, too. The last thing is, I wanna thank you all for holdin' me down. Tangi told me how you all kept an eye on me while I bugged out. Even if everyone else lost faith, so what? I have a lot to lose here and I can't afford to look back. I gotta keep movin'."

Much of what Ringo said passed right through the others. They were just glad to see him well again. In a way, he seemed like a kinder, gentler boss to serve. And they didn't mind that, either.

Now that his "Dream Team" was in some type of order, Ringo had to square things away with Brice. He had to be truthful with him—to let him know how miserably things were going, and that he couldn't get ahold of any other performers for the party because of the bad publicity. He was going to have a world of headaches over the next month or so, as the financial difficulies mounted.

"And did I mention that my girl skipped town with my son?"

"I'll tell you what," Brice said on the line. "There's about a week till my party. If you guarantee me that you'll be here, I'll put ten G's in your pocket. That should help ease some of your pain."

Ringo pulled the phone away and looked at it with certain discrimination. As if money could solve everything.

Then he said, "You ain't gotta do that, B. I'll make it somehow." I got some chains 'n' shit I don't really need. Plus, I can liquidate a few—"

"You might be forgettin' somethin', son. Crime pays. You just be here like you promised and I'll make sure you don't have another money problem . . . ever."

"If you say so," said Ringo, still with some gripe in him.

"What's that?" asked Brice.

"What's what?"

"That . . . the clicking sound."

Ringo shrugged, as though this could be seen through the telephone.

Then, before Ringo could speak, Brice said, "I think you should have your phone line checked. Holla." And the line went dead.

Ringo gave his handset another strange look, but quickly dismissed further concerns.

Tangi was posted at the window, bracing herself with hands gripping the sill, watching Butter and Sweets escort Ringo to the Suburban. When the truck rolled away Tangi let out a sigh and went about her business.

Determined and focused, she marched into the bedroom and pulled up the mattress. She always knew that Ringo left the gun there, thinking it was his little secret.

Taking up the weapon somehow refreshed those memories of Bridgeport . . . the State Street Motor Inn . . . the shooting. And for a time Tangi was transfixed with the images, the pistol being a lens into the past. But there was new business now, and Tangi's energy was unstoppable. She went over to a vanity once accessorized with Porsha's jewelry, makeup, and other personal effects, and she raised the gun, pretending to be a hitman or executioner. Then she attempted to spin the gun on her finger, except it wound up pointing at her. She even tossed it from hand to hand until it fell to the floor.

A gunslinger Tangi was not.

Eventually, she did what was easiest, clenching the handle with both hands, pointing the weapon straightforward.

"Pow!"

ST. JUDE HOSPITAL

Finding Audrey was a lot easier than Tangi had expected. Sure, St. Jude was all over the news with the battered and bruised victim under the glare of flashbulbs and bright lights. But getting inside was easier still.

She stopped a hospital worker who seemed to be about her age, and she laid down her appeal. "My brother is lying in there and they won't let me in—some mess about me not being an immediate family member. But we were orphans and we were split up and given different last names . . . Blah blah blah.

It worked. And the hospital worker was kind enough not only to give up her cute outfit, but also her nametag. The tag had a photo of the girl—Tangi's co-conspirator—but she said, "Don't worry; there's so many people who work there, they never check. Plus, the guard on duty is practically brand-new himself."

That was all the assurance Tangi needed. And she cruised through the hospital lobby and onto an elevator with a heavenly ease. On the third floor Jamie had been standing behind a wheelchair in which her friend Audrey was sitting. She had on a blond wig and tinted glasses just so that a zealous reporter wouldn't make the connection—Jamie being the major link between Ringo and Audrey.

The elevator was still climbing, now from the second floor to the third, as indicated by the game show effects there above the closed doors. The ever-familiar *ding!* sounded and the doors spread apart. Jamie pushed the wheelchair into the elevator car. She heard the *ding!* from the neighboring elevator just as she eased over the threshold.

When the elevator doors parted, Tangi stepped out and instinctively looked to her left. A woman with familiar features, although she didn't immediately place her, was slipping out of sight, into the adjacent elevator. The doors closed behind her before Tangi could get a better look.

She was so distracted that she bumped into a hospital orderly, a man perhaps twice her size.

"Watch yourself, Missy."

The warning came without notice and the guy's hands grabbed both of Tangi's arms. Startled, Tangi remembered that the nametag she wore said Missy. But there was still that sense of panic . . . as if she'd been captured. Her face felt flushed, the pistol in her pocket was heavier, more like a brick now, and the slight impression it made in the uniform's fabric suddenly seemed too obvious.

They got me.

But then, the orderly continued on his way, preoccupied with his priorities. Tangi closed her eyes and breathed in relief. The hospital corridor was hers for the having. The nurses' station was occupied by one nurse who was too busy to be concerned about a hospital volunteer.

Tangi finessed the rest of her hospital visit, getting to see the in-patient and out-patient records and the rooms they were in, or had been assigned to, until she finally found that Audrey Pitts was discharged not too much earlier.

The volunteer outfit was abandoned and Tangi marched out of the hospital to hail a taxi.

That had to be them gettin' on the elevator, Tangi told herself. And she thought about the wig and shades, and how Jamie appeared to be in disguise.

She remembered Ringo saying: *Jamie introduced me to her friend Audrey.* And now, no matter that she was employed as Ringo's assistant, Jamie was considered an enemy too.

"Take me to West Thirty-fifth Street, please," Tangi instructed. And she closed her pocket organizer, anticipating her run-in with Jamie (the traitor and her friend Audrey, the extortionist).

"Here's her photo album," said HK, part of Tip Top Hard Knock Cleaners—the company B-Money fabricated as a front for all their various criminal activities.

"Good. At least this time we know what the target looks like. Remember when we tried to snatch Big Larry's—"

"Hey! Easy with that shit, man. We said no discussin' that . . . ever!"

"Right, right."

"And whaddaya mean you don't know what the target looks like? Dum-dum, you got dat newspaper article, don't ya?"

Tip Top turned sheepish.

Don't tell me you lost it. What is it this time? Your three cats ripped it up and ate it 'cause you forgot to feed 'em . . . or maybe you used it to wrap yo' mommy's birthday present by mistake . . ."

"Hey, cut it out with the mommy cracks." HK rolled his eyes and opened the photo album. Tip Top reached over and tugged at the album so he, too, could get a look.

"Isn't this that Jackson girl? And look . . . Big Joe—I know his stuff."

"Mmm . . ."

"And that's Killer X. Oh shit."

Hard Knock smacked Tip Top's hand.

"Cut that shit out. We're here for one thing, and one thing only. If you don't stay focused and we fuck up this job—oh boy . . . They tell me if you piss B-Money off he don't give no second chances. He fills you with holes on the spot."

"Yeah, I heard what he did to that kid in Jersey . . . what's his name, Rabbit?"

Hard Knock cut a harsh expression at Tip Top and he smacked the photo album shut.

"You just don't seem to learn, do ya?"

"What now?"

"What if the van was bugged? You wanna give up the man's social security number too? Maybe his date of birth and the exact time of the—" Hard Knock wagged his head, thinking that Tip Top was a hopeless case, that he'd one day be the death of him.

"Oh shit!" Tip Top whispered excitedly. "Somebody's comin'."

"Over there!" ordered HK in a hushed tone. "And keep quiet!" *I'll be in the closet,* he mouthed silently.

The two were aware of the job here: B-Money wanted the girl alive.

* * *

Chuck Turner had an office that was a little bigger than a broom closet. There was his desk, a file cabinet full of wannabe photos and, to really crowd things, a used love seat that had been used many times when Chuck decided to sleep or nap in the office.

This, contrary to the opinions of others, was okay with Chuck. Sometimes small was good, especially with the entertainment industry being so damned fickle. You never knew where the next buck was coming from.

Chuck had tried his hand at peddling aspiring ingenues to Broadway shows and child actors to advertising agencies for possible TV commercial work. He represented a country-music band, too, but the novelty of the group wore off and the group ended up on a bus to Nashville, where the atmosphere was more conducive to their brand of music. There were also three models Chuck managed, until he cut out the models altogether. It was the near-scandal that encouraged him, when one of the models (who was actually fifteen years old) tricked Chuck (and the world) into believing she was nineteen. The truth didn't come out until she began appearing in porno movies. When word got out, anyone who Chuck managed disavowed their association with him.

Chuck barely escaped prosecution with his I-didn't-know alibi.

Brooklyn Jones heard about the incident and showed compassion. He helped Chuck get back into the mix and got him hooked up with Jamie, and he inevitably became Ringo's manager. "It's a sure thing," Brooklyn had told him. But now, since this new controversy came up, Chuck was falling into a depression. It was as if it was all happening again—and wait till the press connected the dots! It would eventually surface, Chuck assumed. And the media would follow a new bent on the Ringo story: Rapper Coached by Former Manager of Teenage Porn Star.

To avoid those possibilities, Chuck made the decision to cut his losses and bail out. It was a paranoid choice, but his only alternative was to turn back time and perhaps make some better decisions. But even that was a daydream, an illusion that knocked around in his head.

"I swear to God, Chuck. If you don't open this door I'mma kick it in!" shouted Ringo. And he kicked the door once to show his manager that he meant business.

Damn, Ringo thought, wincing in pain. *I didn't kick it* that hard.

The office door gave, but it wasn't Ringo's kick. Chuck had opened it, and now he stood there singing: "R-I-NGO, R-I-NGO, R-I-NGO, and Ringo was his name-oh!" And Chuck let out a horselaugh before he went on to say, "Didn't think I had talent, huh? I can hold a tune better than an opera singer, buddy . . . I don't need to manage nobody." Chuck had the hiccups mixed in with his exaggerations.

"Yo, man, what the fuck's wrong with you?"

"I'm Lincoln Center material . . . Radio City . . . even Carnegie Hall! Fi-ga-ro, Figaro . . . Fi-ga-ro-!" Ringo sucked his teeth when he noticed the empty liquor bottle.

"Dude, you're twisted," Ringo said when he picked up the bottle, its label explaining everything: Jack Daniels, 100% Proof.

"Better me than the rest of the world . . ." Chuck's latest hiccup was followed by phlegm, and then he barfed up a soupy vomit, its rich stench so sour it irritated Ringo's nose tissue. The desk was foul with half-digested cookies, liquor and spaghetti.

"Oops . . . lunchtime!" croaked Chuck, and he attempted another laugh, except the vomit pushed up from his throat once again.

"Aww, damn, Chuck! That shit is nasty."

Chuck ran his shirtsleeve across his soiled lips.

"Life is nasty, kid." Chuck snickered and sobbed all at once. ". . . And so is the rent, the empty refrigerator, the car note—oh gee, they already repossessed that this morning . . ." He suppressed a chuckle. "But now I have an even bigger, more dependable car . . . the subway!"

"Fuck, Chuck." Ringo wagged his head.

"Fuck Chuck, hey that rhymes! Lemme guess . . . you're the

rapper, right? Platinum one day and broke the next . . . hand me that—I need another drink."

Ringo pursed his lips and gave Chuck the bottle, instead of hitting him with it.

Tangi got to 35th Street in time to see two scruffy-faced men. One looked like Barney—short, beady eyes, a box for a head and a long, pointed nose from the Flintstones cartoon, while his partner was heavily scarred about the face, with a buzz cut and a tattoo of some heart-shaped design on his neck. Both men had on painters' coveralls and there were rolled-up carpets flopped over their shoulders.

For an instant, Tangi imagined that those were corpses the men carried. But she soon shook that idea and slipped through the doorway they'd just stepped from.

She had her head turned and didn't realize a resident was in her path. He was a larger man—big enough to be a basketball player and 49er, both—and, like the hospital orderly did, he grabbed ahold of her to prevent the collision.

"You should be careful, young lady." And just like that, he excused himself and went about his business.

Her heart leaped inside of her chest, Tangi cupped her breast, caught her breath, and regrouped.

What am I doin', running into walls all of a sudden?

There was a wall of mailboxes where Tangi discovered the confirmation to her suspicion. Pitts . . . Horton. They both lived in the same building—Audrey Pitts and Jamie Horton. And how convenient! They both lived on the sixth floor, too.

Tangi put her pocket organizer away and stepped across the lobby, into the building's sole elevator. As she was taken to the sixth floor, she tightened her grip on the 9mm in her pocket and painted a picture of deceit and conspiracy in her head—how these women must've been scheming on Ringo for some time now.

Up on six, she found Jamie's door locked. Nobody home.

Audrey Pitts . . . apartment 612.

Tangi strolled the length of the hallway, passing 612, and

blending in with the midday silence. People work . . . they vacation . . . and who knows why else it was so quiet.

Hoping she hadn't aroused neighbors with her knocking at Jamie's door, Tangi was more conscious now, and she eased up to the door, apartment 612. There were no sounds coming from inside and she wondered if it was possible, again, that nobody was home.

Her leaning on the door forced it open, and it was obvious to her that it wasn't locked. *Too easy,* she thought, her head swinging back and forth to check the hallway. She wondered if anyone was peeping through the many peepholes in any of the apartment doors—and if they were, what would they assume anyhow?

Now the self-talk: *You can do this, Tangi. You did it before . . . this is easy for you . . . like riding a bike . . . Do it for Ringo, just like he'd do for you.* Then she crept through the door. Tangi, the trespasser.

The first thing Tangi noticed was the lamp, broken on the floor. A chair was down on its side and a table had been bared, most likely where the houseplants had been.

Tangi stepped over the broken pottery, scattered soil, and hopeless plant life to get a better idea of what transpired. A robbery? A fight? It was an assumption, but she could envision a struggle of some sort. Either that or someone had been looking for something.

Quick thinking made Tangi wonder about the two painters. Were they even painters at all? And she shuffled over to a window for an aerial view of the street where the van was parked. Gone.

A loud beep caused Tangi to grab the gun from her pocket and whip it out. She swung it around, aiming at nothing but inanimate objects that furnished the apartment. She sighed when she realized it was an answering machine, and her eyesight rested on the device, presumably the only thing "moving" in such a dead atmosphere.

"Hey! It's Audrey. Leave a message. Smooches!"

Smooches? Who the hell uses that word?

Another beep.

"Audrey, it's B.J. Jamie called and said she'd be taking you home from the hospital, so I thought I'd call you to see how you're doing. Where are you two? Anyway, I tried Jamie's cell phone and yours . . . but I just wanted to say you did great work. A huge sacrifice on your part. But trust me, you're gonna see huge rewards for your end of this. I just wanted to say thanks, and that you two make a hell of a team. Next target, the president of Arista . . . or the United States! Imagine that!" There was energetic laughter. Then the caller, B.J., finished his message. "I'm talkin' too much. Anyway . . . get at me as soon as you get in. I'll be in the office till eight tonight. Gotta sell records, y'know. Peace, baby. And get well soon."

Tangi fell back onto the couch, her arms (and the gun) uselessly drooping between her legs as she stared at the answering machine. She repeated the message, and sat idle again. When the message was done with, when she was done deliberating, Tangi rose to her feet with great determination. She pried the cassette tape from the well of the recorder and left the apartment.

Jamie and Audrey were no longer important to Tangi's cause.

She mumbled to herself as she proceeded to the Seventh Avenue subway. The PGD buildings and Brooklyn Jones' office weren't more than fifteen minutes away.

Triflin' mothafucka.

Chapter Thirty-three

He was dazed.

Everything with respect to his comfortable home and his newfound career was falling apart. There seemed to be more problems now than ever before—before the fame and the money. And now Ringo understood what the Notorious B.I.G. was talking about when he coined the phrase "Mo' money, mo' problems." More stress, more shady characters. It was hard to find people who would keep it real with him. He was tired of the phones, the fair-weather friends, and the so-called soldiers who bailed out when it got too hot in the kitchen . . . when his chips were down.

"Kujo, pull over. I need to make a call," said Ringo. The request drew strange expressions from Butter and Sweets since there was the mobile phone and the portable cell phone to make things more convenient. But no one questioned it.

This was personal, obviously.

Ringo climbed out of the truck and gestured to Sweets that he'd be fine. Sweets made a face, but he remained posted there by the truck, still on the job. And besides, the pay phone was but ten or so feet from the nose end of the Suburban.

After a second, Ringo recalled a phone number, then dropped two quarters into the slot. He punched in the math and waited.

Twelve rings vibrated in Ringo's ear before he heard the background sounds of a busy barbershop.

"Domepiece. Who you need to talk to?" It was a young boy's voice. Ringo assumed it was the hired help who generally swept the floor.

"This is Ringo. My pop there?"

There was no response at first, but Ringo thought he heard the kid asking for his father. The cocky voice was soon replaced by a confused one.

"Ringo? Ringo, is that you?"

"It's me, Pop."

"Oh, my God! I was just thinkin' about you! Oh my God! Hold on, lemme take this phone in the back room . . ."

Ringo could hear the urgency in his father's voice and it touched him so that his insides quivered with anticipation. It was at that instant that Ringo breathed freely, more so than he had in a long, long time.

"Ringo, what's going on with you? First, I'm watching you on *FN Music* and *106 & Park*, and the next thing I see is you in handcuffs—about some girl in the hospital. My God, son. What's happening? I thought I lost you. Are you out of jail? I heard something about bail, and some nonsense about not leaving the country."

"Pop, easy. I'm fine, I just . . . I'm fine." Ringo hesitated, not because of the phone conversation. It was the sedan about four car lengths behind the Suburban. He could see at least two men in the front seat—although he wasn't obvious about it.

The vehicle was idling there, half in and half out of the parking space.

Five-0, Ringo told himself. And his heart began to pound faster.

"Ringo, the police came by here asking all kinds of questions about you. I told 'em you were a good kid, but that you left years ago, and that I haven't seen you since, truth be told. So they left me alone. But—"

"Pop, lemme call you back, all right?"

"Ringo?"

"Yeah, Pop?"

"Everything okay? You safe?"

"Of course. Look for my call, okay?"

"Ten-four, kiddo. I love you, son."

Ringo dwelled on that for as long as he could stand, before he finally responded.

"I love you too, Pop."

Ringo hung up, found another quarter, and he made a second call.

"Hold on," said Butter. Ringo could see him answering the phone through the truck's front windshield.

"Butter, it's me, Ringo."

"Uh . . . oh. Okay, I get it."

Ringo looked at the mouthpiece and then over at Butter in the truck. *No you don't.*

"This is where we split up," said Ringo.

"Huh?"

"I'm gonna disappear down into the subway. Just take the truck back home—business as usual. I'll see you all later, aight?"

There was a hesitation on the line until Ringo turned to look through the front windshield, eye-to-eye with Butter.

"N-no problem. You okay?"

"Yeah. But we're being followed." Ringo pushed down the receiver, but didn't hang up yet. He pretended to continue his conversation until he felt a rumbling from the sidewalk where he stood. Then, without the slightest hesitation, Ringo made his way down the nearby staircase to where the train was coming to a stop. He slid two dollars into the tray, where the token booth was stationed, and he didn't bother to wait for a token. Ringo hooked around and made a run for it, hurdling the turnstile in time to make it through the closing doors.

He was sure there was nobody following him now—not unless there were ghosts who could sprint faster than he could.

Domepiece was a somewhat weathered establishment—weathered by the traffic that passed through over the years on Francis Lewis Boulevard in Queens. It was sandwiched between a liquor store and a laundromat. Ringo spent many an afternoon here as a youngster, where he was once like Sweepy, sweeping up hair from around the barbers' chairs and answering the telephone.

"Wassup, Sweepy—you ain't hollerin' at cha boy no more?"

"Is it true what they say 'bout you? That you be beatin' women? My old man beats on my momma—"

Ringo cut Sweepy off. He could see where this conversation was going. *Kid probably thinks I'm a creep.*

"Lemme school you on somethin'. I might be grimy, aight? But I ain't never beat up no woman."

"But the TV—" he began to protest.

"Forget what you seen on TV. That box tells a lotta lies. And too many people get tricked by the lies. Don't you get tricked too. You know me, Sweep. You know my pop. So . . . who you gonna believe? The TV? Or me?" Sweepy hesitated, but eventually warmed to a confident smile.

"I knew it wasn't true, Ringo."

Ringo felt like the Earth just stopped spinning even if only for an instant.

"Am I still the man?" asked Ringo, his fist stuck out.

Sweepy balled his own fist and hammered Ringo's.

"Yeah. You still the man."

Now all he had to do was wait for Pop to finish the head—the customer whose hair he was cutting—so that they could talk: that long-awaited father-son discussion.

Tangi was a somewhat familiar face at the PGD building in midtown Manhattan. Whereas most others had to show identification and wait for their appointment to be confirmed, Tangi would generally walk right through the atrium with its marble floors and long stone reception desk.

In the past, a confident smile did the trick, and she'd simply traipse through, either to drop off or pick up something important for Ringo. So today was no different. With so many hundreds of visitors and PGD employees—PGD had twenty subsidiary record companies all housed in the same forty-eight-story complex—entering the building lobby, there was no way to stop everyone . . . no way to check everyone's identification with absolute scrutiny. To do so would congest things to a virtual standstill, and that would ultimately interfere with business as usual.

Even then, it was simply a case of familiarity with the building's security personnel, leaving them to address the less-familiar faces on a random basis. Otherwise, there were no security measures such as metal detectors or fact-finding inquiries that would stop Tangi's mission.

Tangi remained focused and headstrong as one of twelve elevators carried her upward.

PGD's affiliated labels included an array of musical tastes, including jazz, classical, alternative, country, rap, pop, rock, heavy metal, gospel, and an even larger variety of international music.

The labels all represented brands—boutiques that operated independently of one another, but also as arms and legs that supported and fed the same Goliath: PGD.

When Tangi reached the twenty-first floor she sidestepped the procedure of pulling up to the receptionist's desk. The woman was busy manning the switchboard, juggling calls, and transferring others to their appropriate parties. Another phenomenal woman.

More than that, there was a FedEx driver standing over the receptionist with a clipboard, ogling her cleavage and pointing to where she should sign for a delivery. The way he was conveniently blocking the receptionist's view, Tangi thought him to be the perfect cohort. Tangi took advantage of the opportunity and secretly thanked him as she joined the employees already milling through the corridors that branched off of the twenty-first-floor lobby.

She assumed the mind-set of a participant and blended right in with the activity. Her determined expression led her past the departments of retail, promotions, A&R, video promotion, publicity, and into the rear corridor, where she knew Brooklyn Jones and his executive assistant were situated.

Tangi remembered B.J.'s executive assistant to be a fine woman who was diligent and worked hard to serve her boss.

I hope she doesn't get in my way. If she does . . .

Ringo and his father did their best to close the communication gap that existed—years of separation. The barbershop eventually closed and the two sat in the back room, designed like a living room, with a sectional couch, an entertainment center, and a small dining table. The couch and chairs were covered with plastic so that the barbers who came back here for a break wouldn't get clippings on the furniture.

For now, it was just father and son back there. Everyone else had gone home for the day.

"You still closin' shop, huh?"

"Don't see why I shouldn't. I'm an owner. And when White moves down to Dallas it's gonna be just me and Del."

"Wow, Pop. I don't wanna say I'm impressed 'cause, damn, I'm your son. It's supposed to be the other way around—you're supposed to be impressed with me. But I have to say, you came a long way from—"

"From what? Being a drunk?"

Ringo didn't want to agree with his father, but he knew what the man spoke was the truth. Maybe that was the best indication of him being a changed man.

To save face, Ringo changed the subject.

"What's that?" he asked, watching his father pour a glass of soupy orange something into a glass. There was a huge color difference, but the moment reminded Ringo of Brice and his wicked concoction.

"Carrot juice. That's how I dried up. I substituted it for the hundred-proof, know what I mean? I been alcohol-free for almost two years now, so. I even feel like a new man."

"And you look like a new man, Pop," said Ringo with little doubt in his voice.

"Wanna try?"

"Shoot—will it make me a new man. 'Cause I could stand some magic right now."

"I ain't gonna say all o' that. But it's a start. The real trick ain't a trick at all. It's just about eatin' healthy and livin' healthy. You gotta take care of your body, so it can take care of you. If you don't, nothing else matters. I woundn't be able to cut hair . . . you wouldn't be able to rap."

Ringo nodded and his mind wandered.

"Ringo . . . tell me everything gonna be all right with you. I mean, is there anything I can help you with?"

After rubbing the question in like a face lotion, Ringo pulled his hands away from his eyes to respond.

"Pop, sometimes I think I'm in the wrong game."

"How do you mean?"

"I mean, I'm stuck with a name, a record label . . . a certain fan base that goes crazy over my stuff, and it's like my life revolves around these things. My image is a hyped-up image . . . my sound and lyrics are, I don't know, my signature. And I just don't have a choice. I can't grow out of it like I want to because the record label—those good white folks with the suits and ties?—they depend on me to be consistent with the meetings we have. I'm like some voodoo doll that they manipulate as they please. And if I don't do what they want . . . boom. End of game."

"I don't know what to say, Ringo. You're not a boy anymore. You're old enough to sign contracts that are legally binding . . . to make your own decisions . . ."

Listening to the truth reddened Ringo's eyes, and he felt himself stuck somewhere between defeat and the urge to press on—teetering there in the middle of that so-called decision.

Only his tendencies were stronger where the challenge was calling, and he would not allow himself to cry. Not in front of his father not in front of anyone.

"Oh, I aint givin' up or nothin'. It's just . . . I guess this rap thing ain't all I thought it would be. I busted my ass, Pop. I hustled day and night, until the next thing I knew, I was in another world. Back in the day I was scrapin' for subway fare, but once I signed the deal? I was on the record company's private jet landin' in Atlanta, swept off by a motorcade with my security, my publicist, my assistants, and my manager. We're stoppin' at radio stations and TV stations for interviews . . .

"Then there's what we call an in-store promotion with a line of fans two blocks long, shoutin' 'Ringo! Ringo! Ringo!' One girl, I'll never forget. She's in tears and can hardly talk. And she's a white girl too, so you know I was freaked out. Probably some high school cheerleader. But she's babblin' about how she loves me to death, tremblin' like she's naked in Siberia . . . I mean, damn, Pop! I'm comin' from a ghetto full o' sugar-water babies and wish sandwiches . . . all of us powerless, hatin' on each other . . . drugs and violence killin' us off little by little . . . no money, no hope, cryin' in church like that's gonna change somethin'. You know the deal, Pop. I don't have to tell you, it's a cesspool of misery here . . .

"But, all of a sudden I'm bein' treated like a million bucks—only, I ain't got a million bucks. A million records sold don't mean I'm a millionaire. That's what everybody thinks. But the Real Deal Holyfield is that it's the record company gettin' paid. A million records means maybe ten million dollars in revenue that they get to play with however they want. And me? Out of all that money, I probably get a hundred thousand dollars."

"That's good money."

"Nope. Not out of ten million in revenue. Not if it's mostly my work . . . my lyrics. They give me two hundred and fifty thousand dollars, Pop."

"Now, that's really good money."

"Nope. It's long-term money. That hundred I make off of the first million? That goes toward the front money they gave me. Then, I gotta sell another million and a half units just to pay off the rest. All it is is a loan, Pop. They banked on me. But now, most of that's gone. And if you add in the scandal, things get worse. I'm in a lot of debt if you really calculate things. Plus, people don't even want to talk to me now. It's like I was never here. Like I never mattered. Even the record company president who used to sweat me to join his team—he won't take my calls anymore. Here today, gone tomorrow. I'm like a broken Christmas toy . . ."

"I'm listening to you, Ringo. And you know what I think? I think you're sinking into a black hole—one you made yourself. But I also think it's all an illusion and that you're not really seeing the big picture. Okay, so you got sucked into somethin' you really weren't planning for . . .

"I think you have a gift, Ringo. A way with words. And it's okay if you wanna be angry, outrageous, spittin' fire. But you also need to know that while words can give life, they can also be deadly. Look at the big picture, Ringo. Are you lookin' for success? Fame? Money and security? How about love? It's important for you to know this, because very rarely does a person achieve all of those things if they don't have a plan or an objective to focus on. It's the big picture, Ringo . . .

"Just as an artist has a vision to paint a masterpiece, being an artist has to make her happy. That's the only way she'll be able to express herself—her true self. So painting is her vehicle, and rappin' might be yours. But you have to be happy doing it, Ringo. Otherwise, your vision is distorted, like mine was at one time. And guess what? The masterpiece is really what life's about. It's our destiny. It's all that we want—all of our values and dreams. You are that masterpiece, son."

Ringo went home with his father and didn't mind sleeping on the couch. Not for a long time had he had a chance to ignore the rest of the world—quality time during which he could think about things his father said, time during which he could consider what he was given life for.

Why am I here?

No telephone calls, no television, and no radio. Ringo just relaxed without the conveniences or the external influences to interfere with his peace.

Pop had a small selection of books that Ringo picked through. He hadn't sat alone with a book in quite a while, since the days he was holed up in Bridgeport, and even holding a book felt good.

One book, *The Celestine Prophecy: Your Purpose in Life*, seemed right up his alley, and he took it on as his pet project.

"Good choice," his father told him at one point. "That book changed my life."

And Ringo absorbed the various concepts. They made him stop and think about his past, his present, and his future.

When his father came home early enough from the shop, the two would eat dinner and talk about how things were when his mom was around. His father also helped him to plan for his future, according to the guidelines set forth in the book.

For Ringo, these had become the five most important days in his life. He was determined to go back and make things right. He wanted to find Porsha and Quentin, and affirm what kind of father he'd be, and maybe, if Porsha would have him, what kind of husband as well.

"How are you doin' with money?"

"I can make it. There's eighteen thousand in my bank account, but I'm sure that'll be gone within a couple of weeks just with the rent and the truck note. It's a big mess at my place. But on the positive side, I'm hosting this party in a few days—a guaranteed ten grand. So maybe I can work things out until this woman tells the truth."

"The truth? How's that gonna happen? She'd be askin' to get arrested herself."

"I haven't figured that out yet, but I gotta fix things. If she's gonna have my third child, cool. I can live with that. But this other assault shit? Uh-uh . . . I can't live with that. She gonna clear my name. Believe that, Pop. Believe it."

Chapter Thirty-four

CHELSEA, 13TH STREET

The Freaky Deaky Ballers Ball was absolutely nothing like the dream that Brice sold to Ringo. "I'm plannin' a little underground party," he told Ringo two weeks earlier. And now, here it was, party time, and this was a world away from the way things were "supposed" to be.

To begin with, the basement of the 13th Street commercial building was incomplete, nowhere near the Jewel—that illusion that Brice projected.

"As soon as we get this place lookin' like paradise . . . on some real upscale tip," was how he put it. But by the looks of things. Ringo's suggestion about the mirrors along the interior walls seemed to be the only improvement. So the basement where dead rats once ran now appeared twice as large.

However, there were none of the other elements that might be customary for most any club or dance hall—no elevated VIP areas, no incredible laser light show, and the so-called dance floor hadn't even been tiled; it was left as a bare concrete foundation.

Ugly, Ringo thought.

And, as if Brice could read his mind, he made an attempt to clear the air.

"A little rough, I know. But my people are okay with it. They just come for the excitement anyway."

And that was another thing. His people. Ringo wore some sharp jeans and a New England Patriots football jersey. The pendant hanging from his neck and a diamond-studded Rolex completed his look so that he measured up to Brice's request: "I need you to look like you do in the videos . . . I want you to stand out so the girls—" And Ringo said, "Girls? I thought this was for ballers?"

And Brice replied, "Well . . . yeah, that's what I meant . . ."

Whatever. Ten grand, dawg. I'll wear Spandex if you want.

So Ringo dressed the part and stood at the entrance to the basement. He also had the opportunity to shake hands with almost everyone admitted. Rascal. Spider. Tip Top. Crock. HK, Johnny Boy, and maybe two dozen other shady characters. Certain names stood out.

Some guy named One Tooth was a memorable sight to see. Ringo winced when he saw one guest's scar, the keloid curving from his temple, down to his chin. Then there was a dude with a mouth full of gold teeth that glistened when he smiled . . . glistened with an odor that was worse than a baby's soiled diaper. But One Tooth had his one tooth positioned dead center on his lower gums. And furthermore, when One Tooth shook hands with Ringo, he got close enough for the rapper host to feel the tool hidden underneath his jacket. That idea of guns on the premises—how many, he couldn't imagine—sent a chill through his body.

And then there was the entertainment.

Spook led a group of young women—Ringo counted eighteen of them—into the basement. They had on one-shoulder tops, tied-off T-shirts and baby tees, and those tops that appeared to be two sizes too small and wrapped the body like a second skin. On their lower halves they wore short shorts, stone-washed jeans, and a miniskirts, leaving their midsections bare so that Ringo could see navel rings or the waistband of their thongs showing. And their hair was either pulled through the back sides of baseball caps or braided or simply left to fall freely.

These girls had a sense of fun, sass, and impulsiveness about them—the gum-smacking, the Minnie Mouse backpacks, and the ready-for-excitement desire in their eyes all felt rather promising. And Ringo saw them as no different from concertgoers, representing a variety of cultural origins. Not only that, but they all apparently knew of him, especially the ones who were loud about it, recognizing Ringo with a squeal, a shriek, or that up and down jumping that a person did when they had to pee.

Already, some of them had been allowed close enough to ask for a hug, a kiss, or an autograph from the rap star. And Ringo at once recalled the white girl who went crazy for him down in Atlanta, or the frenzy of contest winners who were admitted backstage in Kentucky or Los Angeles, or even the most extreme fans who had his name tattooed on their bodies.

"Let's keep it movin', girls. There's plenty of time for this later," explained E.J., who came to help Spook guide them down into the bowels of the makeshift social club with its loud music and unruly shouts and whistles.

"Ringo, I didn't believe you'd be here," one girl called out. Another said, "I told you he would. Now don't you feel dumb?" "Ringo. I loved 'Just Cause,' and 'Push,' too. And I don't believe a word they said about that woman," said an Asian girl. And before she was pulled away by her friend, another girl whispered to Ringo, "You can beat me any time."

Then Brice showed up with a no-nonsense attitude.

"Okay, girls . . . please follow the others to the dressing rooms. We can't wait to see you audition. Ringo's been expecting this all week long, isn't that right, Ringo?" Brice pulled his homeboy in for a shoulder-to-shoulder hug.

Ringo managed a smile, more a confirmation than a denial, but he also tried to get an eye-to-eye understanding with Brice. Audition? Brice was nonchalant about the questioning look and simply patted Ringo's shoulder, winking at him as well. It was that go with the flow message.

Brandishing a sinister smile, Outlaw eventually came through the doorway.

"Sorry we're late . . . playin' taxi driver isn't the easiest job in town . . . Oh, here's my card. Call me if you have any more girls to pick up."

Outlaw was in motion, passing a business card to Brice, who quickly crunched it in his fist before anyone could get a peek.

"That Outlaw—he's always playin'," said Brice as he tossed

the crumpled business card. Ringo's eyes followed the ball of paper as it fell through the air, diving way down to the cement floor where guests milled about.

"Come on, lemme show you your seats. You don't need to stand up here anymore."

Ringo shook free of his curiosity and followed Brice down the steps and over to a designated area where a handful of chairs were set in a semicircle.

"This is our VIP area," said Brice. And Ringo saw that his friend was serious. An array of chairs were scattered behind the semicircle, with half-assed cocktail tables that could've once been some nursery school's oversized building blocks.

No sooner were the two seated than the raw table service began. No waitresses, just E.J. hustling around the place, pulling bottles of champagne from a barrel of ice, setting them on tables alongside wicker baskets of mixed peanuts, nachos, and pretzels.

Brice turned around to his guests—the notorious, the nefarious, and the ne'er-do-wells among them.

"You all good?" he asked aloud.

In a broken chorus they all muttered or else openly pronounced their agreement.

"Let's get on with it," one voice barked.

"Yeah!"

Ringo turned some and saw that, by and large, these men were hungry and fiendish.

Brice made a gesture to relax as he replied, "Should be starting any minute now." Yet the expression he issued to E.J. wasn't appeasing, but more of a summons. And just then, E.J. rushed off through a door.

Inside the makeshift dressing room, the lanky brown-skinned girl copped an attitude.

"This one don't fit." She held up the two-piece bathing suit to her body—nothing more than thinly meshed lace that left little to the imagination.

Outlaw prayed for patience as he turned to her. It was that set of juicy lips and the huge doe eyes that seduced him and tamed his urge to step over and put his hands on her.

"Squeeze into it the best you can, would you? Ringo's gonna wanna see you in that. Trust me." And the girl's attitude immediately softened. Another girl, this one with braids, pretty dimples, and a self-important expression in her eyes, held up her swimsuit as well.

"This one must have holes in it," she said.

"Nah, boo. That's just the style. Ringo picked that one especially for you."

"Yeah, but ain't my nipples gonna show? My momma didn't raise—"

Outlaw stopped "Dimples" before she said another word.

"Come here."

His directive had the majority of girls at attention. Then he whispered in the girl's ear. Her frown soon turned into a gradual smile, and she went about her business as usual. Not another peep.

Outlaw swept a gaze across the others, encouraging them to hurry along. He breathed relief when he saw all the reconsideration, and that the girls were going with the flow.

Submission . . . I love it.

E.J. entered the room and his presence provoked some shock—the violation of yet another stranger seeing their varying states of undress. Outlaw saw this and clapped his hands loudly and abruptly.

"Come on! Come on! Listen, Ringo don't need no scared actresses for his videos. If you gonna be models, you gotta be bold girls! You gotta get used to men seein' you—that's all there is to it. Now . . . anybody who's afraid and you don't wanna hang with the big girls, speak up now and pack your stuff. Otherwise, we got a show to do."

There was a sigh or two, but overall, the tension in the room lifted and the dressing and undressing continued with little apprehension. Outlaw and E.J. locked eyes, sharing that satisfied leer.

A minute later E.J. said, "Okay, who's ready for the big time?"

Two of the most ambitious girls raised their hands high. A third girl also shot up a hand, but her top hadn't been affixed yet.

Outlaw withheld his laughter when the bikini top fell to the floor and the girl crossed her bare breasts with her other arm.

"You two—front and center."

Obediently, the two drew near, barefoot and ready for whatever.

"Don't worry about makeup," said E.J., his hand reaching out for a purse that one of the two held. "That's not where your talent is."

Outlaw stood before them now for a mini pep rally.

"Okay. I want you two to go out there and get the party started. Show everybody you got what it takes. And remember, this entertainment business is all about tits and ass. So you better make those men out there cream in their pants. Got it?"

"What about Ringo? Will he see us?"

"Of course. He's right there in front. He'll be lookin' right at you. He wants the works: sexy eyes, sexy dance moves . . . and he loves seein' a lot of skin."

"Yup," added E.J. "Skin. He loves it. The more the better."

"And don't pay attention to what the emcee says. Remember, this is all part of an act. It's a . . . a rehearsal for the real thing. So do your part, and let us do ours. Got me?"

The girls' heads nodded nervously.

Outlaw softly swatted both their asses after he opened the stage door.

"Okay. Move out. You know what to do." As directed, the two cuties—one with tapered golden hair and a cream-colored doll face, the other with a darker complexion and braids—shuffled out into the musky, darkened room of men.

They immediately distinguished Ringo from the others—the ones with bald heads, crew cuts, jheri curls . . . hats of every sort pulled down over eyes, turned to the back or to the side . . . bug-eyed men, lizard-eyed men, puny-eyed men . . . scars, tattoos, earrings. Bucktoothed. One-toothed. Snarling tongue flicking. Noisy. Hootin' and hollerin'. Stompin'. Hungry for flesh.

"What's yo' name, girl?" asked the emcee, dressed in a white T-shirt, a gold rope chain, and baggy jeans. His eyes drooped some, his head gleamed, and his nose was something like a link sausage.

"Billie McDonald."

"And you?"

"I'm Althea Greenwood." And Althea pushed her braids back over her shoulder so Ringo could get a better look.

"Good, good," said the emcee. And into the mic, he announced, "Fellas . . . heeeere's Billie Gold, lookin' like a college chick . . ." The emcee swatted Billie's ass cheek. "Okay, babe. Go up there and shake that ass."

Billie did.

"And fellas . . . check out Alfie too." Again his hand reached out to hit her ass after the name adjustment. Alfie stepped onstage—just a foot-tall platform, and squeaky from many uses—and joined Billie, the two of them putting their all into this, using every muscle, exhibiting their every curve and pretending to be part of Ringo's harem, the concept that Outlaw said would be used for the rapper's forthcoming video. Alfie got a little excited by the crowd, and now she, too, was gyrating and bending over. The two girls with their pubescent figures drew roars from the crowd.

"Okay, y'all . . . time to start the bidding," barked the emcee. What do I get for Goldie? Two fifty? Okay . . . what about two twenty-five?" The emcee searched for a signal. When he got it, he pointed to the back.

"Buster in the red Kangol hat offers two twenty-five. Do I hear three? Three hundred for this fine piece of Gold here. Bend over, baby. Show some more o' that ass. Now . . . does that look like it's worth three hundred? Come on, man! That's gotta be worth at least five hundred. Now who's biddin' five . . ."

"Seven!" shouted the big-faced cat with the slicked-back waves.

"Seven! Now, that sounds a lot better. Who's challengin' Slick Willie, huh? Who's biddin' nine? Do I hear nine for a bump n' grind with Goldie?"

Ringo's eyes widened in amazement.

Goldie took it as a sign of appreciation.

"A thousand!" called out a husky brother with big bulging eyes set deep inside of their sockets.

"There it is there! Booty from L.A., Rascal's peeps, puttin' up a G. Goin' once . . . twice . . . sold to Booty, Rascal's peeps. Okay, Goldie, you're done. Step down. Now how 'bout this trick, y'all. Alfie . . . ready to wrap you in her long braids, tie yo' ass up, and . . . bang bang bang! So I hear five to start . . ."

E.J. helped Goldie down from the platform.

"Good job, Goldie. Come with me. This is part two of your audition."

"Did Ringo like me? Do you think he saw his name I got tattooed?"

E.J. held in a chuckle.

"Of course he liked you. He even liked the tattoo—said he hoped it wasn't too painful."

Goldie smiled at E.J., then back over her shoulder at Ringo. The thousand dollars changing hands was irrelevant. The smile vanished when Goldie asked, "What'd that guy mean by a thousand? And bump 'n' grind?"

"In here . . . I'll explain later; there's work to do."

"Damn, B . . . these girls actually sell themselves like this? They don't even know these dudes."

"It's the freaky-deaky, Ringo. That's what they all came for—to be freaked!" Brice spoke so that he could be heard above the bass-heavy music. There was a slow jam on now: Teddy Pendergrass's. "Turn Off the Lights" was motivating the audience to wind and grind in their seats.

"Girl, there's somethin' that I wanna do! I wanna do to ya, baby!"

Ringo couldn't help but to get his sing on.

And Alfie fed right into it, eating every word.

"Look at this girl smilin' at you."

"I'm lyin' here, waitin' my dear . . . ," Ringo sang.

"You like a cherry pie she wants to eat!"

"I wanna give you a special treat."

Brice laughed at how hypnotized Ringo was—so caught up in the moment.

"You might even want one of these for y'self.

I got mad rooms set up in this building."

"Nah, man. I pass," Ringo replied, despite the champagne in him and how erect this performer had him. "I'm tryin' to get my life together. I might even propose to my girl."

The emcee shouted, "Okay, Alfie! Bend over and show that ass!"

"Propose! Dawg . . . look at all this pussy in your face. How you gonna pass all this up?"

"Easy . . . I got two, maybe three children to think about. A future, know what I'm sayin'? What my kids gonna be like if they follow in my footsteps? Me stickin' every piece of ass that passes by. Nah, dawg, I can't do it like that."

Brice wagged his head. "Have some more champagne. You trippin'."

Ringo took his bottle by the neck and pressed his lips to the mouth of the bottle.

"Matter of fact," said Ringo, "I'm tryin' to get up out of here soon. How much longer you need me?"

Brice put down his own bottle and went to the edge of the stage. Crock smacked a girl's ass and she copped an attitude. Just as Crock reached in his jacket, Brice gave him a friendly bear hug from behind.

"Easy, Crock. Easy. We just here to have fun, man. Don't take this shit so serious. Can't blow my spot up over some trick."

And just like that, potential violence was suppressed.

"Thanks, Crock. I'll straighten her out . . . that's a promise."

Once Crock was settled, Brice gestured for one of his subordinates.

"Take that bitch to a private room."

The girl was helped down from the platform, consoled with a song and dance: *Don't worry . . . we're gonna make sure you get into the video . . . don't pay any attention to them.*

Afer the fifteenth staged exhibition, Brice invited Ringo to the back.

"Come on, Ringo. Lemme show you a few other surprises."

Meanwhile, the mob began chanting "Diamond! Diamond! Diamond!"

"I got you, don't worry . . . I gave you my word, right?" Brice spoke to the crowd of men that stood between the stage and the door.

Ringo was disturbed by the words exchanged, and until now, he'd forgotten all about this label mate . . . the girl he once used as a shield on Queens Boulevard.

"She here? You actully got her here?"

"I did better than that, buddy. Much, much better," laughed Brice.

During their discussion, they left through a doorway, down a corridor.

Someone—a girl—was crying.

Brice approached a door and stopped short before pushing it open. He said, "Now, what's my name?" The question was no more than a proclamation, just an opportunity to make a big show of this, a way of rubbing in (again) the fact that he would always have his way.

When the door swung open, so did Ringo's mouth.

Diamond.

And while all types of alarms rattled his body, Ringo froze. This was worse than in Newark . . . worse than the captive detectives and flying bullets . . . maybe even worse than his own arrest. At least, that's how it felt to see Diamond like this.

Inside of the gloomy atmosphere, nothing but a twenty-watt bulb casting its glow on the cinderblock walls and cement floor, Diamond stood out as the only colorful feature in such a miserable circumstance. She looked so helpless and abused there in that glittery green strapless dress and her trademark fuck-me pumps. Her back was against one of the basement's many support beams and her wrists were bound behind her back.

One of Brice's goons stood by Diamond, his hand gripping her forearm so that she'd remain standing. Three feet away, Justin Lewis was against a wall, his upper body partially exposed under a ripped shirt. He was handcuffed to an overhead pipe and bleeding where the iron bit into his wrist. Justin's face had also been beaten to the degree that his cheeks and lips were swollen and his teeth bloodstained.

Another thug stood beside Justin, slapping a hard plastic bat into his open palm, waiting to deliver his next blow.

Brice's unexpected appearance put a halt to the activities in the room, even as the fuck thinned from the sudden draft.

"She change her mind yet?" asked Brice.

He was speaking to Gaze, the thug who was closest to Diamond. He had on dark sunglasses and a scar that curlicued from one side of his bald head to the other.

Ringo couldn't say for sure, but the scar seemed to affect the man's left eye, and in light of the sunglasses, he imagined that there might not be any left eye there at all.

Andres was the other thug, the one nearest Justin. He had an unruly crown of dirty brown hair, a horrendous pockmarked complexion, and a nervous condition that had his right eye twitching and some other body part, whether a tapping finger or a wiggling foot, on the constant move.

"She's hardheaded, B. The cop keeps sayin' no, don't do it. He wants us to beat him. But I think we gonna start beatin' her now."

Justin made a remark and was immediately disciplined with the plastic bat smacking his jaw. A cry of pain followed.

"You fucking bastard! Leave him alone!" wailed Diamond.

"Remember him? He's like a fuckin' headache—just keeps comin' back," said Brice.

Ringo was too startled by all of this to respond, and yet he was ever grateful that Diamond had a scarf blindfolding her.

Brice was apparently amused by these circumstances, how everything was so much under his control, to whatever extreme they had to unfold.

"Nah, Gaze. Do what you want with the cop, but don't mess with the girl—we need her . . ." Brice left Ringo back by the doorway and strolled in until he was up close and personal with Diamond. "Whether she likes it or not she's gonna be up on that stage tonight."

Brice smoothed his hand along Diamond's face, then went on to explore her neck, collarbone, and . . .

Diamond wiggled herself away from his touch and yelled. Her yell provoked Justin's yell.

The plastic bat swung again.

"See what you're doin' by denying me what I want? What I will eventually have?" Brice moved even closer and his volume was out of Ringo's range.

"Suck an egg, you pervert!"

Brice turned to Justin now, smirking at his desperate attempts.

"Feisty bitch you got here," said Brice. "You shoulda taught her some fuckin' manners!"

He slapped Diamond, provoking her tear-stained cheek to redden.

"I didn't wanna do that, but you, mister, ain't been doin' your job." Brice turned to leave and simultaneously made eye contact with Gaze, a signal for him to turn up the heat in here.

"No!" Diamond cried. "Please let us go! Leave him alone!"

Brice pulled the door closed, but even so, the punishment could still be heard.

Ringo squinted here and there with the blows, somehow feeling some of the pain himself.

"Now," said Brice. "Let's see what's behind door number two."

Number two?! There's more?

Brice led Ringo farther along the hall.

"Did you like that? If you did, you're gonna lose your mind when you see this."

"But . . . how'd you find Diamond?"

"Easy. She had a show scheduled at the Town Hall. We went to the rehearsal early today—my boys did. That's why you see her in that skimpy dress. But huh . . . she wore that for the ballers, didn't she?" Brice hee-hawed loud enough for his voice to carry down the hallway.

"Don't worry . . . her boyfriend gettin' his ass whupped will get her. You'll see."

"Where'd he come from?" This Ringo had to hear. With the snicker, Brice said, "My boys HK and Tip Top are not to be fucked with. They carjacked the singer's limo." Now, they got themselves more than they bargained for."

Justin . . . in the wrong place at the wrong time. By now,

Ringo had a new talent, how to take that deep, nervous wealth of air without it showing.

Brice took a moment to inhale the joy of those cries and moans coming form Diamond and Justin. He even closed his eyes, as if to imagine the play-by-play activity.

"Ahhhh, the smell, the sound . . . the experience of pain. How sweet it is."

And now, Ringo decided, it was confirmed: Brice had most definitely been snorting that shit again. And another thing: Brice was 1,000 percent a certified nut—more vicious a man than Ringo ever realized.

"Okay . . . ready?" Brice had to unlock this next door, and Ringo could already picture a dead body in the room, but whose?

The door was pushed in and that whole abracadabra effect happened when the lights came on.

Ringo's head rocked back on his neck. It was Jamie, his assistant, and Audrey, his accuser.

They were bound to a support beam, sitting back-to-back on the cold concrete floor.

Jamie was the first to recognize Ringo.

"Ringo! Oh, my God. I am so sorry. Please . . . you have to believe me. Don't kill us . . . it was all BK's plan. He made me all kinds of promises. I feel so . . . so used and so horrible for what happened—"

"Who the hell is BK?" asked Brice.

"It's . . . his name is Brooklyn Jones. One of the big boys up at my record label."

"We'll go to the press if you want. We'll tell the whole truth. Everything. I was the one who hit Audrey . . . to make it look good. Pleeease, Ringo. Don't do this to us." Jamie's screams were a loud confession that bounced off of the walls and floors, sucking at Ringo's mind like a vacuum.

"Hold up!" barked Brice, more confused than ever. "You mean your own assistant was in on the scheme? With this, uh, BK character?"

"I knew it. I fuckin' knew it."

"Knew what?"

"That I was being set up. I just didn't know how or who was involved."

"So, it was this BK at the steering wheel?" asked Brice, his eyes leaving the women and turning to Ringo.

"Yes yes yes!" screamed Jamie with nowhere near the composure she usually exercised.

"Shut the fuck up," commanded Brice.

"He's the only one who could've done it . . . the man with all the power and resources. I just don't understand why." Ringo's lips were tight and he thought of all the early stages of his quick claim to fame, how Brooklyn introduced him to Jamie, and Jamie introduced him to—

"Hey, what about Chuck? Is he in this with you all too?"

"No, Ringo. It's just Audrey and me. And Brooklyn calls the shots."

Ringo tried to see past the present circumstances. He certainly knew how a person would do most anything—and say most anything—in desperation. Brice began to glue things together.

"So . . . she whipped her ass so that Brooklyn could set you up? I don't get it. Why would they wanna destroy your game when they eat because of you? How they benefit from that?"

Ringo didn't have the slightest idea.

Jamie spoke up again. "He was trying to create controversy, Ringo. He said it would send the sales through the roof . . . that it would guarantee four or five million units sold."

"But I'm already platinum-plus. Couldn't you all just be patient? Have a little faith?"

"It's all smoke and mirrors, Ringo. The street teams set up deals with the mom-and-pop stores . . . they make it so the SoundScan reports are exaggerated. On the surface, everybody sees the platinum . . . but the record label is gonna report you as a loss by the end of the year.

Ringo—I'm sorry to say this, but you were never a platinum artist . . ."

"Well, ain't that a bitch," said Brice, his hand on Ringo's shoulder. "They didn't give a fuck about you no way, dawg. And ain't this Brooklyn dude the one you told me about? The freak who spits all the time? With the feather earring?"

Ringo was still wallowing in the revelations, his head nodding and wagging.

"The same guy who said to make your lyrics more violent . . . more gangsta?"

"Yeah," Ringo muttered. "He's the one."

"Well, damn . . . we shoulda grabbed his ass too. Here we are, thinkin' you the star of the story, and all you really are is anotha fuckin' pawn. A fall guy. They played us, Ringo." The way Brice said that created the illusion that they were partners all along.

Ringo was too angry to think straight.

"Don't worry. We'll fix things," said Brice. "You two just hold tight. My boys'll be in to see you in a few minutes." Brice closed and locked the door even as the screaming and shouting carried on inside the room.

"So, ahh . . . whatcha gonna do with 'em?" asked Ringo, showing as little concern as possible. At the same time, he tried to figure out the damage caused, wondering if things had gone too far to repair.

"It's not what I'm gonna do with 'em." Brice hugged Ringo, shoulder-to-shoulder, escorting him along the hallway, farther from the cries of desperation.

"It's what Gaze and Andres are gonna do with 'em. Only thing I wanna do is stick my spoon in Diamond's jelly before we finish 'em."

"Finish 'em?

"Don't sweat the small stuff, dawg. Diamond—ain't no way on Earth she can go back to the streets now that she been kidnapped. The whole world would be at my door. And your two friends?

They fucked you, kid. This is simple: We'll get some videotaped confessions, send 'em to the newspapers and TV stations, then we sprinkle parts of their bodies out on the Cross Bronx Expressway . . ."

All Ringo heard was *we, we, we*.

"Okay. Now get ready," said Brice, his hand on the doorknob, a door two rooms away from the last. "Door number three is a doozy."

This door wasn't locked like the last. And the room was carpeted, a lot warmer than the others, and dimly lit inside. There were two video cameras, both of them on tripods and operated by cameramen. Past the cameras, beyond a one-way glass wall, there were virtual studios.

Oh shit! Ringo exclaimed to himself, his eyes protruding and his body moving closer.

"Now this . . . is a real show," said Brice. Ringo vaguely recalled this girl standing at the entrance to the basement. *Ringo, I didn't believe you'd be here.* She was entirely naked, and there was a red ball wedged in her open mouth, strapped in so that she was gagged. There was an older man standing behind her with his pants to his ankles. On closer look, Ringo realized the girl was propped up in some kind of harness so that she was some ways from the floor in a doggie-style position. The man had a strong grip on one of her arms, holding it behind her back, and with his free hand he spanked her bare ass, turning her flesh even pinker.

Just before Ringo sidestepped over to the sound studio, he saw the guy touch the business end of his cigar to her opposite ass cheek. And the man's burst of laughter filtered through an overhead vent. The girl's reaction, meanwhile, was stifled.

In the other arrangement was the man that Ringo definitely remembered—the husky one that had the altercation with a girl on stage and who Brice had to jump up and stop from attacking her. And the girl—

"Isn't that the same girl who pushed his hand away and cursed him out?" asked Ringo.

"Yeah, but . . . you know girls and how they change their minds so easy," explained Brice. But Brice couldn't keep pulling the wool over his eyes; Ringo knew he was lying.

The girl looked so pretty . . . so innocent, lying there on the mattress. Goldie. But in her eyes there was a dreamy expression, like she was somehow put under a spell. And she was put in a most awkward position, with her ankles bound to separate ends of a pole, with the pole chained to a pipe above so that her lower body was suspended, her legs apart and her genitalia exposed for the large man.

Goldie's wrists were also strapped and pulled back behind her head.

"You'd be surprised what we get chicks to agree to down here," Brice said. Ringo saw it as an attempt to gain his approval. Meanwhile, the bear-sized man was beyond the glass, spanking Goldie's pink folds with precise aim. Her cries were also suppressed with a red ball.

And still, Brice kept explaining away.

"The bottom line? They all whores. It's just a matter of bringing it out of them."

The way Ringo was feeling, floating somewhere between his common sense and his own lust, it wasn't easy to pull himself away from this. However he knew it was twisted—the girls, the atmosphere, all under a roof established by Brice, the maniac.

A wall phone chirped and Ringo jumped some.

"Relax, son. It's just the phone. Have a seat. Enjoy some of the show."

I gotta get outta here, Ringo thought.

It wasn't only common sense or lust tugging at Ringo's mind. He could still imagine those cries and screams from down the hall. And his inner vision explored the bowels of this virtual dungeon, the various pipes snaking along the ceilings, the exposed wire, and the slightest sounds echoing to and fro.

"Shit!" Brice slammed the phone back in its case and started for the door. Another door.

"Make yourself at home, Ringo. I got a little problem in another room." And Brice disappeared. It made Ringo wonder just how many rooms, passages, and doors there were in the complex.

"Man . . . he's tearin' that ass up," exclaimed one cameraman to the other.

"Whew-eee, you ain't never lied."

"Listen, I'm . . . I'm headin' out to the bar. I . . . need a drink," said Ringo. All the while, in his head there were the messages: *I think you're sinking into a black hole—one you made yourself . . . Ringo! Ringo! Ringo! . . . Ringo, the police came by here asking all kinds of questions about you . . . Lemme guess—you're the rapper, right? Platinum one day and broke the next . . . Ringo! Ringo! Ringo! . . . I'll put ten G's in your pocket. That should help ease some of your pain . . . He was trying to create controversy, Ringo. He said it would send sales through the roof . . .*

One of the cameramen nodded, but neither of them were much interested in Ringo or his whereabouts. *Lemme get my ten Gs and split,* thought Ringo as he slipped back into the hallway.

"Ringo, help us!" The wailing seemed to get louder. It echoed, all the time with his name involved. *Leave my name out of this!* Ringo wanted to yell at them, but he also didn't want them to know he could hear them. And yet, somehow he was sure that they knew he could hear them.

"Ringo, I'm sorry! Please don't let them hurt us!"

A part of him was at odds with all that he'd witnessed—the bidding war, the bondage and torture, and his own presence. Ringo just being there was somewhat of an endorsement. So much mayhem in this snake pit. But even if he did go down there to help, what could he do? He didn't have keys to the handcuffs. And he definitely wasn't gonna challenge those two goons with Diamond and Justin.

I gotta get the fuck outta here.

Ringo turned in the opposite direction, away from the shrieks of agony—agony either real or imagined. He was getting away . . . leaving this madness behind, and that's all that mattered now.

Farther along a woman with pretty dimples and crimped black hair pulled back into a fountain of curls came straggling out of a doorway. Ringo had to lunge forth to keep her from falling over.

"You okay?" Ringo asked, wondering if she was drunk.

"Uh . . . yeah. Just a little . . . lost," she managed to explain, trying to stay upright in her pumps. Ringo wondered what extremes this one might've gone to in her effort to make money, catch a thrill, or for whatever reasons that made these young women do what they did. *You'd be surprised what we get these chicks to agree to down here,* Brice had told him. And considering all that Ringo had witnessed in the preceding hours, that statement seemed to be true.

"Just, hee hee . . . tiny thing, I know . . . can you tell me how to get back to the stage?"

"Uhh . . . yeah . . . It's that way, I think."

"Hey! You're Ringo, right? Can I get your autograph?"

"Listen, sista—"

"Ringo! Plee-hee-heease!"

"I gotta get movin'. Maybe later, okay? You move along now. I'm sure they're waitin' for you out there." The words were unconsciously leaving Ringo's lips, almost like a rap he was spitting from off the top of his head, without any serious contemplation. But he merely wanted to get this latest confrontation behind him. He just wanted to get out of this haunted house of horrors.

He pointed the woman in the other direction and trotted off.

It was darker down this way, but there was a sense of peace in that he was moving farther from the drama.

He came to an exit door marked GARAGE. Ringo put his weight against the push bar, but the door wouldn't give.

Something made him turn around. When he did, his body experienced a jolt, as if a million volts of electricity zapped him all at once.

It was the girl with the dimple, right there behind him, within arm's reach, and her face was only faintly visible under the poor lighting. Ringo had to catch his breath.

"Where you goin', Ringo?"

Ringo's eyes fell down to her feet. *She took off her shoes?* Then he looked back up to her face.

"The fuck out of here, that's where I'm—" He made another attempt at the push bar. No dice.

"Who are you? Why are you followin' me?" She had taken off her shoes to creep after him, and it left Ringo frazzled. *Autograph, my ass.*

"What . . . no S and M for you? No slave shows?"

"What? Girl, I don't know how you get down, but this ain't my thing. When you see Brice, tell 'im I'll see him another time. I'm gettin' outta here."

* * *

Shonna King certainly got around. This had been her mission for a few days now—to infiltrate the 13th Street building where all the construction workers were streaming in and out. She considered gearing up in a construction hat and tool belt, but that might call too much attention—a woman construction worker among an all-man crew. But then she noticed a fella approaching a young woman. She had a shopping bag in her hand and a book bag on her shoulder. He talked her into a coffee shop at the corner of 13th and Houston.

Shonna went into the same coffee shop and sat at a nearby table. She figured the guy was either soliciting the girl for a date, or something more sinister. It took some time, and Shonna was about to leave, but she caught a lucky break. The same guy who ran down the student shopper came after Shonna. He put on his whole mack attack, trying to be smooth with his compliments: "You look good, girl. You ever think about bein' in a video? The money's good and you can be famous." And he passed her his business card.

So that was it. He was recruiting girls.

"I'll think about it," Shonna told the guy.

One phone call and a cup of coffee later, Shonna was another one of those eighteen girls who had been ushered into the old Centipede building. She noticed that the surroundings were undergoing renovations. Walls had been torn down or erected, and there was a gloomy mood lighting from the street entrance to a basement door where the recruiter—some guy named Outlaw—was taking everyone.

Shonna took it all in with a naiveté, wearing that certain wholesome smile that, throughout her youth, had attracted so many pinches on the cheeks from relatives. It was a sweet sensuality that she could never shake. But she also used the same appeal to her advantage. And no matter how naive these thuggish characters took her to be . . . no matter how much Outlaw thought he had tricked her into this massive lion's den, she knew how sadly mistaken they were.

Shonna was grinning inside—a little flame that was burning

in her mind just to stay aware of men and the many fiendish games they played. Sure, if she hadn't had a strong father, the values, and the street smarts to boot, she might have been swallowed up by all of this—the promises of being in a video and fame. And these men seemed to be all-too-ready to victimize the next fine young thing. But no, Shonna wasn't the one to fuck with. She kept in contact with McDoogle with her cell phone and had a .45 automatic in her purse. Indeed, nobody was gonna be having their way with her.

This run-in with Ringo was more coincidental than anything else. Shonna managed to slip out of the room where girls were changing into the skimpy two-piece bikinis that were provided. She got to see a lot of this commercial building, although the best she could come up with was that some kind of studio bedrooms were being constructed. She also got into a garage where she kept out of sight enough to see a number of expensive cars and two vans—the ones that brought the girls to the so-called audition.

Shonna went room to room looking for the senator's daughter, knowing the girls must've been lured and tricked. But she had no luck. No sign of Christine Lieberman.

Back down in the basement, sneaking along these puzzling corridors, Shonna had gone undetected. And now there was Ringo. The first time she saw him was at the entrance to the basement—the club full of men and the platform stage that was positioned in the middle of it all. But now that she'd heard those screams . . . now that she'd run into Ringo alone . . .

"Ringo," she said, grabbing his wrist to keep him from running away. "I don't know where you're going or what part you play in all of this, but—"

"What part? I don't play no part in this. Don't try 'n' hook me in with this mess."

"Then what's this?"

Shonna handed Ringo a business card and she used a cigarette lighter to offer him a better look.

"Man . . . so this was why all them girls came—they were hoping to be in my video."

"I thought you knew."

"Well, I didn't. Hey . . . you were one of them girls, weren't you?"

"Ringo . . . the business card."

"I'm tellin' you, I never saw that before in my life . . ." Again, Ringo looked at the card. TALENT SCOUT FOR RINGO THE RAPPER.

"That's silly. Besides, I ain't got no talent scouts."

"And you're not holding auditions for your next video?"

Ringo sucked his teeth. "Here? Tonight? Hell no. Auditions for a video is the last thing on my mind. I don't care about none of this . . . the dancin', the girls . . ."

"Was that Brice who was back there in that room?" Shonna took out her cell phone and pressed a speed dial option.

"Wait a minute. Who are you? You never answered my question."

Shonna put her index finger to her lips. *Shhhh.*

"Bill? Shonna here. You told me to push the go button if I think— Yes, yes, I'm pushing it. Get in here now. Now."

"You're not one of those dancers, are you?" Ringo asked.

"No. I'm afraid not. And this building? It's about to get hit hard in the next five minutes," said Shonna as she stashed the phone away.

"Hit?"

"Yes. By a shitload of NYPD. Now . . . can you help me find the girls?"

"Hey, they're down that way. But you gotta know," said Ringo, taking his own defense, "I didn't have nothin' to do with this shit. Kidnappin'? Torture? Leave me outta this."

"Is that an order?" she asked sarcastically.

Ringo took Shonna's shoulders in his grip with enough intensity for her to charge him with assaulting an officer.

"I'm not with this!" Ringo growled urgently.

He wasn't hurting her because Shonna was a gymnast in her spare time. But she still wanted him to.

"Let go of me, Ringo. Put me down." And perhaps her order carried more weight because Ringo didn't hesitate. He released her at once.

"You have to believe me," he appealed to her once more.

Shonna appraised him with that look she learned to use like a weapon, allowing her to judge a person's honesty and intentions . . . an appraisal that was fine-tuned in determining one's human nature. And her diagnosis: Ringo was afraid, but he was also sincere. He was desperate, but not stupid. If anything, Shonna concluded, he was the one who was tricked.

"You've been drinking."

"I ain't gonna lie to you. I had a few."

"So how do I know you're telling me the truth?"

"Because the girls are down the hall. Trust me. You can hear their voices. If you're talkin' about Diamond, she's all the way down on the left. Some dude is beatin' the shit out of her boyfriend. And next door, Jamie and Audrey are cuffed to a pole. They're roughed up, but they're alive. But . . . as far as those other girls—those rooms on the right? I don't know any of them. I swear."

"What about Christine Lieberman and her friends?" Shonna took out her firearm—safety off.

Ringo shook his head. "I got no idea who you're talkin' about. Now, please . . . I just wanna get out of here."

"What's wrong with that door?"

"I think it's stuck."

Shonna helped Ringo shove the door and it finally gave. Dried paint and rust had sealed it tight.

"Good luck, whoever you are," said Ringo.

"You too."

"And just remember what I told you . . . I didn't have no part in this."

Shonna nodded as Ringo measured the passage ahead. He looked determined to find a way out. Ringo, the escape artist.

With her work cut out for her, Shonna King headed toward the screams, her pistol by her side.

Chapter Thirty-five

It was all over the morning news. And Ringo would've missed it except that the disk that he slid into the DVD player was only two hours long and the Repeat mode wasn't pressed. So sometime during the early morning hours, the meditation scenery of waterfalls, rain forests, and lakes had shut down to be replaced by the earliest news reports.

There were arrests. A lot of them. And if Ringo didn't know who they were then, he surely knew now.

The characters and their mug shots were flashed on his television one after another, representing a who's who of the underworld. A number of them were from out of state, found to be in possession of illegal, unlicensed guns, or else small amounts of drugs for their personal use. Nonetheless, they were all gathered and jammed into a paddy wagon, all of them booked and charged for one reason or another. Fat Stan, a drug kingpin out of Philadelphia, was one of the catches. So was One Tooth, aka Thurston Mathis, from Virginia, who had warrants for his arrest scattered from Miami to San Francisco.

More than half the girls questioned in the raid were underage and that meant even more charges, including rape and sodomy.

Ringo still didn't know her name, but he swore he saw that woman with the dimples wearing dark glasses and helping escort one of Brice's goons—one who Ringo recalled was named Gaze, who also had on dark glasses.

In the video footage there were the news reporters lobbying for comments from the arrested as well as from the on-scene law enforcement. And despite many of those taking their perp walks with their head lowered, Ringo experienced the déjà vu of recognizing the scars, the hats, and the tattoos of these figures.

"The most bizarre criminal bust in decades," the newscaster called it. "One of the young women who was abducted is decribed as a multiplatinum R & B singer whose identify has been tightly guarded to help preserve her image . . . Although authorities report that the singer will provide her full cooperation in the effort to convict the men who are said to have organized this event . . ."

Ringo's heart raced. He thought about the business card that had his name on it and how it was used to lure those women into the frying pan.

The dark cloud was following him again.

Beyond those men who patronized the 13th Street activities, and the others who helped to facilitate them, there was no mention anywhere about Brice's capture. They did show his photo, indicating him as one of the perpetrators, and they even added how he was wanted in connection with the Just Right robbery and homicides. But Ringo shrugged that off, knowing that Brice had been dodging capture for this long, and that *America's Most Wanted* even did a whole big story on their show. What would a little more exposure hurt?

Ringo could easily picture Brice escaping arrest, considering how vast the building was and how many ways there were to come and go—doors, windows, tunnels . . . Who knew where he was?

The press, instead, spent much more time showing the arsenal of weapons, drugs, money, and cars that were confiscated. There were watered-down accounts of the sexual activities and how girls were bound and enslaved, all of them influenced by the bait. And there he was, right there on the television screen. Ringo's video and a superimposed snapshot of that business card.

"There was no sign of the rapper when police arrived. However, most of the young women who were ushered to Thirteenth Street talked of being greeted by Ringo when they arrived . . ."

A girl's face was hidden from full view as she spoke. "If Ringo's name wasn't used I never would've agreed to go along . . ."

Another girl explained, "I thought this was legit. I saw the business card, the man I spoke to seemed to be on the up-and-up, and I really wanted to be in Ringo's video. But then they tried to sell me like I was a piece of ham. When I rejected, I was grabbed. They hit me and . . ." The girl, whose face was also hidden from camera, began to sob and couldn't finish her interview. A few others shared similar stories.

"Shit!" Ringo barked at the developing headline story.

"Authorities have now launched a full investigation, including the missing daughter of Senator Lieberman and how this latest incident is directly related to young Christine's disappearance . . ."

Ringo's head pounded as the broadcast continued on. They spoke of Christine Lieberman, showed her high school photo as well as those of her friends . . . They explained how the girls attended the Hip Hop to Fight Hunger concert at the Beacon Theater. They added how Ringo was a featured performer at the event, showing footage of his performance and then a snapshot of him in the company of Brice with the missing girls circled in the background. Ringo felt like a sitting duck in front of his monitor—as if someone would inevitably reach out from the screen and pull him in. But he was already in! Within the space of minutes, they linked him to more criminal activities than took place in a week's worth of *Cops* episodes. And all of it—the robbery, homicides; car thefts; shooting; body parts; missing girls; enslavement; first-, second-, and third-degree kidnapping; rape and sodomy—pointed to Ringo.

Ringo picked up the phone while his name and image was dragged through the quicksand. "Can I speak with Madelyn Young, please?" Devoted soldiers, Butter and Sweets stood by while Kujo was out in the truck, the lookout. Nobody knew when, but for sure they'd be coming to get him.

When Ms. Young came to the phone, Ringo begged for her help.

"That's what I'm here for," she said. "Can you come to see me?"

The attorney's words fell on deaf ears. Ringo was caught up in a subsequent broadcast, his eyes once again glued to the TV.

"In other news, PGD record company executive, Brooklyn Jones, who was shot and killed days ago is being laid to rest tomorrow. Sources say that his funeral is expected to attract some of the music industry's most notable celebrities . . ."

"When did this happen?" Ringo cried out, then quickly apologized for being so loud on the telephone. "Yo, Butter!" Ringo brought the phone to his face again. "I'm sorry, Ms. Young. Can I come down today or tomorrow?"

"Ahh . . . sure." Then, as calmly as the start of a snowfall, she asked, "Is everything okay, Ringo?"

"No," he said with a trembling voice. "But I'll talk to you, okay?" And he hung up.

Butter and Sweets were before him now—the king's jesters.

Ringo repeated his question.

"Tuesday," said Butter. "But we thought you knew. We thought that was . . . well, why you cut out on us. And we didn't know where you were going, so we assumed . . . when we heard the news . . ."

The news again.

". . . The young woman, Tangi Stokes, who was found with the smoking gun—"

"Goddamn!"

"—is now undergoing psychological evaluations to determine her competancy . . ."

"No! No! No! What the hell does she have to do with this!? No! Not Tangi. Jesus fucking Christ!"

Before Ringo could lose his mind, Sweets explained how things happened. And since Ringo only came home late the night before and crash-landed on his bed, there was no opportunity for these revelations to surface.

Ringo marched back and forth. He fell back onto his bed. Then he was up and about again. All the while, his soldiers merely followed him with concern in their eyes . . . hoping he wouldn't hurt himself.

Sinking back onto a couch, Ringo stared up at the ceiling,

wondering what he could do or what he should do. Butter switched off the TV. Nothing but trouble.

Can things get any worse? he wondered.

Just then, Ringo hopped to his feet again.

Something crossed his mind.

"Sweets! The gun! I know didn't . . ." Ringo dived over to his bed, his hand wedged between the mattresses.

"No no no no no! Not again! She took my gun again! Fuck!"

All Ringo could think about was the track record of his gun. The bodies it could be linked to.

How much worse could things get, indeed.

"Where you goin', Ringo?"

"I gotta . . . oh shit!" It was Ringo's pager: 911-911-911.

"What's wrong? Ringo, talk to us. We're here to help you."

What was wrong was that Ringo was feeling very much like a caged animal. And there was little he could do about it.

He was a fugitive, as far as he knew, and it was only a matter of time before the world he created came crashing down on him. If it hadn't already.

The 911 message was from Kujo, who was serving as a lookout, sitting in the driver's seat of the Suburban truck outside. He was barely able to dial the emergency code before officers converged on the vehicle.

"Get your hands up!" they were shouting with guns pointed. Kujo hoped that Ringo got the message.

Chapter Thirty-six

Drug deals gone sour. D-packs that exploded in the getaway car following the bank robbery. Fingerprints all over the bad checks. Madelyn Young could swear that she'd heard and seen it all before. She figured that she'd represented more thugs with their foul-ups and errors than she could ever dare keep track of. But sitting in the company of Ringo, her first so-called celebrity client, had to be the most captivatiing of all the sit-downs she'd ever experienced with an alleged offender. From the mess with his ex-girlfriend, to the relationship with Brice, to the fabricated rap success, his story just didn't want to stop. Even when it seemed to come to an end, there was so much more for him to say and for her to consider.

"And you actually swung down from your patio? Nineteen floors up, down to the eighteenth floor, and . . . you were able to avoid capture to come here to see me," Madelyn asked with disbelief in her voice, having to confirm what she'd just heard.

"Don't make it sound so easy," said Ringo. " 'Cause you gotta know, this gash on my leg wasn't easy." It made Ringo wince just to think of the injury.

"You know, as a general principle, Ringo, I have been skeptical and even disbelieving of every crime story I hear. And I've heard a lot of them. But your story? I have to say it's truly too incredible to be a lie. I can't say I'm one hundred percent sure, but a ninety-nine percent bet I'll take any day. Queens. Bridgeport. Porsha and then you hit the big time, only to find out it's been mostly fabricated? Young man, you sure have been living an amazing life during the past few years. Maybe you've done things you can't be totally proud of, but . . . nobody's perfect."

Madelyn Young's smile somehow made all the difference in the world to Ringo. He couldn't quite put it into words, but he trusted Ms. Young. He felt her to be his ally at a time when he needed one most. She seemed to have good judgment and a firm manner in how she addressed things. She had confidence in her walk, in her gestures, and in her tone of voice, and that comforted him. It made him feel secure—more than the money, the celebrity status, or even the wisdom that his father offered. Not that Mr. Valentine didn't offer Ringo sound advice. It was just that a wing and a prayer sometimes worked better with a strong, consistent wind.

In Ms. Young's presence Ringo even imagined her filling that void in his life. She'd be the perfect candidate . . . a mother figure. It was in her words.

"I'm only interested in your well-being and I want to make sure that justice treats you fairly," she had explained. "You should have every affordable option that a Wall Street trader or a Mafia boss has."

Ringo wondered if that was good or bad.

"And in order for me to represent you to the best of my ability you're gonna have to trust me. You've gotta come clean . . . and that means I need to know the absolute truth, if at all possible. And rest assured, what you say to me will never be repeated at any time . . . to anyone."

And, call him a pushover, but Ringo spilled the entire story to her. He poured his guts out to the point that he felt talked out and exhausted. As far as he was concerned, Madelyn Young was his counselor, confidante and Catholic priest. A person to whom he felt ready to surrender for advice, support, and correction.

"It's crazy, ma'am," said Ringo after he emptied his soul.

"Call me Madelyn. Please. I think we know each other a little better than when we first met."

"Okay, well, Madelyn." Ringo smirked to soften the discomfort of being on a first-name basis. "Things just went haywire."

"Just some bad choices, that's all. Even I make those from

time to time. The trick, Ringo, is to try and not make those same choices again and to identify the lessons that are hidden within your challenges. And do know that everyone has challenges." Ringo uttered a subtle grunt.

"I don't know if there's a lesson coming out of this mess. Unless you call a bad hunch a lesson."

"I could pick a few."

Ringo waited.

"What about making better choices in friends? What about tightening up on the people who come into your life? Like, maybe a background check? Oh. And how could I forget? Your bad habit of leaving guns around. What was it, twice that your friend Tangi has used your weapon? You could've just as well posted a sign near your mattress for her: Gun . . . this way." Madelyn's ridicule was punctuated with a sarcastic grimace. "And that's not to say that I advocate guns being stashed, or not owning guns at all. But it seems to me that to have one requires a certain, dare we say, intelligence?"

Ringo was reminded of the night he ran into Brice at Zanzibar and something he said on the way to his hideout on Drake Avenue. *You gotta dump that gun, son. What are you thinking?* Of all the people to give valuable advice, Ringo told himself.

"Okay . . . so first things first, Ringo. Now that I have a better picture . . . we've gotta clear things up with the police. Since you weren't a part of your homey's Thirteenth Street schemes with the young girls and whatnot, you shouldn't have any major issues such as arrest warrants."

"But they were coming to—"

"To what? You don't know what the police wanted. They could've been coming to pick you up for questioning."

Ringo wagged his head. There was just no way he was going for that.

"But even if they were there to arrest you, we need to know why. Otherwise we're in the dark, and you're a fugitive."

Ringo rolled his eyes to the ceiling, indicating that he'd been there, done that.

"I still don't believe you have anything to be concerned about, unless you haven't been up front with me. The DA can sell all the bridges he wants to the media, and they'll mostly eat it up. That's just how it goes. But the reality is, if he doesn't have proof that you were, in fact, involved in these crimes, then he's got no case against you. And I'll challenge him to come up with anything that'll stick."

Ringo tried to settle for that.

"Ringo, I'll stake my career on your liberty and your right to a fair shake in court. However, you must trust me. I'm the best friend you have right now."

"Can I ask you something?"

"Ask away."

"Can I go see my son before I turn myself in?"

"Ringo, you're not turning yourself in. Merely going to have a discussion with the DA. That's it. But I'll do you one better. Would it be helpful if I go with you to smooth things out with Porsha and Donia?"

"I'm a man, Ms. Madelyn. I can handle mine."

"Okay, Mr. Man. You wouldn't mind if I tag along, would you?" Madelyn didn't give Ringo a chance to reply. She just went on to say, "Good. I'm glad you agree. Now, let's go."

So that there would be no surprises, Madelyn offered to chauffeur Ringo around, allowing him to address those few concerns that topped his list of last-minute priorities. It was important for him to see his father, as well as the children he had by Donia and Porsha. Madelyn realized that Ringo was being paranoid, but she was also understanding when he said he didn't trust the police.

Not that the law wouldn't support her promises of fairness and justice, but Madelyn had to agree with Ringo. Sometimes things had a way of "popping up." And when that happened, the game and all of its rules changed.

They were in her car, an avocado green Mercedes Coupe, waiting for Ringo to finish up with Donia. This conversation, Ringo assured them, wouldn't take as long as the one with his father. But that was all fine by Madelyn.

"Take as long as you want," she told Ringo. And besides, Butter and Sweets were such interesting company. "Oh!" she'd said upon meeting them. "So you're the action heroes who helped Ringo escape." Even more amusing was what a wealth of information these two were, having taken this spin with Ringo from the very beginning. Only now did she realize that men in their positions—those who provided personal security—had a wider perspective, often observing details that the star would otherwise overlook or take for granted. What they shared with Madelyn included everything from the NBA stars and movie actors they bumped elbows with, to the encounters with crazed fans and how these young women threw themselves at rappers, willing and ready to do almost anything—oral sex being at the top of the list—to get near celebrities. There were the complexities of traveling in a now security-conscious society and how rappers were stereotyped as common criminals because of the images they projected. There were even stories of backstage shenanigans that led to fights, accidents, or bodily harm.

By the accounts that Madelyn heard, Butter and Sweets had become living, breathing video recorders, experiencing the rap world vicariously as Ringo's employees. She also came to realize that there were many myths, lies, and truths that molded hip-hop into a culture whose pistol-packin' realities, rituals, and icons were deeply rooted in pain and suffering as opposed to joy and pleasure. It had its own dogma that devotees regarded and worshipped much like any formal religion.

Whether myth, misconception, or mystery, Madelyn was left to formulate her own opinions, no different than she had to do both in and out of the courtroom. And, as usual, she was left to bare the burden of dissecting what she'd learned. Because, as she well knew, everything wasn't always what it seemed. What compelled the lawyer most was Ringo's day-to-day activities, his work ethic, and the types of challenges he faced. Perhaps these were bits of information that could assist her in seeing things from a rapper's point of view.

What made Ringo think or act the way he did?

While the three considered the adventures and the misadventures of Ringo's world, there were also phone calls made to

Bridgeport, where Kujo was on a mission to start things up for a Porsha-Ringo reunion.

Butter was now disconnecting the latest call, just as Ringo was exiting the front door of Donia's place, trotting back to the busy Mercedes.

"What'd Kujo say?" asked Ringo.

"He got her to leave the house."

Ringo slammed his fist into his palm. *Yes!*

"She doesn't know about me coming, does she?"

"Nope. But he said it wasn't easy—something about being harder than putting a three-piece suit on a codfish."

And they laughed about that as they cruised up I-95, destination Bridgeport Park.

Quentin recognized Kujo the minute his grandmother opened the front door. And just as the three-year-old ran toward him, so too did Kujo extend his arms to receive the excited boy. Kujo scooped Quentin up and hugged him, and he also flashed that warm smile upon Porsha's mom to say that her daughter and grandson would be in good hands. Porsha wasn't far behind, shoulder bag in tow, passing her mother with one of those "see ya later" pecks on the cheek. She floated down the walkway as effortlessly as she would've done in the months past, as if she missed having a hired escort to drive her here and there. She hopped into the rear passenger seat of the buttermilk yellow Dodge Caravan to be whisked off on an outing that Kujo promised would be no longer than an hour and that wouldn't reach beyond the city limits.

"Nice van, Kujo."

"It's temporary. Something I can use for a taxi."

"A taxi? I thought you still worked for Ringo. What happened to the Suburban he bought for you?"

There was no lie he could tell for that question. "I decided to think smart. Things haven't been too pretty back in New York. I sensed a layoff coming and . . . well, there's no way I can afford the gas on that guzzler. Not on a taxi driver's salary, anyway. I just had to liquidate . . . cut my losses, y'know? Maybe if things pick back up with his career . . ."

Porsha put her palm up as a stop sign. "I don't even wanna hear any more about it. I'm sorry I asked," said Porsha. "And hold up. If finances are such a problem, then what's all this about a shopping spree?"

"I had some extra cash after I sold the truck and I wanted to get a nice toy for Quentin—a little somethin' for the lady too. I know you've been through a lot."

"Kujo, I don't believe you."

Kujo didn't know what to say. He didn't think she'd see through his lies so quickly.

"You're so . . . so sweet." Porsha lifted up from the back seat to kiss Kujo's cheek.

Whew.

"Thank you for thinking of us, Kujo."

The two made small talk on the way to Bridgeport Park and Kujo peeked up into the rear-view mirror every now and then to be sure Ms. Walker was neither too close nor too far.

"So your mom's okay with you back at home?"

"What's she gonna do? Disown me? Plus she loves Quentin to death. She didn't really wanna let 'im go just now . . ." Porsha scratched her head. "Umm . . . where exactly are you taking me, Kujo?"

"We're almost there. Just a quick stop I need to make. Hope you don't mind."

Porsha shrugged it off as Kujo looked over his shoulder to smile at Quentin.

When the caravan reached the park's entrance Porsha said, "This is a park, Kujo. What business do you have here?"

"I'm, uh, putting a . . . a flier up to advertise my taxi service. I've been getting a lot of business lately from the park folks."

Porsha shrugged.

Kujo put the van into park and disembarked, never mind that he had no such fliers in his hands. In the meantime, Porsha turned to give her attention to Quentin.

"How's mommy's little bubba, hmmm?"

Quentin responded to his mother's tickles, giggling, and twisting his body.

"Daddy," said Quentin, his eyes starry and his smile in the 500-watt range.

"Huh?" Porsha didn't realize that Quentin was looking not at her but past her. She was so busy burying her nose into her son's neck—a playful attempt to win back his undivided attention—that she didn't realize they were no longer alone.

"Nononooo . . . Mommy. Mommy, Mommy, Mommy . . ." Again, Quentin called for his father, and this time Ringo wasn't outside; he had quietly slipped into the driver's seat.

Porsha turned to see Ringo and her head jerked back some, startled but not surprised.

"Sorry to scare you," said Ringo.

"You don't scare me," snapped Porsha. At the same time she pivoted her head back and forth, cursing Kujo under her breath. "And to be perfectly honest, you don't do nothin' for me." As Porsha said this, she also removed Quentin from the car seat, hugging him to her, partially shielding herself and partially protecting him.

"Porsha, I know you're angry with me—I don't blame you. If I were you—"

"You know I'm angry. If you were me. Please, Negro. You have no idea how I feel about you."

"I know I fucked up, Porsha."

"Watch your mouth around my son."

"Oh. He's not our son anymore?"

"Just 'cause you know how to plant the seed don't mean you know how to grow the tree."

Whoa.

Porsha didn't seem to lose momentum in her attempt to discourage Ringo. But he wouldn't give up.

"Porsha, I made some mistakes—"

"That's the understatement of the decade."

"But I'm not here to make excuses. I really have none to give you. If I could turn the clock back I would change a lot of things."

"Oh yeah? Would you change me too?"

"Yeah," said Ringo, allowing some dead air to keep things dramatic. "As a matter of fact, I'd change you into my wife."

And he reached back to put a hand on Porsha's knee, the first touch in weeks.

Porsha's eyes watered and she appeared choked up.

"I mean it, Porsha. I slept on a lot of things in my life. A lot of opportunities. But if there's one thing, one person I should've never slept on, it's you."

Ringo took a deep breath and went on to say, "I realized that you were the one to make this career happen for me. I know you set it up for that photographer to come down to Bridgeport . . . plus those calls to *The Source, XXL,* and whatnot. If you didn't put your hand in this I might've never left Bridgeport. And I wouldn't have the fame, the money, the nominations, the concerts, or the platinum plaques. Even the money I blew, the apartment and the expensive lifestyle . . .

"Porsha, you don't know how long I dreamed about winnin' with rap. The fancy cars, the fans. It's the only way I knew out of the mud. But after you left I finally saw the light. It was your energy and your spirit that helped lift me up. Yeah, I was reading and dreaming and planning. But I was in a shell. I might've stayed in that motel room forever, stuck in Bridgeport, if I didn't have you. You gave me somethin' to dream about, bigger than rappin'. And then when you got pregnant and almost gave up the baby . . ."

Ringo wondered if Porsha also recalled the close call and how he prevented her abortion.

"Porsha, do you know that I went through a hundred-and-eighty-degree turn that day? Where I came from, jokers walk away and turn their back on shorties. I dunno . . . it's just how we think in the hood. We think dumb. We don't think long-term. All we think about is ourselves."

Ringo held Porsha's hand. Silence embraced the encounter even if their hearts were making a racket. "Sorry I had to trick you to get you here alone. I just wanted to apologize . . . and to see you both again. I have to go and stand up for myself. I have to go and be a man. I gotta be James Valentine . . ."

Ringo opened the door. But before he left, he said, "Someone I hope you and Quentin will be proud of one day."

Ringo closed the door and strolled across the parking lot.

* * *

Porsha shivered. She was at a crossroads between her own stubbornness and the dreams she once held dear to her; the imaginings of her complete family, with both male and female role models for Quentin to look up to. And here he was, half of that vision, walking away from her. Quentin put his palm to the window, touching nothing but the fading image of his father.

"Daddy?"

Shuddering and in tears, Porsha scrambled to get to the door handle. "Quentin! I mean—Ringo!" Porsha's confusion with the names was captured inside of the van until she finally got the door open.

"Quentin, you hold on, baby. Mommy be right back." Porsha secured Quentin in the car seat as he huffed, building up for a big cry. She kissed the baby's forehead and ran for Ringo. "Wait! Ringo, wait!"

Porsha jogged to him, her hair whipping about and her winter coat falling open in the rush. The two held each other in a tight bond, vines of emotion, passion, and longing, wrapping their limbs for dear life.

"I must say, Ms. Young . . . this is an interesting proposition indeed. You've brought us a wanted man, you're offering to address these issues and charges, but on the other hand—do I understand you correctly?—Mr. Valentine here, alias Ringo, is not willing to cooperate in our capturing his partner, his accomplice? Now I ask you, is this really a deal at all?"

Bill McDoogle had been pacing behind his desk, but now he was seated on its edge, folding his arms across his chest. A wall full of certificates was behind him.

"Mr. McDoogle, first of all, my client is not a partner with, nor is he an accomplice of, this wanted man you're looking for, no matter how you paint the picture, the colors won't flow. Secondly, my client is no more a wanted man than your son is or your father or your brother . . . Don't you look at me crazy, Bill. I've been doing this much too long. I know who I'm dealing with as well as you do. If my client is wanted for questioning, then say that. Don't try and intimidate him with vague blanket statements, because I'll be honest with you . . . I'm ready to leverage every available resource, every intelligence at my disposal, to clear him. I'll not allow you to pigeonhole him as some statistic you can manipulate at your whim. I just won't allow it. This is no deal we're coming to the table with, it's simply the truth."

"What about Queens?" asked Detective Dobson.

"No, what about Drake Avenue!" growled Detective Blair, his wrist and hand bandaged, all in relation to his severed finger.

Ringo spoke up, unable to contain himself. "I told you! I didn't have anything to do—"

Madelyn gripped Ringo's wrist, interjecting. "You have no evidence regarding those claims. And that's the last time we'll address those issues, unless you plan on pressing charges. And detectives . . . sir, I'm very sorry about your pain and misery. It was a tragedy what happened to you, indeed. But you need to know, again . . . my client merely witnessed your situation. He was not armed as the others were, and he was in no position to stop what they were doing. Not without endangering his own life. If you think beyond your anger for a moment, you'll recall that my client was just as powerless as you were . . . not to mention that he was the one to rescue you." She turned to the other detective. "And you . . . and even your intern, Bill. So let's call this what it is; my client is not only innocent of your charges regarding kidnapping and car theft, among the list of other allegations, but he's also innocent of the assault on the woman. Now . . . I understand that there was a confession. If I can read between the lines, I'd put all my money on the hunch that your so-called rape victim has changed her story." Madelyn had one brow raised high with both eyes cutting into Bill McDoogle like a sharp blade and her arms folded. "If we were playing chess, this is where it would be your move."

McDoogle had defeat in his eyes and he unfolded his arms, turning away toward the window and the New York City skyline. He looked as if he had nothing left to fight with. He looked at the detectives, at Ms. Young, then toward the floor. Finally, he looked at Ringo. "There is the small matter of this," said McDoogle as he slid open his desk drawer. From it he pulled out a plastic bag. He said, "I'm sure you're familiar with a young lady we have named Tangi Stokes." The plastic bag held a 9-millimeter automatic, the very gun that Tangi was holding when police came to arrest her at the PGD building. "Poor girl went and shot some big-wig record producer. Dozens of witnesses . . . smoking gun . . . We've got the girl red-handed. No question."

Ringo was staring at the gun with its evidence tag attached inside of the Ziplock, just dangling there like a fish on a hook.

"Interesting thing about guns and bullets . . ." McDoogle lifted a second plastic bag with shell casings. "These sorts of things are studied by what we call ballistics experts who can match a bullet that's been pulled out of a cop to the exact gun from which it's been fired. A very unique profession these experts have. Sometimes I'm just flabbergasted by the things they come up with . . ."

Ringo's heart began to thump harder. His throat contracted over and again, but there was nothing to swallow, and his mouth was too dry, besides.

"Do you know that we can actually match a weapon to, say, a robbery-homicide that dates back as far as ten years earlier? I suppose that's why criminals and murderers lose them in the Hudson River. But some . . . shall we call them the stupid ones? They keep them for Lord knows what. Maybe souveniers?"

Ringo tried to maintain, but his throat tickled and he was forced to clear it. He also reached up to wipe his eye, but it was just an excuse to bring his wrist to his forehead . . . to wipe the perspiration away.

"And there's more that might interest you . . . You see, sometimes these same weapons show up in other people's hands. Let's look at one particular case—like our friend Tangi. She's not more than nineteen years old. And can you imagine how she came to have possession of this gun? It's a nine-millimeter, in case you were wondering. An automatic, actually. Hm . . . it's my job to know all the little details."

Ringo's stomach was queasy, like two pounds of spaghetti had suddenly turned to live worms. He could feel his arms and back slick with sweat. Again, he wiped his brow.

"Maybe you'd like to get to your point, Bill?" said Madelyn.

"My point." He looked over to the detectives, taking pleasure in this. "Humph. I'll give you my point. In fact, I'll make you an offer, Mr. James Ringo Valentine. In my hands I have enough evidence to try and convict Ms. Tangi Stokes for premeditated murder. I can also be the devil and tie in a certain three-year-old murder case up in Bridgeport. Of course there's all sorts of other charges that ride with those, like trespassing, illegal possession, etcetera. But my biggest connection is dragging that girl into the robbery homicide in Queens. She could've been one of the suspects that got away. How do we know? A mask was worn. So, I'm thinking . . . if we can get even half of the charges to stick, then for the next, ohh, twenty-five years, at least, our nineteen-year-old Tangi will be one hopeless, childless woman who can count on making eleven cents an hour sewing prison uniforms. And if she's lucky, she just might find—ahem—a friend who can send her a money order and accept her collect phone calls from the penitentiary . . ."

The detectives' expressions changed to hopeful ones, a result of the power in McDoogle's dramatic presentation.

"Or . . . ," McDoogle continued, "you can be her hero. I understand that Tangi's one of your best friends . . . someone near and dear to you. What do you rappers call it? Your ride-or-die chick? I also understand that you might've rescued her from some unmentionable harm at one point in her life." McDoogle turned to the detectives. "Would you two excuse us?"

Without question, they left the office.

"Your point, Mr. McDoogle?" asked Madelyn, losing her patience.

"A trade-off."

"A what?"

"You heard me right. I want your client here to cooperate with us in finding Brice. And I want him to assume some responsibility for the unsolved Just Right armed robbery. If he agrees, I let the girl go on an aggravated manslaughter charge. With a six-month out-patient program, she'll get off with a misdemeanor, a suspended sentence, and probation. But she'll never be in custody more than three months.

"Can you please run that by me again?" Madelyn looked at McDoogle as though he'd lost all of his marbles.

"Without going too deep into this, Ms. Young, you know how this game works. It's not always about conviction. It's also about politics and public opinion and votes. I get the votes, I keep my job and my four-hundred-thousand-dollar home. I'm the ultimate do-gooder. Taking down the rapper would be my biggest win to date. It would mean that, despite not finding Christine Lieberman, all of my efforts are somewhat justified. There's a lot of publicity at stake here. A lot of reporters waiting for results. One phone call to Ted O'Reilly and he'll convince the world that I'm God. And we all know how Ted O'Reilly hates rappers . . ." "Mr. McDoogle, I am thoroughly convinced that you have gone completely out of your mind. You must be—"

Ringo pulled at Madelyn's wrist a second time before she got the message. "I need to talk to you. Alone."

Chapter Thirty-seven

After ten minutes alone with the attorney, Ringo followed her back into McDoogle's office. Madelyn had suddenly turned into little more than a light switch that had been flipped, and she went into negotiation mode. She had to work the best deal possible for Ringo.

"Bill, this is crazy . . . and for me, it's a first. But Mr. Valentine would consider—" Madelyn appeared to shift thought patterns. "Wait a minute. You said you wanted him to assume some responsibility. What exactly does 'some' mean? What would the charge be?"

McDoogle shrugged, as though that was of little concern.

"A conspiracy charge. Conspiracy to commit would be sufficient."

"And what kind of time are we talkin'? I hope you're not thinking up any crazy numbers."

"Fifteen years. He'd be up for parole in ten."

"Oh no. No, no, no, no, no . . . he'll give you four, and not a day more, and no cooperation. He's totally against that. You're on your own with Brice and the Christine Lieberman case."

"No deal."

"You're being unreasonable, Bill. You've got nothing to work with here. Mr. Valentine has got everything to lose and he's coming to you of his own free will. He only cares about Ms. Stokes."

"And so do I, which is why I'm willing to accept his guilty plea in return for her misdemeanor sentence. She'll get a light out-patient commitment to a psychiatric program, and she's on the street before we can blink an eye. But him? The deal is that he does time. I don't care what he is now—platinum rapper, fans all over the place, whatever. He was a damned tyrant gunslinger a few years ago! Now . . . before I lose my patience, I'll accept thirteen years. Parole in ten."

Again, McDoogle held up the Ziplock bag—the noose that would likely fit snug around Ringo's neck.

Ringo nudged Madelyn's foot with his, but she ignored it.

"Six, Bill. Parole in four," she haggled, and afterward she looked down at Ringo, seated with his hands cupping his face in agony. She wondered if he could really handle the consequences he was committing himself to. Madelyn went on to say, "And no cooperation."

Ringo wagged his head. His life had come to this: being negotiated over like used furnishings at a foreclosure auction.

"Ten and eight," offered McDoogle. "With ten years probation. We can go after Brice ourselves. Ten and eight—take it or leave it."

Again, Ringo tapped her with his foot.

Madelyn bent down, her breath tickling his inner ear, she was so close.

"Ringo, I've represented some of the most notorious criminals in the city. We can hold out for a better deal. You are not a criminal and you do not deserve hard time," she said in a whisper.

Ringo spoke up, addressing both his lawyer and the DA.

"We'll take it," he said hastily.

McDoogle smiled.

Madelyn stomped her foot. "What is your— No! Eight and six, Bill. Five years parole. And community service for any crimes known and unknown . . ." Madelyn swung her head toward Ringo and at the same time she clutched his wrist. *Let me do this,* she implied without words.

"Sorry. Ten and eight, or no—"

"Then we walk. Let's go, Ringo."

She pulled at Ringo's wrist, but he wouldn't budge. He was determined to take this deal and get this monkey off of his back once and for all. Moreover, he knew what Madelyn didn't. He knew just how tragic the Just Right robbery was. He knew that, if it ever came down to it, there was a lot more than "some responsibility" to be assumed; after all, he was the one to pull the trigger that killed at least one out of the five victims. He could still feel his fingertips on the trigger . . . could still see the rounds penetrating the woman's body, one after another. Again, Madelyn tugged at his wrist, and again Ringo resisted.

Madelyn turned back to McDoogle who, it turns out, was the puppeteer at the moment.

Angry now, Madelyn sneered, "Eight . . . and . . . six!" Her teeth clenched behind her sour expression as she repeated her demand, and her voice trembled as if she were bargaining for her own son's liberty.

McDoogle let it marinate.

"I have to discuss it with the judge."

"Bill, don't you play me. You seem to be forgetting that I used to work in these same offices. I know exactly what goes on around here and what you can and can't do. Now confirm." And before McDoogle realized it, his wrist was in the woman's grasp.

Such deals were easy to make orally, but then there were always the politics that were neccessary to solidify the agreement. Back-office politics involved borrowing from Peter to pay Paul and you scratch my back, I'll scratch yours. It was part of the usual everyday events that took place within the magnificent machine called justice.

And while Bill McDoogle saw to those under-the-counter schemes, Ringo was permitted twenty-four hours to tend to personal business before he was to be fingerprinted, booked, and arraigned. Sentencing would be swift.

Porsha and Kujo were seated at a picnic table in the outside courtyard of Jacobi Psychiatric Center when Tangi and Madelyn emerged from inside. Tangi threw herself at Porsha, then hugged Kujo before they were all seated.

"How did the evaluation go?" asked Porsha. The question was directed at Tangi, however Madelyn addressed it.

"It looks as though she'll be cleared for out-patient status by Friday." Madelyn shook her head as if to rid herself of an annoying insect. "Just rountine evaluation. I'm sure everything will be fine."

Tangi's mind was elsewhere.

"I'm so sorry, Porsha. I heard what Ringo did for me, but I never wanted that. I only wanted you two to be happy, to . . ."

Porsha squeezed her eyes shut, but tears still managed to escape. There was just no winning in all of this.

Tangi pulled her friend to her with all of her might.

"Kujo? How about we go to the cafeteria? I saw some delicious sandwiches there—at least, they looked delicious."

Kujo got the message and the two went off, affording Porsha and Tangi time alone.

"Ms. Young says you put your name down as my guardian. I didn't think you'd wanna see me after . . . well . . ."

Porsha wiped her eyes. "Come, Tangi . . . you know we go back like suede Pumas."

Tangi's red eyes laughed.

"That's suede Adidas, Porsha."

The two laughed inside their tears, overwhelmed to be in each other's company after three weeks of court appearances, pre-trial detention for Tangi, and Ringo's surrender and guilty plea to the conspiracy.

"You'll be stayin' with me, Tangi. You know I need my friend back."

"Me too . . ."

It was the following Saturday when Tangi was once again settled—out from under the skeptical appraisals of Jacobi's doctors and anything having to do with handcuffs, keys, or iron bars—in the luxury of Ringo's residence. She felt queasy at first, to see freedom again when it seemed that hers was guaranteed to be replaced by a lifetime of slavery. She didn't even make sense out of half of what Madelyn Young explained to her, only that Ringo had made the ultimate sacrifice. Those were the only words she understood. And now, in return (although it had always been this way) Tangi vowed to help look after Porsha and

Quentin. It was the least she felt she could do: the price of her getting away with murder. Again. In the meantime, Porsha was instructed by letters and phone calls—Ringo still doing his damnedest to hold on despite the obstacles.

Sell whatever you have to, keep whatever you want. Just send me photos of you and Quentin if you wanna be with somebody else."

But it was difficult for Porsha to let go.

The electronic grand piano seemed like such a centerpiece in the living room. The elaborate multimedia center had provided so many hours of enjoyment—it was like having their own in-home theater. And Lucy, the housekeeper, had been such a tremendous help during the lean times as well as the prosperous ones. It was heartbreaking to even think of letting her go, much less to see it actually happen.

"I'll be available whenever you need me," Lucy explained, her emotions choked back as she made her final walk out the door.

Quentin held on to her leg, not wanting to let her go. Porsha produced an iced fruit stick to lure him out of the hallway where the good-byes were exchanged.

"Well . . . that leaves you and me. We gotta decide what to do with this big apartment . . . all this stuff," said Porsha once the excitement died down.

"I don't think you should get rid of the piano, Porsha. It's not hurtin' anybody by sittin' in the living room." Tangi seemed pressed for an excuse. "Plus, Quentin likes it," she blurted out.

Porsha smirked at the sight of her son slurping at his frozen treat. At the same time she ran her hand across the surface of the photo albums stacked there on the piano seat.

"I don't know when I looked at these last," said Tangi as she took up the albums and sat beside Porsha. It was only natural for the albums to be opened, the flames of their experiences fueled once more.

"Oh, God. This is the first picture of you and the baby."

"I look like shit."

"Don't say that. You had just given birth. That's a beautiful thing . . . and Ringo looks so in love!" Tangi squealed.

"He's not in love," Porsha said after smacking her gums. "He's just glad it was a boy."

"Wow . . . look at us," Tangi drawled and pointed at the group photo. It was the first big party at the apartment—a month after they arrived in New York. "Now this is the truth, Porsha. Before all of those others came into the picture. Look at us . . . all serious with our ready-for-the-world expressions."

"Especially you," Porsha said, chuckling.

"Remember this? Our first time going to California . . . We looked so stupid—L.A. or bust. We musta been the tourists of the year . . . sunglasses and beach shirts, ha!"

Porsha couldn't help but laugh along. It was their first big trip, first time on an airplane, first everything.

"Remember First Avenue?"

"Do I? That club was off the hook! Just straight sexy. And how 'bout this one, the Playa's Mansion on Miami Beach."

"Now girl, how could I forget that? I could finally wear a two-piece bathing suit again."

"Oooh! And you wore that thing, too! Men was hollerin' like you were a star."

"Baby, I was a star. Ringo was nowhere to be seen." Porsha and Tangi exchanged a high five.

"You betta go, girl!"

It was approaching midnight and the two were still flipping through the photo albums, eventually moving to the floor, with the piano serenading them.

The phone rang.

"Who's callin' this late?" Tangi asked as she crawled over to the couch for the cordless phone. "Hello?"

"Oh . . . uh, I'm sorry. I expected to get the answering machine or voice mail. This is Chuck Turner."

"Hi, Chuck. It's Tangi."

There was a silence.

"Chuck?"

"W-wow . . . I . . . I never thought I'd hear your voice. How did . . . but I . . ."

"Chuck . . . it's a long story. And it's late as fuck. Could you get to the part about why you called?"

"Um . . . sure. It's regarding Ringo's checks. I wasn't sure where to send them . . . I didn't know the status of his apartment."

"Checks?"

"Sure. He's in the black, you know."

"What's that mean? In the black."

"It means he doesn't owe the record company anymore. All the publicity within the past month with, uh, the death of . . . Well, let's just say that sales of Ringo's album have shot through the roof. In fact, when the year ends, Ringo may well reach four times platinum if he continues to receive the public's sympathy."

"Hold on, Chuck." Tangi covered the mouthpiece and turned to Porsha. "He wants to know where he should send the checks from Ringo's record sales. Supposely, Ringo's CD is gonna go four times platinum."

Porsha made a face expressing disbelief.

Now Tangi rolled her eyes and went back to the call.

"Chuck? I think Madelyn Young, Ringo's lawyer, is the best person to speak to. You need her number?"

"No. I think I can find it. Sorry to bother you so late."

"It's all right, Chuck. We're just chillin'. Kickin' it about old times."

"Mmm . . . Tangi?"

Tangi's response dragged. "Yeees, Chuck?"

"I . . . just want to say that I can't blame you for what you did. I only wish I had your guts."

Tangi said nothing.

"Well . . . if there's anything I can do, please call me, okay? You're the best, Tangi."

"No, Chuck. Ringo's the best. I just stand by him."

"That he is. And that, you do."

Just a half hour later there was a knock at the door.

"That should be the pizza. I'll get it," said Porsha. As she went for the door, Tangi went to the kitchen for plates, sodas, and napkins.

"You must be Ringo's girl."

"And you must have the wrong apartment," said Porsha,

immediately swinging the door closed. Why hadn't she checked the peep hole first? The stranger stuck his foot out, creating a wedge that allowed him to force the door despite Porsha's weight.

"Now, you should be a lot nicer to your man's homeboys." And now Porsha realized the guy wasn't alone.

Homeboy?

"I ain't come for no drama, momma . . ."

He was inside now—he and his sidekick with the scar and Commodores afro.

"I know how it is—yo' man all locked up, leavin' you home alone. I just stopped by to, ahh, help you out. You know . . . see that things go smooth for you and—"

"You're Brice, aren't you?"

"With all my chocolate goodies," Brice replied, pulling open his leather blazer. He was muscular under the mesh brown shirt. He had on a gold rope chain, and a shiny black handle was obvious in his waistband.

"Well, I don't know how you found me or how you got up here, but you must be smokin' something as foolish as you sound."

Brice laughed. "Don't knock it till you try it, sweetheart." He roamed past Porsha and tried to caress her cheek. She whipped her face out of reach. "A little blow can make you disappear into the clouds for the next . . . oh, eight years." The way Brice said that was an intentional stab—it was about as long as Ringo would be in jail.

The audacity of him, barging in here like this, Porsha thought.

"Excuse me," snapped Porsha as she snatched a foot-high sculpture from Brice's tag-along.

"Oh, you'll have to forgive my buddy. He's not used to such luxuries. Man! Ringo wasn't jokin'. This spot is the bomb."

Arms folded, Porsha said, "And I bet you'd just love to come and be my sugar daddy while Ringo's away."

"Why not? No sense in you bein' locked up too. And besides . . . based on some things I heard, Ringo's not exactly the one-woman man you thought he was. But it's all good, baby.

That's the life of a rap star. I'm sure you expected as much, right?"

Brice came close enough to touch Porsha, but this time she didn't flinch or back up. "I would expect Ringo to do the same for me, you know . . . keep my honey warm and protected."

The scar was touching shit again. This time it was the unmanned piano. Something had to be done.

"Oh, really? And how may I ask would you keep me warm and protected?" Porsha asked this with half-closed, sultry eyes. There was a promise in her attitude—a change of heart. But all the while she was merely trying to relax the intruder so that he was comfortable and off-guard. When she was ready, she'd pull him close and put her swift knee right up into his groin. It must be deliberate, Butter had told her.

"First thing I'd do is—" Brice was interrupted.

"Pizza here, babe? I'm starvin'! Oh! We got company? Friend of yours, Porsha?"

Porsha muttered, "Hardly." Then she turned so that only Tangi could see her face, hoping that her best friend could read her mind. "It's Brice—a friend of Ringo's. It looks like he might just be our future lover . . ."

Tangi's face went dry with misunderstanding.

"Hunh?"

"Sure. Tangi? Meet Brice. Brice, meet Ringo's other woman, Tangi. Tangi can you believe this man came by just to look after us? What was it you said? To keep us warm and protected?"

Tangi's eyes rotated back and forth between Brice and Porsha. Finally they settled on Scar, who was poking through the photo albums.

Porsha could pretend but so much.

"And this . . . this one hasn't been house-trained. Do you . . . mind?" Porsha grabbed up the armful of photo albums and reproached Brice. "Is it at all possible that"—she switched her steel attitude to a soft cotton one—"we could be with you . . . alone?" Porsha winked at Brice.

"Shit, boo. You ain't said a thing." Brice then turned to his flunky. "Out in the truck. Wait for me."

Like an obedient mutt, the riffraff strolled out of the apartment. Porsha flashed a counterfeit smile at the guy as he crossed the threshold. She practically slammed the door behind him.

"Now . . . where were we?"

"Damn. You mean . . . Ringo was bangin' you both? Shit. I always knew that nigga was a pimp down to the bone. I just didn't know he had it like this. Damn."

Porsha was beside Tangi now, arm around her shoulder and eyes still toying with Brice. She whispered into Tangi's ear until both of them giggled and looked Brice over with a head-to-toe examination.

"Whatchu freaks whisperin' about over there? Come and welcome me like a real playa deserves."

Porsha and Tangi shared a knowing look before they made their advances—Porsha in a face-to-face confrontation, and Tangi easing up from behind.

Brice became excited and put his arms out to accept Porsha, as if to say "Come to daddy." Measuring the distance, Porsha slid up to Brice and thrust a knee into his groin.

Direct hit.

Brice growled in pain and buckled over. Tangi lifted his leather jacket over his head and pulled it forward so that it became an instant straightjacket, entangling his arms and preventing any chance of a clear view.

"You bitch!" Brice had no choice but to chew his words as he did his damnedest to yank free.

Just then Porsha looked to Tangi for some moral support. Tangi nodded and smiled mischievously Encouraged, Porsha swung a sharp kick to the thug's head, but it merely grazed him and she fell off balance.

Free from the jacket, Brice focused his rage on Porsha.

"Comere you—" Brice didn't get the entire command out before he dived on top of her.

"Hey!" Tangi shouted. Her words fell on deaf ears. Within seconds Porsha was in a headlock, gasping for air.

The next thing Porsha heard was a gunshot blast, and Brice's full weight collapsed on top of her.

Electrified with fright, Porsha jerked and pulled herself from beneath the body. The gunshot left a dark bloody gash at the rear of Brice's skull, and the sight vice gripped Porsha's ability to breathe or to move.

Overcome with the sudden reality before her, Porsha turned to Tangi—Tangi with her wide gaze. Tangi with Brice's gun, and the gun smoking.

Porsha reacted with little or no sound. She merely uttered a winded word, a silent prayer: "Tangi."

Detectives made it to the scene of the shooting before the ambulance. Two uniformed officers were already upstairs, doing their best to calm a pizza delivery man, still shaken from having walked in on the bloody mess. Soon thereafter, many others came spilling into the apartment. Ringo's was already a very familiar address.

"Officer, could you give us a summary before we talk with the ladies?"

"Well . . . it's like this. See the body there? That's our wanted man—name's Brice. The woman there on the left is Porsha Lindsey. It seems that the dead man forced his way in, attacked Ms. Lindsey, and Ms. Stokes just happened to walk in on the event."

Both Dobson and Blair cut a second peek at the couch.

"That's Tangi? But I thought she—"

Dobson finished Blair's guess. "—Was at Jacobi. She was only there for a brief stay.

"So we understand. According to the ladies, the notorious Tangi Stokes was released just today into Ms. Lindsey's supervision," said the officer.

"Oh brother."

"You can say that again. And to top it all off, guess who the shooter was?"

"Say it ain't so," said Dobson.

"It is so. She slugged him—one right to the back of the skull. The pizza guy there walked in just minutes late. He confirms at least his end of the story," said the officer.

"She strikes again," mumbled Blair, looking over at Tangi like some surreal vision . . . like a beast. "Teflon Tangi," he snickered.

"Somebody better call a lawyer," said the officer as he turned to carry on with the procedure.

"How's that?" asked Dobson.

"Well, someone's gonna need to do the negotiations for the movie rights." The officer smirked and turned away.

When the smoke cleared, Tangi became the recipient of the $1,000,000 reward that Senator Lieberman and friends offered for Brice's capture. "Dead or Alive," the poster said, but in a related press interview the senator mentioned that the "Dead or Alive" statement was a misprint, and that he never meant for such extremes to be carried out.

Politics.

Just two weeks later, Porsha and Tangi found themselves walking into a Long Island church. The jazzy "Wedding March" had already begun as they came to a sudden stop outside of the chapel doors.

"How do I look?" huffed Porsha.

"You? What about me?"

Porsha played with Tangi's hair while Tangi straightened the collar of Porsha's attire.

"Okay . . . ready?"

"Yeah."

An usher rolled his eyes and led the latecomers into a rear section of the chapel. From their spot they could see the backs of two dozen attendees, half of them celebrities, the other half, family.

And in time there were the sacred vows.

"Do you, Justin Lewis, take Jesse Chambers to be your lawfully wedded wife, to have and to hold, in sickness and in health, for better, for worse, for richer, for poorer, until death do you part?"

Tangi realized that Porsha was crying and there was no need for explanation. She took ahold of her friend's hand and squeezed, hoping to transmit some strength her way. She knew this might be difficult and that Porsha needed this occasion to offset her own guilt over being in love with a man who caused

Diamond so much pain. To see Diamond and Justin in wedded bliss would help—at least someone was happy now that so much had been said and done.

But the look in Porsha's wet eyes was much different: It was a look of loss and longing . . . a look full of her own pain and suffering. Sure, there was a man in the world who would give his life for her . . . who would endure great sacrifices for her and her child. But Tangi couldn't help wondering along with Porsha: What good is that if they were separated? And does a man consider all of his victims when he makes choices in life?

The thoughts brought tears to Tangi's eyes, but she wouldn't let them fall. They welled up and dried. After all, somebody had to be strong for the two of them.

Don't miss these other novels by
RELENTLESS AARON

PLATINUM DOLLS
ISBN: 978-0-312-94968-6

SEEMS LIKE YOU'RE READY
ISBN: 978-0-312-94963-1

SUGAR DADDY
ISBN: 978-0-312-94964-8

TRIPLE THREAT
ISBN: 978-0-312-94966-2

TO LIVE AND DIE IN HARLEM
ISBN: 978-0-312-94962-4

THE LAST KINGPIN
ISBN: 978-0-312-94967-9

PUSH
ISBN: 978-0-312-94969-3

Available From St. Martin's Paperbacks

EXTRA MARITAL AFFAIRS
ISBN: 978-0-312-35935-5

LADY FIRST
ISBN: 978-0-312-35936-2

SINGLE WITH BENEFITS
ISBN: 978-0-312-35937-9

Available From St. Martin's Griffin

Coming soon...

Look for Relentless Aaron's next novel

BURNING DESIRE

ISBN: 978-0-312-35938-6

Available in December 2009
from St. Martin's Griffin